WILDWOOD FLOWER

A NOVEL

ANNE LOVETT

WILDWOOD FLOWER

Published by Words of Passion, Atlanta, GA 30097.

Editorial: Nanette Littlestone
Cover and Interior Design: Peter Hildebrandt

ISBN (print book): 978-1-7364640-0-7
ISBN (e-book): 978-1-7364640-2-1

Library of Congress Control Number: 2022913273

To all the wonderful friends along the way who have helped me in my spiritual journey.

I'll twine 'mid the ringlets of my raven black hair,
The lilies so pale and the roses so fair,
The myrtle so bright with an emerald hue,
And the pale aronatus with eyes of bright blue.

I'll sing, and I'll dance, my laugh shall be gay,
I'll cease this wild weeping, drive sorrow away,
Tho' my heart is now breaking, he never shall know,
That his name made me tremble and my pale cheek to glow.

I'll think of him never, I'll be wildly gay,
I'll charm ev'ry heart, and the crowd I will sway,
I'll live yet to see him regret the dark hour
When he won, then neglected, the frail wildwood flower.

He told me he loved me, and promis'd to love,
Through ill and misfortune, all others above,
Another has won him; ah, misery to tell
He left me in silence, no word of farewell.

He taught me to love him, he call'd me his flower
That blossom'd for him all the brighter each hour;
But I woke from my dreaming, my idol was clay;
My visions of love have all faded away.

(Maud Irving/J.P. Webster – 1860)

Chapter 1

Bow Creek, North Carolina, 1990

How could he ever tell his wife about Molly?

The day God took the matter out of David Wilder's hands began as a chill November morning in the Blue Ridge. By afternoon it had warmed into a rare Indian summer. Standing in hip boots in the rushing Quanasee River, David felt his soul magnify, breaking loose from its familiar constriction. An unfamiliar lightness, something near to ecstasy, lifted him as he floated a stonefly nymph into a quiet eddy where a trout might lurk. The fish didn't matter as much as the wide space of peace, the rustling of the water, the drifting scent of pine and balsam, the rising mist from the autumn hills.

The mystics of old took to the mountains to meditate, and he felt it was in the swirling mists of the mountains that he could feel at one with nature, at one with God. The mountains had helped him keep his faith, in spite of everything.

The moment evaporated in guilt as his mind returned to Tallulah. He loved these delicious hours out here, alone, with nothing to do but fish. Not that he didn't love his wife, God knew he did. But day in and day out she was there, and when he wasn't with her, he had the flock, always the flock, and now, he had the letter.

Should he have mentioned the letter to Lu? The time never seemed to be right. Lately, after her last radiation treatment in Asheville, someone else was always around, or she felt weak, or she was enjoying a TV show, and he didn't want to spoil her enjoyment . . . or . . . who was he kidding? *He didn't want her to know about Molly.* It was all so long ago. And he thought he had buried that past disaster. Seeing Molly would anguish him, and heaven only knew what Lu would think. She was so quiet, so contained, so gentle. She bore the illness she didn't deserve stoically, not wanting to give him cause for worry. Sometimes he felt as if he'd never really known her.

The lure bobbed on the surface of the Quanasee. The river swirled and gushed, flowing along knee-deep before it tore into foam over rocks further downstream.

The rod bowed; at the tug, David stepped back and let the line out, watching the arc of the rod. He waded downstream, working the fish, and then the trout, a fierce big one, circled back within vision.

His momentary peace was shattered by a hollow hoot and a piping voice from upstream. David guessed a couple of teenagers were fooling around on the rocks. Then a sudden tug on his line nearly pulled the rod out of his hand. He gripped the rod, but the fish lunged downstream. The line went slack.

David reeled in the line and waded back to the bank, cursing silently. He'd let himself be distracted by those kids. Tourists, flatlanders—more and more of them, every year. But he'd been one of them, once upon a time, a million years ago in a land called Hana Lee.

He settled his rod on the bank, pulled a yellow rope out of the river, and twisted a can of Budweiser from the six-pack on the end. He popped the top and took a long draw. Tallulah, raised Baptist, had been surprised to find a preacher who drank beer right out in the open, neither teetotaler nor closet drunk.

She'd shooed him out of the house today, told him she'd be fine with Nell to keep her company. He hadn't taken a day off like this since the surgery. How could he tell her about the letter? She needed peace in order to heal.

He looked at his reflection in the quiet pool along the bank and felt older than forty-six; both his beard and his dark brown thatch of hair were shot through with gray.

A scream again. Those kids. Then the scream became louder, shriller, more urgent. "Help!" A high girl's voice. "Help! Is anybody there?"

Heart pounding, David jumped up from the bank. That wasn't any ordinary scream, and that voice sounded familiar. One of his church teens? "Here!" he called. "Where are you?" Sound in the hills could ricochet from the rocks.

"Here, here!" Something was desperately wrong.

Now he pegged it as upstream. He sprang to his feet, hustled to the truck, and grabbed a length of sturdy rope from his tool locker. The loop over his shoulder, he raced along the path, vaulting a fallen tree and plunging through rhododendron thickets.

A girl in wet-bottomed jeans and a sweatshirt met him, eyes wide. "Oh, Uncle David. Thank God," she gasped. "Come quick. Please."

What was Tallulah's niece doing out here? "What happened, Clover?"

"Come on, *please*." She hurried ahead, words tumbling out. "Crossing the river up there at the flat rocks. Looked easy. Foot slid—right out from under him—he went in."

"In the water? Who is it?"

She didn't tell him. "He grabbed—tree." She skidded on wet leaves and steadied herself. "Don't know how long—he can hang on."

David knew the drop was about twelve feet or so, not too bad, but the water was icy and jagged rocks lurked beneath the black water of the pool below. He gave a silent prayer for skill and strength, for courage, and for Riley Clyde's safety.

Panting, they climbed the steep path to the top of the falls, dodging low-hanging rhododendron and mountain laurel, churning through the thick layer of forest floor. From the highway that ran near the creek, a truck sputtered and a car whined, making their way up the mountain road.

David and Clover reached the clearing. Here, the river and the big flat rocks looked inviting and safe—a dangerous illusion. And there was the big fallen trunk of an oak, its roots clinging tenuously to the opposite bank, for the bank had washed away near the roots. The boy, soaked to the skin, his wet hair matted to his head, was hanging onto a limb and trying to get a foothold on the tree itself so he could work his way back to the bank.

The fallen oak swayed with his weight. The boy was Riley Clyde Summers, a seventeen-year-old troublemaker that Clover's grandmother wouldn't like her keeping company with. She'd just turned fifteen.

"Hang on, Riley!" he yelled.

One of the boy's hands slipped; he grabbed a curving branch. He gritted his teeth, trying not to show fright. But his wide eyes looked desperate.

David weighed his options. He could wade out among the slippery rocks himself and extend a hand, or throw a rope. But one false move, one panicky move, and they might both go over. Riley Clyde was closer to the opposite bank. David could make his way across the stream and try to reach him from there. Going for ranger rescue wasn't an option. The tree looked too treacherous. Any moment it might tear loose and plunge below, taking the boy with it.

David would be putting himself in danger, and his wife needed him now more than ever. But he would never forgive himself if he made the safer choice and the boy died. That would be another death on his conscience.

"I'm heading upstream where there's a shallower point to ford," he told the girl. "Then I'm going back to him. You stay here and keep his spirits up." He looked back at her. "Stay calm and you'll help him more."

"R.C.," he heard her call over the rushing water. "Hold tight. He's going across to help you."

David strode uphill about a hundred feet to a point where, in the fading orange late-afternoon light, he could see pebbles on the sandy bottom. He waded across and pushed his way through dried brier canes and underbrush, slogging as fast as he could with the cumbersome boots.

Finally, he emerged at the point where the tree had fallen. Riley Clyde was trying to swing one leg over and haul himself up on top of the log.

"Don't move," David called. "You're rocking the tree."

With each sway of the tree a little more dirt fell from the roots, loosening a shower of rocks and pebbles into the water below.

"I can get it," the boy said. He swung the leg again. The tree creaked ominously.

"Stop, dammit," David yelled. He lashed the rope he'd brought around a sturdy river birch and tied the other end to his belt. He edged out along the sandy spit behind the tree as far as he could and reached out. Not far enough.

"Let go, push, and catch my hand."

The boy swayed there, paralyzed, watching David's outstretched arm.

The tree creaked, and David felt sweat break out on his brow. His breath came shallowly. If he failed—if he failed—but he couldn't fail. He steeled himself.

"Son," said David firmly. "You're going to have to jump. I'm here to catch you." He *had* to catch him. He prayed for the strength to catch him.

Dark hair plastered to his head, the kid worked his hands down the limb. The water rushed, hissing. The sun was going down and it was getting colder. David was close enough to smell fearful sweat, and he didn't know how long Riley Clyde could hang on. Showing off for the girl got him into this.

"Let go," he called. "Let go!"

He lunged forward and grabbed one of the boy's hands, prying it from the log. The rope seemed to slip, and David's heart went to his throat. How did that happen? Then he realized that the knot had tightened, and now he had Riley Clyde's hand. The other hand shifted to a side branch.

"I've got you," said David. "Let go."

He knew the kid didn't want to miss with the girl standing there. David grabbed the boy's hand, leaned backward, and heaved with all his weight. Both of Riley Clyde's hands slipped loose and the boy landed in the water, gasping with the cold. David splashed back on his rear as he'd planned and got a firm footing on the bottom. He pulled Riley Clyde to him, now shivering and shuddering.

They still had to make their way to the bank. David's boots felt like concrete overshoes, but he waded, supporting Riley Clyde, and at last they reached solid earth, where Clover was waiting for them.

She fell on Riley Clyde and hugged him, and together they sank to the ground. Just then the tree let go of the bank in a crackling rush and disappeared over the falls. It landed with a deep, rumbling splash in the pool below.

Thank you, Lord.

"You two need to get out of those wet clothes," said David, feeling his own cold-soaked jeans. "Can I take you anywhere? Let your folks know you're okay?"

The girl looked sheepish. "Our folks don't know we're here."

"I can get back by myself," Riley Clyde said sullenly. "My truck's parked up a little ways."

"Could you please take me home, Uncle David?" Clover said. "Mama Hattie'll kill me if she knew I was . . . was out here."

David saw the situation clearly. Riley Clyde Summers got up, straightened, and extended his hand. "Thanks, Preacher," he said. "I 'preciate you saving my damn fool hide."

David didn't feel like smiling. He wanted to smack the boy upside the head and pound some common sense into him. But where was the compassion he ought to have felt? The understanding? It had vanished the moment he'd been plummeted into the past, as the headstrong young man he used to be. "It's okay," he said.

He needed to get back to Lu and the quietness of his hillside house. Back to the David he was now.

David gathered his fishing gear, and he and Clover walked back to his truck in the half-darkness, reaching it just as night fell, black velvet all around him. Driving back to Clover's grandmother's house, he remembered what it was like to be boy and girl, wanting to be alone in the woods together, taking foolish chances. It could have been him. It could have been him, once upon a time.

His knuckles whitened on the wheel.

Hattie Holley was standing on the porch when David pulled up in front of their tidy cabin, old but kept as clean and neat as an oiled shotgun.

Clover hesitated.

"Better get it over with," David said, not unkindly. "Want me to come in with you?"

Clover shook her head and slid hesitantly out of the truck.

"Clover Holley, you get in this house right now," David's mother-in-law said. "I was expecting you home two hours ago." She frowned. "Who's that? David?"

Clover ran into the house and Hattie strode up to David's window. "What happened? Edison dropped her off at the soda shop and she said one of her friends would bring her home."

"Hattie, don't be too tough on her. I think she learned a lesson today."

Hattie propped her hands on her hips. "What're you talking about, David Wilder?"

David sighed. "She and Riley Clyde Summers were at Quanasee Falls and he was showing off. Almost went over. If I hadn't been there fishing and heard her call for help, he might have drowned."

"Or broken his fool neck," Hattie said. "I'm going to get Edison to tell that boy to stay away from Clover. Put some fear into him."

"Hattie, that'll just make it worse. Teenagers love to rebel. It's part of their journey."

"Long as they come out of it in one piece," Hattie huffed. "I'm training her up in the way she should grow." She paused. "How's my Tallulah today?"

"About the same," David said. "She practically shoved me out the door. Told me she'd be okay with Nell there. Guess I'd better get on back."

"She's a good woman, Nell is," Hattie said. "But she sure did pick a doozy this last time, that Taggart."

David laughed. "I tried to talk her out of marrying him. I wasn't surprised when she'd had enough."

Hattie snorted and was just about to say something when Clover burst through the front door. "Uncle David! Miss Nell is on the phone looking for you. Says come quick!"

Chapter 2

Atlanta, Georgia, November, 1990

Molly Westbrook took a deep breath as she stood before the white-columned President's House, half-hidden behind tall magnolias. A long walkway lined with drifts of wine, mauve, and yellow pansies led to the front door. She halted and checked her appearance. Black skirt. White top. Tweedy black-and-white wrap that went all the way around, sort of disguising her condition. She patted the barrette holding her impossible red curls. It hadn't slipped, thank goodness.

Paul hadn't wanted her to come. He'd been afraid she'd deliver the baby right there on the floor of the university president's house, and that was *not* the kind of attention he wanted, up for tenure as he was.

Paul. She adored Paul. She'd do anything for Paul, except stay home from this university women's coffee. He didn't know what it was like to have a spot inside that felt empty, a spot that was missing a mommy and daddy she'd never known. To be mistaken for a babysitter instead of her three siblings' sister.

She was going to be suave and elegant and say all the right things. That is, if she could find a way to talk to Mrs. Wilder, and this was maybe her one chance to meet that lady, the guest of honor, wife of Philemon T. Wilder, university benefactor.

She stepped onto the walkway, rehearsing what she'd say if she got a chance. She knew she couldn't start with the Thanksgiving she was thirteen and had overheard her aunts talking about a man named David Wilder. That might be disaster.

She didn't want to hurt Daddy, but what if this David Wilder was her "real" daddy? She'd carried that name in her heart for years. She loved her stepmother, Hedy, but she had an ache to know about her birth mother. The times she'd tried to ask her father, she'd been met by stony silence. "She died in an accident," was all he would say. The only thing Molly knew for sure was that her mother was from Glencreggan too. And Molly could do the math. They must have married young.

And if she talked to Mrs. Philemon T. Wilder, would the lady tell her what she needed to know? Did she have a son or nephew named David? And would talking to her at all be a risk for Paul?

Paul was so smart, and he made her laugh, and had done so ever since he'd been her grad student lab instructor when she took chemistry in college. He even forgave her when she ruined her lab experiment. Well, she hadn't been paying attention. She'd been laughing at something he'd said and let the solution she'd been evaporating catch fire. And then he'd become furious at her, and she knew it was because he'd cared so much.

She walked up the broad brick steps and knocked. Mrs. Naomi Ragsdale, the college president's wife, threw open the door and, beaming with delight, grasped Molly's arm with her plump fingers.

"Mrs. Ragsdale . . ."

"Come in, come in, you're . . ."

"Molly Westbrook. My husband's Paul Westbrook, Chemistry . . ."

"We're so glad to have you!" Gray-haired Mrs. Ragsdale, short, stout, in a dusty rose dress and matching pumps, hustled Molly across the wide entrance hall to the parlor, where three women stood talking. "I want you to meet . . ."

The women were sociology professors, and Molly, a biology teacher, couldn't think of anything to add to the conversation. She felt out of place, as usual. She excused herself to go for coffee, searching the crowd for a woman who might be Mrs. Wilder. How would Molly know her? Would she have red hair?

Molly maneuvered through the crowd of well-dressed women to the buffet table in the dining room, brilliant with yellow and orange chrysanthemums. She inhaled the aroma of sausage and biscuits on the table and noted the stack of warm Danish pastries on a silver platter. She was always hungry these days.

She filled a small plate and headed to the bowl of orange punch, accepting a cupful from the uniformed server. "Why, Molly Westbrook. How nice to see you."

Molly nearly choked on the first sip when she heard a familiar voice behind her. She turned and tried to sound delighted. "Hello, Aletha."

Aletha Higgins's smile was friendly, but her eyes were cold and fishy. "I'm amazed you're here."

"Oh? Why?" Molly sipped her punch.

Aletha shrugged, eyeing Molly's belly. "Well, really. Something could happen."

"I'm sure there's a telephone in the house."

"You wouldn't want to cause Mrs. Ragsdale any problems, would you?"

Molly furrowed her brow at the snarky remark. Aletha worked in the Public Relations Office. Both Paul and Aletha's husband, Drew, were up for tenure this year, and there had been talk of budget cutbacks.

An excited murmur came from the living room. Aletha peered back over her shoulder. "What's going on?" Her eyes lit up. "There's Jonas!" The university photographer was plowing through the crowd, a heavy video camera on his shoulder. Mrs. Ragsdale came to the dining room arch and beckoned everyone to join her.

Hurrying out, Aletha's elbow caught Molly's elbow. "Sorry," she threw over her shoulder and rushed out, pretending not to notice that Molly's punch had leapt out of her cup and landed right on Molly's blouse. Molly felt the cold liquid seep through the material and onto her skin.

"Oh, no," Molly gasped. "Oh, no." Her throat grew thick with tears. A server in a black and white uniform looked up from the chocolate-capped strawberries she'd just placed on the table. "Oh, honey. Let me bring you a washrag." She disappeared through the swinging door to the kitchen and was back in a moment with a damp towel. She handed it to Molly. "Nasty woman."

"It was an accident. I guess." Molly dabbed at the spreading blotch of sticky orange punch, knowing she couldn't possibly stay at the coffee. Tears stung her eyes, and she blinked them away. She had to leave now.

The path to the front door was blocked by the photo-op crowd. She handed the cloth back to the server. "Thanks so much. Is there another way out?" She looked hopefully at the kitchen door.

"No guests allowed that way," said the server. "President's orders. Wait 'til they get called for a group picture on the front steps. Then go through the living room and out the sun porch."

That sounded all right to Molly. She lingered by the table and drank a cup of coffee. She really didn't have an appetite anymore.

Finally, she heard Aletha urging the women outside.

Once the front door had closed, Molly whisked through the living room, dodged plants on the sun porch, and opened the louvered door. She found herself outside in a small Japanese-style garden. She gazed, entranced, on pebbled walkways and pots of bonsai, a stone lantern under a red maple. Water trickled into a small pool.

"Good morning."

Her heart gave a leap, and she turned. A tan, slim woman, in her late sixties, perhaps, sat at a small wrought iron table, an unlit cigarette in one hand and a small gold lighter in the other. Her short copper hair fluffed above gold-and-pearl earrings. A cropped jacket of silk tweed looked perfect with her bronze shantung dress.

The woman looked up at Molly, a wry smile on her face. "Naomi is so particular about smoke. Did she send you out here?"

Molly wished she had a fan. She wished she could disappear. "Oh, no, ma'am, I . . . just dumped punch all over myself. I thought I'd better leave."

"Ma'am? I'm not the Queen of England. Come here. Maybe I can help."

"I'm afraid it's hopeless." Molly took a step backward.

"Nothing's hopeless." The woman placed the cigarette and lighter on the table and from her bag extracted a moist towelette packet. She ripped it open and held it out to Molly. "I was once a Girl Scout."

Molly had no choice but to accept. "Thank you." She took the towelette and dabbed at the spots again, amazed to see more of the orange come out. She rubbed the towelette over her hands and arms, wiping away the last of the stickiness. Then she dabbed at her wrap. "It's better."

The woman nodded. "I knew it. See?"

"Thank you so much, ma'am. I'd better be getting home." She eyed the wooden gate that led out. Now was the time to get out before anyone else saw her.

"Wait. There's no need to leave," said the woman. "Naomi doesn't bite, and neither do I." Her gaze slid over Molly's belly, undisguised by the wrap. "You look like your feet hurt. Come sit down and talk to me. I'm Evangeline Wilder." She flared the lighter at the cigarette. "Smoking has gotten so lonely lately."

"Mrs. Wilder?" Molly's heart raced and her palms felt sweaty. The actual Mrs. Wilder?

The smiling woman raised her eyebrows. "In the flesh. Tell me about yourself. And the baby." She patted the chair next to her.

Molly walked over and sank down, dazed and giddy. How much to tell? "I'm Molly Westbrook. My husband's Paul. In Chemistry. I teach high school biology, but right now I'm on leave. I'm not doing much of anything except waiting."

"Is it the first? Congratulations! Waiting is good, and don't sell yourself short. So Paul's with the university?"

Molly leaned forward. She could do this. "Paul specializes in natural products chemistry, and a wild berry he's investigating is really exciting. It's a possible tumor-reducing agent. His job is to find the active substance."

"Wonderful," said Mrs. Wilder. "What sort of berry?"

Molly could talk about Paul's berry all day. "A type of huckleberry from Tibet. It's very rare. What's so exciting is that a variety of it has been found in western North Carolina. Why, there are so many species of plants there—"

The louvered door from the sunroom swung open. A surprised look on Aletha Higgins's face changed to a frown and then changed just as quickly to a wide smile.

Mrs. Wilder glanced up, then back at Molly, ignoring Aletha. "You said North Carolina?"

Aletha ducked back inside, almost slamming the door behind her.

Molly nodded. "Yes, ma'am." She wished she didn't feel so queasy.

Mrs. Wilder picked up her cigarette and lighter. She flared the lighter, drew in, and let the smoke drift out. "You know, we've spent our summers in the mountains for as long as I can recall."

Molly's heart pounded. She had to get it out quickly, before Aletha came back with others in tow. "Where? I was born in Glencreggan."

Mrs. Wilder studied her. "Really, now."

Molly noticed the way the lady shifted in her chair and leaned forward slightly. Molly had better hurry and get it out. "I've only been there a few times since I was a baby. My dad was in the Army, and I've lived in so many places I've almost lost count." She closed her eyes, took a deep breath, and then opened them. She licked her lips. "Do you—do you know a David Wilder, by any chance?"

"Why do you ask?" Mrs. Wilder took a draw from her cigarette and let the breeze take the smoke.

It was now or never. She took a deep breath. "Because—"

The door banged open, and a gaggle of women filed out into the garden, along with Aletha, Mrs. Ragsdale, and the photographer, this time with a still camera.

"Mrs. Wilder," said Aletha, "we'd like to get your picture with Mrs. Ragsdale."

"I'll be right with you," said Mrs. Wilder, then she turned back to Molly. "I've enjoyed talking with you, my dear. My best to your husband."

Molly's head was spinning and her insides were lurching. She thanked Mrs. Wilder, pushed herself awkwardly from the chair, and made her way across the pebbled pathway toward the gate that led to the driveway.

Molly's shoulders slumped as she closed the gate behind her. Mrs. Wilder knew something. She had reacted when Glencreggan had been mentioned and tried not to show it. And then when Molly asked about David Wilder, the lady had seemed relieved when they were interrupted. Molly's eyes filled again, and she found a tissue. *That won't do, Molly*, she told herself, sniffling. She hoped Paul wouldn't be angry when she told him what she'd done.

Just as she stepped onto the path leading down from the house, she heard someone call, "Mrs. Wilder! You're wanted on the telephone!"

A busy, important woman, the lady was.

Molly walked down the long pathway to the street. She'd almost reached the pavement when a Lincoln Town Car sped out of the driveway. That's when she saw Mrs. Wilder in the back seat, lighting her cigarette.

Molly trudged back to campus, her stomach in knots. Had something terrible happened?

Chapter 3

Bow Creek, November 1990

David numbly watched the mourners leave the churchyard in the misting rain. How was he going to get through the rest of his life without Tallulah? Only four days ago he had held her close and kissed her.

For three years he had watched her decline, with always hope in his heart that she would recover, that a miracle would happen, and the hope had been the main thing that kept him going.

She was the one who had picked him up out of the mud of his own loneliness, afraid to love again. He'd loved his work, he loved helping people, helping them to build faith in their lives, but when he came to Bow Creek it had been a long time since he'd ventured to have any kind of meaningful relationship. The last time had not turned out well, and he'd just concentrated on work, on people in need. Still, sometimes the longing for love overcame him, and he took to the hills for a day to meditate.

And then a year and a day after he had arrived to become the rector of St. Ninian's, the day he was interviewing a new teacher for the church preschool, the kind and gentle soul that was Tallulah walked into his life. A widow five years older, husband lost in Vietnam, with a deep love for children, having none of her own. She hadn't taken his interest in her seriously. He'd spent a year convincing her to have dinner with him.

He swallowed the lump in his throat and took the hand of an elderly woman who had come to comfort him.

Lonnie Tucker, the sexton, waited with his shovel and pickaxe at a respectful distance. They couldn't use heavy equipment in this old cemetery. David's mother, dressed in an impeccable black suit and pearls, held his arm as they picked their way between the old headstones and mounds of gravel.

David turned to his mother. "Would you and Phil like to follow me to Edison's? I won't ask you to ride in my old truck."

"Edison?"

"Edison Holley, the tall man with the salt-and- pepper beard. Tallulah's brother."

"Oh, yes, I remember him." She appeared to be thinking about something else. Her clear green eyes searched the faraway mist. "David . . ." Then she stopped and folded her hands. "David, I'd like to have a word with you." She glanced over at Jake Halsey, David's mentor and an old friend, standing nearby.

"Go ahead." Jake smiled affably and gestured with an upturned palm.

David nodded and walked his mother to the shelter of a huge oak.

She met his searching eyes. "A young woman at Naomi Ragsdale's coffee interested me, and I struck up a conversation. She asked if I knew a David Wilder. She said she was born in Glencreggan. She said her father was in the Army."

David felt his face go cold. His palms grew clammy and his gut knotted, primed for a kick.

"I'm sorry to have to tell you now, of all times," his mother continued. "I didn't tell her anything. But her husband is a professor at Westbury. She's a bright girl, a biology teacher. She might try to find you."

"I know," said David.

His mother arched her eyebrows. "You know?"

David plunged his hands into his pockets and hunched his shoulders. "She wrote me a letter. I haven't replied."

"What will you do?" his mother asked. Then she gripped his arm. "David, see her. She's a lovely girl. You'd be proud of her."

He couldn't bear the thought of seeing her. Maybe she would judge him harshly, once she knew the whole story. She might hate him. Better she never knew. And then there was Owen. . . "No," he blurted. "I made a promise."

His mother waved her hand dismissively. "Surely, after all these years."

"Mother, I can't think now."

Her fingers gripped his arm. "David, for God's sake, face it. She has a reason for wanting to see you. She's—"

David interrupted. "No, Mother." Anger flared up, the anger he'd felt so long ago, anger he thought he'd overcome. *What about that other time? Were you so understanding then?* He had hoped his parents would support him when the trouble first began, and they'd kicked him in the gut. And because of that, everything had gone to hell.

He wiped his brow with the back of his hand.

"Very well." Evangeline drew her lips into a thin line.

David said a silent prayer for understanding and walked with his mother to rejoin the others. Harry Claymore, a churchwarden and an old friend of his brother Phil, was talking to Phil some distance away.

David caught Jake's eye, and Jake came to rejoin them. He laid a comforting hand on Evangeline's shoulder. "We're going to the wake. Coming with us, Evie?"

Evangeline looked up at him. "No, I don't think so. Phil's got a meeting, and I need to get back to Lem. Angina again. I really wish he'd keep his doctor's appointments."

Jake nodded. "I'll come to see him if you like."

"He wouldn't listen to you," said Evangeline. "You know he's a heathen to the core."

"If I couldn't help somebody without talking religion I'd be a poor pastor."

Evangeline smiled. "A person would think you're a heathen too. I'll have you to dinner." She glanced over at the couple approaching David and gave him one more hug. "I'll try to get your father to call you."

David stiffened, hugged her awkwardly. "He'll never change."

He felt his mother's smooth kiss on his cheek. "Be generous with your father, David," she whispered. "He's not well. And think about what I told you. Call me if you'd like to talk about it. I'll even give you my car phone number." She scribbled the number on the memo pad she always carried and gave it to David.

Phil came over to collect his mother, and Harry Claymore joined them to say good-bye. "Good to see you again, Phil, buddy. Just wish it didn't have to be here. David, I'll see you at Edison's. Sure I can't do anything else for you?"

"You've been great, Harry. I couldn't ask for a better senior warden."

Harry walked off, and Phil gave David a quick hug. "I'll be here if you need me, brother," he said. "By the way, your church is beautiful. I'd like to know its history some time."

"Of course," David said. "I'm glad you came."

Feeling heaviness deep in his soul that his family should still be divided, he watched his mother and brother walk across the parking lot to Phil's gray Mercedes. "Let's go," he said to Jake.

Jake glanced over at him. "Is your mother all right?"

David's shoulders slumped, all the energy he'd used to get through the day leaving him. He said woodenly, "Nothing is all right."

Jake frowned with concern and put a hand on his shoulder. "You look as if the earth is caving in before you. Tell me about it."

It took all his grit not to break down. The day had been too much. "I don't know what to do, Jake. My daughter's looking for me."

He had told the story to Jake years ago, when he had felt he had a call to the ministry, and Jake nodded his understanding. "You never thought this day would come, did you? I can see why you're torn. You want to see her, but you're afraid of the consequences."

"Yes. I need time to think."

The two walked into the wind, up the rock-studded path leading to the broad front porch of Edison Holley's house. Needle-sharp blasts of cold whipped David's hair and rattled the leaves of ancient hickory trees. A wind chime on the front porch clanged in desolate cacophony.

"You know," said Jake, "Evangeline wants you and your father to reconcile before it's too late."

"I've been right here all these years," said David, hunched, hands thrust into his pockets.

Clover opened the door for them. Her eyes widened when she saw David. He smiled and put a finger to his lips quickly, and she relaxed. How pretty she was, with her glistening brown-gold hair, smelling faintly of apples, and her shy smile. She'd attract admirers, and David hoped life wouldn't hand her trouble, wouldn't hand her a hard-bitten face she didn't deserve.

The cozy house, packed with family and friends, smelled of warm bread and chicken casseroles. One of his stalwart parishioners set down a platter of fried chicken and greeted David with a hug.

"If you need anything . . ." said another aproned woman.

"She was one of God's own," said someone else.

"She's at peace now."

David nodded silently, churning inside.

Clover, who had disappeared for a time, returned with heaping plates of food for David and Jake. "There's some chairs for you in the dining room."

"Come eat with us," said David.

She grimaced. "I'm not hungry." A strange look crossed her face. "Maybe I'll get a drink."

"The funeral was hard on her," Jake concluded, after she'd gone. "Were she and Tallulah close?"

David found it hard to say the next words. He swallowed. "Yes. Clover was the child Lu never had. Lu's sister died from a drug overdose and Hattie wanted to take Clover. The sister said she didn't know who the daddy was, said she was high on drugs when it happened." David blew out and clenched his fists. "Lu would have taken Clover, but after our baby died, Lu was fragile."

Jake gave him a sympathetic glance. He'd helped David bury little David Ethan.

When the two men finished their meal, they took their plates to the kitchen, where they were whisked away. An aproned woman scraped the remains into a brown paper bag and splashed the dishes into a sink full of soapy water.

Jake smiled and nodded at the bustling parishioner. "I wish I had a dozen like you at my church."

She blushed with pleasure. "You can stay here with us."

Jake kissed her cheek. "Thank you, my dear, but I've got a meeting in the morning. I'll slip out the back door."

"I'll walk out to your car with you," said David. He needed to get out of the house, needed to be alone, needed not to hear anyone telling him Lu was in a better place.

He and Jake stepped out onto the back porch, where firs tossed in the breeze, the cold scented air like a refreshing balm. David clicked the back door shut.

"Don't you have women like our stalwart Marthas?"

"Of course, but they're growing old," Jake said. "The younger ones have careers and less time for the larger community."

"It's coming to our small town too." David gazed out toward the mountains, where the sinking sun spilled shadows in the hollows. They walked around the side of the house to reach the driveway.

"What will you do now?" asked Jake.

"Stay here and do my work, as long as they want me."

"Have you thought of leaving?"

David gave Jake a sharp glance. "Where would I go?"

Jake took his pipe out of his mouth and smiled. "Come home."

"The city's not my home anymore. This is home now. It has to be."

Jake knocked his pipe against his heel, letting the ashes fall to the rocky ground. "All that was so long ago."

"It's what Trilby would have wanted."

Jake tucked the pipe into his pocket. "How do you know what she would have wanted? Why won't you see your daughter? Acknowledge her?"

"I made a promise to Trilby. People could get hurt."

Jake sighed. "Your daughter must have a good reason for wanting to find you. I've known you a long time, David. Remember, I knew you when it happened, and I saw you just withdraw into yourself. You wouldn't let me help you."

David gave him a rueful smile. "Well, you were rector of St. Anselm's. You were the establishment. How could I trust you, even though I liked you?"

"Seriously," Jake said. "I've always felt you've never moved past what happened. Maybe meeting your daughter would start you on the road to healing the past."

David's cheeks warmed and he clenched his fists again. "Jake, I've done all I could to heal that past. That's why I'm here."

"Maybe God is talking to you."

"Don't bring God into it," David snapped.

Jake's eyebrows rose. "David. What makes you say a thing like that?"

David put a hand to his forehead and his neck warmed. "I'm sorry. That just came out. That's how I felt back then. That a good God would never have let . . . oh, you know. You'd think I'd never learned a thing from you or my other teachers. It was a reflex."

The murmur of voices floated faintly from the house. "I see." Jake nodded slowly. "Have you ever been back to Glencreggan?"

David shook his head. "My father sold the house the year after . . . the year after it happened. He bought another at Pinehurst. Said the golf was better, and he still would be in North Carolina."

Jake gazed at him with compassion. Meeting that gaze, David felt his soul in danger of being ripped from its moorings. In Bow Creek he had redeemed himself for what had happened to Trilby. Hadn't he? He couldn't bear for the wounds to be ripped open once again. It would happen if he went back to the town that had wrecked him.

David and Jake walked on silently through the dry grass, leaves scudding across their path, until they reached the black Lincoln.

"Nice car," said David.

"It was left to me by a parishioner." Jake stroked the shining finish. "Not really my thing, but I could get used to this kind of luxury."

David's father had driven a car like that once. He could imagine what his own congregation would say if he drove such a car. "Do you get criticized for it?"

"Criticism doesn't bother me." Jake laid his hand on David's shoulder. "Look, David. Perhaps I'll be leaving St. Augustine's. You'd be good for them."

Stunned, David didn't need that kind of shock right now. He tried to laugh it off. "Come on, Jake, a country parson at that big church? I told you the city's not my home anymore."

"You've got the background," said Jake. "You've handled a social situation here I wouldn't envy. Search your heart. Maybe leaving Bow Creek would be the best thing for you."

Leave Bow Creek? How could he? "Jake, my life is here. No question. But why do *you* want to leave your church?"

Jake looked down for a moment, then looked David squarely in the eye. "This is hardly the right time, but I don't think you knew my plans. I've put in my name for bishop. Of your diocese."

A cold breeze rushed past David's neck, giving him a chill. The unexpected death of Bishop Windermere a few months back had caused a stir. David, preoccupied as he'd been with Tallulah's illness, had hardly been aware of the goings-on to find his successor.

"Jake, that's wonderful news. You're the most qualified man I know. Having you as my bishop would be all I could ask for. "

Jake nodded. "Thank you. I'd better be getting along. We can talk of this later."

"I'm just thankful for friends like you, Jake. It meant a lot having you take the service."

Jake gripped David's hand with both of his in farewell. "Think about what I've said."

"I will."

Jake climbed into the Lincoln and drove away. Watching the car snake down the long rocky drive, David slumped with exhaustion. He wanted to go back home, back to Bear Lick Mountain, to the farmhouse he had shared with Lu, to the bed he'd slept in alone these past three years.

A beige van lettered with *Nell's Antiques* rumbled up the driveway and swerved onto the grass, just missing Jake's exiting car. David waited as the van pulled to a stop beside him. Dressed in a dark gray coat, her light brown hair under a gray beret, Nell slid out of the driver's seat and walked over to David.

He hugged her. "I didn't see you at the funeral."

She shook her head. "I couldn't make it. Sophie's sick, and even though she's ten, I didn't want to leave her alone. I finally found someone to stay with her for an hour so I could at least come here. I had this ham. . ." She gestured helplessly toward the van. "Lord,

I'm going to miss our Lu so much. Is there anything I can do for you?"

Nell had been a rock these past three years. She was a practical sort, could see things clearly when his own mind was up in the clouds, or down in a pit. "Just keep on being the friend you are." He felt so blessed to have had her company, especially with Lu these past few years.

He was sorry her marriage to Hampton Taggart, the country singer hadn't worked out. David had warned her not to marry him; it had been too soon after her divorce from the architect Lyle Heatherton. When David had come to Bow Creek as a single man, she'd been married to Lyle and living in a house suspended off the side of a hill. She'd spent winters in Raleigh and come back in the summer to run her antique shop, Lyle commuting as his business allowed.

And now she was back in Bow Creek full time, back in her antique shop, and Hampton Taggart was still touring the country, making women cry over his lonely ballads. Among other things.

David cleared his throat. "I hate to run off, but I need to go home. I'll say goodbye to everyone."

Nell smiled sadly and took his hand. "I'm sure you need some rest."

He squeezed her hand, let it go, and walked with her up to the house.

He arrived back at the old farmhouse just as the sun was going down.

The fading golden light filtered into the big room opening out onto David's wraparound porch. A stone fireplace built of stones that David had gathered from the gullywashes of Bear Lick dominated the room. Bookshelves that he'd hammered together lined the alcove where he sat and wrote his sermons on a big wooden desk, a hand-me-down of his father's.

A rag rug, braided by Lu out of their jeans and dresses and shirts and sweaters, lay under the pine coffee table, a record of their life together beneath his feet. Among green and blue and white and tweedy brown, he spotted flecks from the bright red blouse he'd bought her. Ever modest, she wore it only to teach her preschool classes, and it had become covered with paint and peanut butter and eventually made its way underfoot.

Landscapes hung on the walls. He'd done the paintings years ago, after he'd taken lessons at the art colony north of town. Tallulah had insisted on hanging them, even though he knew they weren't any good. Over the fireplace hung the charcoal sketch he'd done of Lu just three years before, the one thing he'd drawn that he liked.

It had been a fine Saturday afternoon in September, a little crisp, when he'd seen her under the apple tree, resting from gathering a windfall. Her old straw hat hung by a cord on her back, and her dark hair was feathered by the wind. He'd brought charcoal and pad out to the porch and tried to capture the far-away look on her face. He didn't, but it was a decent likeness. He wondered whether she had known even then of her illness and had wanted to spare him.

The sun dropped, and he watched the colors of the room shade to gray before he turned on the electric light, filling the room with a dispirited glare. David had been looking forward to coming home, but tonight even the memories were empty. A home was where somebody else was.

He sat in his chair, closed his eyes, and tried to rest. But a vision of Trilby, her tumbling dark hair, her nimble grace, danced before his eyes and then receded, as behind a cloud, teasing him, haunting him.

Chapter 4

Glencreggan, 1963

All David had wanted to do that day was go fishing.

His father had other ideas. While his father lectured, David took his Swiss Army knife out of his pocket and fooled with a small blade. Dammit, the day was perfect, sunny, with the freshness of mountain evergreen on the breeze that riffled across the porch. He thought a summer house was to relax in, not to harass your son about what he was going to do with his life. Maybe David wanted to figure that out for himself. He liked people, not numbers.

His father was saying, "Phil's been working for me for three years, learning the business, and you've goofed off all summer."

"I've earned a little money." He looked off past the golf course. The emerald hills to the west, shading into a smoky blue in the distance, showed shifting shadows of darker green.

A snort. "Lifeguarding? That was just for fun."

David shrugged. "Yeah, Dad, but look at my tan. The girls love it." He knew they also loved the way his thick mop of brown hair looked after a summer in the sun, because they were always running their fingers through it. It had been a very good summer.

"Don't be a smart ass," said Lem Wilder.

"Just being honest, Daddy-O." What a square his father was. He wondered if he could risk flipping the knife over the porch railing to land in the grass.

His father flashed him a warning look. "I still wish you'd come back to the city with me tomorrow, David. I could teach you a lot about the banking business in three weeks. It would be good to have that experience under your belt when you're deciding on college courses."

David wished his father would can the lecture. He really wanted to go fishing. "Maybe I don't want to be a big-city banker, Dad. Maybe I'd like to be something else."

Lem's mouth tightened. "I've worked all my life to give you boys security. A place in the world."

David clicked the knife shut, shoved it into his pocket, and looked away. A knot of anger tightened in his stomach. This conversation had been the endless tape loop during his senior year at Westwood Academy.

David wasn't as tall as his brother or his well-built father, whose graying hair was trimmed by a stylist near his office building every three weeks. But he worked out, played a mean game of tennis, and felt he could take on any kind of bully. He'd be off to college before long, out from under his father's thumb. Freedom! Seconds ticked by as David calmed himself. This time he wasn't going to fight.

He straightened. "If that's all, I'm going fishing."

"Go ahead." There was the slightest note of contempt in the firm voice. Before David could get away, a rusty black pickup, its back jacked high, rumbled into the driveway, and a red-eyed man stuck his leathery face out the window. "Hey, Mr. Wilder. You want some produce today?"

Lem Wilder walked over to the porch railing. "What do you have?"

"Tomatas, beans, squash, a few pints of berries. Your missus likes them berries."

The banker put down his pipe and dug out his wallet. He gave David a ten. "Get some tomatoes and raspberries from Tully. His wife usually comes by."

David took the ten, went down the steps, and walked over to the truck. He'd seen the old truck, driven by a plump woman with a cloud of salt-and-pepper hair, stop by the house before. She'd been friendly and cheerful, but her husband reeked of alcohol and his dark hair smelled sour.

Tully heaved himself from the cab and extracted two pints of raspberries and two pounds of small ripe tomatoes from the crates in back. One more crate was covered with a threadbare quilt. David paid him, eyeing the crate. The man took a small wad of bills from his back pocket and counted off the change carefully.

Waiting for the five dollars, David glanced into the truck's cab. A rifle lay half-concealed on the floorboard. He'd heard Tully was a moonshiner, and David had a thought as to what might be under the old quilt.

He looked up to find Tully's eyes boring into him. "Something you want, son?" David's cocky expression disappeared. This was not a man you would want to meet in the deep woods on a moonless night.

"No, sir."

The man nodded. David took his change and the produce, bid good-bye, and glanced up at the porch. His father had gone. David shoved the change in his pocket.

Listening to the truck roar away, he took the berries and tomatoes into the kitchen, where his mother was pouring tonic into her afternoon glass of gin. A dish of limes waited beside the bottles on the bar.

Evangeline's flaming red hair caught the sunlight from the window, giving her a halo. Saint Evangeline? Hardly. He placed the tomatoes and raspberries on the counter. "Dad bought these from Tully Gaddis. I'm going to the lake. Then I'm taking Pam to the early show and I guess we'll get something to eat at Danny's."

"Pamela Dodge?" asked his mother. "Kind of wild, isn't she?"

David shrugged. "You know her folks."

"Nice people," said Evangeline. "Too nice. She's a bit spoiled and I heard—" His mother stopped. "It's just gossip. Be careful, David."

"I'm a big boy." He turned and went down the back steps, pausing to pick up a small bucket, and continued down the steep path through the rhododendron forest that led to the lake. He stopped at the stream where the minnow trap was set.

He scooped minnows out of the trap into the bucket, reset the trap, then scuffled down the steepest part of the path until he reached the lake shore, where a ramshackle boathouse and a dock stood. He breathed in the smell of the woods and the damp earth, so deep in its loaminess, its primitive sensuality, that the hair on the back of his neck prickled.

The boat was a quarter full of water from the last night's rain, and he bailed it out quickly with an old coffee can. He didn't bother to check the gasoline level. He'd just filled it the day before, and the sooner he put some distance between himself and his father the better.

He stowed a paddle, cast off, and yanked the cord. The motor sputtered and then purred. He guided the boat to the middle of the lake, boats bobbing at dock after dock in his wake. On the far shore, yellow pine beams of new construction jutted through the trees. The pounding of hammers rang in syncopation. He headed away from the sounds, east, toward the waterfall.

The waterfall wasn't one of the high, rushing ones that spilled over rocks like a bridal veil. This waterfall was a sloping rocky spill, its flow just strong enough for a water wheel. Around the next bend David cut the motor and drifted into a cove, where he heard the rushing of the distant cascade. The low sun cast gold paillettes on the green-black water, and a mallard paddled around the shallows where blackberry canes arched, heavy with fruit, their tips kissing the glassy water. He dropped his line and almost at once felt a tug. He pulled in the fish, a small rainbow trout. He tossed the undersized fish back.

After half an hour, he caught nothing else. Ready to try another cove, he tugged on the rope of the little motor, but it sputtered, coughed, and died. David yanked on the rope again. And again. And again. Then he remembered his brother Phil had taken a girl out in the boat the day before.

He'd get Phil for not refilling the tank. He grabbed the paddle from under the seat and plunged it into the water, cursing as the splatter hit his cheek. He swiped the water away with two fingers. He'd try the cove by the falls and then go home.

He didn't want to be late for his date with Pam Dodge. He'd wanted to go out with her the summer before, but she'd been going with Judd Coulton, a guy from South Carolina whose father bought him another Corvette every time he wrecked one.

He glided through the sun-dappled water, around the bend and into the cove where the waterfall tumbled and glided over a slope of boulders, spiraling into eddies of dust and rhododendron blossoms.

Above him, the abandoned grist mill stood beside the falls. Twenty years before, tourists had come by cable car from the highway above to buy cornmeal, but now the cable car swayed in the wind, red with rust, creaking eerily. The flume that had carried water to the big overshot wheel had collapsed, and the mill was boarded up.

He gazed at it for a moment, then raised his paddle to head for quieter water. A motion in the woods near the falls caught his eye, and he lowered the paddle.

A girl in cutoffs, dark hair giddy in the wind and water spray, leaped from stone to stone at the base of the falls. Their eyes met for a brief moment before she stepped to the opposite bank and disappeared behind the mill.

Was he dreaming? Girls who looked like that belonged in the movies, not around dilapidated mills. "Hey," he shouted. "Hey." The noise of the falls swallowed his words.

He paddled to the bank and tied the boat to a root of mountain laurel. A path led uphill to the old mill, and rickety steps gave access to its catwalk. A sign had been nailed across the door. HAZARD. KEEP OUT.

He climbed the path and mounted the stairs to the mill's entrance. He followed the catwalk around the mill, peering through the cracks. The single room was empty except for scattered husks of grain and piles of rotting bags.

He turned back, wondering if he had imagined the girl, but she was down by the lake, peering into his boat.

He ran down the rickety steps, shouting, "Hello!"

She raised her head in alarm and hurried back toward the shallow place where she'd crossed the falls. She leaped onto the first stone. It teetered with her weight, and she threw out one arm to balance herself. She jumped back toward the bank and landed awkwardly, dropping to her knees. The bucket slipped from her fingers and tipped into the lake.

He was at her side in an instant. "Are you hurt? Let me help you."

"I'm all right." She scrambled to her feet and brushed off her shorts. Wet dirt caked her knees and brown mud spattered her T-shirt. But her eyes, glowing as deeply as star sapphires, regarded him with burning contempt.

She tossed her head and pointed. "Look-a there!"

Blackberries, whole and squashed, lay half-buried in the mud and scattered on the bank, the rest bobbing on the lake's ripples. David dropped to his knees and began to pick up all he could see. "I'll help you."

"Can't put them in nothing; the bucket's in the lake."

"I'll get it." He dropped the berries in his hand.

The bucket, slowly filling, floated just beyond the water's edge. He stepped into the shallows despite the cold water seeping into his shoes. Just as he reached for the bucket he slid knee-deep into a hole. He grabbed the bucket and waded out, his shoes sucking mud, his shorts soaked.

Triumphantly, he held the bucket out to her. She snatched it and began to scoop berries off the ground. "This was an afternoon's work. My ma will tan my hide when I get home."

"Well, I've got to go home all wet."

Her eyes traveled his body from his reddish-brown hair to his mud-soaked sneakers. David felt a blush rising in his cheek at the inspection. "I sure have pity," she finally said and knelt into the mud to continue her work.

David went to the boat and washed out his shoes and stowed them under the seat. Then he went back to help the girl. Many of the berries had been smashed, and many were unrecoverable.

They worked silently for a while, not talking, berries plunking in the pail and the waterfall rushing behind them. He watched her out of the corner of his eye, trying to see the face below the mass of curls.

"I'm David Wilder," he said, wishing she would say something.

She looked up at him quickly. "I seen you around." He was surprised; he couldn't remember seeing her before. Maybe she'd been on the street, in the soda shop, and all he'd noticed were his own friends. He wished she would smile.

"Look, I'm really sorry," he said. He leaned closer, close enough to smell girl sweat and Ivory soap. "Can I do anything else?"

"No, thanks, you done plenty." She stood up and brushed herself off. She walked over to a nearby laurel bush and reached under it. She pulled out a brown paper bag and a pair of boots. She sat down and tugged on the boots.

"Can I give you a ride anywhere in the boat?"

"I reckon not."

He cleared his throat. "What's in the bag?"

"You sure do ask a lot of questions," she said. She tied her boots and got up, then picked up her bag and began to climb the rocky trail up to the roadway.

"Tell me who you are," David called out, but she didn't turn around. She gave him a funny feeling. He'd never met a girl like her before. So quick to judge him, so dismissive. He wanted badly to show her she was wrong.

He looked at his watch's foggy crystal. He was going to be late. He paddled faster. Pamela would be furious. All because of a girl who wouldn't even tell him her name.

Time, for him, had stopped. A half-sun glimmered on the tops of the hills. He got into the boat and paddled out of the cove, away toward home.

Chapter 5

The City, 1990

Molly Westbrook paced back and forth by the telephone. What had Daddy always told her? That she could do anything she wanted to do in life? That she should be brave, never hold back?

She picked up the phone and punched in the numbers she'd found in the phone book. Two rings, and then a voice answered, deep and plummy. "Wildwood, Junius Johnson speaking."

Molly took a deep breath. "Hello, is Mrs. Wilder in?"

She heard the gentle regret in his voice. "No, I'm sorry. She's had a death in the family. May I take a message?"

A cold knife sliced through Molly. "Oh, no!" she blurted. "Was it her son?"

The voice didn't lose a beat. "No, ma'am. It was Mr. David's wife."

Molly felt cold and then hot. "I'm so sorry."

"Thank you, ma'am. I'll tell her you called. Whom shall I say?"

"Molly Westbrook," she said. "I met her at Mrs. Ragsdale's."

"I'll tell her, Mrs. Westbrook."

"Thank you." Molly hung up the phone, hardly breathing. Her shoulders felt heavy and tight, and her chest hurt. Oh, yes, Mrs. Wilder did know a David Wilder! And she hadn't wanted to say. Why not? When would Mrs. Wilder return? And where had she gone? Molly could've asked, but it didn't seem like the thing to do. Maybe the next mail would bring a letter, just one letter, from the David Wilder who was the Reverend in North Carolina. Or would he be in mourning, and not inclined to answer her?

She hadn't really believed her David Wilder could have any connection with Philemon T. Wilder, the philanthropist. Why would the son of a man who lived in an estate like Wildwood near a big-city university become a clergyman in the rural mountains?

Two years ago the Wilder family had sponsored a university-wide function on the lawn of Wildwood. When she and Paul wandered through the grounds, Molly thought the Tudor mansion was lovely, but she had seen castles and palaces in Europe and wondered why people wanted to live in places so big. She'd learned that often these palaces were built by kings who squeezed the peasants for money and didn't pay their soldiers. Kings who lusted for land and power.

And her father was a soldier. A good man. An honest man. What would this David Wilder be like? She wasn't sure she wanted him as a father. But she had to know.

She'd first heard of him when her family had gone to Glen-creggan, North Carolina, where her daddy's folks, the Fergusons, lived. She hadn't seen the place in years. She'd lived most of her life on far-flung Army bases, too far away to take the whole family back for holidays, or so Daddy had claimed. Glencreggan was as pretty and quaint as he'd said, but it was beginning to bustle.

"God, it feels good to be home!" Daddy had said, standing on Uncle Jimbo's back porch, sniffing the cool evergreen-scented air, gazing at the autumn-colored mountains fading into blue.

Home, Daddy called it, but it didn't feel like home to her. Her two boy cousins told her she talked funny and tried to tickle her. She finally chased them out into the backyard and challenged them to a fight, but Daddy put a stop to it.

The aunts just laughed. "She takes after Owen," they said.

Later, she escaped out to the back porch to avoid the girl cousins, who kept talking about the boys they liked and asking her about boyfriends. She didn't have any; Daddy was way too strict about that.

She sat on a wooden bench near the kitchen window and watched Aunt Annie's gourd martin houses swing on the T-bar of a pole, wondering what it would be like to live in one place all your life. The longest they'd ever stayed in one place was three years.

The smells of turkey and dressing and sweet potato pie came drifting through the window along with the hill cadences of her aunts' voices. She was about to starve, and wished dinner would hurry up. And then she heard her own name.

She caught her breath and slid along the bench, closer to the window.

"Molly sure looks like her momma, don't she?"

"The spittin' image. But where'd that red hair come from? Trilby's hair was black, as I recall."

"Red just crops up in some famblies."

Heart racing, Molly strained to hear. The voices dropped. "Them Wilders have got red hair in the family."

"Not the boy. That Davey."

"That boy had red in the brown like my Uncle Ike. His momma was a carrot top."

"You better hush, Myrtice. Don't say nothing like that around Owen."

"I still can't get over him not suspecting. She don't look like him a-tall."

"Hush, I tell you! She looks like Trilby. Don't go making trouble."

It seemed that they'd left the troublemaking to Molly herself.

When Evangeline Wilder returned home to Wildwood the evening of the funeral, her husband was sitting in his favorite leather chair, feet propped on a brass-studded hassock, watching the Bulldogs play the Gators on television. In the old days, she'd accompanied him to games, and they'd taken Phil and David a few times. More often they'd attended football games with friends or business associates and gone to a party afterwards. Where were those friends now? Scattered like the autumn leaves across the grass and, like the leaves, blown away in the celestial wind.

It was past time to reunite their family. They needed each other.

She stood behind his chair watching an end run for a loss. Lem loved to watch football. Teamwork. That was what made a man, Lem said. Phil had played football in high school, and David had excelled at tennis, and the basement was full of their trophies. A few stood on the shelves here in the paneled study. Their father hadn't had the time to attend their games, and now Phil didn't care all that much about the sport.

"Lem?"

He turned the sound down a notch. "Hello, Evie."

She leaned down to kiss him. "How are you feeling?"

"A little better. Tommy saw me this morning. He says I'm overdoing it again."

"Tom knows what he's talking about. Did he give you a new prescription?"

"Umph." Evangeline knew this meant yes.

Lem watched a pass, a reception, and a run for a touchdown. After the conversion kick succeeded, he turned to Evie. "How's the boy?"

She patted his shoulder. "He's all right. I get the sense he's not showing what he really feels. On the surface he's taking it well."

Lem peered into his empty beer mug. "Had a lot of time to get used to it."

Evangeline squelched a sigh and walked around to sit on the sofa next to his chair. "Yes, Tallulah was sick for a long time, but do you ever get used to it?" She placed a hand on her husband's shoulder. "Please take care of yourself."

Her husband grunted. "Don't you worry about me, Evie, I'm fine."

Evangeline stroked her husband's shoulder. "You know, Lem, it would mean a lot to him if you called him."

"I don't know what I could say." Commercials interrupted the game, and he brandished the remote, flipping through channels. "No good at consoling people. Leave that up to you. Have J.J. bring me a cup of decaf, would you, hon?"

Evangeline went into the half-light of the empty, enormous kitchen and glanced at the clock. Junius had left long ago. He took evening classes at the university downtown, planning to go into hotel management. She turned on the electric kettle and measured one careful spoon of fresh ground decaf into the French press, then added another for herself. Tonight David would be numb. Tomorrow might be harder for him. She'd give him a call then.

She looked through the notes Junius had left. So many people had called to express condolences. Molly Westbrook? She set her lips in a thin line and poured the coffee. She would have to think of a way to handle Molly, even as she yearned to tell the young woman everything. She looked very much like that girl of David's: there was no mistake. Staying quiet was what David wished, and yet she felt he was wrong.

The next morning David blinked awake, groggy, to an intermittent patter of rain on the roof. He shoved the covers aside and stumbled to splash water on his face before he went to get Lu her glass of juice. When he stepped out of the bathroom, he stopped short. The hospital bed across from his own was neatly made, green corded bedspread pulled tightly across the top, cream-colored blanket folded at the foot.

The jolt at not seeing her there took away the fog of sleep, took away his breath. He awakened fully to the cruel reality that he would never see her again.

He made himself go through the morning routine. He dressed in jeans and a flannel shirt; he brewed a cup of coffee the way she'd taught him to like it, grinding the beans fresh. She'd told him her grandpa had even bought his beans green and parched them. David walked out onto the porch and watched the rising mist sift into the sun. He sipped the coffee slowly, unwilling to get on with the day. He didn't feel like food just yet. He wanted to take down the bed where she'd been trying to recover from her latest surgery before the stroke took her life.

He hated the bed, a symbol of her suffering and decline. The sooner he could get it out of the house, the better. And it was painful to look at her clothes, the glasses resting on the bedside table, her favorite coffee cup. He fingered the robe draped across the back of the chair, the robe waiting for Lu, who would not place her hand on its soft folds again.

He found a set of socket wrenches in the tool shed by the barn. He went into the bedroom, took off the bedspread, and folded it neatly. He folded the white sheets, then the sheepskin pad that had kept her from getting bedsores, then the mattress pad. He lifted the mattress off and took it out into the front room. He began to wrestle the frame apart.

The telephone kept ringing. Friends and parishioners wanted to come by, to bring him casseroles and cakes, to stay the night with him; they felt that loved ones should not be left alone to grieve. But he needed to face this time alone, and he fended off the offers of company. The food he could not refuse, and gratefully accepted it. He told them they could leave it at the church if they didn't feel like driving all the way up to his place. Some would drive anyway.

He took the frame rails to the porch and then walked back to the bedroom, over to Lu's closet, and opened it. He gazed at the blue print dress she wore to church, the rose striped shirt she used to garden in, the green corduroys she wore at home by the fire. Each one brought back a painful memory of her in happier days, doing the things she loved.

He pulled out one garment after another, willing himself not to remember. He piled them on the bed, the dresses and the skirts and the blouses and the coats, then the shoes, until the closet was empty.

The clothes filled three green leaf bags. He'd take them to the thrift shop the Methodists ran, but not today; people would say it was too soon. He took the bags back to the closet, shoved them in, and shut the door. He realized he was sweating, though the cabin was cool.

He pulled nightgowns and underthings and pantyhose out of the dresser and stuffed them into smaller trash bags for discarding. The nightgowns, too familiar. Seen too many times, associated with pain. Then he opened a drawer of Lu's little writing table. There, stacked carefully in a rubber band, were all the letters he had ever written her. He slipped off the band and carefully opened one, unfolded the yellowed paper, read it. It was a love letter. "Please believe me, I will never hurt you . . ." The words were an empty wind blowing through him. He folded the letter shut and dropped it. He had not hurt her. He had never hurt her. Except, perhaps, by not giving her everything he could have, the one thing he did not have to give: his whole heart.

All those years that had gone by since he'd tucked his heart away. Had they been wasted? He had loved once, a long time ago, with all his being, and it had ended in disaster. And he had loved Tallulah, but always holding something back. And now he wished she could be here again, so he could try again to tell her how much he cared. But then she was reserved too, never complaining, and had made it too easy for him to stay in the prison he'd constructed. Still, the house felt so empty without her soft mountain voice, without the way she sang old songs as she cooked, without the excitement she radiated when she was happy.

Resolutely he went back to the drawer and pulled out another packet of letters, somewhat larger, somewhat more tattered, tied with a red ribbon. These were from her first husband Leland, from Vietnam. Perhaps he should give them to Leland's mother, who was eighty-four. He laid them on the table. Under the letters there were a few snapshots of Lu and Leland. He started to lay them on top of the letters and then on impulse looked through them. They had been taken just before Leland was sent overseas.

Leland stood in his uniform, looking down at her. He'd been a tall man, taller than David, and he was looking at his Tallulah with love, and she was looking back at him with the same love, smiling, both of them, not knowing that three months later their smiles would be shattered in the steaming stench and cry of an explosive jungle night.

David looked at his own letters a long time. And then he took them to the fireplace, stuffed them in, and set a match to them. He watched the smoke spiral up the chimney as the letters blackened and curled and flaked away. Then he walked over to his desk and picked up the letter from Molly Westbrook. Maybe he should toss it in too. But something held him back. He carefully placed the letter on his desk, walked over to the fireplace, and poked the ashes of his letters, watching the bright sparks taking his words to heaven.

He took a last sip of his cold coffee. He shouldered the bed frame and took it out to the barn. He'd call someone to come pick up the bed.

Outside, the chickens in their coop squawked and gabbled, fluffing feathers against the crisp, cold air. He needed to see to the cow first.

He hunched on a milking stool, cheek against the cow's flank, fingers on her warm teats, urging milk into the steel bucket, too much milk for one man. Could he live here alone? He had five acres, the remainder of a farm. He'd bought the cow so that Lu could have the fresh milk she had loved as a child, and he'd carried on with her vegetable garden. She had looked after the chickens as long as she was able, but David didn't like the work involved with chickens and thought he might give them to Hattie, along with the cow.

He needed to go to the church, lose himself in work. He couldn't stay here today.

Before he left, he put on a warm jacket and went out to tend the animals. He tossed the cow some hay and fed the chickens and the barn cats. They were all a part of his life: the cow, the cats, the chickens. Tallulah had been fond of the critters. She'd had a mongrel dog when he married her, and the dear creature had died about the time Tallulah got sick, and she didn't want another pet, since she couldn't look after it. He wondered what his new neighbors, the Florida people building a three-level house just down the rise, would think of his farm animals.

David backed the truck out of the driveway slowly into a fog of exhaust and clatter. The truck was showing its age and needed work. It occurred to him that if he sold the place, he could buy a new pickup.

On the outskirts of town he slowed near a hog wire-fenced field where shells of automobiles rusted in tall grass. RECYCLE read the sign next to HERMAN'S GARAGE. He turned into the driveway of a corrugated metal building, stopped the truck, and got out uneasily. Herman was one of Tallulah's cousins, one who'd never quite accepted him.

"I heard you coming, Preacher," called Herman from the bay of the shop and ducked as he ambled out, wiping his hands on his green coveralls. "You might have a hole in that muffler."

"Could you take a look at it today?"

"I'm kindly stove up with work this morning, but I might could get to it by this evening."

"I'll drop it off another time." David gazed up at the sky. "Looks like rain anyhow."

"How are you getting along?" asked Herman.

"All right," said David. "Thanks."

"That was a good funeral."

"I appreciate your coming, Herman."

Herman stood there as though he had something else to say. David waited patiently as he'd learned to do, to ride with the rhythm of the town. Finally, Herman said, "You planning on staying?"

"I hadn't thought of leaving," said David.

"Preachers got a habit of moving on, and Bow Creek's a mighty little place." Herman pushed his baseball cap back on his head with a grease-stained hand and narrowed his eyes. "Talk is you might be happier someplace bigger."

"Maybe my job's not finished here yet."

"I hear you," said Herman.

"I'll see you later." David climbed back into the truck.

Leave? He'd been here fifteen years, most of them good. He'd started out with controversy, and he'd always be an outsider to people like Herman. He'd presided over the decision to sell the old rectory next to the church to a couple who wanted to convert it into a small bed and breakfast inn.

He'd thought it was a perfect solution. The upkeep to the old house had been draining the church coffers, and the beautiful, historic old church had badly needed a new roof. The leaky parish hall was also showing its age.

At that time, the small church provided one service each Sunday and two services during the summer months. Now, the summer attendance increased with each new summer house built for residents from Georgia, Florida, and the coastal Carolinas.

There had been lean years until this uptick, and only the stubbornness of the McGarry family had kept the church going. Nell was the only McGarry left in Bow Creek now, operating her antique shop out of her old family home. She'd opposed him when he wanted to sell the rectory. It had been built by her great-grandfather.

After Nell had lost the rectory fight, she'd been unhappy but seemed to get over it. And then she and Tallulah, both fiercely loving Bow Creek, had rekindled their schoolgirl friendship. Nell had become a friend to them both.

Then Bow Creek had started to grow, and with it, the church. And the difficulties.

Light-headed, realizing that he'd never had any breakfast, he parked the truck across the street from Nell's Antiques and walked down to Happy Mac's Cafe. He plunked two coins in a blue metal box and pulled out a copy of the *Citizen-Times.*

He slid into his favorite booth, the second on the left. Sandra, the waitress, came over. "Same thing, Preacher?"

Grits, scrambled eggs, toast, bacon. "Sure. And orange juice. Coffee."

"Gotcha."

He opened the newspaper. One of the old-time self-sufficient mountain men, who had lived up on a ridge all alone, had died. He'd been dead for three or four days before anyone found him. The story sent a shudder through David. He wouldn't want to die alone up at the farmhouse. Sandra slid a steaming plate of goodness in front of him, and he laid the paper aside.

He'd just finished the breakfast, downing the last sip of juice, when a hand touched his shoulder. "Mind if I join you?"

Nell McGarry, her light brown hair pulled back in a ponytail, smiled down at him. She'd dressed for work in a soft wool skirt, boots, and a blue tweedy sweater.

"Nothing I'd like better," David said affably She was already sliding in.

"Just coffee," Nell said to Sandra.

"Don't you eat?" David asked.

Nell shrugged. "Not breakfast."

"You ought to."

"Stick to spiritual advice, David," she said, raising an eyebrow. "Leave my diet alone."

"Would you take my spiritual advice?" Though he'd meant it jokingly, he was surprised to see her blush. After he'd advised her not to marry Hampton Taggart, telling her she'd have to get permission from the bishop, she'd sweetly ignored him and married Hampton in a chapel down in Greendale, in a blue gingham dress, music by a country guitarist, and the church full of Hampton's fans. And now Hampton was gone with his latest lady and Nell still didn't have a divorce. "Sorry," David said. "I shouldn't have made that remark."

She shook her head. "It's all right. I didn't stop to talk about my personal life. It's about the church."

He shrugged. "That's what I'm here for."

Nell leaned forward and gazed at him searchingly. "Well, here goes. Has anyone spoken to you about buying back the old rectory?"

He sat back in his seat and folded his hands. "No." He waited, saying nothing else. The ball was in her court.

She took out a pen and drew a flower on a napkin before she raised her eyes. "Since I opposed you on the sale of it back then, I've been elected to talk to you about buying it back."

Well, this was interesting. "So is the B&B for sale?"

"Not yet." She took a sip of coffee. "Harry Claymore found out that the Johnsons want to retire from the B&B business and move near their children in Charlotte. Harry talked to Frank Johnson, and Frank will agree to give us first option. He'll give us six months to come up with the money. They want to move by next year."

"And if we can't raise the funds?"

Nell bit her lip. "I hear Transmontane Properties is looking for a site to build a new complex of shops."

David shook his head. "The house will be toast if they get it, Nell."

She nodded. "I know. My great-grandfather's ghost will haunt the place forever. No one will ever rest again."

David managed a smile, but this news was like a punch in the gut. "Refresh my memory. Didn't he build your antique shop too?"

"Yes. My great-uncle wound up with the B&B house and my grandfather the house where I live. My great-uncle left his house to the church for a rectory. His only child died in World War I, and he wanted to memorialize him. It was called Fenimore House then. The plaque fell off and everybody forgot."

David's face warmed. Maybe Nell had told him once, and he was embarrassed that he'd forgotten. The vestry meetings had been unpleasant, to say the least, when he'd first proposed selling the rectory fifteen years before. Nell had finally given in when the B&B buyers promised to keep as many of the original fixtures and woodwork as possible, only making changes to qualify the kitchen as commercial and rewire and replumb the place.

He sighed. "All right, Nell. Bow Creek is growing, the church is growing, and we very well may need the property. But where would we get the money to buy it back? And would it split the church? The new summer people want to improve the church and parish hall, and the old-timers like to keep things as they are."

She gave him the ghost of a smile. "Old-timers like me. I was furious when you sold the rectory. I almost left the church."

"I'm glad you stayed." He returned her smile, wider. "We need your spirit. And I need your friendship."

Nell looked at her hands for a moment and took a deep breath. "David, you never talk about your father. Lu told me he's kind of . . . rich." David tried to interrupt, but Nell pressed on. "Do you suppose he'd help us get a loan?"

David's eyes slid away and he tightened his jaw. "I don't ask him for anything."

"But surely . . ."

"That's a subject best left alone, Nell," he said, not unkindly. He glanced at his watch. "Now I'd better be going. There's a pile on my desk, I know." He reached out and clasped her hand with both of his. "I can't thank you enough for all you've done for my wife."

Nell waited in the booth until he had paid the check and left. She liked David and wished they didn't have to be at odds. Especially now that he had to deal with this when he was still mourning poor Tallulah. Thinking of her friend saddened her. The painful thing she remembered was how Tallulah had seemed resigned to her fate. Why hadn't she fought harder?

Chapter 6

Bow Creek, November, 1990

Breakfast with David. Walking back to her shop, Nell was concerned about him. If it was just a case of money, she didn't see why he couldn't use some of his family connections to find a way to finance buying back the rectory. Approaching the old house, the beloved old house of her growing-up years, she brightened just to see it in sunshine and decided to go ahead and hang cranberry bows on the front porch railing. It was time for early Christmas shoppers.

Nell unlocked the back door and walked into the kitchen, remembering the days before the divorce, when she ran the shop during the summer months only and spent winters in Raleigh with Lyle. And then a dark time had come in the marriage, a time when she'd dreaded closing the shop. She'd stayed open later and later each year, postponing her return home, and wasn't surprised when her best friend in Raleigh called with the news about the woman in Lyle's office, which she had known but not wanted to admit.

It had been a messy divorce, but she had lived through it, and the shop still gave her a giddy pleasure. Bow Creek, her hometown, where her roots ran deep, had saved her life after the divorce, giving her somewhere to belong.

But had she ever really belonged in Raleigh? And after having spent time in the wider world, could she ever totally belong here again, with her family scattered? The church and Sophie were her family now.

She started a pot of coffee and assembled a plate of cookies to take to the parlor for early customers, her mind still on David. He'd advised her to wait a year when she told him she was going to marry Hampton Taggart. Hampton Taggart! What had she been thinking? With a school-age daughter, she couldn't always go on the road with him. Though he grinned like a lovesick fool when she was by his side, though she loved the feel of being his girl, in the end they had each thought the other was someone else.

She shook her head. If she'd only listened to David. He did have his good points.

She walked around the shop, checking the eye appeal of her displays, straightening a faded blue and rose quilt on an antique mahogany rack. She pulled back the curtains to let in sunlight and turned the front door sign to OPEN.

She'd headed back for the cookies when the door jingled an arrival. She turned to welcome a new customer, and, instead of the woman she'd expected, a husky blond man with the build of a former athlete stood grinning at her. "Ms. McGarry?" he asked, holding out a hand. "I'm Kip Hogarth, from Transmontane Properties."

She pasted on a smile she didn't feel and shook his proffered hand. "Hello, Mr. Hogarth. What can I do for you?"

"It's what I can do for you," he boomed. "Can we talk for a few minutes?" He surveyed the room. "Nice place you've got here."

"Thanks. I can talk until a customer comes. My assistant's not in yet. Please, come back to the kitchen." Nell kept her pasted-on smile and beckoned him to follow her. It might be good to see what he was going to say.

The coffee was ready, and she offered the visitor a cup. He agreed, and she poured her second cup of the day and one for him. Facing her guest across the antique pine table, she took a sip of the fragrant brew. "Well?"

He leaned forward, radiating enthusiasm. "I'll come right to the point. They told me you might have some connection to this property that's coming on the market soon, this B&B next to the church."

She smiled, lifting one shoulder slightly. "A purely historical and sentimental connection. I don't own any part of it." She didn't feel like telling him it was the house her great-grandfather, Magnus McGarry, built when he'd moved here from Charleston to get away from the heat and malaria.

She also didn't feel like telling him that Magnus opened the Mercantile Store and ran it until his death, and that Magnus gave her great-uncle the first house and built himself another one, which was her shop now. Or that when her great-uncle's son died, he left the first house to the church for a rectory.

But now Hogarth was clearing his throat. She gave him her full attention. "The owners tell me they'll give the church first option," he said.

She sipped her coffee again. Her shoulders were getting tight. "Yes. It was the rectory once, and it was sold because it wasn't needed at the time. But that was then." Did he know she was a church member, or was he fishing? She glanced toward the door, hoping to see her assistant come flying in, late as usual and full of apologies.

"Look," Hogarth said. "We've been looking for a place to build a shop complex in Bow Creek, and this location is ideal. The house could be the centerpiece and serve as the restaurant, perhaps. It would be a perfect use of this property. Do you know when the church will make a decision?"

Nell gazed into her coffee cup. She didn't want to lie, but it was all right to fudge. "You've caught me at an awkward time, Mr. Hogarth. I don't know the answer to that."

"Perhaps you could find out?"

Nell sat back, grim. He knew she was a church member and was trying to test her loyalty. It wasn't right. Much to her relief, the front bell jangled. She glanced up to see two women plunging through the door, shaking off drops from the mizzling rain.

She stood, smoothing her skirt. "I don't think I can help you, Mr. Hogarth. Now if you'll excuse me? I have customers."

He reluctantly got to his feet. "Nice talking to you. Here's my card."

"Thank you for coming in," she said. "Just leave it on the table." He placed it by his cold coffee and left by the front door, shutting it a little too hard.

Nell's well-dressed shoppers wanted to browse for Christmas presents while their husbands were out hunting wild turkeys with a guide. Hoping the women didn't plan to roast those tough old birds for Thanksgiving, she showed them some hand-fired turkey platters as well as some Victorian glass ornaments and some handmade quilts and pillows.

These shoppers weren't concerned too much with the cost of things, just that they were authentic, and Nell specialized in authentic. It was so important to keep local crafts alive, crafts that historically had grown out of necessity, giving mountain women and men a way to bring beauty and artistry into their plain and precarious living.

Nell loved anybody who appreciated crafts, and today the ladies were in a buying mood, arranging some of her most finely wrought items on the counter. She wasn't envious of their affluence, because they had good taste, and she had everything she needed—almost.

Sometimes it got lonely, with her family out of town now, but she was just fine by herself. She had the shop, the church, and Sophie. But she would miss Lu a lot.

Once again she thought of David.

She spread wrapping paper for a soft blue and lilac lambswool throw. She folded the paper and sealed it with a sticker. She shook out a tote bag. If David's father was Philemon T. Wilder, head of Wilder Bank and Trust, then why did David live so simply? Lu had kept teaching preschool as long as she was able, and Nell knew good and well what St. Ninian's had paid both of them. It must have been some real falling-out he'd had with his family. His perfectly groomed and stylish mother had come for Lu's funeral. Not his father. Why?

The women approached the counter, and Nell cleared her mind. David's family situation wasn't her business, except for the possibility of getting a loan for the church.

She gave the women two large tote bags filled with treasures. After they'd gone, she gazed out the window at the church steeple down the street. She thought she knew David, but he had secrets.

Chapter 7

David opened the side door of St. Ninian's and entered. *Maybe this day will be better.* At least the sun was shining and the air was clear. He enjoyed walking past the preschool classrooms, alive with the babble of the children. On the walls, crayoned lions and lambs and cows and horses, God's creatures, hung. He remembered with a pang that those drawings had been posted a week ago, when Lu was alive. He'd meant to take some home for her. *The things we put off . . .*

"Good morning, Father David." Jane, the white-haired church secretary, glanced up from a computer screen. "This new computer takes some getting used to."

Meticulously dressed, Jane was a South Carolina transplant, a widow who'd seen her social life shrinking, wanted to be useful, and could afford to accept the small salary St. Ninian's was able to offer.

"Jake Halsey was surprised we'd waited so long to upgrade," David said.

"I think I'll like it," Jane said. She pointed to the screen. "Anything to add to the Sunday bulletin?"

David scrutinized her copy. “No, I don’t think so. Did the altar guild call you about the request for flowers?”

“I have it.”

“I’ll be in the office.”

“Oh. A Kip Hogarth from Transmontane Properties called, wanting to see you.”

David paused a long moment. “Did he say why?”

“No. I didn’t think you’d be in today. I went ahead and penciled him on your calendar for nine Monday morning.” She looked at him with concern. “How are you?”

“I’m all right,” said David, giving Jane a rueful smile. “Happy to be at work.”

Jane cleared her throat. “Oh. Bad news. I hate to tell you this. Sudie Conway is back in the hospital.”

Oh, no. Sudie’s overweight and diabetes had plagued her for years. “I’ll go see her.” After Lu’s illness, David found hospital visits took all his strength to stay positive and hopeful, but Sudie was a local, a former evangelical, who was now more Anglican than the Archbishop of Canterbury. She’d wandered in one Sunday out of curiosity, just to see if they really worshiped devils, and never left. Now she was his goodwill ambassador to all of Bow Creek.

Jane pursed her mouth. “Better go soon. The last time I talked to her she sounded so strange, so unlike herself. I hate to think she’s giving up.”

David laid a hand on Jane’s shoulder and gave it a squeeze. “I’ll go this afternoon.”

In his office he took a call from Tom Wilkins, his junior warden, a county surveyor who lived in Greendale with his Baptist wife and widowed mother.

“I’m surprised to find you in,” said Tom. “Why don’t you take some time off, a couple of weeks, say?”

"Well, Tom, we're short-handed here." David riffled the stack of letters on his desk and glanced at the notes on his memo pad. It was a bad time for him to be out of the office.

"Let Harry Claymore and me carry some of the load, and get one of those retired priests over in Cashiers to take the service."

"I think I'd better be here for the vestry meeting next week."

Tom hesitated for a moment before he replied, "Oh, sure. I'd almost forgotten."

"We'll have lunch soon, Tom."

They said their good-byes. David hung up the phone bemused. Had they meant to have a vestry meeting without him? And why? Did it have to do with the rectory? And if it did, why didn't they want him there? Were they thinking it was time for new blood?

He tasked himself with replying to the many consolation messages that had come in. The phone kept ringing, and he took most of the calls. Finally, he laid down his pen, stretched his hands out in front of him. He'd go to Greendale to see Sudie Conway now. He hoped he could do her good and help her faith to carry her along.

The sweeping curves of the road east to Greendale led through stretches of fallow farmland and hillsides filled with young Christmas trees, their fresh smell scenting the air. The leaf season had come and gone, save for a few brilliant red oaks. On rocky slopes, tall hardwoods spread bare gray limbs, while the undulating distant hills shaded into blue smoke and sky.

Twenty-five miles, descending. Soon he passed by a waterfall cascading over a rocky slope and he slowed to admire the rush of water playing in the sun. The sight jolted him into a remembrance of Trilby and the letter from Molly Westbrook. How could he reply? How could he begin? *Molly, I met your mother by a waterfall.*

He'd gone out with Pamela that evening. He smoothed over her anger at his lateness by telling her how great she looked, and he wasn't lying. He admired her smooth bronzed skin, her killer figure, her pouty lips, her perfect teeth, her sun-streaked hair caught in a ponytail. They went for fudge ripple ice cream after the movie, made out a little, and Pam even agreed to a tennis date later that week.

But the lady of the lake . . . he couldn't let her go. Not yet. There was mystery there. There was a challenge in the way she'd looked at him.

The next afternoon, he filled the tank of the outboard motor and puttered out on the water, wanting to race, forcing himself to idle along. He cut the motor when he rounded the bend to the waterfall cove but saw only a gray-haired man and a small boy fishing out of a shiny aluminum rig. Did he imagine the mystery girl? But there had been blackberry stains on his wet clothes, and Celesta, his mother's "help" she'd brought with them, had caught him trying to smuggle the bundle into the laundry room. Rotten luck she'd still been awake. Her room was across from the laundry room on the ground floor.

"What you doing, young'un?" she said, fixing him with her gimlet eye.

"Um, I just fell in the lake, and I was picking blackberries . . ."

"I never knowed you to pick blackberries."

He shrugged. "I wanted one of your delicious cobblers, Celesta. They're the best, with some whipped cream on top."

A smile broke her frown, and she took the bundle and set it on top of the machine. "Go on with you. You up to no good, I reckon, but I won't tell the folks."

"Thank you, Celesta, you're the greatest."

"Hmph," she said, and he knew he'd been dismissed, and he also knew she wouldn't tell. She'd practically raised him, and sometimes he'd play with her son. Edward. She wanted Edward to be a preacher.

Not for him, he'd thought. He surveyed the cove once more. No mystery girl today. He might as well fish. He caught four nice trout.

On the following day he met Pamela at the Glencreggan Country Club's new tennis courts. They played a fast and hard set against the threatening dark clouds to the west. Pam was a canny, strategic player, but David was a better one, with the advantage of strength, and he took the win. She fought him hard, though. He admired her spirit.

After it was over, they sat sweaty and flushed on the green courtside bench drinking bottled Cokes. A cool breeze carrying the smell of rain filtered over them, feeling good.

"Nice game," David said.

Pamela playfully swatted him on the shoulder. "You weren't a gentleman."

David grinned at her. "If I'd let you win, you'd have said I was a wuss."

"Next time, buster." She wiped the sweat from her forehead and pulled off her elastic band, regrouping her ponytail. "You know, last year I thought you were a nerd."

David flushed. "Thanks a bunch. I thought I was hot stuff."

"I didn't mean that in a bad way," she said. "I mean, you're always so serious. Got your nose in a book."

He studied his sneakers. "You ought to try it, Pam."

"What do you mean?" She frowned. "Is that an insult?"

Before he could say he was just kidding, a voice broke in behind them, halfway between a sneer and a drawl. "Which one of you wants a real game? My partner didn't show."

Judd Coulton, in tennis shorts and polo shirt, an off-white sweater, the V-neck banded with maroon and navy, slung around his shoulders, stood at the gate. A couple of inches taller than David and tanned, he wore his brown-blond hair longish. He'd graduated from Yale and was planning to attend Harvard law school in the fall.

Pamela looked at the new arrival, a mixture of emotions playing across her face. David remembered how into each other they'd seemed the year before. "I've had enough, Coulton," David said, and spun his racket on the ground.

"Pammy?"

"I'm tired, Judd."

"Neither of you is in my class anyhow. God, how I wish we had a tennis pro so I'd have somebody worth playing with."

"I can beat you any day of the week," said David. He hated that braggart.

"You?"

Pamela placed a hand on his arm. "Don't let him get your goat, David."

Judd Coulton grinned. "I get what I want."

"Do you always?" Pamela's voice was hard.

"You should know."

Pamela winced at the insinuating tone. David clamped his jaw, spun his racket once more, and grabbed it up. He strode out onto the court. "Ready when you are, Coulton."

Pamela sighed, flung her sweater over her shoulders, and crossed her legs, swinging her foot. David vaguely remembered her telling him once that Judd Coulton had been the captain of his tennis team at Yale, but he didn't care.

David aced more serves that day than in a long time, but he couldn't keep up. Coulton's shots spun and slid just out of reach. Sweat poured down David's face, not just from the exertion. After it was all over, Judd Coulton bone-crushed David's aching hand. "See you guys. I've got a date." He walked off the court, whistling, to his red Corvette.

Lips tight and flexing his sore hand, David walked Pamela back to her car. Pamela touched his arm. "David, did you hear me? I said 'Guess who he's dating?'"

"Sorry. I couldn't care less."

Pamela shrugged. "It's Trilby Gaddis."

"I don't know her."

Pamela looked at him curiously. "She's a local girl."

"Holy spit," said David. "Nobody goes out with the locals."

"Obviously, some people do," she said with an enigmatic smile. "Last year I went out with the guy whose father owns the stables. I found he wasn't interested in me so much as seeing if he could make out with one of us. A trophy, you know?"

David's face flushed. "Yeah. Guys are like that. Some of them, anyhow."

"Oh? You too?" She laughed.

David didn't know what to say. He wondered if she'd done it with the stable guy but wasn't going to ask.

He opened the door of her aqua blue Dodge convertible for her and closed it after she had gotten in. Her family wasn't related to *those* Dodges, but they always drove their cars. Let people wonder.

"Are you going to the square dance Saturday night?" Pamela asked.

He hadn't thought about it, but it seemed like a good idea. Maybe the waterfall girl would come. "Sure. Want me to pick you up?"

"I was hoping you'd say that." She flashed him a grin and drove away.

Saturday was a long time coming, but Pamela was ready when he arrived, dressed in madras Bermuda shorts and a white sleeveless blouse, and she'd tied a baby blue sweater over her shoulders. She bounced into the seat of David's yellow convertible. "I like your car."

"Not a nerd car, is it?"

"Oh, forget I ever said that." She smiled. "Come on, let's put the top down."

They drove to town, wind in their hair, past the supermarket and Laundromat, past the post office, the Spinning Wheel Café, and the gray and white St. Anselm's Church. A young man named Jake Halsey was rector there, and his sermons made David's mandatory Sunday attendance bearable. Jake somehow got away with being a haircut shy of a hippie. He'd even convinced them to have a folk mass once a month, though it wasn't called a mass, because that made the low-churchers uncomfortable.

David stopped at the lone red light at the corner of Main and Hemlock. The neon sign of Danny's Soda Shop glowed blue against the darkened storefronts. Inside, he could see kids crowded at round tables and leaning at the counter, where counter girls Glenda and Allene were talking to a big guy with a crew cut.

He drove on past the Spinning Wheel and the Glen Theatre, its red-letter marquee announcing *West Side Story*. A knot of vacationers milled in front of the auction house, waiting for the weekly auction to begin. When he'd almost reached Dell's Barn, he glanced down at the gas gauge. "Pam, I'm almost out of gas."

She laughed. "That's supposed to be your line when we're on a deserted road somewhere."

"I wouldn't be so obvious," he said. He drove on past the barn and turned into Watson's Handy Mart just past a row of hemlocks. He pulled in front of the pump, and Norville Watson came out to fill the tank. "Wouldn't you know it," said David, spotting Judd Coulton's red Corvette sliding up to the other side of the pump.

A dark-haired girl got out of the car and headed in the direction of the ladies' room. David glimpsed a striped, scoop-neck top and short black pants, the kind the girls at school called Capri pants. There was a familiar lilt about her walk.

"Trilby Gaddis," whispered Pamela.

David took out six dollars and a quarter to pay Norville for the tank of gas. Norville went to get David a receipt just as the girl came back from the restroom.

The waterfall girl. David's heart did a double flip. Of course Coulton would pick the loveliest girl on the mountain. He'd feel it was his due.

David licked his dry lips and jammed the receipt into his pocket. He sped away, squealing tires. "Hey, take it easy," said Pam. "You still mad about the game?"

"Yeah, a little," said David. He couldn't let Pam know he had any interest in the girl.

"You'll get him next time," said Pam.

"Sure, sure," said David, glad for the useless encouragement. Two blocks down the street they turned into the driveway of

Dell's Barn and bumped down the rutty rows of cars, looking for a parking place.

"Well, well," said Pam, looking behind her. "I think our friends Judd and Trilby are coming too."

David swallowed. This was going to be one hell of an evening.

The faces from the past faded as the cream-colored stucco facade of Greendale Hospital rose on the hill ahead. David exited the highway and sighed. Sudie Conway was just sixty, ten years older than Lu had been.

Twenty minutes later he sat by Sudie's bed and held her hand as her breathing came in short gasps. Her daughter Willette, thirtyish, her mouth compressed in a thin line, paced back and forth in front of the window. The doctor had said Sudie needed her gallbladder out, usually a routine operation, but with her diabetes and being overweight there could be severe complications.

"We're counting on your prayers to pull her through," said Willette, not looking at him.

"I'll do my best," said David. "It'll take all our prayers, and whatever the outcome, you'll know they were heard."

"I don't know," Willette muttered. The room became unexpectedly still. David realized the tortured breathing had stopped.

He hastened to the bed to press the call button. In that instant Sudie gasped a rattling breath. Her pale eyes opened and she fixed her gaze on David. She wheezed a few unintelligible words, and her gnarled hand reached out to him.

He grasped it. "What is it, Sudie?"

Her gaze shifted to something just beyond his right shoulder. She smiled all the way to her crinkling eyes. "Bessie? Olen?"

David glanced at Willette and raised his eyebrows.

"That's her brother and sister," Willette murmured. "Olen died when he was twelve, fell off a waterfall. Aunt Bessie's been gone a year."

David, still holding Sudie's hand, waited to see if she'd say anything else, but she closed her eyes and appeared to nod off. David let go of her hand and patted it.

Sudie's eyes flew open and she smiled. "Father David. It's so good to see you. You and Willie." She glanced at her daughter. "Come over here, honey," she said.

Willette moved to the bedside and laid her hand on her mother's shoulder. Sudie looked up at David. "It's a blessing to have a daughter, don't you think?"

David, his heart in his throat, could do nothing but nod dumbly.

Chapter 8

After she'd seen Paul off to teach his 9:00 class, Molly Westbrook made the bed and washed the breakfast dishes and then she tidied the apartment and thought about catching the bus to the grocery store while she still had the energy. She got so tired by afternoon, waddling around with all that extra weight. She wondered what it had been like for her late mother, who must have been small like she was.

Her big-boned stepmother, Hedy, had popped her babies out like popcorn, her father had joked. And since Molly had been ten years old, used to fending for herself, when her first half-brother had been born, she stoically bore it when Hedy had little time for Molly once the babies were tugging at their mommy's skirts. Molly had played big sister and offered to help, all the while wishing that she had her own mother to confide in, to help her grow up.

Her outspoken youngest brother, Max, one day asked her, "Why don't you look like the rest of us?" Hedy had shushed him and blushed, but the words could not be unsaid.

But now Molly was about to become a mother herself, and the ache within her, that missing part of herself, nagged. Would she ever know the truth? Perhaps, if she found the man she suspected was her birth father. Maybe he would tell her what had really happened.

Daddy had had told her that her mother had died in an accident, but no more. She was sure that Daddy was keeping something important from her.

She searched for her good pen and some decent writing paper, and found both the pen and a box of pretty note cards someone had given them for a wedding present. She sat down at the clean kitchen table.

"Dear Mrs. Wilder," she began.

How much should she say? Should she write anything other than condolences, or should she refer to their conversation? Wanting to find out who she was lingered like an ache, an ache that wouldn't go away no matter what she did. Why didn't Daddy understand? Why wouldn't he tell her anything about her birth mother? Maybe it was painful for him, like some of those Vietnam experiences he wouldn't talk about.

She had received nice letters from a few of the David Wilders she'd written to, sorry they weren't the man she was looking for, and giving her some family history of their own so she could be sure they weren't even in the running. One of them told her that a single couple from the British Isles in the early 1800s could have had as many as ten children, and if even half of those survived to have ten more children there would be many, many Wilders.

"She looks like Trilby," her aunt had said. Molly often brooded, gazing at herself in the mirror, trying to see in her features what her mother must have looked like. The aunts said her hair was black. If only Molly had a black wig or something.

The only other clue as to what her mother might have looked like was that song, once upon a time. They had been visiting in Glencreggan and Daddy had taken her, Hedy, and the little ones down the mountain to a country fair. They walked into a field of tents and tables to the strains of country music and bluegrass on wooden platform stages, the pickin' and singin' following them as they strolled. There were jams and jellies for sale, there were quilts and woven baskets and canned vegetables in jars and sourwood honey and pickled pig's feet and pie and scrumptious-looking layer cakes. They wandered among booths that sold paintings and wood carvings and walking sticks with feathers on the end and wrought-iron fireplace tools. Little hands tugged the grown-ups over to fishing games and pony rides, ice cream cones and funnel cakes, which reminded her of doughnuts.

Waxed paper-wrapped funnel cakes in hand, the family circled back to listen to folk ballads sung by a guitar duo, a bearded man and woman with braided salt-and-pepper hair. Molly was entranced by the first ballad "Matty Groves," so rich, so full of feeling, so sad. The little kids squirmed, but soon they quieted down and the crowd around them hushed to the story told in music. Hedy said she didn't care for that sad music and she'd go buy some jams and jellies. She took little Max with her, but the older two children stayed.

And then they began one called "I'll Twine 'Mid the Ringlets."

"Oh, I'll twine 'mid the ringlets of my raven black hair, the lilies so white and the roses so fair . . ." Daddy listened, giving the song his full attention, and then his features hardened into the stillness of a statue. "He taught me to love him and promised to love . . ." When the duo sang the verse about the "frail wildwood flower," Daddy stopped listening and turned aside, as if he couldn't bear any more.

He told Molly to watch the kids while he went to get them some ice cream. She wondered at the huskiness in his voice, the frog in his throat. When he got back, the duo was singing another ballad and he managed to smile when he handed out three cones. He said he'd buy cones for Mom and Max later.

As Molly walked away from the stage with her family, slowly savoring her treat, the song echoed in her mind. What about it had bothered Daddy? Maybe that poor girl, that pale wildwood flower with raven black hair, had reminded him of her mother. It was nice to think she might have had wildflowers twined in her ringlets, lilies and roses, most likely Cherokee roses.

But Molly didn't have raven black hair, and she didn't have blondy-brown hair like Daddy. Her hair was rich copper. Like Mrs. Wilder's.

She shook her head to clear it, turned back to her writing paper, and composed the letter to Mrs. Wilder, saying she'd be so grateful if they could talk some more, talk about Glencreggan. Should she bare her heart and tell her how much she wanted to find her mother? How much she wanted to solve the mystery of those hush-hush words she'd overheard on the porch of the Fergusons' house, the porch with the swinging gourds for the swallows? No. She wrote a single sentence that conveyed just a hint of what she was feeling.

Letter in hand, she walked down to the mailbox at the leasing office and, crossing her fingers, slipped it into the slot. She was running out of Davids to ask. She hoped beyond hope this one was the right one, and that Mrs. Evangeline Wilder would understand.

And that Paul would understand.

Chapter 9

November, 1990

On Monday morning, David looked up at the sunny sky with regret. He almost wished for a storm to match his mood, anything to postpone this meeting. Parking in the church's back lot fronting the cemetery, he walked over to the graveyard under drifting oak leaves, the grounds aromatic with their December tang of leaf mold, wet wood, and smoke.

Delaying his entry, he made an inspection. The handsome decorative gate and iron railings looked good, but the sides and the back were enclosed by sagging hog wire. He'd ask Lonnie Tucker to make repairs. He gazed at Tallulah's grave, dirt piled to settle before they laid the stone. At last he walked inside and stopped at Jane's desk. "How's it going?"

She nodded. "Kip Hogarth's waiting in your office. I gave him some coffee."

David set his mouth in a line. "Thanks. Has Lonnie come in?"

"Not yet."

"Well, I've got a job for him when he does."

Jane raised her eyebrows. "All right."

As David entered his office, a bulky young man stood abruptly and extended his hand. "Reverend Wilder? Kip Hogarth, Transmontane Properties."

David gave him a business smile, shook the proffered hand, and walked around to his chair. "Just call me David. Have a seat."

Kip resumed his chair across from David, his back to the window, to the slanting morning sun and Quanasee Mountain. "I'll get right down to business. I understand you people might buy the property next door."

"We might, yes. It's not officially on the market."

Hogarth shrugged. "We're interested in that property too. It's an ideal location for us, right here in town. We'd be prepared to work something out with you."

David sat back in his chair. "Work something out? How?"

"You buy it, you turn around and sell it to us. We could help arrange the financing. Make a good profit."

David felt as if somebody had sucker-punched him. "Excuse me. I'm going on hearsay, but I understand we have the option, and only for six months. You apparently know this too. Why don't you just wait us out? If we don't come up with the money, it's yours."

Kip Hogarth tugged at his ear. "Well, Reverend, time is of the essence. Y'know? The loan rates are on a slide, and when they hit a low point, we can lock in the financing and be ready to start construction when the weather permits. Our new condos up on the hill in town are filling up fast, and we'd like to have a new restaurant and shopping court ready for our people. It's what they're used to, y'know?"

The man actually winked.

David leaned forward on his desk and clasped his hands. "I can't give you any answers today. Kip, do you attend church?"

Kip shifted uncomfortably. "Used to go when I was a boy."

"Maybe you don't remember the story of when Jesus chased the money changers from the temple."

Kip laughed, as if David had made a joke. "Oh, yeah. There was a picture in our Sunday school room, turned-over table, gold coins all over the floor. It's the only time I ever saw Jesus look mad."

"Well, Kip, I don't want to start turning over my desk here, but the thought has crossed my mind."

"Hey, hey, now," said Kip. "No harm intended. I hoped we would have a mutually beneficial talk. Anyhow, I've got another offer for you. Heard you might be in the market for a buyer for your property up on Bear Lick."

"My farmhouse?"

He nodded. "Heard you've got a great view there. Ten acres, isn't it? I've got a client looking for just such a property, with that great view. Wants to build a tasteful, rustic family home, with stables and a nature preserve."

David sat back, shaken. What a vulture. "It's five acres, and it's not for sale."

Kip cocked one eyebrow. "No? I heard you might be leaving town."

"Who told you that?" said David. "I have no plans to leave." He put the accent on leave and stared at Hogarth.

Kip slowly heaved himself out of the chair. "Well, you never can tell what's going to happen," he said. "If you change your mind, you've got my card."

"I'm staying." David rose to see Hogarth out. At the office door, the sound of breaking glass reached him, as if it had come from the nave.

The stained-glass windows? David forgot Hogarth and rushed to the nave door. He jerked it open.

In front of the old-style altar of mountain granite, one of the glass-lined urns that had held flowers for Tallulah's funeral was lying on the floor, flowers and greenery and glass scattered about. Just then Lonnie Tucker crawled out from behind the pulpit, one hand full of white lilies. He lurched to his feet, the smell of sweat and alcohol mingling with the sweet odor of the flowers. "Sorry, Rev," he mumbled.

He handed David the lilies and leaned down and started picking up the sharp shards of glass with his bare fingers.

"Lonnie," said David. "Get a broom."

Lonnie said, "Ah, my old hands're tough as shoe leather. Don't worry about a thing."

"Get a broom, Lonnie."

Jane appeared in the doorway, eyes wide. "I'll help." She held out her hands for the dripping flowers. "I'll find a vase."

David was glad to hand them over. "Thanks, Jane." He turned abruptly, almost into Hogarth. The man stepped back and said, "I wouldn't put up with that. Drunk, isn't he?"

Before he answered, David strode outside, out of Lonnie's earshot. As he hoped, Hogarth followed him. "It's hard sometimes," David said bluntly. "But nobody else'll give him a job."

Hogarth shrugged. "Hope you get it straightened out. Nice talking to you, Reverend." He stuck out his hand.

David politely shook it. "Have a good day," he said.

He was on his way back from washing his hands when Jane said, "Your mother-in-law's on the phone."

Hattie hadn't called him much since Lu had died. Maybe she'd heard about Sudie Conway. He walked back to his office. From his window he could see all of Quanasee Mountain. Hattie Holley lived in the up-valley, near the Quanasee River. When he'd come to Bow Creek, Quanasee had brooded majestic over the town, green in the summer, quilted with red and orange, green and brown, in the fall. Now at the higher elevations, Quanasee stood bare where the red spruces had been killed by acid rain. At all elevations houses and condominiums jutted above the trees.

Hattie was like those higher elevations, bare in the spots where her loved ones had lived. She had lost so much when she lost Lu. He picked up the phone.

"Hattie? How are you?"

"Oh, honey, she told me! Clover told me everything. Lord have mercy! What are we going to do? I tried to raise her to be God-fearing."

"What is it, Hattie? What did she tell you?"

"She's gone and got herself with child!"

"What?" His stomach dropped. He had made a bad mistake letting Riley Clyde Summers off the hook.

Hattie practically growled. "You seen her and that Summers boy t'other day. There ain't no mistake. She's four months gone. Wearin' all them sloppy clothes for a reason."

Hattie always knew things like that. A former midwife, she'd known Lu was sick before anyone else did, including Lu. "Hattie, I can't tell you how sorry I am. I should have been harder on the boy when I got him out of the water."David had been thinking about his own past, and it had clouded his judgment. He felt hollow.

"Honey, if I wasn't a decent woman I'd tell you just what I think of that sorry hunk of steamin' horse manure. A young girl like that and him a jailbird."

"A *jailbird*? Are you sure, Hattie?"

"Oh, you've had enough on your plate, honey. I didn't want to bother you with the trouble with our girl stuck on that boy. He took one of them red Corvettes out of the country club parking lot and rode around in it all night until he ran it off the road and down a mountain. He was lucky to get away with a broke rib."

"I don't think he'd actually go to jail for joyriding, Hattie."

"Well, he got that juvenile probation, and won't be long afore he turns eighteen, and then if he does something it's off to the hoosegow. His daddy and Ruby Lee like t'had a fit. And let me tell you something else, David Wilder. He's got that Indian blood. He's always going to be wild."

He let her get it all out, holding the phone a little ways from his ear. He could explain all day that the Cherokees were more peaceful than some of her kin, but old prejudices die hard. He'd have to try again. And now she was saying, "You come right out here and talk to her."

"It'll be late this afternoon, Hattie. I've got a full day. Maybe I'll stop by the barber shop and see Clyde."

"What?"

"I just remembered I need a haircut."

"Oh, Lordy. Don't tangle with Clyde Summers."

"Clyde's not the tangling type, and neither am I."

"You didn't know him back when."

"No, I didn't. Don't worry." He thought he and Clyde could talk. Clyde was the talking kind, and he knew the Holleys.

"Good luck, son."

"Thanks," said David. He'd need it. Clyde *did* have a temper.

Before he left the church that afternoon, David fielded a call from a parishioner who'd heard the B&B might be for sale and wanted to let him know. David thanked the woman and said he'd check into the rumor. How many rumors were going around town? Maybe Nell would know.

When he called her, she answered on the fourth ring, a little breathless. "I'm sorry, David, but I have a customer. Do you need anything right this minute?"

He should have waited. Of course, this was the shopping season. "How about a cup of coffee tomorrow morning? I've just had a visit from Kip Hogarth. You know him?"

There was silence on the line. And then, reluctantly, "I've met him. Happy Mac's?"

"Sure. 8:30." David put down the phone. She'd met Hogarth? He looked forward to seeing her even more.

Now he'd go to see Clyde. He walked down the sidewalk past Nell's shop. Did a lace curtain move, or was he imagining things?

He reached a grey wooden storefront with BARBER SHOP painted in peeling white letters on the window. A bell rang when he opened the door; mingled odors of bay rum and steam reached his nostrils.

"Be with you in a minute, Preacher," said Clyde, whose bald head topped a long face scored with deep wrinkles. His generous mobile mouth kept up his patter. "I told the colonel, here, don't look at me. I ain't a good advertisement."

He was clipping the steel-gray hair of a man David didn't know, a man about his age. The man said, "My name is Sanders, and I was never in the service."

"You've been handed a permanent commission," David said.

Clyde winked at David. "One of them captains of industry."

"That's a fair assessment," said the man. He introduced himself to David as Ron Sanders from Tampa and said he was just passing through and was going to come back to play golf one day.

When Sanders had paid and left, the shop was empty except for Don Summers, Clyde's oldest boy, who was moving a broom over the floor.

The barber brushed off the chair and David sat down. "How're you doing, Clyde?"

Clyde fastened a cape around David's neck. "Ruby Lee keeps telling me I'm doing fine, but sometimes I ain't so sure."

Ruby Lee was Clyde's third wife. He didn't have good luck with wives. The first one, Don's mother, died of pneumonia. The second one, whom he'd met while visiting an old friend in Cherokee, just upped and disappeared one day, leaving her son, Riley Clyde, behind. Some ignorant people liked to say it was restless Indian blood, but David suspected that Riley's mother might've been made unwelcome by those same people. Ruby Lee was a good woman, and had done her best with the motherless boys, but the younger son had tried her sorely. He'd been only seven when his mother had left.

David knew he would have to approach his subject carefully. He turned to Don. "Catch anything this weekend?"

"Nah," said Don. "I was kind of busy."

"I was out there a few days back," said David. "It was a perfect day. Got some nice rainbows."

"Now Preacher, what you want here?" said Clyde, pointing with the scissors.

"Trim it up," said David. "They're thinking I've turned hippie."

"Want to get rid of the beard?" asked Clyde.

David looked at his reflection in the mirror. Lu had liked his beard, said it suited his calling. He wasn't ready for that much of a change. "Not now. Not in this cold weather."

Clyde got busy with the scissors while Don stepped outside to have a smoke. David watched him on the front bench, smoking and watching passers-by. There had been something in Don's tone, less friendly, more guarded, when David had asked him about the weekend.

The barber liked to fish, but even more he liked to go rabbit hunting with his beagles, and he talked on and on about his dogs while he snipped. David was pondering a way to broach the subject of Clyde's second son when he almost missed his opportunity.

"So Riley Clyde, he says, 'Daddy, why don't you and Mama Ruby take a little vacation, I can look after them dogs,' he says, so I took Ruby Lee up to Gatlinburg and we had a fine time, let me tell you, but when I got back one of my dogs was missing. It was Bluebell, my second best dog, and I liked t'killed that boy for leaving the gate open. I been looking for the pore old girl a week now."

"Well, I hope he helped you."

"By damn, excuse my French, R.C. lit out and I ha'n't seen his sorry ass since."

"Lit out? You mean he took off?"

"You got it, Preacher."

"Oh, hell," muttered David.

Clyde looked down at him with amused eyes. "Well, I always heard you boys over at the 'Piscopals were different."

"Sorry. I wanted to talk to Riley Clyde. You know where I can find him?"

Clyde's eyes narrowed. "If I knew that, I'd'a dragged his butt home. What you want him for?"

"It's about my niece," said David.

Clyde's scissors stopped for a moment before they resumed. "I told him not to be messin' with no jail bait." David glanced up sharply, but Clyde's face had pulled down the shutters and closed the shop.

David decided he wouldn't say anything more until he'd talked to the girl. "Well, just wanted to talk to him, is all."

"If I see the sorry bugger, I'll pass the word," said Clyde. He brushed David off and whisked the cape from his shoulders. "Without them whiskers you might look right nice."

"I don't know about that," said David. He could have said that Jesus had a beard, but then nobody really knew, and historians claimed he probably didn't. He paid Clyde and included a generous tip, then he walked back to the church and told Jane he needed to go to Hattie's. "I'll pick up some lunch there."

"She's planning on it." Jane gave him an unfamiliar troubled look. "She called back to ask you. When I told her you were out, she told me what had happened with her granddaughter."

David gave her a look of resignation. "You bring them up the best you can, but love . . . ah, love is as strong as death, as the Song of Solomon tells us." And Clover was mad with love. As he had been once.

"*Yes,*" sighed Jane. She gave him a searching look. "You would have been a wonderful father."

Mumbling his thanks, David turned away to hide his sudden flush. He had a daughter. He had not been a wonderful father.

Nell McGarry stood at the window of her antique shop, hand on a lace curtain, and watched David's truck pull away from the church. This morning, after one carload of Majolica collectors had kept her occupied for almost an hour, no more customers had arrived, and she'd had way too much time to think.

Despite their disagreements, despite his secrecy about his family, she'd always thought David was one of the best men she knew. Still, there had always been something sad, something tragic about him, even before Lu died. Nell had always dealt with sadness by working too hard, and that had been her undoing with Hampton Taggart.

She'd been in her shop and hadn't recognized the bearded shopper in a cowboy hat buying his mother a very expensive handmade quilt, until he presented his credit card. She smiled shyly at the singer then, and he told her she worked too hard and he wanted to buy her dinner. And she'd blushed and said no, and he'd joked and kidded and made her change her mind. He reminded her of her brother, Andrew, who had died. Her talented big brother, who'd loved life and laughing, and who'd had left the mountain to study architecture after working construction a couple of summers.

She choked back the memory.

Well, she'd be meeting David in the morning—to talk about Kip Hogarth, the man from Transmontane. She bit her lip. She ought to tell David that Hogarth had stopped by her shop asking questions, and that he had tried to convince her the church would be better off selling to him. David wouldn't like it at all. It seemed like dirty pool to her, too.

She picked up her feather duster and began to dust the big grandfather clock in the hall. She watched its pendulum swing back and forth, back and forth, a rhythmical tyrant. Time marched on, and things changed. Things must change, if there was to be growth. But some things were too precious to lose and must be held close to the heart. Love. Honesty. Faith. And old houses.

Chapter 10

David drove along the Bow Creek ridge leading to Hattie's place a little too fast. Riley Clyde Summers had made trouble for himself. But so had David Wilder, once upon a time.

In the distance he spotted a barn, rotten, falling in, a relic that reminded him of Dell's barn and the dance. And Trilby. Would she still be alive today if he had never gone to that dance, to that party? If he had never gone to the waterfall? Would she have kept going with guys like Judd Coulton, and would they have used her and used her, blinding her with the glitter of their promises, until there was nothing left of her but an empty, bitter shell?

Dell's Barn had once housed livestock. Then Glencreggan grew up around the farm, and Rufus Hughes sold all his acres except for the house and barn. His daughter Dell opened a boarding house and then her sweetheart Lincoln Cravey, who played the banjo, talked her into using the barn for entertainment, for square dances and bluegrass. It had been going strong ever since 1946, after the soldiers came home from the war ready to kick up their heels.

"I haven't seen you at the dances," Pamela had told him when they were on the way to Dell's Barn.

David shrugged. "I've been away most of the summer. I'll have to make up for lost time." Even though he felt that square dances were, well, square.

Still, the Saturday night dances attracted local residents, as well as summer people and tourists, and there everyone met on an equal plane. That night he was planning to get out on the floor and give it all he had. *She* would be there.

The dancing was already well underway when David and Pamela arrived. So many cars were jammed into the yard that he had to park by the hemlock hedge separating Dell's parking lot from Watson's gas station.

The plunking of a bluegrass banjo sifted out into the still mountain night, where a quarter moon hung pale as a piecrust high above the trees. Knots of men, some in overalls, gathered outside with smokes between their knuckles and bottles lazing in the shadows.

David paid for himself and Pamela at the door. They walked into the converted barn, where a fiddler was sawing out "Buffalo Gal" on a platform at the far end. Girls in Bermuda shorts, farmers in overalls, ladies with perms and Vera overblouses, girls in green clog dresses and poofy starched crinolines, lick-haired young bucks all spiffed in jeans: they were all there, bobbing and weaving, crowding the floor. *Birdie in the cage, take the little bird out and put the old crow in, promenade, circle up four . . .*

Judd Coulton and the girl, Trilby, swung their way, and Trilby, catching sight of David, broke into a curious smile. Then Pamela touched his back. "Ready to dance, Davey?"

When "Foggy Mountain Breakdown" began, he took her hand. They'd shuffled and coupled up and promenaded halfway around the floor when they found themselves paired with Judd and Trilby. David, heart racing, swung his waterfall girl, pulling her close, whispering, "You looked prettier with mud on your face."

She jerked away, eyes blazing.

"Promenade with your lady!"

Pamela slipped into his arms. "What did you say to that girl? She's furious."

"Nothing," he said, following Trilby with his gaze until the crowd closed around her. "Maybe I stepped on her toe."

"You can stop staring at her. I'm your date. Remember?" She gave him a dig in the ribs somewhere between sweet and nasty.

David shrugged. "Sorry," he said. "I wanted to bug Judd. Let's get a Coke." They were waiting in line at the concession counter when the next set ended. The band took a break, and Judd Coulton steered Trilby past them and out the door. She didn't look his way.

David squared his shoulders and stepped up to the counter for the Cokes. He paid and handed Pamela hers, sloshing it only a little. "Want to go outside?" He swiped the wet hand on his jeans.

"Sure. I could use a cig." She smoothed her hair and smiled at him.

Sallow light atop tall poles illuminated the parking lot, reflecting off chrome Chevy trim and mica sand and sequins sewed carefully onto the cloggers' crinoline-puffed skirts. David spotted four other kids that made up their summer-resident crowd, smoking over beside Eddie's pink Mercury with the big tail fins. Mostly Pam's crowd, but he knew them. One of the guys waved them over.

"Hey, Dave," he said. "Where you been all summer?"

"Lifeguarding back home."

The guy shrugged. "Well, you've come back just in time for the party."

“Party?” said Pam. “So it’s on for tonight?”

“You bet,” said the guy. “My place. The folks are out of town.”

The fellow who drove a Mercury convertible nodded. “All *right*.” He turned to David and Pamela. “You guys coming?”

“Wouldn’t miss it.” Pamela’s eyes shot a challenge at David.

“Sure.” He looked over his shoulder, out into the parking lot. Where had Trilby and Coulton gone?

“How about a light?” Pamela touched his elbow. He turned and lit Pamela’s outstretched cigarette. “I thought you would never notice.” She regarded him under her lashes as the smoke drifted by.

“Sorry. I was just . . .”

“Hey, Judd!” yelled the party host. Judd Coulton, his arm around Trilby, emerged from behind a parked car not twenty feet away.

“You coming to the party?”

“Later,” Judd yelled back. He stayed put beside the car, not coming over to join them.

David muttered, “Why’d you ask that prick?”

The party guy grinned. “Why not? He always brings booze.”

“Think he’ll bring Trilby?” asked the convertible guy, snickering. No one spoke for a moment.

“Do you have any snacks?” asked one of the girls, more to change the subject, David guessed, than to say she was hungry.

“Honeybun, we got snacks out the wazoo,” said their host. The music from inside interrupted with a crash of a chord and thumped into “Wabash Cannonball.” “Yee-haw!” The party guy grabbed his girl’s hand. They stomped out their cigarettes in the dirt and hustled back inside.

David and the partygoers left right before the last dance. Fifteen minutes later, after driving up a steep paved road near the golf course and down a driveway to a half-lit lodge-style house, the group was creeping down a rhododendron-lined path to the basement door of a game room. "Are you sure this is going to be all right?" whispered one of the girls.

"Sure," said another. "That old lady's seventy-something and half deaf."

"She's been my nanny forever," said the host with a wicked grin. "She thinks I'm God." He unlocked the basement door and the group filed in. The room was a little chilly and smelled of pine paneling and dampness. He switched on a lava lamp, and blobs in blue liquid began to rise and fall. The eerie blue glow turned the gold shag carpet to mud.

"Just a minute." An electric heater was clicked on and then the party guy ducked behind the built-in bar. He popped up with a six-pack in each hand. He plunked them on the counter, then opened a cabinet and tossed red and yellow cellophane packs of chips and pretzels toward the counter. He cracked open a fresh jar of pimento-stuffed green olives.

David picked up a packet of chips from the floor. "Won't your folks miss the beer?"

"Nah. There's extra in storage that my dad brought up here from home. It's a dry county, remember?"

Somebody slid a Johnny Mathis record onto the player in the big stereo cabinet. David took Pamela in his arms and began to slow dance, and before the end of "Chances Are" he'd managed to work her shirttail out of her Bermudas and slide his hand up her bare back and under the elastic of her bra. Even so, he couldn't stop glancing at the door.

Empties lined up on the counter; chip packets grew thin; Johnny Mathis and Ray Charles crooned. When the Isley Brothers came on with "Twist and Shout," David and Pamela twisted till they were exhausted and fell, laughing, in a heap. After a few more fast songs, Johnny Mathis played again. Couples paired off. The lava lamp gushed, shapes lifting and dropping in the soft blue darkness. Nat King Cole crooned while one couple disappeared into another room. David led Pamela off to a corner sofa and drew a soft cotton blanket over them. His hands caressed her body, her back, and she didn't resist. The kisses grew deeper and deeper. How far would she go? Breathing heavily, he'd just managed to unclasp Pamela's bra, feeling her heavy breasts swing free, when the door burst open.

David pulled back, pierced with cold, and froze.

A shaky voice, a girl's voice, slurred out of the darkness. "Can I use the bathroom?"

The Nat King Cole record ended, scratch-scratching into the silence.

"My God," said Pamela. She straightened and pulled the blanket in front of her. "It's Trilby Gaddis."

"She sounds strange," said David. "Like she's hurt or something." He stumbled to his feet, blinking. "Hey, do you need help?" he called.

"Are you kidding?" Pamela hissed under her breath.

The voice came back tired, disgusted. "I'm okay. I just want to use the bathroom."

Blue globes rose and fell.

"You don't sound okay. Come on in."

Trilby stood in the door frame, shadowed against the moonlight, hand to her cheek. When she took a step and let in more light,

David saw that her ballerina top was wrinkled, askew, and inside out. Her hair ramped in a vine-like tangle over her head.

Ignoring murmurs behind him, he strode to her side. "What happened?"

"Nothing."

David took in her frightened eyes, saw her sway and catch herself. Something had happened, something that scared her. When he rested a hand on her shoulder, she flinched. He lowered his hand and led her, limping, to the little room off the paneled hallway. She edged in and closed the door. She locked it.

"David?" called Pamela.

He leaned close to the bathroom door and waited. Light spilled from the door frame. "I'll be here," he said to the door.

"David!" said Pamela.

"Maybe you could come and help her," David said.

"No way." He heard Pam's lighter click and then smelled one of those menthol things.

A toilet flushed, water rushed, and finally Trilby stepped out. She'd straightened her clothes and hair, but her striped top was ripped at the neckline. She clutched the seam together, but couldn't hide her trembling hands. She didn't smile at David.

As she reached back to turn off the bathroom light, he noticed a red welt on her cheek. Probably would be a bruise by the next day. "Where's Coulton?"

"Passed out in the car outside."

He'd smelled the liquor on her. "You're not so sober yourself."

"Is anybody here sober?" She tried to smile and edged around him. "Thanks for the help. I got to go home."

David caught her arm, and she ducked away from his hand. He held it straight up. "Wait. How far is home? You're not going to walk in those flimsy shoes, are you?"

She stopped and stared at him. "I didn't bring my boots, city boy."

"I'll take you," he found himself saying.

She gazed at him tiredly, sizing him up.

"I'm a good guy. I want to help."

She nodded in Pam's direction "She's not going to like it."

He shrugged and called to Pamela. "Come on, let's take Trilby home."

"Big white knight," snorted Pamela. He heard her crack open a beer. "Don't expect me to be here when you get back."

"Better stay with your girlfriend." Trilby took a step toward the door.

He didn't know then that he was about to change his life forever.

"I'll be right back," he said to Pamela and jingled his keys in his pocket. He touched Trilby at the small of her back. "Let's go."

They drove off into the star-pointed night, drove with the wind drowning any talk. Cold and sharp and fresh was the wind, soft the moon above the curving road down the mountain.

"Are you cold?" David finally shouted into the darkness. "I can put the top up."

"No." He waited for her to say more, but she didn't, and she didn't hug her arms around her but just accepted the chill air on her bare skin. She directed him down the mountain to a jelly and vegetable stand. "Stop. Let me off here."

"Is your house up that driveway?" David asked, pulling off the road and making out a dirt drive speckled with gravel. "I don't mind driving up. It's dark."

She shook her head. "I don't want to wake up the folks."

He waited while she took a comb out of her shoulder bag and untangled her hair. He thought of her torn shirt, thought of her parents. "Do you want a sweater? There's one in the back seat."

She shook her head. "I won't take your sweater."

"It's my brother's. Take it." He reached for the blue wool V-neck and handed it to her.

She smiled the ways girls smile when they don't approve of what a guy is doing, but they like it, and then she slipped it on. "I'll bring it back next week sometime."

"You can have it."

She gave him another look, a different look. "I'll bring it back."

He got out to open the door for her, the dim car light revealing a smile and soft eyes. "Thanks for the ride," she said. He closed the door, leaned against the car, and crossed his arms.

She took a few steps and turned back. "Well, what're you waiting for?"

"For you to get up there all right."

"You don't have to do that."

"I want to."

"I forgot your name," she said.

"David," he said. "David Wilder."

"That's a nice name," she said. "I'll be all right."

"Are you sure? Trilby?"

She didn't seem surprised he knew her name. "I'm sure. Now get back to your girlfriend." Without another word she left him, dodging away from the lights of the car, ducking behind rhododendrons. In a tangle of laurel, a pair of glittering animal eyes watched him as he watched the girl go.

He didn't like the way she'd walked. Like she hurt somewhere.

David drove back past the Glencreggan Country Club, a low, weathered half-timbered structure on a gentle hill. From the road he could see the giant hydrangeas that flanked the drive, their white flowers glowing ghostly pale in the moonlight. He came to Moffitt Road, the road that led to the party house, and turned.

At the house all the windows were dark, and by the basement door he saw neither dim shadows nor blue lights. The host stuck his head out of a second-floor window. "Oh, it's you, Wilder. You missed all the excitement. Judd woke up and staggered around and pissed in the driveway. Yelling for that girl. Woke up old Tooney and she called security."

"Geez. What happened then?"

"The security guy somehow got in touch with Judd's folks. His dad just left with him and his mom drove the car home. Eddie took Pam home, and she's never going to speak to you again."

"Thanks," said David. He put the car in reverse, strangely exhilarated.

Chapter 11

Watching thunderheads building in the distance, David turned onto a dirt road just past Edison Holley's country store and bait shop and rattled across the rickety bridge over Bow Creek. He hoped fleetingly for a good soaker: the roads were dusty and the turnips in his kitchen garden needed watering badly, but right now Clover's predicament filled his heart and mind. He had tried to be a good uncle to her, a father figure.

Clover. What could he say to her now? He was the last person who should be advising a teenager. Her grandmother didn't know that. Didn't know the half of it.

The moment his truck pulled up behind Hattie's, she burst out the back door and clattered down the steps, hands smoothing her apron, wisps of gray hair flying in the balsam-smelling wind. He slid out of the truck, arms reaching out to her.

"How are you doing? How's Clover?"

Hattie leaned into a hug, then stood back. "Well, honey, I had it out with her. She locked herself in her room, and ha'n't come out all day."

"I'll see if she'll talk to me." David followed Hattie into the kitchen he knew so well: he'd been welcomed at that well-worn pine table many a night while he was courting Tallulah. He sniffed the familiar scent of the potions Hattie made out of native plants. "Been brewing some herb tonic today?"

She cut him a look. She always did think he was too nosy, but David knew she took it for her nerves. Lu's death had to have hit hard, even as stoic as Hattie was. Her husband had been dead for two years, and her other son had been killed in 1984 when a bad tire on his overloaded truck blew out on a curve. And then there was Clover's mother, dead at twenty-eight from a drug overdose. Her rotten husband had never been seen again.

Edison's family and Clover were all she had now. He walked to the girl's door and knocked softly. "Clover, may I come in?"

He knocked again, harder. No reply. Nothing. "What did I tell you," said Hattie. "She won't talk to you neither."

"Are you sure she's there?"

"Try the door."

He rattled the knob, but it didn't budge. The old-fashioned rim lock was rusty. "We're worried about you, Clover," he called. "Let us talk to you." Still nothing.

Hattie sighed with disgust and clomped back to the kitchen, where she fished in a drawer and drew out a string of keys, the old-fashioned kind with an oval loop for a head. David fitted one of the keys to the rim lock's keyhole and worked it until the rusty lock rasped and turned. The door swung open.

The room was empty, and a breeze stirred the calico curtains away from the open window.

David walked over to the window, parted the colorful calico, and leaned out. Four feet below, the soft dirt bore scuff marks.

Hattie came up behind him and peered over his shoulder. "Durn her hide."

David laid a comforting hand on the old woman's back. "Where do you think she could've gone?"

Hattie coughed and resumed her steely expression. "No telling. You go out the back door and holler for her, and I'll go outen the front and see if she's down the road a piece." David headed for the kitchen.

"Lordy, Lordy!" wailed Hattie.

David returned inside and found Hattie staring at the fireplace. She turned to him, lips pale, her jaw set grimly. "The musket's gone!"

Her husband's old Civil War muzzle-loader had always hung above the mantel. David stifled a laugh. "The musket? I'm sorry, Hattie. I know it's not funny, but . . . the musket? At least she can't do any damage with it."

"Little you know," said Hattie. "Keeping that firearm in working order was my man's one hobby. Many's a winter night he oiled and rubbed that thing. He showed her how to use it."

David walked over to the window, where the sun was sinking behind the mountains, gilding high dark clouds. Night was coming, and Clover was out there alone. Why had she taken the gun?

"Hattie, she's not going to shoot anybody." He hoped that was the truth. "Maybe she was worried about bears. Have you seen any lately?"

"'Course not. They're in their dens now. She knows that."

Hattie followed David out to the front porch, and they stared at the darkening woods beyond the drive.

"Do you think we ought to call the sheriff and get up a search party?" he asked.

She shook her head. "Too soon for that. She's wandered these woods since she was knee high to a grasshopper. She don't go far."

David knew Hattie was scared but didn't want to admit it. Darn that mountain folk pride and their independence. Not just that, but with a search party word would spread fast, and then people would talk. Find out about the baby. Hattie didn't want people saying she'd done a poor job of bringing up her granddaughter.

"Hattie, I know Clover's upset and with a weapon. Would she harm herself?"

Hattie didn't say anything. David hoped she was reconsidering. He knew too much about desperate girls.

Back inside, David called Edison at the store, but he hadn't seen her, and neither had his wife. They said they'd be glad to help look for her. David thought that would be a good idea and asked them to come as soon as they could. Edison was used to dealing with his stubborn mother.

That evening Evangeline Wilder, dressing for a dinner party, stood in her lace-encrusted slip and faille pumps listening to the sound of the shower. She selected a jade green silk dress and slipped it on, grateful she was still limber enough to zip it up the back, but it was becoming a struggle. She wondered whether Lem was really up to going out this evening.

It was too late to cancel with the Ragsdales, and Lem never liked to miss an important university dinner. He expended more affection on his alma mater than he did on his own sons. Phil had dutifully followed him to Westbury, graduating with honors in History, and Lem merely tolerated Phil who loved him with the devotion of a sad-eyed dog. Phil, always the reader of the two, had even given up his dream of becoming an historian to please his father.

And then there was David. He'd delighted his father with his brightness and exasperated him with his rebelliousness. First, he'd given up football after junior high. He'd attended Duke instead of Westbury. He'd had that trouble with the girl. And to top it all off, he'd gotten religion, something the old rationalist tolerated in his wife but felt was unsuitable for men like him. Even the religion might have been forgiven if David had married the right sort of girl and had worked his way up in the church. A bishop in the family would please Lem. Power was something he could respect.

But the boy had married Tallulah Holley and holed up in Bow Creek and seemed to like it there. Lem had not seen David in five years, not since the funeral of Evangeline's brother. How could he be so unforgiving, despite her efforts to broker peace between them?

He charged into the room from his dressing room. "You ready, Evie?"

"Are you sure you feel up to it, Lem?" She thought he looked a little flushed. And did his hand tremble, ever so slightly?

"Of course I do," Lem bellowed, his voice as commanding as ever. "Stop treating me like some sort of invalid."

Ironically, that vocal quality of his father's that David had inherited helped him in the pulpit. He could go further in his career if he wanted. Why was he content in that backwater church?

"Come on, Evie, we don't want to be late."

Lem was always so impatient. "We're not going to be late."

Evangeline slipped on her diamond evening watch and fiddled with her hair. Red wasn't so becoming to her anymore. She took her diamond earrings out of the third section of her jewelry box and slid them onto her ears. "I'm ready, Lem."

He clumped down the stairs, and she followed him with misgivings.

Junius had already left. "I'll get the car," Lem said. "Pick you up in front."

Evangeline put on her favorite mink coat and then spotted the afternoon mail waiting on the desk in the library. Lem had left two out just for her.

She slid open a note from her college roommate: was she coming to the Converse class reunion, their fiftieth? Fifty years? Dreadful to think about. The next note, in an unfamiliar hand, carried the return address of M. Westbrook, University Apartments, 3-C. She tore open the envelope.

> *Dear Mrs. Wilder,* she read,
>
> *I'm so sorry that you had a death in your family.*
>
> *I enjoyed talking with you at the coffee at Mrs. Ragsdale's, and I hope you won't mind if I call you in a few days about something important.*
>
> *Sincerely yours,*
>
> *Molly Westbrook*

A loud honk out front interrupted her thoughts. She slipped the note into her evening bag and walked out to the car, the door locking itself behind her.

Gliding through the dark night, dim streetlights above, Evangeline considered what to do about Molly. Molly *had* to be her lost granddaughter. Evangeline longed to talk further with the young woman, who was about to make her a great-grandmother! Of that she was certain. She'd never quite succeeded in putting David's missing daughter out of her mind, especially now that Phil's Thad was all grown up, not needing a granny anymore.

But her son's wishes? That promise he'd made? Would stirring up all that again be bad for Lem's heart? Or would it be healing?

"Lem . . ." she said, looking straight ahead.

"What is it, hon?"

"Why don't we go to Bow Creek and spend a little time with David? There's a nice bed and breakfast right next to his church."

"Hmph," said her husband. "You can go there if you want to. He can come to me if he wants to talk."

Evangeline took a breath to speak and then let it out slowly. She could never reason with Lem. She might as well change the subject. "How was Phil today?"

"All right, I suppose."

"How is Thad working out at the bank?"

"Evie, I don't know. He's been let run wild too long. No discipline. The other employees resent him."

They fell silent.

"Damn!" said Lem. "What's going to become of my bank if my grandson can't take over? Phil's already making noises about leaving to do some fool nonprofit project. He can't handle the job."

"You've never trusted Phil," she said grimly. "He does a good job."

"He can't make a decision."

"You've always insisted on making them for him."

"The boy was always too melancholy," said Lem. "No spunk like David."

Phil was the kind of man who considered the consequences of his actions, not just how to win. He had integrity. "He wanted to please you. He's serious and thoughtful."

"Evie, let's not start an argument tonight."

She knew she ought not to say it, but she had to speak up for what she believed. She had stayed quiet too long. "Please. Let Phil take some of your load. Let him do things his own way."

Her husband snorted. "He can wait and mess things up after I'm gone."

Evangeline felt her neck muscles tightening. "Lem! Why all this dwelling on when you're gone?"

"Damn, Evie, I'm going on seventy-six."

She smiled at him. "You know, I clean forgot. You're so youthful."

He pulled into the Ragsdales's long driveway and drove up to the house. A uniformed valet sprang forward to open Evangeline's door. Lem opened his own door. "Come on," he said grumpily. "Let's get this over with."

Evangeline was surprised to hear him say it. He usually enjoyed these University dinners. Maybe he felt worse than he'd admitted. Holding Lem's arm, she walked up the steps of the house where she'd first met Molly Westbrook.

She knew one thing. She couldn't ignore the letter.

So Owen Ferguson had taken the child for his own. She had often wondered what had happened to David's child. She was happy that the girl had turned out so well, so pretty and brave, and so educated. Everything she would have hoped for in a granddaughter. But she mustn't think that way, should she? What was her duty to her son?

Chapter 12

Nightfall enveloped the woods, turning shadows to threatening shapes. A search party of David and Hattie, with Edison, his wife, son, and his two daughters, tramped through the woods around Hattie's place, flashlights scouring the underbrush off the path, calling and calling for Clover.

David, his shoulders aching and knotted, tensed more with each crack of a twig, with each unanswered shout. He left the search and went back to the house to call Clyde Summers, both at the shop and at his house, to see if he'd heard from Riley Clyde, in case Clover knew where he'd gone and was trying to join him. But there was no answer.

He left a note for the others and went to his truck. Clyde's place at the edge of town had the front porch light on. David parked and walked up to the house, neat and practical like Ruby Lee, with pots on the porch and turnips among the flowers in the front bed.

Hearing voices outside, David followed smoke and the smell of barbecue and found Clyde sitting in a lawn chair on the grass behind his house, drinking whiskey out of a glass, while Don turned some chops on a grill. Clyde gave David a salute.

"Don't like your haircut, Preacher?"

David hoped the barber hadn't had too much to drink. "I've been trying to call you, Clyde. Where's Ruby Lee?"

"Visiting. Don and me are batching it tonight. Can't hear the phone out here, thank the Lord."

"Look, Clyde," said David, "Clover's disappeared, and I think she might have gone to look for your son."

"He ain't here, is all I can tell you," said Clyde, his eyebrows meeting, the long face sagging. "The girl ain't been here neither."

"You don't have any idea where he could have gone?"

"Told you I don't know," said Clyde. He looked over at Don and rolled his eyes. "Lacey might."

David's heart picked up. "Who's Lacey?"

Clyde hemmed and hawed. Don grimaced. Finally, it came out that Lacey was an old girlfriend who lived in a trailer park right past Jimbob's Grill out on Highway 46.

It wasn't quite eight-thirty when he reached the trailer park, dressed in his black shirt, white collar, and tweed jacket. The mobile home park was set back a little from the road in a grove of trees, the lighting there dim and greenish, giving it the eerie feeling of a landscape just before a tornado.

A passing vacationer might think the place had been closed down, which wasn't far from the truth. The ancient units were leprous with rust, the newer ones looking tentative, as if they might leave at any time. A yellow FOR SALE sign at the entrance had been plastered over with a red SOLD. David turned in by the sign and followed the dirt lanes until he came to a dusty pink round-backed trailer with a light in the window. Lord only knew how long it had been hunkering in the wiry grass.

David parked his truck, got out, and walked past a white plastic chair, kicking aside a couple of beer cans. A pot of plastic red geraniums gave a hopeful spot of color to the faded door. He walked up two concrete block steps and knocked.

"Just a minute, asshole," returned a husky voice, female, not happy. Feet thumped and scuffled. The door opened on a tousled blonde wearing a neon pink sweatshirt and holding a can of Miller Lite.

Her eyes widened, then she smirked. "Sorry, Pastor. I thought you were somebody else. Something I can do for you?"

"I'm looking for Lacey. Is that you? I'm sorry, but I don't know your last name. I'm David Wilder."

"Just Lacey, at your service." She gave him a flirtatious smile.

"I won't disturb you if you're busy."

She jerked her head toward the muttering from inside. "Oh, that's just Bobby."

Was he supposed to know who Bobby was? "I'd like to ask you about Riley Clyde Summers."

Mascaraed lashes flicked over angry bloodshot eyes. "That god . . . oops, sorry."

"No problem. I just want to know where he is."

She frowned, regarding David with narrowed eyes. "He in trouble again? I don't know and I don't care."

"You sound pretty upset." David thrust his hands in his pockets.

She raised her chin and tossed her hair. She glanced behind her, where country music threw tinny sounds into the night air. "I got my reasons, Pastor."

"He hasn't been here lately?"

"No." She stepped back, her hand on the door as though to close it, and then tilted her head in appraisal. "How important is it for you to find him?"

So that's how it was. His eyes went to her arms, looking for needle marks, but he couldn't tell for the long sleeves. Red nose, red eyes. She might have a cold. Or not.

He had exactly fifty dollars in his wallet. He took it out and noted her hungry look, her lean toward him. He hesitated for a long minute. "One more thing, Lacey."

"What?"

"Have you seen a girl, about fifteen? Looking for Riley Clyde?"

"That kid!" Lacey laughed. "No way."

"She might come by tonight. She might have a gun."

Lacey snorted, finding that funny too. "She won't be the first one to want to shoot his ass."

David dithered for a moment. Go or keep trying with Lacey? He felt she knew something. "Let me know, will you?"

"I might. You're kind of cute. You got a wife?"

He took a deep breath. *Oh, Jesus, help.* "She died last week."

"Yikes, I'm sorry," she said, biting her lower lip. "I gotta get back in."

David held up a folded wad of money. "Lacey. Where is he?"

She looked down. The game was over. "Bobby said he went to Rock Springs to work. Construction."

"Thanks, Lacey." David handed her the bills and a card from his wallet. "Here's how to get in touch with me."

She tucked the money and card into her jeans pocket. "Thanks. Hope you find the bastard. If you get lonesome you know where I live." Right before she closed the door she looked back out and blew him a kiss.

David stood looking at the door for a moment before he left, watching the moving shapes behind the curtains. He wished there was something he could do to help Lacey. Now it was more important than ever that they find Clover. He'd go to Rock Springs and look for Riley Clyde. The boy might be no good, might have a heart as hard as flint. But if Clover had found something to love in him, maybe there was a chance to reach him. David had to try. He wouldn't let Clover end up like Trilby.

David phoned Edison first. He found that Edison had already contacted the sheriff, an old buddy of his, and hadn't told Hattie. He told Edison what had transpired at the trailer park.

"Hell, Davey," said Edison. "Give it till tomorrow and then go look for the SOB. He might have called the girl to meet him and she's on the way there. My posse can keep looking for her here."

The next morning, first thing, David phoned nearby hospitals and morgues and found that no teenager of Clover's description had entered any facility. Thank God.

Then he left home packed for a trip in case he had to stay overnight and stopped by the bank to withdraw more cash. He found his balance was pretty low. When he got to St. Ninian's, Jane told him the messages were just about parish matters. He had calls to make, and when he finished, it was after ten. He finally left for Rock Springs under overcast, shifting skies.

Clouds followed him eastward down the mountain and through the valley. It was over two hour to Rock Springs: fifty miles through twisting roads or eighty miles using I-40 plus more twisting roads. He chose the highway. For long stretches the interstate felt almost deserted; only an occasional car passed, and he had the feeling of being alone, misty mountains rising on both sides. This illusion dogged him for a few miles before he came upon a pack of cars again and then he crested a hill and saw a line of fuzzy red taillights that stretched down a hill and back up again. Fog. The traffic inched forward. David swore softly beneath his breath. Why hadn't he taken the mountain road? Perhaps because it went through Glencreggan.

He'd heard Glencreggan had become even tonier now. Used to be the summer people played it down, thinking it was bad manners to display your wealth, content with a little genteel shabbiness here and there.

Not anymore.

He wondered what had become of the waterfall and the boarded-up mill where he and Trilby had first met. He started to shunt the memory aside, as he had for the past twenty-eight years, but then he let it all come flooding back. For once, he'd take the pain. Without the pain he couldn't remember the sweetness.

Chapter 13

Glencreggan, 1963

David longed to talk to Trilby alone. He'd always had pretty good luck with girls, but this one left him dazed and confused.

The day after he'd taken her home, and the next, he'd driven by the blackberry stand. The first time, the place looked deserted. The second time, her mother was bagging pole beans for people in a blue Buick with Ohio plates. The third time, the charm, he found Trilby leaning back in a folding chair behind baskets of corn and tomatoes, eyes half-closed. He drove past to see if her mother was around. No mother in evidence. He turned back, and when he pulled to a stop in the sandy soil, she opened her eyes and regarded him without expression.

He sat for a minute, gathering his nerve, and then got out the car and walked over. She leaned back in her chair, and he saw that the bruise on her cheek had faded to green.

"What are you doing here, fisher boy?" she said. He wasn't sure if she was teasing him or not.

He shifted his balance and picked up an ear of corn, awkwardly fingering its tassels. "I wanted to buy some corn."

She shook her head. "Try again."

He wished he was in his car, his exoskeleton. He felt as exposed as a dug-up earthworm. "All right. I wanted to see if you were okay. And to ask you to go to the show with me."

She leaned back and crossed her arms. "Well, now. What's on?"

David had forgotten to look at the marquee when he'd driven through town, and so he guessed, because the shows generally ran a couple of weeks. "Some Vincent Price thing."

She lifted her shoulders and arched her brows. "I've already seen it. And it's gone."

His cheeks warmed. "So have I. Okay, I forgot to look. But will you come, no matter what? "

She finally smiled, and that high feeling came over him, that feeling that left him someplace between quivering jelly and a proud lion. "Does that smile mean yes? Can I pick you up?"

Her smile faded. She picked up a tomato and studied it. "I don't know."

David's muscles knotted and his stomach grew queasy. Was she just playing with him? He forced his voice to sound casual. "Why not?"

She placed the tomato carefully back in a basket. "It's my daddy. When he saw this purple thing on my face, he said he's gon' find a way to kill Judd Coulton." She paused, doodling on a pad of paper with a pencil. "I don't think he'd do it, even if he does beat up on my mama sometimes."

"Oh, Jesus. He doesn't . . ."

"No, not on me. Not yet. He told me to stick with my own folk, not you people. Better not t'cross him."

"Yeah. I know the feeling." David pushed the thought of his father aside and spotted a big green flower in a squat fruit jar, a flower with leathery petals. He wanted to buy something, and his mother liked flowers. "What's this?"

"It's a galax rose," she said. "I make 'em out of galax leaves I find in the woods."

"How much?"

"Fifty cents. Shoot, you can have that one. I owe you for the ride."

"No, you don't." He dug two quarters out of his pocket.

She took the quarters, put them in a cigar box, then took the galax rose from him and dug under the table for a paper bag. "Put it in water soon."

He took the bag. His feet felt like lead, unable to step away from her. "Okay. I'll be seeing you."

"I think you asked me to the show." She gave him a small, teasing smile.

His pulse quickened. "So you'll go?"

She shrugged. "I'll meet you there. There's not much else to do around here anyhow."

And then she winked at him. He almost drove his car off the road as he sped home.

Funny how he couldn't remember what had been playing. She wouldn't let him put his arm around her, wouldn't hold hands. But he remembered how she looked, in her black pants and a white shirt belted at the waist and those flimsy flat shoes, hoops in her ears, the wild gypsy hair.

Afterwards they'd walked to Danny's. David had offered to take her to the Spinning Wheel for their famous coconut pie, but she'd told him she really loved the chocolate shakes at Danny's. At the soda shop, David ordered two, collected them from the counter, and took them to a table by the window.

"Did you like the show?"

"Sure," she said, taking a paper napkin from a table dispenser. "What a spooky old house that was, that tumbling-down mansion. Tell me, fisher boy, do you live in a mansion? Back home, I mean?"

A flush spread to David's cheeks. He didn't like to think about the difference between them. "Not exactly, but it is a big house."

She leaned forward, intrigued. "Does it have towers and secret rooms and all that stuff?"

He shook his head and carefully unwrapped his straw. "Nope. It's kind of boring. No secret passageways. No ghosts of any kind."

"Hmph. I'll bet I wouldn't think it was boring." She glanced out the window, then. Her look of wonder disappeared and the sparkle in her eyes faded. He followed her gaze and saw Judd Coulton and Pamela Dodge walking down the sidewalk. They approached Danny's.

David held his breath for a moment and then Pamela stopped in front of the window. Her eyes bored into David's. She tossed her head, said something to Judd, and they walked on by.

David searched Trilby's face, but it had closed against him. She pushed her half-full glass away. "Let's go."

He knew what was wrong. That damned Coulton. David wanted to make it better, but he didn't know how. "Want me to get a paper cup for the shake?"

She shook her head.

David swore under his breath. That guy had really hurt her. He pulled out her chair and gave her his arm.

She dropped his arm when the front door swung open and a bulky crew-cut guy bulled through with two friends.

"Hey, Trilby," said the bulky guy. "Who's your friend?"

"Hey, Owen," said Trilby, without enthusiasm. "David, this is Owen Ferguson. Owen, David Wilder."

Owen inclined his head slightly, not offering to shake hands. Then he turned back to Trilby. "I've been trying to find you. Some of us are getting together to ride to the Greendale dance next weekend. Want to go?"

"I don't know," said Trilby.

"We'll come by for you," said Owen.

This guy needed to see that Trilby had a date right here. David said, "I've heard that Greendale dance is pretty rough."

Owen glared at David. "Maybe for you." Meaning: Not for us. We belong here.

"I'll let you know, Owen," said Trilby, and she slipped her arm through David's. "We've got to go."

"Oh, yeah?"

"*Please*, Owen."

David's jaw and fists tightened, but Trilby squeezed his arm. Owen slid a measly two steps aside for them so that they had to edge by.

They walked in silence to the car. "That guy a good friend of yours?" David asked, opening the door for her.

"School friend," she said dismissively.

David couldn't think of anything to say that he probably shouldn't say. Maybe she was thinking the same thing. When they reached the jelly stand she said, "Stop here like last time."

David parked the car. He turned to her and took her hand.

She tried to pull it away.

"Wait, wait," said David. "I promise you I'm not going to try anything." He took a deep breath and waited. Just waited.

The moon behind the trees threw deep mauve shadows across the car's yellow hood and set the mica sand shimmering. An owl called from deep in the woods. She half-smiled and finally let her hand rest in his, her soft hand, her hand that jolted him and took his breath.

He let his breath out. "Tell me the truth. Is that guy Owen your boyfriend?"

"Just a friend. Known him since grade school."

"Are you going with him dancing?"

"I haven't made up my mind."

She leaned away from him and rested her other hand on the door handle. He touched the nape of her neck, tentatively at first. When she remained still, he began to stroke her dark curls. He twined his fingers gently in them. Feeling his body harden, he licked his lips. He mustn't frighten her, no, never. But oh, how he wanted to take her in his arms. Did she feel what he did? Almost as though she felt his thoughts, she edged away from him. He let his fingers slide from her hair.

"You don't have to be scared of me," he said, embarrassed at his passion, trying to control his quickening breath. He stroked her back, felt the tenseness in her muscles, heard her breathing slow. He leaned toward her and kissed her throat, felt the pounding of her blood. She gave a shudder and closed her eyes.

He kneaded her back until the tense muscles loosened. Very slowly he stroked her neck, drew his fingers along her jawline, turned her head to face him. When he looked into her eyes, he saw wanting, bare and fierce, and he soared with joy.

She leaned forward and kissed him, kissed him as no girl had ever kissed him before, a slow kiss tasting of vanilla and soul and dew, of flickering flame on mountaintops. It seemed as if his whole body was suffused with light, with yearning for something he'd never had. Not sex. He'd had sex, well, sort of. This was different. And then a light clicked on from up the hill, from the front porch of her house. She drew back from him and in one swift motion opened her car door.

He caught her hand once more. "Trilby . . . do you . . .?"

The moonlight revealed her confusion, and she jerked her hand away. "I'll be at the waterfall tomorrow. About four." She leaped from the car and ran up the rocky driveway, leaving the door open. David reached over and pulled it shut, then leaned back and closed his eyes, listening to the faint sound of her footsteps until he heard from afar, very faint, the closing of a door.

Chapter 14

Rock Springs, North Carolina, 1990

When David finally edged past the overturned tractor-trailer, the traffic thinned, and he rode smoothly past the blue-smoke hills. His mind still on the painful past, he exited onto a winding two-lane highway. For an hour he traveled past farms and fields, crops and mobile homes, people living their lives much as their grandparents had lived them. It could almost have been 1963 again. An hour and two turns later, he saw the sign: *Rock Springs 15.*

Unlike Bow Creek, Rock Springs had originally been a resort town. During the late 1800s and early 1900s, its Victorian inn had been the center of a lively summertime social life, and churches had sprung up nearby to accommodate the huge crowds. The town went into decline during the Depression years, and the inn had been boarded up. The narrow highway became increasingly hazardous to travel.

But with the opening of the Interstates and the completion of the Blue Ridge Parkway, people were discovering the quaint little town again, and it was growing. David had read that the publication of a cozy mystery series set there was helping Rock Springs to become a tourist mecca once more.

He followed the cliffside road past budget motels and then a Holiday Inn. The road climbed again and then, rounding a bend, the newly refurbished Rock Springs Inn glistened white, its green shutters and front porch rockers picturesque. Distracted, he almost missed the sign just beyond: *Transmontane Properties: Misty Valley, Terriquo Falls 5 miles ahead.* That must be it. He might have known it was Transmontane.

Inside the city limits, traffic slowed to a crawl along the shop-lined main street. The blue Episcopal Church sign at the next corner caught his eye. He wished he could stop and see his old friend Hubert Grimes, the rector, and maybe put in a good word for Jake as bishop, but he had a mission today.

He passed a small mom-and-pop motor court of twenty rooms, a relic from an earlier time. One story, red brick. Portable sign out front. CONGRATULATIONS JIMMIE SUE AND MARVIN. Just past the motel was a convenience store, and he pulled in to fill up.

He asked the clerk if the turnoff to Misty Valley and Terriquo Falls was marked. She didn't know; she was new in town. But a man standing behind him told him that it sure was. He knew some people that were planning to buy there. David asked if there were any more construction projects in town, and the man said no.

He headed out.

David saw the Transmontane sign, turned, and found himself on a fairly straight country road leading past farmland. Mist was rising toward the high sun, the valley warming, wisps of cloud floating above. Now Terriquo Falls came into view, a narrow veil of water plunging down the rocky face of the mountainside. He turned left at the next dirt road. A half mile further, houses in various stages of completion rose out of somebody's back forty.

David drove into the bulldozed dirt clearing and parked beside a house that was being framed. He got out and looked around for someone in charge. Before he could ask, he spotted Riley Clyde across the lot, carrying boards on his shoulder. The boy was small and wiry, all springs and tanned muscle, and his sweaty hair fell lankly to his shoulders under his hard hat. He'd let his sparse beard grow since David had seen him last.

David walked toward him. "Riley Clyde Summers!"

The young man stopped and stared. "Good God, Preacher, what are you doing here?"

"Take a break, can you? I need to talk to you."

"How long?"

"Ten, fifteen minutes." The other workers were glancing at the man in the black shirt and clerical collar.

The supervisor was heading their way. Riley Clyde said a few words to him, walked away from the site with David, and took off the hard hat. He stuck a cigarette between his lips, then lit it. "Has something happened to Daddy or Mama Ruby?"

"They're fine."

"Lacey okay? She and Bobby's only ones knew where I was."

"She's all right."

His face became guarded, as if he knew what was coming.

David nodded. "Clover's pregnant. She's fifteen."

"Oh, Jesus God. Uh, sorry, Preach." He took a drag on his cigarette and blew smoke. "I'm supposed to come back and have old Hattie clap my ass in jail, is that it? She told me she was sixteen."

David clenched his teeth to keep from blessing out the boy. *God, please give me strength to keep calm and say the right words. Let me get through to him for Clover's sake.* He forced himself to speak calmly.

"She's disappeared. Run away. We thought she might be coming to you. Have you heard from her?"

Riley Clyde recoiled as if David had hit him. "Shit, no."

David, hands in his pockets, regarded the young man. "She thought you loved her."

Riley Clyde took another drag. "Clover, well . . . I didn't tell her where I was headed. This may sound crazy to you, but I didn't want to hurt her. I knew I wasn't good for her."

"Do you care what happens to her?

"What's it to you?" the boy said sullenly.

"Clover's my niece, and I'm fond of her. My wife loved her dearly."

"She ain't blood kin."

David took a step forward, slapped Riley Clyde's shoulder a little harder than he meant. "I'd help her if she were no kin at all."

Riley Clyde gave David an amused smile. "You gon' fight me, Preacher? I always heard you was the peaceful kind."

David wanted to grab Riley Clyde by the throat and shake him. He made a fist and raised it, pulled back, ready to lunge, and the boy's eyes narrowed. "Hey. You don't wanta do that, Preacher."

David flushed. The boy knew him better than he knew himself. He looked down at his hands, at the wedding ring he'd never removed that was tight now and bit into his flesh like a penance. His hands could not do violence.

"I've got to get back to work," said Riley Clyde. He flipped the cigarette from his grimy fingers and stomped it flat then looked at David uncertainly. "Look. You gonna be around? Let me know if they find her?"

David had made no plans to stay. Clover was not here. But maybe if he stuck around, he might find a way to get through to this boy. And the girl still might show up, though he winced to think of her hitchhiking, what might happen to her if she climbed into a stranger's car. Musket and all.

"I might be. If you want to talk about things." David held out his hand. "Tell you what. I'm going to check in at the Falls Motel. If you come by after work, I'll treat you to a beer and something to eat."

"I ain't making no promises."

One of Riley Clyde's workmates whistled at him, a long piercing shriek. "So long, Preacher."

The Falls Motel didn't look very busy. He checked in. The room, reeking of dampness and mildew, didn't improve David's mood. The brown shag carpet had seen better days, as had the bedspread and curtains patterned with horses and cactus. He turned up the heat and hoped it was working.

He tried to call Edison at the store, but Edison was out looking for Clover, and the boy who answered didn't have any news. Hattie wasn't at home, either. Jane answered at St. Ninian's, told him he had no new messages, and he gave her his motel room number. Four o'clock, and he didn't want to sit by the phone. Bad news had a habit of finding you wherever you went. The sunny, windless day tempted him outside. Maybe he'd hike Terriquo Falls and be back when Riley Clyde got off work.

He changed into jeans, flannel shirt, and hiking boots. He stopped by a convenience store and bought peanut butter crackers and a chocolate bar to stuff in his daypack with the canteen and Swiss Army knife he always carried on a trip, in case he should have a hiking opportunity. Then he drove to the trailhead a couple of miles on the other side of Terriquo Mountain. He wasn't alone on the trail. He passed a rangy guy and equally rangy girl in cargo shorts and sweatshirts and then a gaggle of migratory-bird watchers with their binoculars.

The trail got steeper, people grew fewer, and then he was alone, climbing over rain-washed rocks and skirting lichen-lined gullies. He scrambled ahead, into sky, finally arriving at the top of a boulder overlooking the valley. To the east rose the pine frames of the Terriquo Falls project.

He pushed onward. In half an hour he had reached the top, where a sudden whistling wind sucked the late-day warmth out of the air. He dug a nylon parka out of his pack and shrugged it on. Resting on a granite outcrop, he drank half his water.

The view of the valley below with the tops of the trees reminded him of the view from the top of Whitecliff Mountain, back in Glencreggan. Now he remembered the night his father had confronted him about Trilby, the beginning of a wound that had never healed. He wondered what his father was doing now.

He guzzled the rest of his water, got to his feet, walked slowly back down the trail to Rock Springs and the Falls Motel. He figured Riley Clyde would be getting off work about now. This time he reached Edison on the phone and found there was no news. Hattie seemed to be the only one who didn't seem worried. Her simple faith was something David wished he had. Jake had always told him that faith was in the heart, not the head, and David couldn't yet let go of his complicated relationship with God. To Edison, he related a short version of his conversation with the Summers boy.

No need to tell them that he might not be finished with Riley Clyde yet.

Chapter 15

The boy wasn't coming. David was tired of waiting for Riley Clyde, and he was hungry. Just in case, he left a note on the door that he'd be at Jewel's Kitchen, a barbecue place in town. In the smoky din of the eatery, he demolished a vinegary, peppery barbecue plate with one eye on the door, but Riley Clyde didn't show. David stopped on the way back to his room and bought a cold six-pack of Budweiser.

Just as he reared back in the lone motel chair with a brown bottle in his hand, the phone jangled. Pulse racing, he picked it up.

Edison told him they'd found his father's Civil War musket about two miles down the mountain, in the woods, and the sheriff was going to bring in the search and rescue dogs.

David gritted his teeth. "How's Hattie?"

"Better than you might think. She has faith that Clover's all right. But I swear I don't know."

"There's worry in your voice, Edison."

"It's hunting season. And the nights are cold."

"Should I come back now?"

"No need to. We got the sheriff and the deputies and half the folks in the county out looking. Maybe they'll find her by morning. Alive and well." There was a long silence. No one wanted to say anything different. "Good luck with that bastard," Edison finally said.

David hung up the phone, a tight knot of fear in his stomach.

He drank his beer while he scribbled notes for a sermon in the small notebook he carried everywhere. Finally, he shoved the book aside and reached for the Gideon Bible in the drawer. Which verse was the one about being lost and found? And then he remembered. He turned to Luke and read again the story of the prodigal son. He had always skipped over that one for a sermon. Maybe because his own father would never welcome him back.

The motel's curtains did not quite meet in the middle, and the yellow sign of congratulations burned brightly outside. Who were Jimmie Sue and Marvin, and why were they being congratulated? Maybe it was a wedding, maybe a fiftieth anniversary. If he had married Trilby, they would have been married twenty-eight years. If he had married Trilby. If.

The afternoon she slipped away to meet him, he'd taken the boat to the old mill, tied it to an overhanging branch, and waded to the rocks. Waiting, full of hope, he plunked pebbles into the shallows where water beetles surfed the ripples. Under the shifting sun and clouds, a trout flashed its rainbow and a bullfrog drummed its cadence from the bank. David's heart expanded when a hummingbird thrummed out of the woods and plunged its beak into a cardinal flower. The air, the heady fragrance of leaf and flower, the music of it all.

A voice broke his reverie. "Hi."

He leaped to his feet and there she was, smiling shyly in the sunlit clearing. "Hi."

"Been here long?"

He shrugged, though he'd been waiting half an hour. "Can I ask what's in the sack this time?"

She reached into the bag she was carrying and pulled out a well-oiled pocketknife. She pointed to a patch of low, round galax leaves. "I cut leaves with this," she said. "I found it one day in the woods, and my daddy showed me how to sharpen it on a stone. Ain't it pretty?" She handed it to him.

He hefted the smooth weight and turned the knife over. "It's really nice." He'd seen knives like it, expensive knives, in the town shops. This one was black with age, the carved bone handle cracked and darkened, and she was proud of it. He almost envied her. Owning something had never meant much to him. Objects were always available, always replaceable. Like girlfriends.

He handed the knife back to her. "So how do you make green roses out of this skunk cabbage?" He'd never liked the smell of galax.

"I'll show you directly." She sat beside him and pulled out a cigarette and matches. "I ain't allowed to smoke at home. My ma is a strict hard-shell Baptist. You want one?" She didn't offer the pack.

"No thanks," he said. He took the matchbook from her and lit her cigarette. "What did you do all day?" The day to him had been endless.

She took a long draw, and a slow ribbon of smoke curled around her face. "What else? Worked at the jelly stand. I tell you one thing. I don't mean to be selling jelly the rest of my life. I want to get out of this place."

"Out of Glencreggan?" said David. "It's a wonderful place." He wished he never had to go back home. The only bad part was having to stay with his parents.

"For you people, maybe," she said. "And then you go back where you make money for them fancy houses."

David's face warmed and he leaned back on his elbow, out of the path of the smoke. "Don't you love the mountains, though?"

"You can love something," she said slowly, "and not love it too." She took another drag off the cigarette. "I love these woods. I love ever' little flower that grows here. I love the air in the summertime and that smoky blue of the mountains. My folks, they say they'd never leave. But I want to go places. Do things. See houses that look like them ivory palaces they sing about in church. I've hardly ever been off the mountain, 'cept to go to square dances in Greendale."

David looked at her. "But this is your place. You know the woods. I saw you skip across those stones like a mountain goat. You belong here."

"Shush." She held the cigarette, studying the ripples of the lake, as though she were trying to make up her mind about something. Then she turned her face to his, looked him in the eye. "Daddy don't work steady. Can't do construction no more after he broke his leg and got the shakes. He plants the garden and he makes the shine, and he lands in jail from time to time, and when he gets drunk, he beats Ma. I try to keep out of his way. After I finish at school next year, I'm on my way. I'm not going to wind up stuck in these hills, tied down with a bunch of young-uns and getting old before my time."

David picked up a stick and raked it across the ground. "Why doesn't your mother leave?"

Trilby hit his stick with hers, then undercut it, popping it into the air.

David watched the arc while Trilby's face grew angry. "Where would Ma go? All the kinfolks are here. Kinfolks tell her a good Christian woman stands by her man. How would she get by? Can't even get maid work with the teeth she's got. Besides, she's got your kind of attitude. Just looks up at those green mountains and she's in heaven." She paused. "Anyhow, it ain't your business."

She picked up the knife, got up, and moseyed along the path, finally stopping at a patch of galax. David scrambled to his feet and followed her.

She kneeled and cut a handful of the leathery rounded leaves, all varying in size. "Look here. The light ones are too soft. You want them good and dark. And don't get none like this." She pointed to one that was mottled with a brown webbing.

When she had a handful, she took a small leaf and curled it tightly. Then she took one a little larger and curled it around the first. A third was added, and a fourth. "Hand me that string, will you?"

David obliged.

Her hands working swiftly, she wrapped leaves around and around the stems and secured them with twine. Finally, she held up a finished rose, the size and shape of a large cabbage rose. She trimmed the stems to an even length and handed it to David.

"Beautiful. But I'm not going to smell it." He laughed and handed it back to her. She smiled at him, and the memory of the kiss she'd given him the night he'd taken her home came flooding back. There was a mischievous look in her eyes, and once again he wanted to stroke her hair. He picked a fallen rhododendron blossom and tucked it in a dark curl. She laughed, shook her head, and it fell out.

His heart gave a leap. He had to get away from this spot before he made some move that would drive her away. "Come on, let's walk."

She looked at him quizzically. "You sure?"

"I feel like walking. Where do you usually go?"

"Up the path to the top of the falls, up to the stream. I can find some good leaves along the way."

He remembered vaguely his mother telling him not to go there last year. "Hey. Wasn't that where that Westbury student got washed over?"

"Yeah, so? Are you scared?"

No way would he mention he'd been warned off. "I know my way around the woods."

"You city folk. Think you know more than you do."

David felt as if there had been a tectonic shift between them. They gazed at each other, and David caught his breath, almost undone with yearning, with confusion. Did he see yearning in her parted lips, her look of surprise? And then the moment was over. Trilby lowered the rose and the knife into the bag, and they stepped onto the path Trilby had taken from the roadway. They climbed until they came to the fork, then veered left, deeper into the laurel forest.

David hadn't used the narrow path that summer. They ducked under arching blackberry canes, overgrown in the sunny places, thorns tearing at their clothes; they climbed over fallen logs and slipped on slick wet leaves. Trilby paused a couple of times to cut galax. Finally they came to the stream's edge, where buckberry bushes grew in a clearing.

Trilby regarded the bushes with satisfaction. "A good stand of buckberries. I'll have to remember that."

"Your mom makes jelly out of those?"

"Sure."

"I thought they were poisonous."

"I'd'a been dead a long time ago if they were." She picked some and put them in her mouth. "Yum, yum." She picked half a handful and held them out to David. Open up." He trustingly opened his mouth, and she put them on his tongue. He bit down and immediately spat them out. "Ugh."

She was laughing. "I didn't say they were real sweet."

"You . . . I'll get you for that." Grinning, he grabbed at her, and she giggled and dodged, darting away, but he caught up with her and tripped over a root as he reached for her. They fell to the path, tussling, laughing. She struggled to get loose, but not very hard.

"Want to get up?" David said softly. Their eyes met, and the playfulness turned searching. Their lips met and lingered, the kiss growing deeper. Her tangled hair lay in the shifting dapples of sunlight, her eyes reflecting sky. Reflecting him.

Afraid she would run, his heart expanding, he gently pressed his hard body against her, and then when she molded herself to him and her breathing quickened, tightly. He slid a hand up the side of her shorts, just under the cuff. "Please," he begged. "Please."

She closed her eyes tightly, as if in pain. "I don't want to get in trouble. Let me go."

He let out a long breath. He didn't want to lose her. He couldn't lose her. Numb with disappointment, he rolled away. She leaped up, gathered her things, and tramped toward the waterfall. He watched her skip over the stones and disappear into the thicket of the forest.

He waded back to the boat, confused and unsettled.

When the knock came a little after eleven, David, surprised but not shocked, heaved himself off the bed, set his Travis McGee mystery down, and opened the door. Riley Clyde stood, head cocked, thumbs in his pockets. "Any news?"

David shook his head. "Come on in."

Riley Clyde perched uncomfortably on the chair by the drawn curtains, wary, his eyes narrowed, posture stiff. He glanced at the door from time to time. David went to the cooler, lifted two cold ones out, and handed one to the young man, who twisted off the cap and took a long swallow. David hunched on the edge of the bed with his beer and told Riley Clyde what Edison had told him.

"Shit."

"Do you have any idea where she might have gone?"

"With a musket? Good Lord."

"To Lacey's? Was she jealous?"

Riley Clyde gave a short laugh. "Clover wouldn't kill nobody."

"They're bringing in the dogs."

The boy looked stunned. It had finally sunk in that this was serious. "Oh my God," he choked out. "I hope they find her."

David had been thinking about how to get through to the boy. It was time to challenge him. "Do you love her?"

Riley Clyde raised his eyebrows and turned the beer bottle in his hands. He shook his head slowly. "What's love, Preacher?"

The boy was trying to hide how much he felt for Clover. David had to go carefully. "To me, it means caring what happens to somebody and backing up that caring with action. Think about this, Riley Clyde. If you love this girl, really love her, then come back and tell her you'll stand by her. Maybe on your day off, if you need the job here.

"We can try to work something out. If all she was to you was a little fun, then stay far away. Let her get on with her life. Let her get over her broken heart. And I really mean this."

Riley Clyde sat for a moment, considering. Then he raised his chin and challenged David. "Why do you care, Preacher? Really?"

David stared at the brown bottle in his hands. It was time he got this off his chest, and what better than to someone who could learn from it? "I'm going to tell you a story."

Chapter 16

Later that evening, David lay back on the pillow, wrung out and almost trembling. What he had told Riley Clyde was only part of the story, but it was the part that mattered. It was the part that had followed him all his life. The part he couldn't shake.

1963

When he'd finally made his way back to his parents' house through the dark and fragrant woods, evening lamplight glowed in the windows and a thin plume of smoke drifted from the chimney. He walked across the porch and entered by the sliding door. His father stood with his back to the stone fireplace, hands in pockets. His mother sat in a yellow armchair, turning the pages of a magazine. She glanced up.

"Where have you been, David? Dinner's been over for an hour."

"Fishing." David hoped his expression gave nothing away.

His mother studied him. "The fishing poles are still in the boathouse. Your father went down there to look for you."

His father waited for him to speak. The room took on an empty stillness, punctuated by a shower of sparks when a log shifted.

His belly clenched. He couldn't lie again. He couldn't face telling the truth. He hated to think of the lecture that was sure to come. He had to get away and get his mind straight. "Just a minute." David walked over to the fire, shifted the fire screen, and jabbed an iron poker at the glowing logs until they blazed anew. He set the screen in place. "I'll be right back." He went to the kitchen, past a plate covered with aluminum foil lay on the stove.

He walked out into the backyard and took a few deep breaths, letting the air swirl around him, siphoning the heat from his body and the giddiness from his head. He kicked at a mole tunnel, then gave the wooden seat of his old swing a shove. He gazed up at the long thick ropes as the plank swung back and forth, back and forth. The moon came out from behind a smoky cloud, hazing the night.

Trilby. Where was she? Was she thinking of their day? Was she glad or sorry that she'd run away?

His father's voice split the night. "David!"

David shoved the swing once again and walked back to the porch, where his father sat in the shadow of the moonlight, smoking a cigar, its red glow puncturing the darkness. "Sit down for a minute," his father said.

David sat on a hard bench, his elbows on his knees, hands clasped. Expecting the worst. "What is it?"

"David, why did you lie? Where were you?"

He felt the heat rising to his cheeks. He'd better tell a little of the truth. "Why does everybody have to know my business? I was hiking with Trilby Gaddis."

"Tully Gaddis's girl?"

"We lost track of time."

"I see. Things can happen when you lose track of time." He paused and puffed on his cigar. "I've known Tully a long time. He was on the crew that built this house."

"So what?"

"Tully's a drunk and a moonshiner."

"Maybe he can't get any other work. It's not Trilby's fault."

"You aren't making this easy, you know." Lem Wilder took another draw on his cigar.

"Dad, don't give me that old class crap. I don't believe in it." And yet it was there, like a boulder in the road, between him and Trilby. He clenched his fists.

His father sighed. "David, I don't want to see you get into trouble. I've heard tales about that girl. You've got a good future ahead of you. Protect yourself."

David bit his lip to keep from saying something he'd regret. "Judd Coulton's a shithead who's been spreading lies about her. She wants to make something of herself."

His father studied him for a moment. "Be careful, son."

"I'm always careful." But it was so hard to be careful when you were dancing in the moonlight on a rickety bridge, over a gully, and if you stepped off, it would be on a cloud . . .

"I'll remember that," said his father.

Damn, thought David. It would be better if the old man would just rant and rave. But he was trying to be *reasonable*, and that was harder to fight.

Just in time, his mother called, "Don't you want something to eat?"

"I'm not hungry."

"You'd better eat something so your mother won't worry," said his father. "We'll talk later."

David, smoldering, barricaded himself in his room, but it wasn't anger, or hunger, that kept him awake most of the night.

So full was he of Trilby—the way she talked to him, the way she had looked, hair wild from the wind and wet with stream-mist, the way she had melted into him . . . and the way she had fled.

He couldn't call her. She'd told him they had no telephone. And the first thing his mother did the next day was command him to take the boat motor to the repair shop, then dry-dock the boat for a paint job. He spent all morning painting the hull with spar varnish. Finally done with the job, he was just about to ride over to the jelly stand when the phone rang. He leaped to catch it, just in case, and was glad the folks were out.

"Hi."

"Trilby?"

"Sorry I ran," she said.

He sensed she wanted to say more. "I want to talk to you," he said. "Away from the house or the lake. I don't have the boat today. Can we hike somewhere?"

"What about Whitecliff?"

"Lots of people there," he said.

"Maybe it's better that way," she said.

"Can I pick you up?"

"No!"

By this time, David knew better than to insist or question. She told him where to meet her.

Thirty minutes later he sat in his yellow convertible in front of Matt's Grocery and Laundromat, restlessly watching cars roll by and disappear around the curve. She'd said she might have trouble borrowing the truck.

He got out of the car, walked up to the Coke machine in front of the store, and put in a quarter. The small bottle clunked out. He picked it up and snapped the cap on the opener with one smooth motion. He leaned against the building, drinking the Coke, eyes on the passing cars.

A baby blue Dodge two-door coupe turned into the lot and stopped in a parking space in front of Matt's. Pamela Dodge got out and smiled at him.

He swallowed the last of his Coke while she walked up and then grinned. "Howdy, Pam. I thought you weren't speaking to me."

She flipped her hair with her hand. "I changed my mind. Want to play some tennis? I've got to pick up some groceries for Mom and then I'll be free for the rest of the afternoon."

"Go play with Judd Coulton."

Pamela pouted. "Oh, come on, David."

"Look, Pam—"

Just then a black Ford truck with a short bed, big cab, and hiked-up springs rattled into the parking lot. It made a slow circle and pulled up beside David's yellow convertible.

"Excuse me, Pamela," said David. "My hiking date's here. Good to see you." He walked over to the truck, and Trilby leaned out the window shyly.

"I had to tell Daddy a story to get the truck."

"Why?"

"I don't want Daddy to know who I spend time with."

"Why?"

She stared at him as though he didn't have good sense. He opened the truck door and helped Trilby down, then opened the passenger door of his convertible. He had this weird sensation Pamela was watching him. He glanced back toward her, but she was talking on the pay phone at the front of the store.

He drove away uneasily, not looking back.

About three miles past the town limits, they turned into the dirt road that led to the well-marked trailhead. Hell, yes, there would be people here, and he didn't care. Pamela could tell everybody in the world.

With a canteen over his shoulder and a bandanna in his pocket, he took her hand. Hand in hand they walked the rocky path until the trail became steep and narrow, then he let her climb ahead. The clouds lifted, dappling the path with sunshine.

Growing warm, they stopped to rest against a boulder. Sweat trickled down David's chest and back. Trilby glowed, her face flushed and damp. She asked for his bandanna and wiped her face with it. He tied it around his neck and caught her scent, and a wild bird broke loose in him, beating its wings.

The notes of a hearty German song burst from above them, and two men wearing lederhosen and carrying hiking sticks emerged from over a ridge. The men greeted them with *Guten tag* and broad smiles and went on. After the voices had died away the fragrant trail was hot and quiet, the silence broken only by the hikers' footsteps and the distant song of a wood thrush. They climbed another twenty minutes before they saw the roof of the pavilion that marked the high point of the trail.

They stood in the pavilion's shade looking out into the valley, at the spires of churches thrusting through the trees. David passed the canteen to Trilby. She drank and passed it back to him, and then he leaned back, pouring the water into his mouth, splashing his face, and they both dissolved in a fit of laughter.

"My uncle probably helped build this place." She looked in her pack for a paper towel and blotted her mouth with it. "He had a job with the WPA, building things like this, building roads through the mountains. It was a godsend for them, after the Depression. He used to call it the Hooverdepression, one word." She laughed.

"Your uncle?

"He's dead now." She sighed, folding the towel and stuffing it back in her pack. "He had a little farm once, down in the valley. The bank took it."

David looked away, thinking of the clean smell of his father's bank: crisp dollar bills in bands and rolled coins, the polished marble tiles of the floors, the sleek brass of the old-fashioned teller cages, the plump blond secretary who offered him candy from the dish on her desk. He had never thought much about loans and the people who had to repay them. Not really.

Trilby looked at him with curiosity. "Did I say something wrong?"

"No. Let's sit down."

They sat on benches and David reached in his pack and handed her a box of Junior Mints. "Hope you like these." She nodded, peeled back the wrapper, and took a bite, filling the air with the aroma of mint and chocolate. David unwrapped his own bar. "What kind of job will you look for when you leave here?"

She licked chocolate from her fingers. "I've been selling jelly since I was ten. I signed up for business classes. My best subject is bookkeeping."

He grinned. "Bookkeeping? So work for a bank."

He loved the way she laughed, all the way to her eyes. "Listen at you. What about you? What are you good at, city boy?"

He looked into those eyes of hers, blue and smoky as the hills beyond, and lifted a shoulder. "Doesn't matter what I'm good at. A bank's where I'll end up."

She gazed back at him, serious now. "You don't sound real thrilled. Why?" She picked up a stick and poked the ground with it, loosening pebbles.

David shifted uneasily. He picked up one of the pebbles and threw it into the trees. "I'm not sure I want to be a banker. What if I had to take away somebody's farm? Maybe it's better to be poor and happy."

"You're crazy." Trilby tossed the stick away, sat back, and crossed her arms. "There's no such thing."

Elbows on knees, David watched an industrious woodpecker spiraling its way up a tree. "There must be more to life than pushing dollars around."

She snorted. "It's a sight better than breaking your back hoeing and plowing, cooking jelly all day, or folding towels at a motel. What else is there for me here?" She finished the candy, licked her fingers, and threw the wrapper at a green-painted trash drum.

David made what he thought was a reasonable remark. "Why don't you go to college?"

A small plane droned overhead and disappeared. The woodpecker kept tapping while she studied him, her expression incredulous. "Go to college! You have no idea what my life is like, do you?"

David realized that he really didn't have any idea how she lived. Her house was hidden behind trees on top of a rise. "Surely there are scholarships, or something."

"Not for the likes of me. Not with a father who thinks girls were made for nothing but cooking and washing and . . . well, you know. I've got two sisters married to men just like him." She sighed and got up and walked to the edge of the pavilion.

His face warm, sorry for his clumsiness, he followed her, stopped behind her, and rested his hands on her shoulders. "What would you be if you could be anything in the world?"

She whirled around and met his eyes. "I think I'd like to be you."

He stepped back, stung. "Trilby, that's a stupid thing to say."

"Is it?" Her voice was bitter." Who's the one in the ivory palace?"

"Hey, let's not fight." Not that class crap again.

"Come on. We came to hike." She headed toward the trail with long strides. David started after her, but she picked up speed, skipping from rock to rock, leaping over gullies, clambering over fallen logs. She was halfway down the trail before he caught up with her.

"Trilby," he said. "I'm sorry I said that." He slid his hand into hers, and she held it fast. He gazed at her, and she gazed back, softening, and he leaned forward. He might have kissed her, but he heard high voices, the crunch of leaves and twigs down the trail. He stepped back just as Pamela Dodge and two of her cronies came into view, swinging tanned arms in sleeveless shirts.

"Well, well, well," said Pam.

"A deep subject," said the second girl.

Pam held up her binoculars. "Hmm. Lovebirds."

"Hi, Trilby," said the second girl. "Been teaching David all about the hills?"

"And valleys?" That was the third girl.

David looked at Trilby, expecting her to give back as good as she got, but she dropped his hand and walked away.

"She won't talk to us," said the second girl.

"Come with us, David," said Pamela. She walked over and touched his arm.

He shook off Pamela and hurried off down the path. When he finally caught up to Trilby, her face was streaked with tears.

"Go back to your people, David," she said fiercely. "That's where you belong."

Maybe he didn't belong with them—his father and mother and those shallow people at the party. "They can't teach me anything," he said, hearing the hurt under the anger. "Maybe you can." He stood still, not wanting her to run again.

"You know what she meant with that crack." Trilby took a swallow of water from her canteen. She wiped her face with a scrap of cloth, then stuck it in her pocket. "No fancy bandanna for me."

David ignored the last remark and spread his hands. "Show me something this afternoon I don't know about. Please. Show me some of your mountain."

She cocked her head and gazed at him, and he wondered if she was ever going to answer. "We'll see," she finally said.

They trekked on until the voices had faded away. Then she stopped. "All right. Just one more hour or two I'm going to spend with you, David Wilder, and then you'll be on your merry way, back to wherever it is you come from."

He did not want to go back. He wanted to follow wherever she led him. She veered off onto a side path, and they wandered to where the wild raspberries grew, and the hidden *'sang*, as she called it, the ginseng with its broad lobed leaves and man-shaped roots. She made him vow to keep the location a secret. 'Sang robbers dug the roots and shipped them off to China.

She showed him foxfire growing in the shade of rotten logs and nests of ovenbirds hidden in the brush. They climbed over and under tangles of rhododendron along a stream and finally came to a clearing where water rushed over jagged rocks into a deep pool.

"What's this?" David touched a shrub festooned with spiky green balls.

She smiled. "It's called hearts-a-bustin'."

"But why?"

"Those are pods," she said. "In the fall, they turn sort of red and open up, and the seeds are redder than holly berries, red like blood. You can kind of see a heart bustin' there."

"My heart is bustin' right now," David said.

"Oh, is it, now? Trilby asked, with a smile. "You know, I'm hot and tired. Maybe a dip would cool it off."

"A dip?"

"Haven't you ever been skinny-dipping before?"

She must be kidding him. "Sure, but not with a girl."

"I'm going in. Suit yourself. Just behave," she said. She ducked behind a laurel and came out without her shorts and shirt, bra and step-ins, socks and shoes. She ran out, plunged in, shrieking with delight. "It's freezing cold!"

David stared in awe at the perfection of her pale body with its rosy points and dark shadows against the shimmering blackness of the pool, and he became suddenly shy at the thought of her appraising his body likewise. He slowly peeled off his shirt, his shoes, his socks, and finally his shorts and briefs. He plunged in, gasping at the feel of the chill on his skin.

It was too cold to stay in long, and when they finally clambered onto the bank, a sweet warmth stole into him. On the big rock, naked, they shivered and laughed and dried themselves with their T-shirts.

"Guess we'd better get dressed," she said.

"Maybe we'd better let our shirts dry." David took both and flattened them on the rock.

She glanced shyly at his body, and the stream burbled and gurgled behind them. "Oh."

"Touch me," he murmured. He didn't feel in control of himself any longer.

Looks of mischief and longing crossed her face. She reached out and then dropped her hand.

He embraced her then and kissed her, warming him all over. Choking out the words, he told her that he'd never felt about any girl as he had about her.

"Don't you dare say you love me if you don't," she said. "I'll know."

"Is that what it feels like, love? Like never ever wanting to let you go? Like wanting to know everything about you, like flying without an airplane, sailing without a boat, taking off like one of those rockets to the stars . . ."

She touched his cheek. "Hush with those pretty words. You'll forget them when summer's gone."

"I won't forget," he said, kissing her hand. "I've got two more weeks before I have to go. We'll explore these forests, every inch. I'll take you to places I know. And I'll be back for you next year."

She shook her head. "A year is a long time." She rolled away and patted her shirt to see if it was dry. "Anyhow, Momma expects me to work at the jelly stand the rest of the summer. We'll have a little time here, and lots of time apart. Maybe by the time you come back I'll be somewhere else. Or you will."

A faint grumble of thunder in the distance underscored her words. "It's going to rain," Trilby said. "Your car top's down."

David laughed, rose from the rock, and pulled her to her feet. "We're already wet."

He gazed into her sapphire eyes. "For always, Trilby." Her lips parted and her eyes grew large and moist. He pulled her against him, felt her hot and cold against him, and kissed her very gently, and then she leaned into the kiss. She shivered a little and laid her dark curls on his chest, warming it with her breath.

The rock was hard beneath them, and he rose and pulled her to her feet. He led her into the glade and they sank to the forest floor and lay together on the cool leafy ground that smelled of moss and rain. Water rushed over rocks and the wind changed; sunlight glimmered though rhododendron and faded, and then sweet rain began to fall. It misted softly over them and dripped crystal from the canopy above; it drummed them with wet lace and lost itself in the stream.

After a time, David rolled to the soft earth, breathing hard, tasting raindrops and salty tears.

"Trilby," he said, lost. "I love you."

1990

In the quiet of the motel room David closed his eyes. He was tired, and it was late, and he had drunk more beer than he had intended. And he had told Riley Clyde what finally happened, the first time he'd told anyone since he'd told Jake those years ago.

He picked up the notebook again and tried to write what he was feeling. Anguish speared him when he thought about those weeks that followed, those weeks of finding out that they could laugh together and hike together and share stories about their horrible parents, of finding out she had never tasted asparagus and oysters, of finding out he had never eaten fiddlehead ferns and cornpone. And there was that magical feeling when he saw her, as if she had been lit by that strange stuff in the woods, the foxfire.

He wanted to write all that down, and he could not write. He jammed the pen into the paper, scratching jaggedly across the page, furious tears creeping down his cheeks. Had he never grieved for Trilby? Shock had made him numb, and later a dull ache followed him wherever he went. But now he wanted to bellow in anguish for Trilby, for Tallulah, for Molly, for everyone he had lost, for the whole damned world and all the suffering. He had ministered to those who were suffering, had held their hands and spoken soothing words to them, had seen their burdens lift a little when he had given them hope. But he had not really known what they were feeling, because he had not seen his own suffering.

Chapter 17

Rock Springs, 1990

The dream woke him. Trilby, sinking beneath the rushing waters of Bow Creek, calling to him. He reached out his hand. She took it but could not hold on and slipped away into the rushing waters. He knew the feel of that cold hand. There would be a gray day ahead, no matter the weather.

Sweating and shaking, David pulled aside the curtain and blinked at the blushing dawn. He rubbed his throbbing head. He knew the headache wasn't from the beer.

He tossed his few items into the knapsack, paid his bill, and took the road out of Rock Springs the way he'd come. The mountains loomed before him, serene, complacent in their secrets. No wonder the ancient mystics saw the mountain as the dwelling place of the Deity—on the mountain, in the clouds and closer to heaven, looking down on God's creation, far from man's despoiling hand.

He wanted to be on a mountaintop far from anyone, breathing deeply of clear, fragrant mountain air. Maybe then he could let his mind empty, let peace creep into his heart. Maybe then he could feel closer to God.

He was almost to the highway when he spotted the turnoff for Glencreggan. Jake had asked him if he'd ever been back and suggested it might be a way to heal. He'd left the town at eighteen and never looked back, not wanting to stir up those memories. Now the memories tugged at him, compelled him. Maybe now was the time to face the pain. Maybe that would help the loneliness he felt, the isolation.

A shiver went down his back, and he made the turn. Fifty miles to go on winding roads. He felt wrung out; his head still throbbed: a hangover more emotional than alcoholic. He wasn't sure how much he'd accomplished in telling Riley Clyde what happened to him and Trilby following that afternoon by the creek. He didn't talk about the best three weeks of his life, weeks of getting to know what made her laugh, how they were alike, how they were different. They'd taught each other what it was to love, and he wanted to give her that better life she'd longed for. But first he had to get his education. When he left, he was certain he'd come back for her.

No. He didn't mind telling Riley Clyde that. It was what came after that.

1963

He'd gone to Duke and was plunged into a new world of classes and parties and fraternity rush. It was easy to make friends as

the students circulated, looking for kindred souls. Here he wasn't known as Phil's little brother, and he reveled in the sensation. He wrote to Trilby at once. He wasn't sure how much to tell her about his new world, because it might make her think of the *class* thing, so he wrote about the magical time they'd had together.

He mailed it to her friend Jenny, as she had told him. Because she didn't want her father to know David was writing to her.

Before he knew it, a week had passed before he thought of her again, and he quickly sent off a letter telling her how much he loved her and how much he wished she were with him. The next week, a pretty girl in class flirted with him, and it made him feel both good and guilty. He ignored the girls he met, thinking only of Trilby, dreaming of her, and his ignoring those girls seemed to intrigue them.

He found himself not knowing what to say in the next letter. He wrote that he'd decided to major in Philosophy. He knew he wasn't going to major in Economics or Business, as his father had suggested. Then he was afraid he was talking down to her, but sheesh, that was who he was, and he just couldn't hide it. Then he said he couldn't wait to see her, he loved her so much, and he was still waiting for a letter from her.

No letter came.

He told himself it was hard for her, with a father like hers. He wondered if she'd given up on him, started seeing that big guy he'd seen in the soda shop. That Ferguson guy.

He wrote her another letter, told her he loved her, and then he had a pile of tests to study for and essays to write and he didn't think of writing letters. He started studying with a girl in his Philosophy 101 class. Before he knew it, the calendar read November.

Finally, when he opened his campus mailbox, a letter from her was waiting.

He joyfully tore it open. When he read the careful, hesitant writing on notebook paper, a word or two misspelled, the joy he'd felt turned into a cold chill. She had to talk with him, and they didn't dare talk on the phone. If she didn't hear from him soon she would take six dollars out of the money she'd saved from selling her galax roses, catch a ride to Greendale, get on a Greyhound bus, and he could meet her at the bus station. Maybe they could get married.

David, to his everlasting shame, had panicked at the thought. Panicked at the thought of her riding all day and into the evening to get to Durham. At his new friends wondering what was up. At dropping out of rush. At the thought of his college education, gone. He didn't have anyone to talk to about it, certainly not his freshman adviser. There was nowhere to turn.

He'd called his parents. He felt like a traitor and the worst kind of jerk.

They had canceled all their engagements and met him in the lounge of the Queen Elizabeth Inn, located not far from the university, furnished Tudor style with blues and deep browns and russet reds. Lem and Evangeline Wilder leaned back in their chairs, fingering glasses of Scotch. David sat across from them on the banquette staring at the prints on the walls of gentlemen in puffy sleeves with swords by their sides. His father was like that, sword at the ready. David picked up his glass of lemonade and drained it.

"I think you should marry her," said his father, leaning forward. "Drop out of school. Go to work at the bank sweeping floors. That would teach you something about responsibility." He paused for a moment. "Are you sure it's yours?"

"Good God, Dad." David shook his head.

"Well? I told you about her reputation."

"I can't be positive," said David sullenly, thinking of the night he'd taken her home from the party, hurt, probably raped by that scumbag. "I'm sure she wouldn't lie about something like that." After those golden weeks with her—no. Now the bubble of that beautiful time out of time had popped, and reality came crashing down.

"Would she have an abortion?" asked Evangeline, ever practical. Her lighter clicked and flared toward her cigarette.

David paused. "I don't like the idea." A child. *His* child. And now he saw Trilby's face, as it looked in the forest, the tears on her cheeks. Pain tightened in his chest, and he could hardly breathe.

"Be logical," said his mother. "Didn't you say she wants to better herself?"

David didn't want to discuss Trilby's dreams with his parents, but he finally admitted that she had hopes. That she'd wanted to leave Glencreggan and make something of herself.

"Let's just give her a good sum of money and let her do what she wants," said Lem. "I'll square things with Tully."

"No!" David leaned forward. What in hell could he say to make them understand?

"Why not?"

David took a deep breath, trying to think of a reason his father would accept. "He might beat her."

Lem snorted. "Tully's a drunk, but not a violent drunk."

David set his jaw. "She told me he beats her mother when he's had a few."

His father said nothing, appearing to consider, and David wondered how much he knew about Tully and wasn't going to say.

Lem laid his hands on the table. "All right, David, what do you think we should do? One thing's certain, I won't have a bastard Wilder, a child of yours, running around Glencreggan."

David looked down at his feet. The thought of a real child slammed him, and he looked up, his stomach clenching. "There's no other way? Maybe I could raise it myself and let her have her life?"

No one said anything for a long moment, as if he'd made a bad joke. Maybe he had. He twisted in his chair.

"It's done my way quite often, David," said his father reasonably. "Just pay her, and that's the end of it."

David slowly shook his head. The one thing he didn't want right now was his father talking to Trilby, or to Tully Gaddis. That would be a disaster on top of disaster. He swallowed. Get married? Drop out of school? Go to work at the bank? Everything his soul rebelled against.

It would be hell on earth for them both, married with a child to raise. Hadn't she wanted freedom? To make something of herself, not to be stuck at home with children? Maybe she'd agree with his mother. Did he have the right to stop Trilby if she didn't want to have the baby? He swallowed. His child . . .

He could hardly bring himself to say the words. "If that's the way it has to be, I have to be the one to talk with her."

His father shook his head. "She's an ignorant girl. You'll botch the job."

"It's her body. And she's not as ignorant as you think." Heat crept up David's neck, and he clenched his fists, struggling to keep his seat. He wanted to strangle the old man.

His mother's eyes met his, willing him to hold back. "Lem, David's right," she said, in a voice that didn't invite argument. "It's his duty."

David leaned back and his hands dropped to his sides.

"All right," his father growled. "Here's how it's going to happen. I'll rent a car and drive you to Glencreggan tomorrow." He turned to his wife. "I'll get my secretary to book you a flight home and a taxi to take you to the airport. I'll have Albert meet you at the terminal. David and I will have time to talk on the trip."

Talking to his father was the last thing David wanted. He trudged back across campus to his room and read Trilby's letter again. If she didn't hear from him by Wednesday at the latest, she was coming. Some of the Ferguson boys went down to Greendale every now and then to buy for the restaurant and could give her a ride. He could leave a message for her at her friend Jenny's. He picked up the phone. Funny how he sounded almost normal when he said, "Hello, Jenny?"

1990

Almost before he knew it, David was driving through the familiar curves, past the city limits sign of Glencreggan. On first glance, the Glencreggan of 1990 looked much the same as it always had. And then it hit him. The stream of cars that snaked through the two blocks of town—in November? November had been dead in the sixties. Danny's Soda Shop was now a real estate office, and a shopping plaza stood where the motor court had been. Dell's Barn was still Dell's Barn, but it was filled with boutiques; the general store that had sold toys and housewares and cotton underwear had been replaced by a lingerie shop called Scarlett's Ribbons.

The Spinning Wheel Café looked unchanged.

David slowed the car to a crawl and peered out at the café. The red-lettered wooden sign over the entrance gave him an eerie feeling of déjà vu; even the daily specials were still taped to the glass.

He parked on a side street and walked the block and a half to the Spinning Wheel, past old couples and honeymoon-looking couples and families with children that skipped and hopped, all wearing nice clothes. Scarlett's Ribbons had expanded the shop, and now a slinky red satin gown in the window caught his eye, the kind of gown Lu would never have worn. He overheard a woman on her way into the shop tell her friend that Hampton Taggart bought nighties and things there for his new girlfriend; she had seen him with her own eyes.

When he reached The Spinning Wheel he paused at the door. The penny scale still waited in the doorway to tell fortunes. He opened the door and walked in. He was greeted by the familiar smell of coffee and bacon and the same hat rack standing at the front, a tweed cap its only occupant. At a little after nine, the café was half full, customers eating eggs and bacon or pancakes at tables instead of the booths he remembered. Lace café curtains, not gingham, hung at the front window; teal walls were hung with sepia-toned photographs of Glencreggan's mule-and-buggy days. So much for the tan walls and waterfall pictures.

Seeing no hostess, he took a two-person table by the window and lifted a plastic menu from its holder. A teenaged girl with curly brown hair and pudgy cheeks, big like all the Fergusons, came to take his order of pancakes and sausage and coffee.

She gave him a friendly smile. "Will that be all?"

"Yes, thank you. Coffee now."

She brought the coffee right away. The café's ambiance, with a swiftness that surprised and anguished him, brought back that snowy November morning in the fall of 1963.

Chapter 18

Glencreggan, November 1963

That morning in November, icy patches glistened like black mirrors on the roadside, and a thin layer of rime crusted the weedy banks. His eyes gritty from his sleepless night, David inched the rented car toward town from the summer house, where he'd left his father drinking coffee and reading a day-old *Wall Street Journal.* For two miles David saw no other cars on the road, and in town most of the shops were closed for the winter. A gray pall hung over the streets.

The warm yellow light from The Spinning Wheel was the only cheer he saw, and it mocked him. He pulled into a parking place in front and emerged from the car into a swirling wind that dusted his face with tiny cold-sugar snowflakes.

Inside, a lone customer hunched in a booth near the kitchen, forking up eggs and sausage and grits. The aromas of coffee and bacon should have made his mouth water, but to David it might as well have been sawdust. He slid into the booth second from the door, out of the draft, so he could see her when she came.

"What do you want, Wilder?"

David frowned and looked up. Owen Ferguson stood above him, wearing a white apron over a football jersey. He held an order pad in a huge hand.

"What are you doing here, Owen?"

"What does it look like? This is my grandpa's place."

"Jeez. Coffee." David closed his eyes. A headache was coming on, and he touched his forehead.

"Hung over, huh?" Owen scribbled something on his pad and stalked back toward the kitchen.

He felt the cold air before he saw her. Breathless, pink-cheeked, Trilby slipped in wearing a knitted tam that covered her hair, the heavy door shutting behind her. Owen appeared from the kitchen carrying David's coffee. When he set it on the table, what passed for a smile flickered across his face. "Coffee, Tril? How about a doughnut? The old man's got some fresh."

"Sure, Owen." She gave him a cheerful grin, yanked off her tam, and shook out her dark curls.

Owen smirked and headed back to the kitchen.

"Nice friend you've got," said David, thick-throated, struggling to sound unconcerned. How he'd ever get through this, he didn't know. He wasn't all that religious, but he prayed *Dear God, help me.*

"He's going into the Army," Trilby was saying. "Right now he's the only one from our class with plans to get out."

She slid into the booth facing David and unfastened the toggles on her plaid coat. Neither spoke for a moment. David's heart felt as if it was sinking through the floor.

"I've missed you," she finally said.

"I've missed you too." *But* . . . it was left unsaid for now. "It seems like a long time." What should he say? That college life was a world away from the past? A world of professors and exams and hard work and new knowledge that was exciting, a world of new friends that liked him? A world that had no room for magic? He could not say those things.

Owen Ferguson brought Trilby's coffee, steaming in a brown-striped mug, and set it in front of her with three hot powdered doughnuts. She picked one up and pushed the dish over to David. He shook his head. Trilby munched the doughnut, watching David.

David glanced over at Owen, who gave the customer in back his check. After he'd rung the man up, Owen went to sit at a corner table facing them. He picked up the man's leftover newspaper.

To say something, anything, David talked about his classes and the school. He said that he had met students on scholarship and not a one of them was smarter than she was. Her eyes gave nothing away. She finished her second doughnut and licked the powdered sugar from her fingers. He knew she was waiting for him to say something about her letter. He reached across the table and took her hand in his. "This is hard to say."

"What do you mean?"

"Don't hate me," said David. He felt miserable. Like the bottom of a septic tank. He licked his dry lips. "Please, Trilby, try to understand."

Trilby stared at him, animation gone, her face as frozen as black ice on the roadside.

Owen in the corner turned pages, crackling newsprint. Eavesdropping. In a few minutes he'd come over with the coffee pot.

David lowered his voice. "We can't talk here."

She glanced toward the table in the back and gave him a hard stare. "Are you afraid of Owen?"

"Come on. We're going to Whitecliff." David slid three dollars, twice the cost of the coffee and doughnuts, onto the table and held her plaid coat for her.

A bitter wind gusted across the trail, bending the pines near the pavilion. David and Trilby huddled on the bench, looking out to the mountains where leafless oaks and hickories patched a grey fretwork through the pines. David cupped his hands around a match to light Trilby's cigarette, and she inhaled deeply, smoke streaming out into the gathering wind.

"More snow, it looks like," she said, her cheeks reddened by the chill, tendrils of dark hair tumbling from her knitted white cap.

The words David had planned to say choked him.

She laid her free hand on his. "Well? What did you bring me up here for if you aren't going to talk?"

He coughed and mumbled, "I said it was hard. Look, Trilby, it just wouldn't work. You and me, I mean." He closed his hand around hers and couldn't let go.

"Don't hold my hand and say that." She jerked her hand away, took another drag off her cigarette, and threw it down. She stomped it hard, grinding it into the dirt. "It would work if we wanted it to. It would have to work, because there's going to be a baby. One that belongs to you and me."

David's rehearsed speech melted away, and he gazed at her with anguish and shame.

Her voice became low and gentle. "Remember what I told you? That I liked you too much? It was more than that. Remember that bush you asked me about, hearts-a-bustin'? My heart was like that." She faced him then, glints of tears in her sapphire eyes. "Oh, David, I didn't want this, I didn't plan it. I couldn't help myself from wanting you close to me."

He hadn't been able to help it, either. He had been drunk with her very being, unable to get enough of her. Yet it seemed so far away, another time, a dream. He closed his eyes and saw his father. "What about Judd Coulton and all those guys like Owen you go dancing with? Did you want to get close to them?"

She shook her head. "Never. It was fun, at first, going around with Judd, riding in that fancy car, until . . ."

The night she came to the party, her shirt ripped. David felt as if he'd been punched. "I know. I'm sorry."

Suddenly she crumpled, tears streaming. "I should'a listened to Daddy. He didn't like me going with you people. Said I ought to stick with my own kind. That's why I had to sneak around to see you. I only did 'cause something about you was different. I thought we were meant to be together. I guess I was wrong."

"Oh, God, Trilby. Don't . . ." He wanted to put his arms around her, to comfort her. When he turned toward her, the money, the cash, the payoff, crackled in his pocket. He knew his father was waiting for him back at the house, probably pacing the floor, impatient to get the deal done and life back to normal.

"Don't what? Don't ask you for anything?"

"No!" He could hardly breathe, he hurt so badly. "I want to make it up to you, however I can. I've brought you something."

She shook her head and reached in her pocket and mopped her tears with a crumpled yellow napkin from the soda shop. "Oh, there ain't nothing you can give me. All I want in all the world is you."

David felt himself trembling, and he coughed. He had to get it out. Fast. "Trilby, I've . . . I've brought you enough money so you can leave Glencreggan like you wanted."

"And get rid of the baby?" she murmured. "Is that what you mean?" She covered her face with her hands. He grabbed her by her cold hands, pulled her close. He swallowed hard.

"Don't you see?" he said, his breath coming in jerks. "It would never be any good. Your daddy would want to kill me. Your folks here would hate me. My father, my *people*—Pamela, those girls, Mother, Phil—would find ways to make you feel an inch high without ever saying a word."

The wind sliced past them, icing his tears. He pulled out his handkerchief and wiped it across his face, then hers. She pushed his hand away and got up, as if to go.

He stood and faced her. "Please look at me, Trilby. I have to tell you this."

She didn't leave, but tears still trickled down her cheeks. "What?"

"Listen. It would be stupid to get married. My father would cut me off. I'd have to quit school and get a job. You'd be stuck at home with a baby. Is that what you want?"

She swiped at her tears with what remained of the napkin. "Don't holler at me, please."

"I'm sorry." He stared at the ground. It took every ounce of will for him to stand there and not take her in his arms.

She turned aside, and when she looked at him again, her eyes had lost their softness, lost their terror, lost their sadness. They were glistening sapphire, hard as the gem. "Yep, you're sorry all right," she said, hoarse from crying. "You're sorry like Judd Coulton. You just hurt me slower."

He swallowed. He wished an earthquake would come and pitch him off the mountain. "Trilby, I'm thinking of you. I want you to have the kind of life you hoped for."

"You're thinking of David."

He spoke the words very slowly, through numb lips. "There's a thousand dollars here."

She didn't change her expression. "Tell me, David. Tell me one blessed thing. Did you ever love me?"

A lump welled in his throat. "Oh, God, Trilby. I still love you. That's why I have to do this."

"Then why can't we be together? Why not?"

He studied his shoes on the frozen snow. "It's not enough," he said.

"Love is not enough," she repeated woodenly.

He gazed out at the gray clouds, the snow clouds.

"Look at me and tell me that," she said.

He turned to see her swollen face, and, overcome, he took it between his hands and kissed her. She pulled back, then finally collapsed in his arms, shivering. He held her tightly against him, as though he could warm her body in place of the hidden sun. "You're so cold," he said, "like rock."

The snow began to fall in earnest. The money—the cash—he was to give her was in his pocket. He fingered the envelope, looking at her as glistening flakes fell on her plaid wool coat and settled in the curves of her long dark hair, piling up flake by flake, as he stood in the snow and held her to him with one hand and held the money with the other and did not want to let any of it go, wanted the moment to go on suspended there, hung in the balance. She finally drew away from him and took the envelope from him, had to tug it from his frozen fingers.

"Goodbye, David," she said.

She tramped through the snow away from him, heading down the trail. This time he did not run after her.

After a moment or two he trudged on through the wind, and he could not rid himself of the feeling that he had left something of himself behind on the top of Whitecliff Mountain.

1990

When the waitress brought his breakfast, with the blueberry syrup he remembered, she spoke, and for a minute he could not hear what she was saying.

"What?"

"I said, are you all right, mister?"

He shook his head to clear it. "Fine. Fine."

"Do you need anything? More syrup?" She lifted the bottle and checked it, then set it back down.

"It's fine. The Fergusons still own this place?"

"Sure do, and I'm one of 'em." She laid the ticket on the table upside down.

"I've been away for a long time," he said. "I used to know Owen Ferguson."

She smiled with genuine affection. "Uncle Owen. He's just retired from the army. My daddy runs the café now. Granddaddy's gone."

"Owen stayed in the army?"

"Oh, yes," she said. "He's been all over the world."

David swallowed. "What about his family? Does he have kids?"

"Gosh, you sure haven't seen him in a long time," she said. "Molly, Bradley, Brigit, and Max."

"Molly? I . . . I remember a Margaret."

"Molly's her nickname. My only redheaded cousin." A customer walked in the door and a bell rang in the back. "Have a seat," she called and then turned back to David. "Can I get you anything else?"

"No thanks," said David. He finished his lunch, leaving the last bites of syrupy pancake on his plate, and got up to go. Behind the swinging door that led to the kitchen he saw Owen's brother staring at him as though he knew him. He laughed to himself. He was getting paranoid. No one would recognize him after twenty-eight years and with this beard.

He was putting on his jacket when the girl came back to ring up his ticket at the front. "I'll tell Uncle Owen you asked about him next time I see him," she said. "Tell me your name."

He couldn't lie. "It's David Wilder." The check was for $5.20. He pulled a ten-dollar bill from his wallet and gave it to her, his heart racing ahead of his mind. "Is he in Glencreggan now?"

"No," she said. "He went to the VA Hospital in Asheville."

"Is it serious?"

Her eyes clouded. "We don't know yet. He's on leave to get some rest and the doctor told him to go there."

"Oh," said David, thunderstruck.

"We all hope it's not bad. But that's kind of what happened to Uncle Odell, started feeling bad and then he got worse and worse."

David laid a sympathetic hand on the girl's shoulder. "I'll pray for him. Keep the change."

Molly. Her adoptive father might be seriously ill. Or not. That's the last thing he wanted to happen. He decided to head for the church, sit in the pew, and pray. Walking down the street, he passed by the jewelry shop where he had bought Trilby a ring. A ring she would never wear.

He looked through the glass, and the same jeweler sat behind the counter, loupe in place, examining a gemstone. David grimaced.

Why had he stopped here? Seeing these places was like picking at a scab. He walked on.

The dress shop was a bookstore, and the five-and-dime sold upscale European toys. He crossed the street and hurried past the inn, where painters were brushing on a new coat of white paint, and headed past Matt's Market to the church where Jake had been rector so many years ago. The door to the beautiful old chapel was unlocked and he went in, knelt, and felt some of the tension leave him as he talked with God, asking for guidance as he navigated the thorny path before him.

Matt's Market was twice as large as David remembered, and as he threaded his way through the aisles to the back, he passed imported goods in jars and bottles, and now that Mason County was no longer a dry county, the store carried French wines. Grits and cornmeal sat cheek-by-jowl with rotini and linguine. Matt, a stained white apron over his well-fed figure, presided behind a meat counter stacked with glistening rib eye steaks and thick pork chops as well as country ham and lean-streaked fatback. Matt's once sandy hair was mostly gray, and he'd grown a droopy mustache.

David walked up to the counter. Matt asked, "What can I get for you?" in a hearty voice; if gloomy butchers existed, David had never met one. He ordered a juicy T-bone, something he could grill for supper, and a couple of smoked sausages. As Matt lifted the sausages out of the case, David said, "A long time ago, there was a jelly stand out on the Nacoochee Highway. Is it still there?"

"You'd be talking about the Gaddis place," said Matt. "After the old man died the old lady sold out and moved on down to Georgia where her sister lives. She sold that place about, oh, fifteen years ago. Hard to sell, supposed to be haunted." He lowered his voice. "Their daughter got shot up there."

David shifted uncomfortably. "Haunted?"

"Yep. Terrible tragedy. S'posed to be her ghost roams the mountain there." Matt shrugged. "I don't believe in ghosts. Listen, I've got some good homemade jelly up near the front. My cousin's."

"Thanks." David felt as though a heavy weight were pressing on his chest. He made himself reach out and take the package wrapped in reddish butcher paper. Matt looked at him keenly. "Do I know you?"

"Oh no," said David. "I was just passing through." Matt nodded and turned back to the side of meat he'd been cutting.

David bought a jar of Matt's cousin's apple marmalade on the way out.

Out on the Nacoochee Highway, he slowed almost to a crawl as he approached the familiar curve, though logic told him there would be nothing to see. He rounded the bend and pulled over on the broad graveled shoulder. A long asphalt driveway lined with lush catawba rhododendrons replaced the dirt road that had led up to the green frame house. Through the trees he glimpsed three new upscale rustic-style houses.

He turned off the engine. No cars passed for a few minutes, and he imagined the summer sounds of the past, the hum of bees among the rhododendrons and the trickling of the stream. The humming and the rushing seemed to grow louder and louder. He felt as alone as he ever had in his life. "No!" he yelled, and the present came back with a jolt with a truck rumbling down the highway.

It was all there, everything that had happened that night, everything he had tried to push down into the deepest recesses of his memory. It was all there crowding in, the smell of old houses, the cry of a fox, the rattle of a truck, the screams, the blood.

Then he felt a strange presence beside him, a warming presence pushing the emptiness away. He looked around to see if anyone had walked up beside his truck, but the roadside was empty. He murmured a prayer, shoved the truck into gear, and bumped back onto the highway. He passed the road that led to the lake where the Dodges had lived. If he had not run into Pamela Dodge the following April, would it have still happened? Would Trilby still be alive?

Chapter 19

The City, 1963

He'd seen Pamela during the Easter holidays. Phil was going to be married in May to Betsy Kirkpatrick, daughter of the family lawyer "Buffalo" Bill Kirkpatrick, and so, when his older cousin invited him to a sherry party for Phil and Betsy at a house by the river, he knew he had to go for the sake of family solidarity. And there Pam was.

"What are you doing here?" David sipped on his sherry, glad to see her, one of the few people he knew. "This is a command performance for me, but you?"

"Same here. My sister Marcia's a bridesmaid." She took a glass of sherry from a passing waiter. "Sherry party! Your cousin likes to be original, doesn't she?"

David smiled. "She does." They exchanged updates about classes and activities and who-have-you-seen, and then the conversation stalled. David felt awkward. Was she still angry with him about that summer party? She'd never seemed serious about him.

Pamela looked around and then leaned closer to David. "Can we talk somewhere?"

"What's wrong with this room?" They were standing in the living room by the fireplace, watching guests come in and be greeted, then work their way to the dining room and wet bar for sherry and cocktail nibbles. David wasn't sure he wanted to hear anything Pamela had to say in private.

She fixed him with a deadly serious look and spoke quietly. "I have something to tell you. You might not want anyone to overhear."

Before she could say more, her sister Marcia skittered over and laid on hugs, gushing about how cute they looked together and that they ought to be next. When she finally dashed to the next victim, David laid a hand on Pamela's shoulder. "Follow me." Maybe they ought to clear the air. They'd never had a chance to talk after that night.

Sherries in hand, he led her out a French door and across a patio. They stepped down to a path through the woods back of the house. A wren scolded as they passed, and in the distance a screech owl called. David gulped his sherry, appreciating the warmth, and tucked the glass under a bush to be retrieved later. He urged Pamela down a steep path. "Wait, David," she protested. "Where *are* you taking me? Mud's getting on my white boots."

"Are those what they call go-go boots? Walk on the pine straw. Come on, you'll like it."

Still sipping her sherry, she followed him gingerly past the bright Christmas fern, past mottled greenbrier vines, stealthy thorns tearing at their clothes. Pamela stopped to pick beggar-ticks off her short red dress. She had told him it was a genuine Mary Quant. Whatever that meant. "Have we gone far enough?"

"It gets better."

She finished the sherry, tucked the glass into her shoulder bag, and followed him across a footbridge. One more plunge through brush and then they stood beside the Chattahoochee. Water tumbled and gushed over the rapids, and the eddying shallows reflected the new leaves' pale green. The hush of the forest gave way to the distant hum of the highway. Then they heard the heavy drumming of a pileated woodpecker.

"Look," said David, catching Pam's arm. "You don't see many of *those.*" He pointed to the huge red-crested woodpecker, easily sixteen inches. The great bird lifted its wings and flapped gracefully away into the thicket of trees.

He was still grinning at seeing the rare bird when Pam folded her arms. "Okay with the nature study. Are you ready to listen?"

The grin disappeared. "I guess."

"First I've got to ask you a question."

He waited. He wished the woodpecker would come back.

"What was going on with you and Trilby Gaddis last summer?"

David stiffened. "Nothing."

"Not from what I saw." Pamela tilted her head. "Was it serious?"

"Forget it." None of her damn business.

"I have a reason for asking." The pale blue of her eyes told him nothing.

He attempted a grin. "You like me after all?" He knew it was a lame joke.

She gave him the exasperated look meant for a hopelessly square parent. "If only it were that simple. Remember that freak snowfall last month? My whole family went up to the mountains for a little fun in the white stuff. I saw Trilby Gaddis in The Spinning Wheel."

Pamela stopped.

David wished she'd just stop goading him. "So?"

"David, she looked pregnant to me."

He froze. His stomach clenched and he felt the blood drain from his face. "Did you talk to her?"

She narrowed her eyes. "Of course not. Should I have?"

David turned away from Pamela and booted a rock so hard that it sailed across the path, bounced, and rolled down into the water, where it splashed and sank. "I'm not the only guy she went with."

"I *know*, David."

He didn't like the way she said it. "What did Judd Coulton tell you?"

"Nothing. But he didn't have to."

David picked up a bigger rock and heaved it into the water, the splashback hitting the two of them.

She whisked the water off her legs. "You two were glued together those last weeks. Everybody knew it. You weren't exactly subtle."

When David didn't reply, she said, "Okay. I told you. If you're mad, too bad."

She turned and started picking her way up the path, mindful of her boots. David trudged behind her, trying to make sense of things.

Trilby hadn't left Glencreggan. Her father hadn't kicked her out. She was having the baby. What did this mean? One thing for sure. Things would never go back to normal. They had never been normal. Another dimension. Her body against the black water.

The fog, the smoke in the air, the slow heavy tap of the woodpecker, were all a part of his life as were the crystal raindrops on the rhododendrons, the high spark of cold mountain sunlight, the snowfall on her hair in the anguished days before the end of

Camelot. He knew then that he had to see her. He wanted her with him, no matter what his father said.

It was Friday night in late May, a night when the Milky Way had spread its soft brilliant cape across a black and cloudless sky, a night when spring coolness still hung in the air. David hiked in the damp woods of the valley trail for most of the day, waiting for the jelly stand to close.

Now he'd arrived and the stand was empty, flanked by a stack of baskets and cartons. He parked the car, locked it, and walked up the steep hill. Hopefully the old man would be out in the woods making moonshine by starlight.

David didn't see the truck in front of the house and quickened his pace. A lone lamp in the front window cut the darkness, outlining the railing and the steps. He caught a feral odor, fox maybe, and heard rustling to his left. Maybe golden eyes were watching beneath the rhododendrons.

He took the wooden steps two at a time and knocked on the door. It wasn't latched, and it creaked open. Mustiness leaked out: damp wood and old quilts and cabbage, a hint of boiled jelly. A screech owl's cry trembled from the woods.

"Anybody home?" he called.

Mrs. Gaddis was at the door at once, rubbing her reddened hands. "What? You? What you want here, David Wilder?"

"I want to see Trilby."

The older woman set her lips in a thin line. "Trilby can't see you. You done caused enough trouble."

A baby wailed somewhere inside. Trilby yelled, "Who is it, Momma?"

"Trilby!" he shouted.

Mrs. Gaddis gave him a scowl and clutched her robe. "It ain't nobody, honey," she called.

"Please. I've got to see her." He had to make right what he had done. He nervously patted his pocket where the gift rested.

Trilby appeared behind her mother in T-shirt and jeans, her face pale in the dim light, her dark hair shading into the shadows beyond.

He took a step forward, hung his head, and then gazed at her. "I've been a jerk, Trilby. I've come back for you." He hated the words as soon as he'd said them. They sounded like a line from a black-and-white movie on the Late Show. But he didn't know how to say it any better.

The angry look disappeared, and Mrs. Gaddis regarded him with something like pity. "Hit's too late."

Trilby stepped into the light, her face tired and greyish, her sapphire eyes as dull as an uncut stone. "You come to see your baby?"

"I came to see you," he said.

"You can see her," she said, "and then you can go." Mrs. Gaddis stood with her arms folded while Trilby faded back into the house and returned, cradling a blue-wrapped bundle. She swayed side to side, rocking the infant in her arms.

He could not believe that he was a father. It was too unreal. He glanced at Trilby's mother. "Can I talk to you, Trilby? Out here?"

The two women exchanged glances. "It's all right, Momma," said Trilby.

Mrs. Gaddis snorted. "Don't be long. Your daddy will be home soon and he won't want to see this'un." She left them and closed the door behind her.

Trilby pushed back the flannel blanket. The baby was plump and pretty, with soft red spiderweb hair. "She looks like you," Trilby whispered.

David thought she looked like Trilby. He reached out and touched the baby's tiny fingers, and goosebumps crept up his spine. He did this? "What's her name?"

"I called her Margaret Rose, after that princess who didn't get to marry the man she loved. But this little princess is going to get everything I can give her."

David, overcome with shame, blurted, "I want to give her things, Trilby. You too." He reached into his pocket for the ring and brought it out. "I have a ring for you."

She pushed his hand aside. "Put it back. You heard Momma, David." She kissed the baby's forehead. "It's too late."

"Why? Why won't you look at me, Trilby?"

The baby whimpered, and Trilby murmured to her. "Hush, hush, honey. This man ain't gonna hurt you. He's just stopping by. He's kind of your long lost uncle, you know, and he'll be far away pretty soon. Not gon' bother you."

When the child had quieted, Trilby held out her left hand, where a gold band gleamed softly in the porch light. "I had a good offer."

Stunned into silence, David finally croaked, "Who is it?"

Her eyes flashed, angry. "Why the peaturkey should you care?"

David shook his head. He couldn't take it in. *Married?* "Jesus, Trilby . . . does he know she's mine?"

"She ain't yours anymore," Trilby said. The baby stirred and fussed and clutched at Trilby's T-shirt. Trilby looked squarely at David. "Owen Ferguson thinks she's his. I started up with him right after you left me with that . . . that *money*. He's been after me since ninth grade. It's the only thing I could do. He'll take me away from here."

"Oh, God," said David.

"Daddy thinks it's Owen's too," said Trilby. "Only one counted on her fingers is Momma." Trilby rocked the baby, calming her. "I'm staying here until Owen finishes basic training. Then I'm leaving here for good and follow him. Like Ruth in the Bible. I saved that money you give me for this baby. I don't want no more from you."

David stroked the baby's hair. He had made this child, and he was struck with wonder. "Owen's not her father," he said.

Trilby's mouth hardened into a tight line. "Don't you never say different, David Wilder. You paid me off. Now get out of here and leave us alone." She fished in the pocket of her jeans for a packet of cigarettes. She tapped one out and put it between her lips.

David didn't smoke, but he carried a lighter for girls and his mother. He flicked it now for her, watching her draw in the smoke, eyes closed and lips pursed. He missed the soft way she used to look at him. He missed the love she had poured out on him, love he didn't deserve.

"Do you still love me?" he asked.

"Don't talk to me about love," she said.

The night was cooling off, and a breeze feathered by. The baby began to cry. Trilby raised her eyes to David's. "I got to feed her." She made no move to get up, but handed David her cigarette, and their hands touched. A wisp of a smile crossed her face. "You might as well stay," she said softly. "You're her daddy, after all."

Was she trying to torment him? He didn't care. Heart racing, David sank onto the steps beside her and, in one slow motion, took the cigarette out of her hands and crushed it beneath his heel. Trilby raised her T-shirt and guided the baby's small mouth into place. It sighed as it settled in, with soft contented gurgles.

David sat on the porch steps, one step below Trilby, transfixed, watching the mother and child under the stars. All was quiet except for a sweet high chirring in the distance and a rhythmical whispering like the beating of a heart.

The baby, replete, fell asleep.

"Do you love Owen?" David finally asked. When she didn't answer he leaned over the sleeping child and kissed its mother. She resisted only slightly, then not at all. He lifted the white T-shirt, whispering against the pale veined skin. "I love you, Trilby."

"Don't, David," she said, pushing down her shirt. He saw by the pale porch light that she was trembling. For one minute she dropped her veil, and he saw the longing in her eyes.

He wanted to seize her and crush her against him. But the baby lay there, nestled in Trilby's arms. She picked the child up, put her against her shoulder, and patted gently. "I've got to get back in."

"Not yet. Please."

"If I don't go in, David, I might go with you. I can't do that to Owen. He's a good man."

"Trilby . . ."

She reached out her hand to him, for what he never knew. For hello, for goodbye. Suddenly headlights cut the darkness, and Tully Gaddis's black pickup rumbled up the driveway and ground to a stop.

The older man got out of the truck and walked unsteadily over to them, small eyes squinting behind a thin nose. In one hand he held a rifle. "What you doing on my proppity?"

David stared at the gun.

"Daddy," said Trilby slowly, "this is David Wilder, Mr. Wilder's son?"

Tully Gaddis took a good long look at David. "Oh, I know this boy. Keep back, girl."

"Please, Daddy." Her voice was soft. "He just come to pay his respects. He's going home now." She crept up beside her father and laid her hand lightly on the gray-blue steel.

"He ain't got no business with you." He jerked the gun away from her.

"*David.*" The way she said it meant *Go. Now. Fast.*

Tully Gaddis pointed the gun at David's feet. "You don't need them feet nohow."

Trilby glanced at David and then back at her father. "Daddy . . ."

"Owen ain't here to shoot you," said Tully. "I ought to do the job." He wheeled the gun around. David backed away a few steps, and Tully pressed forward. He raised the gun.

"David, do what he says," Trilby pleaded.

"Take the baby and go in the house," said David, unwilling to run. He had to show Trilby he would protect her. "I can handle it." He could hear his father saying *real men don't run away.*

The scene felt unreal, as though he'd wandered into some movie set by mistake. He circled around toward the truck, figuring Tully wouldn't shoot at his own truck, but Tully followed him with the gun. Trilby, the baby still propped on her shoulder, ran over to David.

"Get away, girl," said Tully.

"No!"

"I said get away."

"I won't!"

The three stood frozen under the pale light of the stars, no one moving an inch. The screech owl wavered again from the woods. Then a high-pitched welter of squeaking, a scrambling in the bushes.

"There's that fox a'been after the chickens," said Trilby.

Tully leaned toward the rhododendrons and raised his gun. "I'll blast the bugger."

Trilby slipped over to David and gave him a shove. "Go!" she said. "If you love me, go!"

He took off running, and Tully tracked him with the rifle. A few seconds later the gun fired with a resounding crack that seemed to echo forever, and David dived under the broad leaves of a rhododendron, heart pumping wildly.

In a welter of confusion, the baby shrieked and wailed, Trilby cried out "Oh!" and then Tully himself screamed.

"My girl! My baby girl! Oh Lord! Oh Lord!"

To hell with the danger. David burst from his shelter and ran to Trilby. She lay on the ground sideways, crumpled, bleeding, her dark hair fanned on the mica soil.

In the moonlight the old man was rocking and rocking, holding his stomach, repeating "Oh Lord." David felt that all the blood had drained from his body. He knelt and extended a shaking hand to Trilby. Her mother loomed over him, staring down like an avenging angel. "Don't you touch her! Don't you touch that baby neither!"

David, trembling all over, froze. This could not be happening. This was a bad dream. And then he saw Trilby's lips moving. She seemed to be trying to say something, and he leaned closer to hear, closer, touching her shoulder. The half-whispered words came with effort. Before he could promise what she asked, Mrs. Gaddis plunked down beside her daughter and growled at David. "I said get away from her."

David collapsed back on his haunches, sick. Trilby's mother lifted the bloody T-shirt. David saw where the bullet had entered Trilby's back, the blood beginning to congeal.

"She's gone," the agonized woman whispered, then closed her eyes and bowed her head. "It's God's punishment."

"No! Never!" The words forced David out of his shock, forced him to his feet. "I'll go for help!"

He ran down the hill, wrenched his car door open, and squealed tires around the curving road to the town, to the phone booth. He called the hospital and the sheriff's emergency number.

When he got back up the hill, Trilby's mother, trying to comfort the fussy, hiccupping baby, wouldn't let him near Trilby. "She run after you, God knows why."

He sat on the ground, his head in his hands, to wait for whatever was going to happen. He could still hear Tully moaning, "Oh Lord. Oh Lord. Oh, Lord."

No, please no. Oh, God, please no.

Those words would haunt him always. Her last words to him, the words he would remember always, were "Don't tell Owen."

The images rose up in him now. The baby wailing on the ground. Trilby's mother's eyes. The sheriff's hard glare. The inquest. The funeral, where they had buried Trilby. He had never told Lu about her, or about his daughter, Owen's daughter. When they had put Trilby in the ground, they had buried a part of him forever.

His life was framed, he thought, by funerals and farewells, and the loneliness that followed them had shape, form, substance. Now he realized the loss had always been with him, even when Tallulah was alive. It crept into the cracks of his house with the sage-scented air. It slipped under the floorboards in the bars of a sunbeam. It shadowed him as he fished for mountain trout in icy waters. All around him, there was Trilby, always Trilby, as though part of himself had been left on the mountain, shriveling like the flowers on her gravestone.

At the funeral, there had been the wails of her mother and the stony face of her father, stooped and grizzled, in overalls, and smoldering rage on the face of her husband. Owen. David had stood among the trees watching, not daring to go near.

He closed his eyes, a lump in his throat. *Oh, Trilby. You were doing the best you knew how for you and the baby. If I had gone when you told me to go, you would still be alive. Somehow, somewhere, I will atone for this.*

And then there had been the attempt to talk to his own father, to close the vast divide between them that had opened with the death of Trilby, but in the end, there had been no words that could be said, and so he had gone back to his mountains and her people that were now his people, to the mists and the sunrise and the evening echoes across the ridge that sounded hollow, hollow, hollow.

Chapter 20

Had he really atoned? Was the work he was doing here among her mountain people enough? He had thrown aside the life he had expected to live, a life of privilege and money, of clubs and big houses, sleek cars, parties, trips to exotic places, to serve others and help them. How good he had been, he didn't know. He didn't miss the life he'd left behind. He didn't know if he had done enough to be forgiven.

David gunned the old truck, tearing around curves with a heart-thumping screech and a roar of exhaust. He had to let go of the Glencreggan in his mind, the Glencreggan he had known, no matter how much it would hurt. Maybe that's what Jake meant by healing. In his imagination that town still existed, a place where Trilby skipped across stones and ran through the woods, berry bucket on her arm; a Glencreggan that he could reach if he could only find the secret tunnel through the tangled rhododendrons.

The natives called them "laurel hells," and you could lose your way in them. And maybe that was the past, a laurel hell that led into endless roaming. Maybe that was why he had stayed away: so he could believe in the light at the end of the tunnel.

A sign loomed ahead for the trail to the top of Whitecliff Mountain.

He sped past the sign, sped past the entrance, willing himself to be done with the past. Back in Bow Creek there was a young girl who needed him now.

He stopped at a country store where he saw a small telephone kiosk. He leaned into it and tapped in the number of St. Ninian's. Jane answered. "Thank God you've called, David. Everybody's been trying to find you."

"What's happened?"

"Your mother called. Your father's had a heart attack. He's in the hospital."

The wind whipped sand around David's ankles; dust stung his face. He slumped against the telephone, eyes fixed on riffling dry grass, a mound of moldering tires, the shell of a rusted-out car. "What about Clover? Is there any news?"

Jane hesitated. "They've got half the town looking, but she still hasn't turned up."

Bitter gall rose in David's throat. "I wish I could stay and help, but I need to go see my father." It might be the last time.

"Don't worry about the church, David," Jane said. "We'll take care of it."

"You're a blessing, Jane." He hung up and punched in the number at Wildwood. His mother answered on the first ring. "David! Thank God!"

"How is he?" *Please, God, not yet. We have unfinished business.*

"They don't know yet. Please come and meet me at the house. I don't know if they'll let you see him now."

Of course. He had to go. Maybe it wouldn't be too late. "I've been helping to look for a missing girl, and I'm on my way back to Bow Creek. I'll be there as soon as I can." He crammed the phone onto its cradle, vaulted into the truck, and swung it in a wide arc, heading south.

He glanced in the rearview mirror just once. He'd drive straight to the city and call to check on Clover when he got there. Never had he felt so powerless. He couldn't help find Clover; he couldn't do anything for his father. What had Jake told him? Anguished at his helplessness, he pushed the truck to its limit, hoping he'd have time to make peace before his father died. Why had he left it so long? Time to do soul work evaporated like raindrops on a rock in the sun.

He descended through the evergreen hills, through terrain where leafless branches thrust above the green, and swung onto highways lined with pines and ponds, with black-limbed trees tangled and twisted, living desolation against the sky.

He wished Lu was beside him, to help give him strength. Not to have to face his father's mortality alone, not to have to make this decision about Molly Westbrook. *Father, let this cup pass from me.*

Why hadn't he told Tallulah about his past?

Maybe because their child had not lived, the child now buried in the churchyard. His gentle words of comfort, his prayers, could not budge Tallulah's mountain fatalism, accepting the death as "God's will." And it had not been God's will for them not to have another.

He switched on the radio. "In the book of Revelation, brother, it says that the whore of BABYLON . . ." He flicked to another station, where Hampton Taggart was singing his new hit, a rendition of the old ballad "Wayfaring Stranger." *Goin' over Jordan, goin' over home . . .*

Hampton Taggart. He thought of Nell and let the song play on, pushing the truck. Thoughts crowded his mind. Owen Ferguson had raised Molly, had helped to make her the lovely person his mother said she was. Could David just appear in that good man's life and tell him the young woman he surely adored was not his daughter?

Would it help Molly to know how her mother had died? Or would she be horrified? Would she blame David for growing up without Trilby?

And then there was his father. But his father would find a way to bargain with death, to make a deal. Or to bully death away.

The faulty muffler roared under the truck.

Had it really been five years since he'd seen his father? It had been at Uncle Howell's funeral. Betsy, who'd been divorced from Phil for five years, had come with him, and Tallulah hadn't wanted to attend, saying she had nothing decent to wear. Meaning, he realized, she felt ill at ease with his people, as his mother had tried to tell him. He'd offered to buy her a new dress, but she wouldn't hear of it. The old man had criticized Lu for not coming. He fawned over Betsy, the daughter of his old friend, and David felt that for all Betsy's competence and polish, she was not one to show her feelings to anyone. He judged Phil less harshly.

And now flatland air was seeping into the truck, crowding him with its fume-laden heaviness.

David reached the estate a little before six. He drove in past the lake, past gently rolling grassy slopes and then past the broad lawn shaded by hundred-year-old white oaks and red oaks and sycamores. The house, a golden half-timbered Tudor, seemed to shimmer in the afternoon heat, like a far-off castle with its turret. The mullioned panes threw off glistening glimmers of late-afternoon light.

He drove through a Gothic porte cochere and circled back behind the house to the three-car garage. He parked his old truck next to his father's black Lincoln Town Car. The space where his mother's Lexus would have been parked was empty. There was another car parked behind the Lincoln, an old blue Mercury. Whose was that?

He slid down from the truck and stretched, surprised that the garage walls were deeply cracked and streaked with moss. His father must be letting things slide. He was always so particular about the house being kept in top condition.

David ducked down a passageway that led through the butler's pantry and entered the kitchen just as a man wearing a white apron burst through the swinging door on the other side, a man who reminded him of a chef from New Orleans he'd seen on TV.

"You must be the Reverend," the man said in his deep voice. "I'm Junius Johnson. Here I go by Junius, but my friends call me J.J."

"Where are Albert and Celesta?" David blurted. He'd been looking forward to seeing the couple that had helped to bring him up, the ones who cared for the house and for him while his parents carried on their work and social life.

Junius Johnson shook his head. "They retired," he said. "Getting too old to do this kind of work."

David nodded slowly. "You're a Johnson. Any relation?"

Junius smiled. "I'm their grandson. My father's Edward."

"Edward!" David exclaimed. "Is he still preaching?" Celesta had always been so proud of her preacher son.

"You bet," Junius said. "Senior pastor now. My big sister wants to follow him into the ministry. Me, I have other plans."

"Be sure to fill me in later," David said. "Where's my mother?"

"Miss Eva's at the hospital," said Junius. "She said to wait for her here. You're in your old room. Need help with that bag?"

"You look busy. I have it, thank you."

In the chilly slate entrance hall, not much had changed. The same double doors led into the wood-paneled library, and on the right an arch revealed the parlor, forlorn and severe, its cream damask draperies and Aubusson carpet, though beautiful, looking sterile and lifeless compared with Hattie's cozy house filled with loved ones.

He lugged the suitcase up the spiral staircase and down the hall. He opened the door to his old room slowly, not wanting a surprise to ambush him. But on the floor lay the familiar worn Bokhara carpet with its threadbare patch shaped like the state of Alabama. He switched on the captain's wheel lamp beside the maple spool bed, flooding the room with soft light. Every model airplane he'd built, every tennis trophy he'd won, stood on the shelf above his desk.

He didn't want a shrine to his childhood. Or worse, a reflection of the person he'd been, a person who cared more about himself than the one he loved. He gathered the trophies and stuffed them into the empty closet. He would ask his mother if she'd be willing to donate them to charity.

The airplanes he'd take with him. Maybe Mother would redo the room then.

He was glad he'd brought an extra clean shirt in case of rain. He hung it in the closet, then went downstairs to the library.

The clock on the fireplace mantel read six-thirty. He walked over to the sideboard where a tray of bottles and glasses stood and poured himself a drink of his father's Glenlivet. Swirling the amber liquid in the glass, he wandered into his father's study.

In the small room off the library, green velvet draperies covered the one window behind Lem Wilder's massive desk. David pulled the cords and opened them, letting in the last of the daylight. He switched on the desk lamp.

Photographs lined the paneled wall: Father with a trophy deer. Father with an alligator. Father with a brace of quail. Two men and two women in evening clothes. Father with the mayor, Father with the governor, the family at the beach under an umbrella. And then: David and the Bishop at David's ordination. Surprised, he reached out to touch the glass.

Just then a phone jangled on the desk, and as David went to answer he heard Junius take the call. David picked up a photograph of Phil and his mother and himself, so young, all of them. He set it down beside the green marble penholder he'd given his father the Christmas of '62: the Christmas before his life shattered like a crystal vase on a marble floor.

He picked up the penholder, turning it over in his hand.

"Reverend?" Junius stuck his head in the door. "Miss Eva's home."

"David?" his mother called out, her voice shaky and hoarse.

He hurried to meet her, then halted in surprise. Since he'd seen her at Lu's funeral, she'd let her hair go white. He enveloped her in a hug, and the familiar scent of her Elizabeth Arden powder and cologne brought a catch to his throat.

"How is he?" David watched her expression. Her normally impeccable shirt and slacks showed wrinkles and creases, and her eyes were dull.

She shook her head. "They won't tell you anything definite, you know. They just say he's got a long haul ahead of him. With luck he'll be out of intensive care in a couple of days."

"I want to see him," David said. "And talk to him. I'd like to mend fences." It might be his last chance. He hoped his father, considering his end, might feel the same way.

"How long can you stay?"

"I need to leave Saturday; I haven't found anyone to take the service," he said. "That gives me all day tomorrow and Friday." This was a white lie—almost. He hadn't thought about finding anyone. He was worried about Clover, and he couldn't miss the called vestry meeting Monday morning, where he'd have to face Nell and the others who didn't want the church to buy the bed and breakfast inn.

He helped his mother out of her silk tweed jacket and draped it over the back of a chair. She pulled out a cigarette, and David lit it out of habitual politeness. "I'm surprised you still smoke," he said.

She let the smoke drift and gave him a rueful smile. "Now my son's disapproving of me. I suppose I'll have to give it up. Your father's doctors talked of secondhand smoke."

"There's your own health too, Mother. I hope you'll quit."

"Yes." She sighed. "We all wear out."

They sat in the library facing the tall windows that looked out on a smoky blue sky and the stark outlines of familiar trees. While she took nervous puffs of her cigarette, his mother began to tell David what had happened, and he listened, frozen in his chair. This was his invincible *father.*

A bell sounded from the dining room. She glanced toward the kitchen and ground her cigarette into an ashtray. "I'll tell you the rest later. Let's have something to eat."

David knew it was hard for her to talk about it. Maybe a glass of wine would help. "Yes, let's do."

The long mahogany dining table could easily seat eighteen, and often had. They sat at one end, on corners. Junius served chicken gumbo with rice, butter lettuce salad, and a baguette. David felt uneasy having someone waiting on him; he'd done so much for Tallulah these past three years. And now Junius poured California wine into David's glass.

"Mr. Lem's favorite." Junius nodded.

David tasted it and smiled. "Superb. I'm not used to good wine. You know, when I came to Bow Creek the only bottled wine in town was the kind we used for Communion. Muscadine wine, that's what they made there. The place is different now."

"Yes, I know all about muscadine wine," Junius said with a smile. "My uncle made it in the country."

After he returned to the kitchen, Evangeline turned to David, eyes full of concern. "How have you been? Really?"

He didn't want to dump his concerns on his mother. "I haven't had a chance to be lonely. Everyone's been so kind."

"I wish I could have stayed."

He met her gaze. Did she really? Maybe he'd ask her about that later. "So do I. Where's Phil?"

"At the hospital." She paused and said distractedly, "Betsy's been by too."

Betsy? Phil's ex? Another thing to ask about later. "And how are you, really, Mother?"

She sighed. "Oh, I'm muddling through. But it's your father I need to talk about."

Junius opened the swinging door from the kitchen. "Would you all care for dessert? A nice pound cake and vanilla ice cream with fudge or strawberry topping."

David said he was full and thanked him for the good dinner. Evangeline straightened. "We'll have coffee in the library, please." She laid a hand on David's arm. "Let's talk there."

Gas logs lit and coffee brought, Evangeline sank back in the wing chair, fitfully turning her gold-rimmed cup in its saucer. "Your father wouldn't like me saying this about him, David. I think, for the first time in his life, he's afraid."

"Afraid?"

"We had Jake and Emily to dinner. He was polite to Jake, but bull-headed as usual about religion. He told me later that he didn't want Jake or his wife to come and see him in the hospital. Said there was no point in it. Still, I knew he was scared. Can you help him? Can you give him any comfort?"

David leaned forward, elbows on knees, his hands clasped. "He may not accept any help from me."

"Not even now? I had so hoped he'd soften towards you."

Now that Tallulah was gone? David rose from the sofa and walked over to the window. He pulled a cord to close the draperies against the shortness of the days, the dying of the year. He gazed back at his mother, noticing for the first time how fragile she looked, how small against the deep green of the wing chair. But she sat up straight, hands clasped.

"There's something else," she said. "You can change his mind about his will. I know you can."

"I don't want his money." David stared at the carpet, hands clenched, his neck warming. He had built a life without those expectations.

"Stubborn as always, aren't you? If you had only bent a little, he would have come around sooner."

David walked back to the sofa and sat down. He calmed himself. "He wouldn't accept my life. Neither would you."

"You think it was Tallulah," Evangeline said wearily. Her diamond rings sparked firelight as she reached over and laid her hand atop David's. "We would have seen more of you. But Tallulah was uncomfortable with us."

"Lu liked everyone."

"Liking isn't the same as trusting, David. Maybe she didn't trust you, either, down deep. Did you have that kind of love, David? Where you each know what the other is thinking, the kind of love that grows out of shared convictions? Did you find joy in each other? What did you talk about in the middle of the night?"

David turned his face away. "Mother, I won't hear a word against her. Not now. You know I was devoted to her."

Evangeline sighed. "I know. I'm becoming meddlesome in my old age. But what I'm talking about goes further than devotion."

"Mother, what's gotten into you? Maybe everybody can't have what you and Dad have." Sometimes he wondered why she put up with the old man's ways, but then there was one thing about their marriage—they always built each other up, always praised each other to both friends and strangers.

"You haven't listened," she said. "Nobody has. Nobody will. They see the masks, don't they? And after a while the masks become permanent, so that we forget who's behind them."

Astonished, David watched as his mother pushed herself upright, steadying herself on the chair arm. "Wait, Mother. I'll help."

"No, David, I don't need help getting out of a chair. Not yet. I'm tired. I think I'll go up and read for a while. I'll see you at breakfast. Then we'll go to the hospital. I don't think you ought to go tonight."

She walked out, her spine straight, her posture flawless.

David watched her leave.

She was wrong about Lu. Of course.

Chapter 21

David looked down on the sleeping form of his father, trying to will away the hard knot of anger in his belly. Even lying still, the old man dominated the room with his stubbly-jawed presence. David almost expected him to bolt upright, for Lem Wilder had never been a lying-down man. He'd always sat straight in his big leather desk chair, alert, his quick mind scanning for information.

The old lion's eyes were closed now, steel-gray hair slicked back, wire-rimmed glasses resting on a side table. It was clear that David and Phil had been stamped out of the same material as his father's blunt features, though Phil's mustache and David's beard hid the resemblance. How much more of his sire did David carry in his soul? And how hard did he try to hide it?

He sank into a wooden chair at the bedside, an image in his mind of his father as a younger man who, after Trilby's death, had expected David to pick up his college life and carry on. Just a minor stumble on the road to taking his rightful place in society.

Instead, David had become a hippie.

He drifted into relationships with girls who didn't shave their armpits or use deodorant or cut their middle-parted hair, who wore sandals and toe rings and long, gauzy skirts. He excelled in history and philosophy, barely passed math. He smoked pot and marched in anti-war and civil rights protests. His father continued to pay his tuition but cut off any spending money, figuring the prodigal would come home after he got tired of canned beans.

David got a part-time job in the cafeteria.

And then two months before graduation, standing in his father's study surrounded by all the trophies of his father's life, he told his father that he'd been accepted into the theology school at Sewanee. He wasn't sure what to expect. Maybe even praise for having rejoined the conventional world.

His father had roared, "You want to be a preacher? The hell you say. You're trying to avoid the draft."

David felt as if he'd been slapped. "It's not true. I want to help people. I want to make the world a better place."

Lem Wilder took a cigar out of the humidor on his desk and twirled it in his fingers. "I don't understand all this hippie garbage. You make the world a better place by doing your duty. And your duty is to serve your country and then go into the bank."

"You have Phil to help you. Good old married Phil, who'd probably like to join up."

His father lit the cigar and dropped the match, still lit, into the ashtray where it shrank to a blackened stem. "I need both of you."

How could he make the man understand? "Dad, I've seen so much pain."

"If you didn't want to fight, I could have kept you out of Vietnam." He gestured with the cigar, smoke floating in David's direction.

David blinked the stinging smoke away. "I never wanted that kind of privilege. I'd have become a medic, found a way to help people. Haven't you ever wanted to help?"

His father snorted. "The United Way knows my name well."

"Do you get your hands dirty?" David shot out and was immediately sorry.

His father looked at David shrewdly. "You're talking like one of those effete snobs. I built the bank to what it is today with my two dirty hands. It was about to go under because of your uncle's bleeding heart."

Mention of his kindly uncle Jack reminded David of Trilby's struggling uncle. The mountain, the wind, the cold. Trilby's voice, her uncle's farm. The Hooverdepression. Her dream about leaving to make a better life for herself. "Dad. Trilby died in my goddamn arms. I can't wash off that blood. The only way I can redeem myself is to go back and help people. Her people."

His father looked at him hard. "You can't help those people. They don't want to be helped. They're proud and stubborn."

"I can make it right."

"You are who you are, David, for better or for worse. Maybe you'd better realize you can't save the world from itself." Lem Wilder set his lips tight. "There's no use in talking to you. You'll pay your own way from now on."

"Dad, I really don't give a damn."

David's father gave him a long, measured look. "We'll see."

Making it on his own was hard, harder than he'd ever imagined. He scouted for scholarships, wrote applications, worked in the cafeteria, tutored undergraduates, and still managed to make top grades—for the first time in his life.

He loved his student ministry and became ordained, though one member of his committee was suspicious of his enthusiasm. Did he fully realize what would be required of him? But the parish ministry was his calling, and young, zealous men were much in demand. He kept in touch with Jake Halsey and searched for a mountain church.

He served a church in Asheville as youth minister before Bow Creek called him, not believing their luck when he accepted. He'd arrived with a mission, and the church had prospered. When he was thirty-one, an inheritance from his maternal grandmother enabled him to buy the old farmhouse and five acres on Bear Lick Mountain. And then the pretty teacher, the war widow Tallulah Jenkins, had seemed to fit right into the picture.

His father's eyes snapped open; the voice came out a growl. "Umph. David."

David shook away the memory and grasped the freckled hand on the bed.

His father studied him through narrowed eyes. "Why are you here?"

"I wanted to see you, Dad."

"Wanted to convert me before I check out?"

"You'll be coming home in a few days."

A harrumph. "Feet first."

"No."

"You've come to bury me." The old man's eyes met his. "That dog collar's good for something." He let go of David's hand.

A silence hung in the room. David took a pen out of his pocket and turned it over and over. Finally, he slid it back in. "I wanted to talk to you."

His father struggled to sit up, and David sprang to his feet. He found the bed control.

His father reached for it. "Give it to me. I can do it."

David handed over the remote and waited while his father cranked up the head and composed himself. Even in bed, with a paler complexion than David remembered, his father still radiated power.

"So talk," he growled. "What are you living on?"

David raised a shoulder. "I make my salary stretch. I farm a little."

"You're wasting yourself."

David smiled grimly. "At least I've learned the value of a dollar."

His father shifted in bed, and David caught the look of pain the old man was trying not to show. "I suppose Evie will want a big funeral. Waste of money."

"Dad, you're going to be okay."

"Do what she wants. It's for her."

David leaned forward. "Dad, there will be plenty of time to talk about all that. Concentrate on getting well—for her."

The old man's eyes locked with his. "It's going to happen sometime, boy. The cold, dark lake swallows us all, and we go down, down, down."

David fought an urge to get up and go. There was no way, no way he could connect with this man. The silence stretched, while beyond the door of the room people talked, a cart rolled. Then a memory came to him all of a sudden, a hazy memory of his grandfather's farm. A grandfather who wore overalls and lived in the country beside a lake, and a grandmother who liked to sit and talk while she shelled peas on the front porch and would hand you a bowlful too, since you weren't doing anything but rocking in a green chair.

"Remember," David said. "Remember, when I was five, and we fished from the dock at Poppa Daddy's lake early one morning? I caught my first fish that day."

His father nodded. "A decent sized one."

"What did we do with it?"

"Your grandma rolled it in cornmeal and fried it up for supper. We didn't waste good food." He paused. "You fish much now?"

"Every chance I get."

His father wheezed and coughed and reached for a tissue.

David pushed the box closer; the old man whisked one out and settled back. "All of life is catching or being caught. You're fish, fisherman, or bait."

David didn't ask which he was supposed to be. He said, "What happened to Poppa Daddy's farm?"

The old man's lips clamped shut, and then he spoke through his teeth. "I sold the damn place, what was left of it. Now I'm tired. I'm going to take a nap."

"May I pray with you?"

A look of mistrust crossed the old man's face. "What for?"

David unfolded himself and stood. "You do have a soul, Dad."

A gnarled hand reached out from under the covers and grabbed him by the wrist. "Where is it? Answer me that!"

"I can't." David laid his hand over his father's, and the old man pulled it away.

"Yep. Like I said. It's nowhere." The old man closed his eyes, and David knew he was dismissed. He stood for moment looking at Lem Wilder, said a silent prayer for strength and compassion, and then walked out into the hall. His mother, who'd been talking to the nurse, turned to him questioningly.

David knuckled away a tear of anger, of regret at his failure to get through to his father. "He'll live to be two hundred."

When he arrived at the hospital the next day, his father had been moved out of the ICU to a private room. David found him growling into the telephone, the television above showing a stock market graphic. He stood waiting until his father placed the receiver back on the cradle. It didn't take a genius to figure that he'd been talking to Phil.

Lem jerked his head, gave David a sour look. "I hope things don't go to blazes while I'm in here."

"Phil does a good job for you, Dad."

"How in hell would you know?"

David shrugged. "I bank with him."

Lem Wilder snorted. "Fine grandson he produced for me."

David didn't want to get into all that. He wasn't competing with his brother, and he didn't want to get a lecture on how both of them had failed to meet expectations. "Look, Dad. Let's talk about something more pleasant."

"I lost the damn remote," his father growled.

David scrabbled under the bed, found it on its spiral cord, and restored it to his father. He felt the anger, the regret, the rejection, once again rising in him. His father didn't want to talk to him. He wanted to watch whatever was on the tube instead.

Fine. If that was the way it was, he wasn't going to stick around. "I think I'd better be going," he said. "I'm glad you're doing better."

His father cleared his throat and nodded a half-good-bye, still flipping channels.

David, in a black mood when he got back to Wildwood, picked up the phone in the study and pressed a button that dialed Phil's private number. While it was ringing, Junius Johnson came to the door of the library. "Excuse me, Reverend. Your secretary called and asked if you'd call her soon as you got back."

"Thank you, Junius." David cut off Phil's canned message and dialed the church. "Jane, you called?"

"I'm sorry, David. I seem to be the one telling you all the bad news. Oh, it's good and bad."

"What is it, Jane?"

"They found Clover early this morning."

His heart was in his throat. "And?"

"She's alive." Jane paused. "They've taken her to Greendale Hospital. I'll know more when Hattie calls me. Oh, and Tom Wilkins wants to postpone the vestry meeting for a week."

David grew guarded. Tom? He'd been doing his duty as junior warden and checking into the old rectory's building updates. "Did he say why?"

"Said you've had enough on your plate lately, and he wants you to have time to study Harry's report before he gives you his . . ."

So the battle lines had been drawn. David would have no choice but to fight, and that was what he'd been trying to avoid.

Chapter 22

November twenty-first brought a chill gray morning in Bow Creek, a weak sun losing the struggle with the rolling clouds, and still no word from Hattie. Clover must be all right. He'd have heard if she wasn't.

He'd go see her today. But now he had to face that he'd failed with his father.

Tomorrow would be the anniversary of Kennedy's assassination, the beginning of the end of Camelot. The end of his own private Camelot, when the world had been full of promise and love.

David parked his truck in the sandy lot of St. Ninian's. Lonnie Tucker's old truck, a blue Chevy dappled with rust, its back filled with rolls of wire and lawn equipment, was parked by the cemetery gate. Unusual for Lonnie to come to work this early.

The gate was open, and David walked into the churchyard to see if Lonnie was there. He frowned at the plots littered with leaves and grass clippings and at weeds feathering the edges of the granite slabs. Lonnie wasn't doing a good job. A gleam of glass caught David's eye, and he followed it to a tilted gravestone. He reached down, parting the long grass, and picked up an empty fruit jar. He sniffed the jar. Corn whiskey.

He walked to Lu's grave, still holding the jar. He brushed tiny hemlock cones away and stooped to pinch dead flower heads from the bronze chrysanthemum he had placed there a week ago. He was glad Hattie hadn't fought him when he wanted his wife to lie next to their baby instead of in the old family cemetery.

He rose, brushed off his clothes, and left the churchyard, closing the gate carefully behind him. He tossed the fruit jar in the trash. Entering by the back steps, he walked down the hall, his footsteps echoing.

A loud snort, or snore, broke the silence. The door to his office was ajar, and the noise seemed to be coming from there. "Lonnie?" he called out. "Lonnie?" He walked inside and flipped on the overhead light.

"Lordy me, preacher!" Lonnie's wife struggled to her feet from his desk chair, blinking as though she'd been asleep. The gloomy light from the window turned the leathery, copper-colored skin of her face ashen.

"Mavis!"

"Sorry. I must'a dropped off to sleep. Didn't sleep good last night."

"Mavis, did you drive here?"

She nodded.

"Mavis. If they catch you without a license, you might get arrested."

"Sheriff won't arrest me," she said. "Police neither." The town had two policemen.

"Maybe not," said David. "But the highway patrol might. They don't know you."

She looked away.

"Is Lonnie all right?" He didn't have a good feeling about the answer.

Mavis hung her head and twisted her hands together. "Don't fire him, please, Brother Wilder."

He thought of the fruit jar in the cemetery. "What's happened?

"He's t'home, all bruised up with a cracked rib. That Mr. Hogarth took him to the emergency room in Greendale and paid the doctor bills. They give him some pills for the pain but they ain't done nothin' for his head. He's gone plumb crazy, just knowing you was going to fire him."

David sighed. "Mavis, start at the beginning. He fell when he was drinking? What does Hogarth have to do with it?"

She looked David in the eye. "That Hogarth man and some other man was walking around that big old house next door and come over to the cemetery, Lord knows what for. Lonnie was behind one of them bushes with his jar, you know. For some reason Lonnie got in his head they were up to no good. He chased 'em out with his shovel and leaped on 'em. All I can say is, the drink done it. They hit back, not knowing what was happening, and Lonnie hit the ground hard. He's just bruised up a bit. Black eye."

David winced. This could be a problem. "Lonnie and I need to have another talk."

She looked down. "We're almost out of food, Brother Wilder." She shrank back as she said it.

"Drank it up again?"

She nodded. He gave her thirty dollars from his own pocket. He'd already used up most of his discretionary fund. Lonnie was also causing problems among the vestry. Half supported keeping him and half wanted him out.

"Come on," David said. Mavis followed him down to the tiny kitchen of the parish hall, and he gave her a container of chicken and dumplings from the emergency food freezer and a sweet potato pie someone had left for him.

As he walked her to the door, he saw the two preschool teachers getting out of their cars. They watched, bemused, as Mavis walked proudly to the truck, got in, and lurched out of the parking lot.

This was going to be one hell of a day.

The sounds of the preschool children began to fill the halls with laughing and jostling. He was glad to see Jane's cheerful face at her desk.

He made calls to Tom Wilkins and a few others, welcoming the routine tasks. He wrote an outline of his Sunday sermon. At lunchtime he pushed the work aside and walked up to Happy Mac's to have lunch with Harry. They talked about the upcoming vestry meeting. Harry was on his side, and for that David was grateful.

And then he rode over to the hospital to see Clover, thankful that she was going to be all right. Hattie had finally called and told him they'd found her at the bottom of a ravine, the result of a bad fall in the dark. She was suffering from bruises and dehydration, exposure, and a broken collarbone.

He hadn't told anyone he'd found Riley Clyde. Not yet. Perhaps he should let them know the truth, but as long as Clover knew nothing, she had hope for the future. And hope was what he wanted to give her.

Back at Wildwood, around four o'clock in the afternoon, Evangeline Wilder paced around the library, smoothing her hair. An Agatha Christie mystery lay open on her reading chair and a half-finished cup of tea rested on the side table. A good murder puzzle usually distracted her, but this time it hadn't happened.

David's visit had not been a success. She'd hoped that David and his father might be reconciled, but Lem had refused to give an inch. His father's hardness brought out David's stubborn streak, his defensiveness. Sometimes an illness changed people, but not Lem. Did he think that by holding on to his anger he could hold on to life a little longer? It probably worked the other way.

She took a sip of the tea. Jake Halsey had told her once that healing a hurt of the soul was like healing a wound: it has to come slowly, from the inside out. There were very few pathway markers to Lem's heart. Maybe she could have a hand in healing the past. The young woman, Molly, might be the key.

Junius came to the door. "Do you need anything else, ma'am? I have to study this evening." He walked over to the flickering fire and stoked it until it blazed.

"Thank you, Junius. That'll be all. Good luck on the exam."

Junius placed the poker back and left the room. She heard the houseman's footsteps retreating across the marble in the rotunda, the echo like footfalls in a museum. Or a mausoleum. The back door closed.

Since Lem had been in the hospital she'd been allowing Junius to leave early, for there was less work to be done and he needed the study time. She could very well heat herself a bowl of soup. Still, she hated to eat alone and wished she had some company. Albert and Celesta had retired, her brother had died, her sister had moved to St. Simon's, and her sons had their own problems. And she'd gone to too many funerals.

She dialed her friend Alicia Kenmore and listened to the measured tones of a machine. Nobody ever told you the truth about getting old, did they? If you just kept on doing the same things and having the same friends, they fell away from you, one by one, caught up by divorce, dementia, drugs, or death. And she had no daughter.

She sat with her hand on the polished ivory handset, looking down at her Florentine-patterned address book. She opened it to Molly Westbrook's name and number. Why shouldn't she have a relationship with her granddaughter? On the other hand, maybe she didn't need to upset Lem right now, when she was trying to broker peace between him and David.

She tossed the address book aside and went to mix herself a stiff drink.

Chapter 23

By Monday, David had pushed thoughts of his father far back in his mind and worked steadily through the day, meeting with the organist to plan the Thanksgiving Day music and the ladies who collected food for the needy. Everyone wanted decisions today, and he had spent enough time away. It was good to have a busy, ordinary day again.

He was ready to go to his farmhouse and put his feet up, but he had one more visit to make. At five o'clock, he finished his last call, put down his phone, and waved good-bye to Jane. As he was walking to his truck, a fretful gust showered acorns across the church roof, clattering, to land on the ground beneath his feet.

He glanced up at the huge old oak that shaded the church, its stubborn brown leaves waving, clinging to its branches. Of all the trees, that oak's leaves were the last to go, sometimes holding through winter storms.

His father was definitely an oak.

And what was he? Maybe a pine that clung to the high rock, buffeted by winds. The winds changed its shape: the tree grew gnarled, but in the gnarling there was a strange beauty, and the tree still clung.

Maybe he could write a sermon about oaks and pines. He got in the truck, jotted a few notes in the small memo book he carried, and headed out to talk to Lonnie. His mind on the sermon, he hit the gas a little too hard and the truck hit the bump over the washout at the church driveway. The old vehicle shuddered and bounced, metal clanked on the pavement, and the engine roared and sputtered. He killed the engine and got out to see his tailpipe and muffler lying in the driveway. He kicked the parts aside, got back in the truck, and headed for Herman's Garage.

Herman looked at him with mock disgust. "You didn't bring it when I told you. I got a part I took off a wreck, if you want it fast. We can get it done by tomorrow evenin'. Just leave it here. Maybe one of the boys can give you a lift home directly."

"I'll take the part, and I'll find a ride." Lonnie had no phone and he and Mavis would be expecting David. Using Herman's phone, he called Edison, but Edison couldn't leave the store and his wife was off somewhere, as was his son.

He thanked Edison and told him it was all right. He'd just had an idea. Someone who'd be home, because she lived at the store.

Nell answered, sounding a little harried, a little breathless. "Sure, I'll give you a ride. My assistant can mind the store and keep an eye on Sophie."

"If you'll just take me home, I'll get Lu's van. If it starts. I hardly ever drive it."

"Where are you going?"

He told her that Mavis had come to his office before eight to ask him to visit. "In her eyes it's pretty important." He held his breath, waiting for an answer. Nell believed Lonnie should retire before he hurt himself or someone else.

There was a long silence and then she said briskly, "Well, I'll just take you there. No sense in going to your place when Lonnie's is on the other side of the mountain."

David wondered if she was going to try to talk him into firing Lonnie, but her driving him there would save time. "I'd appreciate it, Nell. How have you been?"

"Busy," she said. "And you?"

"Surviving," he said. "My father's had a heart attack."

Nell's voice became soft. "I'll be there in twenty minutes, David."

She was true to her word, pulling up to Herman's in her beige van. When he got in, she squeezed his hand and gazed at him, eyes soft. "I'm so sorry about your father."

He thanked her, not wanting to elaborate. Nell headed out the way he directed her, and three miles down the highway she made a right turn onto a dirt road into a tunnel of green. She spun around curves, passing a farmhouse, a barn, and fields. Small houses and the occasional double-wide dotted the landscape.

"So tell me about Lonnie," Nell said. "I hear there was some trouble."

"You sure found out fast."

"That's Bow Creek." She smiled.

David had to tread carefully. "Anybody with Lonnie's liver shouldn't go around getting in fights."

"Will he be able to work again?"

He might as well get it out on the table. "You're hoping not," said David. "Aren't you?"

"It's not that. I'm just concerned about him."

"I'm concerned, too, but I feel he deserves another chance."

Nell stopped to let a loose dog cross the road. "Maybe it's time to practice tough love, David. Maybe you're enabling his drinking."

Enabling? No. "I wouldn't call it that."

"Wouldn't you? Maybe if you let him sink or swim he'd swim."

David shook his head. I'd have it on my conscience if he drowned. Where's the love? The compassion?"

Nell was silent. She gazed out her window for another half mile. It was hard to know what she was thinking. She was a good person, and he wished she would unbend about Lonnie.

"There's Lonnie's mailbox." David pointed at a rusty box next to a dirt track, almost obscured by mountain laurel. As they bumped over the ruts, he glanced over at the elegant hands that clutched the steering wheel in a death grip. He liked her hands.

The house must have been a simple and attractive cottage once, but dilapidation had outrun Mavis for years. David led Nell up warped wooden steps onto a rickety porch crammed with containers of every sort—pots, pans, washtubs, ceramic holders, old shoes—filled with soil. Some of the pots held chrysanthemums. Lonnie often took the spent ones home from the cemetery and Mavis made them bloom again.

Mavis came out to meet them. "Praise the Lord, you're here!" And then she noticed Nell. Saying nothing more, she led them into a front room of whitewashed planking and took their coats and laid them on a chair. On the hewn mantel—black walnut?—stood carvings of birds and chipmunks and squirrels.

Nell's eyes widened, and she walked over to touch the chipmunk. "Oh, beautiful! Did Lonnie carve these?"

"You ha'n't been paying attention," huffed Mavis. "He sells 'em in a booth at the craft fairs 'round here."

David smiled faintly. Nell kept her shop open during the craft fairs, running promotions of her own, sighing at the out-of-town competition.

Mavis showed them to Lonnie's bedroom, where he lay propped in an old iron bedstead, covered by a faded patchwork quilt and warmed by a small wood fire. A a pitcher of water stood on a rickety table stood by the bed. Another table held a cider-jug lamp with a whipstitched shade as well as a box of tissues, two brown cylinders of pills, and a Bible. On the near wall stood a battered chifforobe.

Lonnie opened his eyes and struggled to sit up. It was hard to tell what he was thinking in the best of times, but the old grizzled face took on a slight smile, and he rubbed his unshaven chin.

"How're you doing, Lonnie?" asked Nell.

"Mighty sore, ma'am." He winked. Then he turned to David. "That was a damn fool thing I did, but soon as I'm well, I'll be back on the job."

"I know that, Lonnie," said David. "We'll find some help in the meantime."

A look of alarm crossed his face. "You know I aim to come back to work if they have to drag me."

"We'll have to talk about that."

"Reverend, you been so good to me all these years. I let you down, didn't I?" He looked up at them with rheumy, repentant eyes. "I swear t' Jesus I'm gone make it this time."

David went over and clasped Lonnie's hand. "You know, Jesus said to go and sin no more." He felt he had to be a little firm this time.

"Yes sir, I do know that."

"Lonnie, we have to talk about your drinking," said David.

Lonnie groaned. “Oh, I do feel too bad to talk about that now. Say me a prayer of healing.”

David placed his hands on Lonnie’s head. “I lay my hands upon you in the name of our Lord and Savior Jesus Christ, beseeching him to uphold you and fill you with his grace so that you may know the healing power of Jesus’s love. Amen.”

“Amen,” echoed Nell.

“Amen,” said Mavis.

“I’ve got coffee and cake in the kitchen,” Mavis said, with a tone that suggested she would be mighty hurt if they refused.

David, hungry, had no intention of refusing. “I’ll help you.”

“You go ahead,” said Nell. “I want to talk to Lonnie about buying some of those carvings for the shop.”

“That’s a nice little gal,” said Mavis, when they were in the kitchen. “Even if she didn’t show no sense about that womanizin’ singer. But Tallulah’s barely in the ground.”

David’s cheeks warmed. “Mavis, Nell’s just a friend. In fact, she was Tallulah’s best friend. She gave me a ride here. My car’s in the shop.” He realized that in a few months’ time, his love life would be more interesting to Bow Creek than any sermon he could preach.

Mavis slid him a side look. “Mmm-hmm.”

It was embarrassing. Just then Nell appeared at the kitchen door to fetch coffee for Lonnie. Mavis filled four mugs and cut them all big squares of apple cake. Nell took a sip of hers, black and scalding. “This is good stuff.”

Had Nell heard what Mavis had said to him? Nell’s face was inscrutable, her aquamarine eyes reflecting sky. When they got back to Lonnie’s room with the coffee and cake, they found Lonnie grinning. Nell then announced that she and Lonnie had made a deal on the carvings for her shop.

They headed back to Bow Creek in the yellow-grey glow of the last of twilight. David reluctantly broached the subject that must have been on both their minds. "What do you think, Nell? I knew you didn't want to keep Lonnie on at the church, but now?"

An approaching car's lights flicked on; the lamplit windows of houses, momentary fragments of other lives, passed by. Hazy outlines of fields and trees gave way to houses. The sky deepened to blue smoke and the first star came out.

Keeping her eyes on the road, she said, "Maybe. If he goes for treatment. You've got to realize the church could be liable if he injures anyone. It's a good thing he didn't go after Hogarth with his shovel."

"Well, who knows what they were doing? Sizing up the church property? But Lord knows I've tried to convince him to give up drinking."

She turned into Bear Lick Road, crunching gravel and bumping over washboard ruts. "If he won't get help, you've got to cut him loose."

Lonnie would shrivel up and die without his job. "You think he can make a living carving? He's too proud to take any kind of charity."

"Maybe he could go on disability?"

David shook his head slowly. "He'd refuse to fill out the forms. He's a couple of years away from Social Security, and he's never made much money. This is going to take some thought. And lots of prayer."

Nell pulled into David's drive and drove around to the back of the house as she'd done so many times during Lu's illness, stopping beneath his yard lamp. He reached for the door handle. "Thanks for giving me a ride. I hope I didn't keep you from anything."

She smiled. "Lean Cuisine is all."

David thought of the lonely ham sandwich he'd probably make. "Let me buy supper for you."

Nell's expression grew thoughtful. "Nice idea. But I've got to get home. It's a school night, and I promised I wouldn't be late. I'll take a rain check, though. Come now, David. I don't want there to be gossip. I heard what Mavis said."

He smiled. "Oh, you know Mavis. She needs her dramas."

Nell shook her head. "Too many people in Bow Creek don't have enough to keep them entertained." She lowered her window to the crisp November air. "It smells fresher up here."

"Fresher and clearer. From my porch you can look out and see lights all over the mountains. People used to say it was fires from the stills. Now it's houses."

"I remember." Her smile was her first of the evening, and it was lovely to see.

"Thanks again for the ride, and I mean it about dinner."

She was quiet for a long moment. "Another time, maybe. Good night, David." She leaned over and kissed him on the cheek.

David, lighter by the weight of an elephant, stood in the yard watching her turn around and drive away, red taillights dissolving into the dark beyond the gate.

The moon was almost full in a cloudy sky, and David caught the smell of wood smoke, bringing the bereavement of a hundred fall afternoons: the backyard leaves when he was a boy, the crackling, fragrant fires in their cozy house during the happy days with Lu.

He turned the key in the lock, noticing the peeling paint on the door.

Now he was seeing through Nell's eyes. She must have known the fence sagged, the roof shingles were curling and balding, and the barn had faded to an anemic shade of red. He had neglected a lot while Lu had been sick. She was the one who noticed things that needed doing.

In the house, the portrait of Tallulah gazed down at him, but she didn't seem to be there anymore. He shook his head. It must be nerves.

"Goodnight, Tallulah," he whispered.

The awful emptiness that had melted away during the trip to Lonnie's came rushing back.

An owl's cry quavered somewhere in the distance.

Chapter 24

The next morning, David got into Tallulah's old van, the one she used to cart kids around for preschool. The vehicle had been sitting over near the barn ever since she had stopped driving, and he hadn't thought about it except considering that it might be useful at church for a youth trip.

He put the key in and turned it. Not a ghost of a sound, not even the crunch of a dying battery. The battery must be stone dead. He called Herman, but the mechanic didn't have anybody free to come give David a jump just then. Maybe in an hour or two. "And you better bring that thing in for me to look at. Could be more's wrong with it.

Herman told David he could pick up his truck that afternoon. David told Herman he'd just buy a new battery for the van when he came and bring the van in some other time. He hung up the phone and called Jane, hoping she hadn't left for the church already, but luck was with him. She was home and could give him a lift to the church and to Herman's that afternoon.

Finally settled in his office, he watched a cardinal on the Carolina hemlock outside the office window, singing *pretty, pretty,*

pretty bird to his mate two branches below. Then he picked up Harry Claymore's report. This was Harry's last year as warden and David was glad he'd been tasked with the report.

Attendance at summer services had reached an all-time high, and they'd needed all the folding chairs they could find. The increased attendance had extended longer into fall than ever. Vestry members were evenly divided between a building campaign and adding an extra service. An extra service might mean assistant clergy, which they felt they couldn't afford yet.

Harry had also included a graph showing projected attendance in coming years as well as a demographic survey of new residents, concluding they'd need to expand eventually. There was no more land—unless they bought back the rectory next door or built a new church somewhere out on the highway.

David had backed selling the rectory after he bought his farmhouse, because the church badly needed the money for a leaking roof and repairs to rotting timbers, not to mention a stained glass window cracked by storm damage. Buying the rectory back now would take money they didn't have. It would take time to raise that much. Could they get a loan?

He wanted to talk the matter over with Nell.

Yet he could imagine one of the church gossips at her weekly bridge club saying, "I saw David Wilder and Nell McGarry at the Frog Pond, and she's still married to that Taggart fellow, far as I know." And another of the good ladies saying, "Why, Tallulah's been in her grave only a couple of weeks . . ."

The phone buzzed. "Someone to see you," said Jane. "Said Tom Wilkins sent him."

"What for?"

"The temp for Lonnie."

David sighed. "All right."

He was not prepared for the man his junior warden had sent. His young-old face was weathered, his blue eyes carried a wise look, and his shaggy amber hair reached almost to his shoulders. He wore jeans and hiking boots and a faded green canvas shirt.

After greeting him, David motioned. "Have a seat. So you know Tom Wilkins?"

The man reached across the desk to shake David's hand and took a seat. "Chris Larson. I'm living up at the arts colony where his sister works. She told me you needed somebody to do cleaning and help out around the church."

"Well, yes. Are you an artist?"

"Actually, I'm a writer." He smiled and shrugged.

"Oh? What do you write?"

"Fiction, mostly," he said. "Short stories, a little poetry, one novel. Got an award. I'm working on another one, more commercial. Art's great, but you have to live."

"Chris Larson," David repeated, searching his memory for any clue to the name and coming up empty. Aside from history and current events, he read only the occasional detective story. They were about good versus evil, and good nearly always won.

He wished he knew the fellow better. He leaned forward and nodded. "Well, Chris, as long as Tom vouches for you, and you understand the conditions, we can certainly use you. It's only temporary, and we can't pay much." He named the figure.

Chris's smile was disarming. "Okay. I was hoping it would last until the summer at least, but right now I'll take what I can get." He told David he'd received a grant to the arts colony for the winter months, but he couldn't write all the time and wanted a part-time job to tide him through. "Winter jobs are few and far between here."

The young man was ready to start at once. David nodded. "All right. Mrs. Smithers will show you where the supplies are kept."

"Cool."

He shook hands with Chris and saw him to Jane's desk and made the introduction. If Tom thought he was okay, David was willing to trust his judgment, but he wished the fellow was a little less good-looking. Maybe it was because Jane, sixty-four if a day, simpered girlishly at him. Hmph.

He closed his door and walked back to his desk. He picked up the phone and punched in Nell's number.

"David!" She sounded happy, and his mood brightened. "I was just thinking of calling you. I've bought the inventory of a small shop in Greendale that's closing. I've got the pieces I can't use in the storage room, and I'd be glad to donate them to the church. Would you like to take a look?"

He knew, and he knew she knew, that one of his stalwart volunteers was in charge of the yearly rummage sale.

"All right, Nell. When?"

"I close at 6:00. Come on by about 6:30, and we can have a drink."

A drink sounded just perfect.

Chapter 25

Mrs. Wilder had not replied to Molly's note, and when she'd called her at Wildwood, the man who answered had told her that the lady was not at home.

And here was Molly, stuck in Apartment 3-C of the University Apartments, steering her dust mop over the living room floor, feeling like the Goodyear blimp hovering over a football stadium. Had she come to a brick wall in her search for David Wilder?

Her father had called. He was on leave, staying in Glencreggan and going into the VA hospital in Asheville. He hadn't been feeling his old self lately, with stumbling and memory lapses and hardly able to rise from his bed some mornings. He was sure it was just overwork and muscle strain, but the doctor wanted him to undergo a battery of tests. Oh, she hoped there was nothing very wrong. Not to the good, gruff, brave Daddy she loved so fiercely.

How could she tell him about her search for that other man? And if it was true that Daddy wasn't her father, did he know it? How could he not, if her aunts knew?

She opened a window and breathed in the cool November air, watching the leaves skitter and tumble across the courtyard below.

She couldn't quit searching now. Before, it had been a feeling of not knowing just who she was, of an emptiness in her being, a space where a mother should be, and a yearning to know something, anything, about this mysterious woman. She longed to fill that void with love.

The search became more important now that Daddy wasn't well. She couldn't bear to lose him, and she hoped he wouldn't feel she was trying to replace him. Never, never, never. If only David Wilder would tell her the truth about her past. If only his mother would answer her letter and help her. Paul had stepped back from disapproval of her quest, busy as he was working late each night, preparing his presentation for tenure, up to his ears in documents to be submitted to the committee and working on more publications of his findings.

She closed the window and walked over to her desk. She picked up the letters from two more David Wilders, each saying he'd never lived in North Carolina. She dropped them and crossed the names off her list. That was all of them except the last one, the Reverend. Why hadn't he answered her letter? He could just say no, as the others had done. But he hadn't done that. Why?

She pulled the vacuum cleaner out of the closet and wheeled it to the second bedroom, the one they'd done up as a nursery. Paul had already bought a magnet board and tacked it to the wall, and she'd filled it with colorful letters. She smiled at the jungle animal-print coverlet on the white baby bed. Nothing pink or blue. They'd chosen not to know the gender of their baby, and there was no health reason for an amniocentesis—or hadn't been until now. She fondly folded tiny camouflage pajamas her parents had sent and glanced up at the magnet board. With an embarrassed laugh, she realized the random letters spelled FUCU. She'd just rearranged them when the telephone rang.

It was not Mrs. Wilder. It was her stepmother, Hedy, asking if she and Paul would be able to come to Glencreggan for Thanksgiving. Molly replied joyfully that they'd love to come, but only if the doctor said yes. She bit her lip when she thought of Paul. He'd want to make her stay home in any case, worried about the baby. But she wanted badly to go. She'd have to convince him. She just had to see Daddy.

Feeling almost giddy, David stood before the intricate lace curtain that covered the glass pane of Nell's front door, right above the *Closed* sign. He turned the old crank doorbell, grinding and clinking out a bell tone. *Grink, grink.*

He shifted his weight and cranked the doorbell again. A moment later Nell opened the door wearing a pale pink sweater, gray skirt, and a pair of pink sneakers. She'd let her light brown hair down, and it fell forward as she leaned to kiss him on the cheek. She closed the door and locked it. "Come on back to the kitchen. Forgive my footwear, but I've been on my feet all day."

David walked into the potpourri-scented hall, trying not to stare at Nell. She looked so beautiful with her hair down. She usually kept it in a ponytail or flipped up in back with a clip. He glanced toward the sturdy oak hall tree on the left. It held an assortment of antique hats, including the trim black hat she'd worn to Lu's funeral. "They're all for sale," she said offhandedly. He followed her down the wide varnished hall through a doorway into a soft yellow kitchen, its walls crowded with sepia photographs of grim great-grandparents in stiff high-necked collars.

David gazed up at the portraits. "Does anybody buy those?"

"You'd be surprised," she said. "Instant ancestors. What would you like?" There was a maple hutch with scalloped edging behind her, and she retrieved a bottle of Jack Daniels from below.

"That's fine," said David. He hung his coat on the back of the chair and sat down. "Where's Sophie?"

"Over at her friend Liza's."

The doorbell *grinked* again. "Who could that be?" Nell set the bottle on the sideboard and disappeared, and David sipped uncomfortably at his drink. He recognized the voice of the visitor, and a roiling black cloud settled over his sunny mood. Nell came back in five minutes. "Sorry for the interruption." She was carrying a roll of something that looked like drawings.

David shifted uncomfortably in his chair. "What did Hogarth want?"

Nell hesitated, her expression guarded. "Why?"

"He came to see me the other day. I'm guessing you know the reason."

She colored"Okay. He came to see me a second time. He offered me the chance to decorate the rectory if they buy it. He says they won't tear it down. They'll use it for a shop and build the other shops in a similar style." She laid the roll of drawings on the table. "Here are the plans."

David picked up the roll and unfurled it, studying the top drawing. "A lot of work for a property they don't own, and may not be able to buy. So what do you think?"

Nell's words came slowly. "It would be a wonderful opportunity for me. I'd get a chance to preserve the house my great-grandfather built and the chance to furnish it with my antiques. My head's been crammed with plans for paint and fabrics. It would help grow my business here."

David couldn't believe what he was hearing. He'd never supposed Nell was motivated by money. He could see that she wanted to save the house, though, and while he wanted to save it too, he couldn't promise what the vestry would want to do. He'd have to tread carefully. "Nell, they're going to hoodwink you. I don't believe they mean to save that house. It would cost more to modify it than tear it down and build something more suited to their needs. You know the damp and the cold here is hard on houses, especially old ones."

She looked down, picked up a fragile china rose, and ran her fingertips over it. She set it back on the table. "He says they'll put it in the contract."

David remembered conversations when he was a boy, a fly on the wall listening to his father's wheeling and dealing. "I'm afraid some lawyer will find a way to put a slip knot in that contract and hope nobody notices. Once people are around the closing table, they're ready for the whole pea-pickin' thing to be over."

Nell raised her chin. "Sounds like you have some experience."

"I could tell you a few things," said David.

Nell reached for the drawings and rolled them back up, then took them back to the nook behind the kitchen, a former spacious pantry that she'd converted to her office. She returned to David with a smile. "Let's have that drink."

David slumped with relief. "I second the motion."

Nell walked over to the sideboard and splashed bourbon into two crystal glasses. "Ice?" At his nod she took a pair of silver tongs and grabbed cubes out of the refrigerator's icemaker and dropped them into the drink.

She handed a glass to him. "Cheers."

"Cheers." He took a sip, welcoming the jolt of warmth.

Nell sipped from her glass and he slid closer. He smelled vanilla and clean hair and the musk of a healthy woman.

She didn't move away but gazed at him, and he found that he wanted to kiss her. No. It wasn't right. It was even dangerous, but feelings were stirring within him, feelings that had been asleep too long, yearnings that had slept through the last companionable years with Lu. Feeling lightheaded and giddy, as though sunshine were flooding the room, he took a step backwards.

She hadn't moved, and her eyes were soft

"Nell, we can't . . ." His feelings slipped loose from their moorings, and his awakened body wanted her, here and now. Closing his eyes, he took a long drink of his bourbon.

Somewhere near a car door slammed.

"Nell. I hear someone outside. I . . . I forgot myself. I should be going, really." He forced himself to take another step away.

She closed her eyes. "I know. I know. But there's still the furniture . . ."

He picked up the drink and downed the rest of it. He had no idea what furniture she meant. "Remember the gossip. It's unfair to you, and there are people in town who think I ought to be moving on somewhere else, now that . . ."

"Now that Lu is gone. I see. Do you want to leave town?"

He shook his head. "No. My home is here. Or at least I think it is. I'm not sure about anything anymore."

"Yes, and we're both still grieving our loss. Grief does funny things sometimes. ."

He nodded. "I've seen that. How about you? Could you ever leave here?"

"It's different for me. I have roots here. My family's been here since my great-grandfather came, and any money he had is long gone. I'll tell you why I even gave Hogarth the time of day. It's not just the house. It's hard, keeping up this old place. The antiques I sell barely do it. And with the town growing, the taxes keep going up, and here I am right on the main street. And it's damned lonely."

"You think I don't know what lonely is?" David's voice was low.

Nell flushed, and he wanted to touch her warm cheek. How could he tell her about the endless nights on Bear Lick? He had to leave before he did something foolish. "I'll be back soon." Inane words.

He grabbed his coat off the back of the chair and jerked it on, then walked with Nell to the front door. She stepped onto the porch with him but suddenly dropped her hand from his arm. Harry Claymore came sauntering around the side of the building, briefcase in hand.

Nell waved a greeting at him and murmured to David, "I guess Harry's stopping by with some legal papers. My divorce from Hamp's been delayed because he's been on tour out of the country."

Harry bounded up the steps. "Hello, Nelly. Why, hello, David." The lawyer smoothed the few black hairs on top of his dome. "Thought I'd save you a trip, Nelly. I'm on the way home."

Nell folded her arms. David knew she hated to be called Nelly. "I was just leaving," he said.

"Nice to see you, Father," said Harry with a smirk. "See you in church."

David strode to his truck, cranked it, and drove off a little too fast, barely making it around the corner without leaving the road. What was that smirk all about? A flush spread across his face and then he laughed. What in the hell was happening to him? Was it grief, or was he going crazy? He drove home, calming when he saw a pale sliver of moon rising above him.

He glanced at Lu's van when he pulled behind the house. In the bed of the truck was the battery he'd bought at Herman's. He unloaded it and set it inside the tool shed but didn't see the crescent wrench he needed on his pegboard. Then he remembered he'd taken the wrench inside the house to take the bed apart.

Inside, he figured a cold beer would be good first. On the porch he took a long swallow, wanting the chill to drive out the last remnants of that forbidden feeling in Nell's shop. When his head cleared, he remembered that he'd gone there to look at some furniture she planned to donate.

Harry Claymore was probably drinking bourbon with Nell at this moment. Harry would make Nell laugh, as he knew so well how to do; and after the divorce papers were signed, what then? Harry would take her to dinner? David crushed the beer can in one hand and walked back inside. He sailed it at a wastebasket, missing. It clanked on the floor. David picked it up. He realized it was nearly eight o'clock and he hadn't had anything to eat.

But then he wasn't hungry.

Chapter 26

Shaking hands with people coming out of the ten o'clock Thanksgiving morning service, David bit his lip and watched for Nell. A week had passed since they'd shared that drink. Would their friendship be ruined? Before now, he'd always felt a warmth in her presence, a calmness, and he wanted to hold on to that.

The case of the old rectory was on hold. A few days after the meeting, the vestry had decided to table the question until the new vestry was elected on the second Monday in January.

He'd been on the brink of calling her more than once, but hesitated because of . . . well, a lot of things. Harry Claymore was one of them. Did he have his eye on her? He'd had been divorced a year, after two years of separation. David hadn't seen Harry's marriage as a happy one, but neither Harry nor Marilyn quite wanted to let it go.

David spotted Nell at the end of the line, a paisley scarf in blues and lilacs draped over her nubby blue wool coat. Two of his stalwarts amused him with tales of their grandbaby before they waved a good-bye, and then there was Nell, taking his hand with a tentative smile. "You know, we never talked about that furniture."

Smiling back, he kept her hand a little longer than necessary. "No, we didn't, and I'm sorry."

"It's still available."

He took a deep breath. "I'll do something about it this week. Come have a cup of coffee in the Parish Hall now. I'd like to talk to you."

Her smile faded. "What about?"

He squeezed her hand. "It's the rectory. Please come."

There weren't many parishioners around the coffee urn. Most were headed to their Thanksgiving dinners, but some dinners took place later than others. He was expected at Edison's around one o'clock. He noticed Chris Larson clearing away used cups and wondered whether the writer would be celebrating Thanksgiving alone.

Nell noticed him too. "Who's that?"

"Our temporary sexton."

"He looks like a creative type. Where did he come from?"

Her intuition had pegged Chris right away. David cleared his throat. "Tom Wilkins knows him. He's a writer up at the colony."

"All alone on Thanksgiving?"

David smiled. It was like Nell to worry about people being alone. "He's probably eating with the Wilkinses. How about you?"

"Sophie and I are going to my sister's in Hendersonville," she said. "My mother's coming up from Florida."

Relief flooded though David, but Chris was walking their way.

"Nell, this is Chris Larson, our temporary sexton." David noted the sunbeam smile Chris gave Nell.

"Ms. McGarry," Chris said.

"Just Nell. Glad to have you with us." Nell shook his hand.

"Thanks."

"Look, Chris," David broke in. "Would you clean this coffee urn after everybody leaves and sweep the hall before you go? I'll lock up."

"Sure. I live to serve." Chris winked and walked away.

David laid a hand on Nell's shoulder. "Let's find a better place to talk so we won't get interrupted."

Nell gave him a questioning look. Only a half-dozen people were left in the room. "David, there's practically no one here."

"We need to talk privately."

She followed him down the hall to his office. The light was gloomy and the furnishings spare, and through the window Quanasee Mountain brooded behind shifting clouds. David closed the door partially and switched on his desk lamp.

"Nice lamp," said Nell. In the soft radiance from the alabaster shade, her creamy skin glowed.

"An old one of my mother's."

"You appreciate beautiful things. I like that." She took one more sip of coffee before she slid the cup onto his desk. "The elephant in the room, David?"

The lamplight became her, and that was the last thing he ought to be thinking. He cleared his throat. "Yes, Nell, it's about the rectory. I'm asking you not to get involved in this. Don't work on behalf of Hogarth and Transmontane. The church needs that property."

She straightened in her chair and leaned forward. "Here's my concern. What will the church do with the house, the old rectory, if we buy it back?"

"Use it for meetings and Sunday School classes, at first, but eventually . . ."

"Tear it down?"

David tried to see things through her eyes, but it was difficult. The old house had given him enough trouble when he'd lived there, with the damp and the mildew and too many worn-out fixtures. The Johnsons had fixed many of the problems, but keeping up an old building in this climate wasn't cheap. "We could name a new building or wing after your great-grandfather."

Finger on her chin, she gazed out at the shifting clouds over Quanasee. "It's a historic building, David. The first rectory in the town." She turned to face him, her face tragic. "My ancestor would probably break out of his grave to haunt us if we bulldozed his house, and it would break my own heart."

David winced at the vision of splintered timbers and torn earth, of the upended gravestone. But would the old man really have cared? From what David had read about the old Scot Alastair Campbell McGarry, the founding father of the church, he would've been practical, not sentimental.

But Nell. It would pain him to break her heart. He could see her point. Houses were hotels where memories and ghosts lived, and once the house was gone the ghosts checked out, taking the memories with them.

And he did cherish a few good memories of his time living there. At the housewarming they gave for him, the fragrance of spice cookies had filled the house and a coal fire warmed the big front room. People perched on shabby velveteen chairs and horsehair sofas, gazing at the Maxfield Parrish print above the fireplace—a cottage nestled beside a stream, a thin scythe of a moon overhead in the dark night sky. The vestry gave him the print when he moved into the farmhouse, as most of them had never liked it in the first place. And Nell? She loved it.

She'd come into his life at that welcoming party. While they sipped coffee, she'd told him of visiting the house as a child, of playing on the threadbare Oriental carpet while the adults talked. He'd been charmed by her then, and secretly envied the architect, Sophie's father.

And then he had married Tallulah and Lu had been there for Nell when she'd divorced the architect, then Nell had paid no heed to her friends' concern when she decided to marry a twice-married country singer. Now she was on the way to divorce again, and he'd been widowed. He must not let his loneliness outrun his good sense.

"I don't want to tear the house down, Nell, but I have to be practical. I'm for the church buying back the house. We can use the house for extra space until we can raise enough money for expansion. Then the house will just have to go. You're for Transmontane buying the property, because they've promised they won't tear down the house. You think they'll abide by that agreement. But what about the church's expansion? Don't you feel we need it?"

Nell met his eyes. "No. I'm not sure we need to expand."

"I'll address that. But you need to consider that Transmontane will find some way to build that retail complex where the house is located, not behind it."

Nell shook her head. "No. That's not right. Hogarth says they're for preservation. They'll transform the house into a restaurant."

David sat back in his chair and his shoulders slumped. "I've lived there. I've visited the B&B. It's not suited for a restaurant. They'll tell you anything, Nell, to get your agreement." Nell leaned forward, her hand on his desk. "David, you know that we don't have the budget for expansion right now. We're not bursting at the seams. And I know more about restoration than you think I do.

After all, I was married to an architect, and I've restored my own house."

Emotion was blinding her to reality. "Summers are already a problem," he said, "and new houses are going up. We need to prepare, and this is an opportunity."

"We can cross that bridge when we get to it," she said.

"Okay," he said, "but consider this. We can't expand into the cemetery. De-consecrating the ground, moving the bodies, would be unthinkable to the families. We're too close to the street on the other two sides. We'd have to sell this beautiful old church and build a new one where we can find some cheap land."

He wondered if he was getting through to her at all.

She settled back in her chair, smoothing her skirt over her knees. "Maybe this past summer was just an anomaly."

Now she was grasping at straws. "Nell, do you really believe that? Transmontane wouldn't want the property unless they saw new customers coming. If we had room to expand, we could start a fund drive for improvements, so we can have our beautiful space for worship as well as fellowship and community." He doodled on a pad, drawing a church, a steeple. "If not, the Presbyterians will be glad to have those folks."

She didn't smile at his joke. "I think we're not getting anywhere, David. I've got to think. Thank you for the coffee."

She rose and left his office, her footsteps echoing down the hall. David sighed and closed the blinds, closing off the gloomy day, and went out, locking his office, something he rarely bothered to do. Did he feel besieged?

Maybe. A number of the congregation still resented that the church had sold the property, and they'd make a point of how much it was going to cost to buy it back. Well, if you were going to lead, you'd better prepare yourself to get kicked in the rear.

Walking to his truck, he just wished the kicker wasn't his good friend.

Chapter 27

Bow Creek, December 1990

On the third Sunday of Advent, a light snow fell. An uneasy peace had settled on the congregation, the members retreating into their views on the rectory matter, not wanting to spoil Christmas with disagreement.

David stood by the front door after the service, snow dotting his black woolen cloak, his hands warmed by the many hands he shook. Almost before he knew it, his hands were holding the slender hands of Nell. Snowflakes drifted and sparkled and melted into the handclasp, and she smiled. "Come to my Christmas Day open house. I'll send you a note to remind you."

David's smile widened and then he hesitated. "You're not going to Florida this year? Is your mother all right?"

Nell lifted one shoulder. "My mother is her usual self, and that's why I've decided to keep Christmas with my friends. It's just too much having to explain to Mom and Patty why I don't want to sell up and move closer to either one of them. I'm all right by myself."

"I don't remember Patty. Did she go by Patricia?"

Nell shook her head. "She married and moved to Hendersonville and never came back."

"If she looked like you, I would've remembered." He realized he was still holding both her hands in his. He let them go, and warmth crept up his neck.

She lowered her eyelashes, pink-cheeked. "Oh, hush. I'd better not hold up the line. Do come."

"I'll try to come, Nell." Best not to promise. If he promised, something might happen where he'd be needed, and he didn't want to disappoint her.

Lucy Bronson stepped forward and told him she liked his sermon and then she said something else while he watched Nell walk away. "Thank you," he said.

"David Wilder, I just asked you when you're going to get rid of those whiskers and let us see your handsome face."

David covered his embarrassment with a laugh. "It's the wrong time of year, Lucy. When I do, you'll be the first to know."

And Lucy laughed too, and the line moved on.

Four days before Christmas, Molly was decorating a tabletop tree in their tiny apartment, resigned about spending the holiday at the university. But she had Paul, and she was determined to make it merry for them, even if their Christmas dinner would be a casserole she'd made a month ago and put in the freezer. Also in the freezer were chocolate éclairs from the bakery and ice cream, and she'd already wrapped Paul's presents, a whodunit by his favorite author and a hand-knitted scarf she'd worked on secretly for months. Now she was confined to quarters, since she was forbidden to drive and it was too cold and wet outside to walk to any store.

Of course, travel was forbidden too, with her due date so near. She was glad she'd been able to spend Thanksgiving with Daddy and Hedy and the kids in the mountains with the uncles and aunts. They'd had turkey and dressing and homemade cranberry sauce, and Hedy had made her special red cabbage and thumbprint cookies to go with the butterbeans and creamed corn and apple and pumpkin pies.

And there had been good and bad news across the table.

Daddy's tests had come back from the hospital, and he was in no immediate danger. The bad news was that he had Huntington's disease, which meant that the stumbling and the weakness and the depression and all the other dreaded symptoms would only get worse, until he hadn't much else to lose. But Daddy had tried to put on a good front, acting as if it didn't matter that he would be leaving a job that he loved, didn't matter that he'd have to be content with thirty rather than the forty years he'd always said he'd serve. And the super bad news? The disease was hereditary. Now it was more important than ever for her to find out who her father might be. She couldn't question him about David Wilder. Not now. He didn't need any more grief.

He'd hate resigning from the Army. Still, he'd told the family that he'd always liked woodworking and thought he might take that up. He'd go back to Glencreggan and work on the family house he'd inherited to give them a permanent home. It was now empty, after his mother had left and moved in with his sister, and it needed some work. His brother, who had inherited the restaurant, was too busy running the business to give him a hand.

How old had her grandfather been when he died? About fifty-five? Way too early. Nobody knew why the accident had happened.

He was the type who, if he felt bad, would clench his teeth and carry on. Maybe he stumbled while he was stacking crates in the back of the restaurant, with a weakness in his legs and arms that made him drop the crates, fall, and hit his head on the concrete floor. No autopsy was done. Everybody thought it was a heart attack.

That was the family story. She didn't remember her grandfather much. He was just a shadowy figure that she had met once or twice in her young life.

And now she was afraid. Afraid for herself, afraid for her baby. As a biology teacher, she knew about genetics, and Paul had brought her a book from the university medical library on genetic diseases. It had chilled her blood. For Huntington's, a child would have a fifty percent chance of having the disease, even if the other parent was not a carrier. The disease didn't make itself known until the person was in their forties or fifties, after they'd already had children.

She shook her head. Trying to tamp down the fear with joyful thoughts, she fixed a silver star on top of the tree and unwrapped some new hand-crafted ornaments she'd bought in Glencreggan. Daddy said the town was getting too touristy, but she loved the little handicraft shop, which had reasonable prices. She hoped the apartment would look nice for Paul's parents, who were coming from Augusta to bring them some Christmas goodies and a good supply of leftovers from their Christmas dinner with Paul's brothers. Reaching out to loop a straw angel on a fragrant branch, she gasped as a cramp seized her. Was that a contraction? She was at least two weeks early, but her duffel bag, packed with a nightshirt, change of clothes, and toiletries, was ready to go. All it needed was her robe.

She scuttled to the bedroom, lay down, and began to count contractions. Her back began to hurt. A lot.

Before she'd finished ten minutes of counting, her water broke.

She grabbed the phone. Paul was at his office, reading proofs for a paper he'd had accepted, one describing the compounds he'd isolated from that rare Tibetan berry she'd told Mrs. Wilder about. She knew it would take a minute for the ringing phone to break his concentration. When he finally picked it up, Molly groaned with another contraction.

"Moll? What's wrong?"

"Oh, love, I hate to disturb you . . ."

Fifteen minutes later, Paul charged though the door. "Where's your bag?" He picked it up while she scrambled into her coat, heart pounding.

When she saw a policeman outside, she stopped in shock and gripped her husband's arm. "Paul, what is this?"

"He stopped me for speeding, and I told him the situation. He offered to lead us to the hospital."

A baby for Christmas! Off they went, siren and Molly both howling.

Chapter 28

Bow Creek, December 24

The late Christmas Eve service took place on a night clear and cold and full of stars, pierced by one magnificent light in the dark sky. Astronomers said it was a conjunction of stars, and that was all right with David. Such an event would have a special meaning for wise men from the East.

He preached on starlight and illumination, the gleam of treasures from dark corners, of hidden fragile loves being the first omen of great and powerful ones, and of the mystery of heaven's flame descending to the heart of a peasant child.

"The message of the child of God born into a humble life, not rich, not powerful, tells us that we must marvel at each new life and each new leaf, because new lives and new leaves are promises, as the birth of Jesus was a promise of love.

"Love is always the answer to our difficulties. Love is when we have to stumble blindly through our terror that out love will not be enough, love is when we must reach out to the unlovable, because God calls us to love them, love is both giving love and letting ourselves receive love, not once thinking we are not worthy, because we are all worthy in the sight of God. Love is making peace.

"God gives us the hope that love can conquer mighty tyrants, and his guiding star above tells us we must wonder at the mystery of it all, and that sometimes we must travel to a place where there are things which passeth all understanding.

"Abideth these three: faith, hope, and charity, which we know as love.

"And the greatest of these is love."

In the crush of people leaving the late service was Nell, alone, wrapped in a blue coat with a fluffy white hand-knit scarf framing her face. "That message was wonderful, David. Shall I look for you Christmas afternoon to join the rest of the strays?"

He took both her warm hands in his cold ones and kissed her on the cheek. "Merry Christmas, Nell. I'll come if I possibly can. I'll be with Hattie and the others, and sometimes it's hard to get away."

She smiled. "Hope you can." She walked on, and David found it hard to turn his attention to the next person.

The bright star followed David home and blazed above his barn. Now the barn looked lonely, for he had given the cow to Hattie, who was happy to have it. He still had the chickens and the cats, and he'd managed to make a pet of a friendly ginger fellow, a practical cat he called Tom Eliot.

After the noon Christmas Day service, David arrived at Edison's house. Hattie and Edison's wife shooed him into the dining room, where they'd laid out turkey dinner with rice and gravy and sweet potato pie, pickles and yeast rolls and cornbread dressing, and a red-and-green congealed salad ring. Coconut cake, assorted cookies, and ambrosia waited on the side table, while coffee brewed in a percolator in the kitchen.

Clover, sitting shyly across the table from him, seemed in good spirits, even though her predicament was starting to show. Nobody mentioned Riley Clyde Summers. The place at the table where Lu customarily sat was empty, and David sat next to it.

The empty chair, without Lu, made him feel odd, out of place. He missed her company, her warmth, at home. Here, her absence was more like a hole in the day.

The whole family dinner seemed different, strained, as though people were grasping for merriment, for normality, when there was none to be had.

After dinner, David wondered if he should leave, but he didn't want to hurt Hattie's feelings by going too soon. He leaned back in a chair in front of the fire. Hattie had shooed him to the holly-decked front room while she and the girls did the dishes and let the old aunts nap. Edison and the boys had left to go hunting.

The fragrant balsam fir twinkled and glittered with colored lights. A plastic Barbie Corvette remained under the branches, Barbie sitting rigidly with her spokesmodel smile, frozen in the good life, already forgotten.

Had he imagined people were treating him differently now, not knowing how to relate to him? Lu had given him the status of family member, and now he felt like an outsider again. He looked up from his brooding when Edison's oldest daughter, Rebecca, came into the front room and gave him a kiss on the cheek. "Bye, Uncle David. I'm leaving now."

He brightened, glad that she'd thought of him. "Have to be back at work?"

"Yep. You should see the place at Christmas. Gotta run." She opened the front door, letting in a chilly breeze. The fire danced, as if angry with the disturbance.

David admired the girl for her ambition. She worked at the Biltmore House in Asheville, and loved her job as an assistant curator, passionate about preserving history. David had mixed emotions. The monumental house, a palace really, reminded him uncomfortably of the life he'd left behind.

He glanced at his watch. What time had Nell said to be there? Four o'clock? It was almost time to go. He got up, stretched, poked the fire, swept the hearth, and rearranged the fire tools. Then he went to the kitchen, stretching out his good-byes, hugging Hattie and Clover and the rest of the family.

He pulled on a tweed jacket over his gray-blue sweater and gazed in the hall mirror before he opened the door. He hoped he didn't look too shabby for Nell's party. It had been a long time since he'd troubled his mind about clothes. He'd go home and change. He needed to call his mother anyhow.

Sitting in his own Morris chair in the cold house, he reached Evangeline in St. Augustine, where they were spending the winter. His father was recuperating well. Phil and Betsy, attempting a reconciliation, were spending a few days with them, and their son Thad had traveled with a girlfriend to the Bahamas. David asked to speak to his father. "I'm sorry, dear, he's not here."

David felt strangely angry. "Not there? Is anything wrong?"

She laughed. "I just told you he's doing well. He and Phil have gone fishing."

"Give him my . . ." He stopped and took a deep breath. "Give him my love."

Now he heard the smile in her voice. "Of course, David. Are you all right?"

"Yes, Mother, I'm fine."

They murmured their good-byes and then he went to change his clothes. Maybe he'd wear that forest green cashmere sweater his mother had sent him a few years back. It had been a long time since he'd felt like wearing something so nice.

He felt guilty going to a party so soon after Lu's death, but these were folks without family for the holiday. He could help other lonely people. That was what he was called to do.

All the windows of Nell's shop were lit up; a huge Christmas fir stood in the front window, bedecked with electric candles and jeweled Victorian baubles. David glanced in the next window past the artificial snow, and he made out streaky watercolor images of people, of red dresses. The sign on the door read *Come In.* He pushed it open and heard the clear notes of a dulcimer playing "Tomorrow Shall Be My Dancing Day."

He hung his heavy coat in the closet near the door. The long polished hallway led past candlelight and greenery and looped ribbons; the fragrance of cinnamon and clove filled the air. He found Nell in the dining room, setting out a tray of lemon tarts. "David!" Her smile brightened the whole room, and she hugged him. "I'm so glad you came. I didn't think you would." She touched his sweater. "Looks nice. You ought to wear it more often."

And then she murmured something he didn't catch, but he looked around and saw Harry Claymore at the sideboard next to a tray of drinks. The town librarian was in the room as well, talking with a couple of the artists from the art colony out near the house where Nell had lived with the architect. Five or six people he didn't know stood around the punch bowl. He didn't see Chris.

"All the Christmas loners of two counties," Nell said.

"It's wonderful of you to do this." David regarded the delicious-looking platters of turkey, fruitcake, divinity fudge, a Plains cheese ring, spiced pecans, lemon tarts, hot biscuits with slivers of country ham, candied fruit peel, a Lane cake, and a sparkling cut glass bowl of nutmeg-dusted eggnog.

"I love doing it. Help yourself."

"Maybe later. They stuffed me at Edison's house."

She headed back to the kitchen, and David wandered over to the sideboard and poured himself a glass of bourbon on the rocks.

"Fancy meeting you here," he heard and looked up. He stiffened a little. "Like a drink, Harry?"

Harry Claymore clapped him on the shoulder. "Don't mind if I do." David gave him the one he'd just made and mixed another one for himself. "Cheers."

"Merry Christmas." Harry raised his glass and sipped. "Well, Brother Dave, tell me one of your thousand tales, those you used to tell."

David hadn't heard that nickname in a long time. Harry had given him the moniker early on when David, new to St. Ninian's, thought he had to start off each sermon with a funny story. Harry had said David was like the old-time comedian "Brother Dave" Gardner. He'd given up the funny business after Lu had taken ill. He didn't even remember any funny stories.

"Not tonight. You did Saint Nick credit at the children's party, Harry."

Harry registered a faint look of surprise. "Why thanks, Brother Dave." He took a long swallow of his drink and looked around the room. "Hell of a Christmas."

"Is it?" David raised his eyebrows. "I'm sorry. Why?"

Harry's jowls grew droopier. "My first one alone in twenty years. The kids are with Marilyn all week." He upended the last of his bourbon and regarded the librarian across the room. "I think I'll go talk to Edwina. Bring a little excitement into her life."

"Harry, you're incorrigible."

"Not to mention irresistible."

David felt that Harry was trying too hard to be jovial. He navigated to the parlor, where much of Nell's stock of antique furniture had been moved to make room for the great Victorian tree. Two artists standing near the fireplace were debating whether their own work, fiber weaving and copper sculpture, might suit Nell's shop. One artist attended St. Ninian's sporadically, and David was glad of a chance to talk with him.

The artist seized the chance and expounded on religion as an art form, suitable for expressing certain modes of feeling. He felt chancel drama might be what St. Ninian's needed. He'd just warmed to the subject of medieval mystery plays when Nell approached and slipped her arm around David's. "Excuse us, gentlemen. He hasn't eaten yet." She led him back toward the dining table.

"Nell, I couldn't eat a thing right now. Honestly. You should have seen the spread Hattie laid out."

Nell's eyes crinkled with merriment. "I just wanted to get you away from our outspoken artist. He was warming up to attack you on the church's position on sex, and I don't mean missionary."

"It might've been more interesting than medieval mystery plays."

"I noticed you kept glancing around and thought you wanted to be rescued. Were you looking for somebody?"

"Nobody but my esteemed hostess."

"I'm sure." She put her finger on his chin. "Come with me. I want to tell you something."

He followed her into the dark hall that led to the guest bath. The powder room door stood ajar at the end of the corridor, a trapezoid of light. They were alone. She laid her finger on his lips. "I may have been drinking too much champagne tonight, but why don't you stay after everybody leaves?" Before he could reply, she went on softly, "Sophie's gone to her father's this year. We can talk about Grandpapa's house."

Whoa. "Why, Nell, I . . ."

"Think about it," she replied.

"Nell . . ."

"Ssh." She slipped away. Now what was he going to do?

It was Nell's offhand comment to Edwina that Chris Larson might come by later that made David decide to stay. Just for a few minutes, he told himself, so that he could check out the situation. It wouldn't do for his temporary sexton and a vestrywoman to get involved. He was coming dangerously close to that forbidden fruit himself.

David sat discreetly at the kitchen table with the drink he was nursing while Nell kissed the two artists, the last to leave, good-bye at the door. Harry had left earlier with the librarian. The time stretched and spun itself out; the ice in his glass melted into coruscating swirls. Perhaps he'd had one too many, but there was warm pleasure in being here and not in the empty cabin where the picture with faraway eyes hung above the fireplace, looking down on an empty chair.

Nell's footsteps behind him were light as misting rain.

"Nightcap?" she asked. She lifted his glass from the table, took it to the sideboard, and poured him a bourbon on the rocks and herself a bourbon and ginger ale. She set the drinks on the table and sat beside him, tucking her legs under her chair.

"So." She looked up at him shyly, and he forgot all about Chris, about Clover, about Hattie and St. Ninian's, and the two men who'd glanced at him in a knowing way when they said good-bye.

He wanted badly to kiss her.

Somewhere, from far away, there was a pale ghost telling him he shouldn't want this. Telling him he'd had too much to drink. He was Father David, and his wife had died only a few weeks ago. But he didn't feel like Father David now; he felt like Brother Dave, the man of a thousand tales.

He reached out for her. The phone rang.

"Let it go," he whispered. He pulled her to him and kissed her. The urgency of the phone shrilled through the urgency of his mouth on hers, the urgency of his yearning, the wax and smoke through a muffled melting haze. But Nell tensed.

"It might be Sophie." She answered the phone in her office. Hello? Oh. Yes. Yes, he's here." She handed him the phone. As he listened, the warmth drained out of his body and the whiskey throbbed at his temples. He hung up the phone. "Sudie Conway."

"You have to go. Nell's hand went to her throat.

David nodded. "We've lost her." His words were thick. He gave her a hug, then took his heavy coat from the hall closet and left, leaving Nell standing by the staircase, her hand on the rail.

Chapter 29

January 1991

On the Monday after Epiphany a thick snow fell, mantling the hills and mounding in the valleys, crusting the stark limbs of the hardwoods with white and riming the firs and pines. David churned through ice and mud down Bear Lick Mountain in a freezing fog, hoping for no more bad news.

The season had fallen hard on Bow Creek and the sun had been hard to find. Half the parishioners were stuffy-nosed, choked up, bedridden with the flu. He'd comforted Sudie Conway's family and seen to her burial, and Nell had left town to collect Sophie from her father. And then he'd had another funeral to conduct. Winter was hard on the old ones.

There were meetings with the two new wardens, both who'd served before. He'd named Wilfred Scoggins, one of the handful of truly good people he'd ever known, as his Senior Warden, his right-hand man, who'd be in charge of the church when he had to be absent. Tom Wilkins remained as the Junior Warden, overseeing the church building and operation. Harry remained on the vestry.

Not to say that goodness did not abound among his congregants; it was just that with Wilfred, what you saw was what you got. He had no hidden agendas.

Now David sat in his office, notebook in front of him, unable to concentrate. He tapped his pen on the desk. Nell was probably back in town by now. Should he call her? It had been a mistake, what had happened at that Christmas party, and guilt nagged at him.

But then he didn't want the upcoming vestry meeting to be the first time since Christmas night that he'd seen her. In this meeting they'd once again take up the matter of buying the old rectory for expansion. Wilfred and Harry Claymore were on his side, but Tom Wilkins was firmly against it.

He hoped Nell understood his dilemma. Yes, they'd had a moment, a magic moment, but, but reality had crushed it. The remains had faded into hung-over January, all grayness and guilt and bare black limbs, empty light that drained the life out of a day.

Jane brought him the mail. "Hope I'm not disturbing you. You look a million miles away."

David forced a smile. "No, not really. Thanks." She bustled out, giving him a worried look, closing the door behind her. Was he so transparent? He picked up a thick envelope from St. Augustine's Church. That was Jake Halsey's church, and Jake had scrawled his initials above the return address.

David ripped the envelope with the sword-shaped letter opener his brother had given him so many years ago. Before he could remove the contents of the envelope, someone rapped at his door. Stoically, he laid the envelope on his desk. "Come in."

Lonnie Tucker, hair trimmed, freshly shaven and smelling of soap, limped through the door wearing his customary overalls and an impish smile. He held his rumpled denim cap in his hand.

"What are you doing back so soon?" David asked. "It's a bad day for you to be out driving."

He patted his cap. "My old woman's pretty tired of me hangin' around, and I heard this new fella ain't here every day."

"He's doing all right," said David grumpily. "What does the doctor say?"

"I don't need no more doctor, and ain't no more pretty nurse coming out to see me, more's the pity. Miss Hattie's helping Mavis to look after me."

"Take another month, Lonnie. I hired Chris for that long." David almost wished he could put Lonnie on the job immediately, but he did not look well enough.

"Don't smell no coffee going."

Chris tended to bring his own herbal tea, and the coffeepot usually sat empty until David or Jane rustled some up. David sighed. "Why don't you make some, then, and have a cup before you go?"

"I can come in and clean up that cemetery. Snow's all over."

Now David got it. Lonnie wanted to get away from Mavis's overseeing. Maybe to drink again? "I can't afford to pay two sextons, Lonnie."

"That's okay. Miss Nell bought some of my critters."

"Okay, just for today, and then we'll see. Go ahead and make the coffee. Clean the cemetery and take some food from the donation basket." David would replace the food himself.

Lonnie brightened and went out, rubbing his hands. Maybe cleaning the cemetery would keep him out of trouble. Maybe not. At least he was sober now. Had to be, with the pills he'd been taking. David would have to keep an eye on him.

A clatter came from outside and David looked out. Chris was perched on a ladder, vigorously scraping the windows. The sight filled David with gloom, reminding him that Chris could do things Lonnie couldn't.

David sat down and picked up the letter from Jake. He'd almost forgotten Jake was in the running for bishop of Western North Carolina, and Jake was telling him he wasn't going to have it easy. The nominees included some excellent men and one woman, and there was a favorite son among the candidates.

Jake ought to win. He was a tireless worker, and he never cared who got the credit, which was somewhat of a disadvantage. The favorite son was a dynamic preacher and somewhat of a seducer, if that was the right kind of word to use. David smiled at the thought. Seducing people to Jesus.

He put the letter down and picked up the phone. Jake was in a meeting, of course. Monday morning. David shuffled through the rest of the mail, found nothing interesting. His calendar was uncluttered, a rare respite after the full December. He'd work on his sermon.

He took out the yellow legal pad he used for first drafts, a sharpened pencil, and his Bible. He turned to the Gospel verses recommended for the second Sunday after Epiphany, John 1:29-41, where John speaks of his unworthiness to baptize the one who is called the Messiah.

David read over the familiar words and then his mind wandered away from Jesus's baptism and back to Jake. Did Emily want Jake to be Bishop? She always wanted the best for him. Oh, yes, the best thing Jake had going for him was Emily. She always urged him to take the credit, backing him up, but arguing with him when he was wrong. And Jake could be wrong sometimes.

Tallulah had been a good woman, but no Emily. She'd always been there for David like a shadow. She'd always let him have the last word, always changing herself like a chameleon, putting her plans aside for him, trying hard to please him. If he'd bought her that scant nightie he'd seen in the window of Scarlett's Ribbons, she'd have blushed and put it away until a special time, which would've been too special to ever happen.

Love with her had been love between clean white sheets, too dear for passion. Passion always required a certain imperfection, and he had not wanted to go beneath the surface, perhaps afraid of what he'd find. Perhaps that's why it had been so hard to sketch her likeness. David came to the shocking realization that he may never have known the real Tallulah at all.

Maybe it was his own fault. Maybe she felt his own reticence and didn't want to reveal her own secrets, didn't want to make herself vulnerable. She, too, had had a terrible loss. Maybe it had been a mistake to keep his shame and regret from her.

He returned to the yellow sheet and the Bible. ". . . *Lamb of God, who taketh away the sins of the world . . .*"

So many sins, as he well knew.

When the phone rang, he was tempted to let it go but knew Jane wouldn't have put the call through if she didn't think it was important. He picked it up.

"Hello, Father."

"How are you, Harry?"

"Won't waste your time. Listen. I've had a brainstorm on how we're going to finance that rectory deal."

David leaned back in his chair, wondering what scheme Harry had cooked up. "Tell me."

"You're going to ask your brother to expedite us a loan. Hell, I know Phil would do it."

David nearly fell over, too stunned to reply. Of course Harry would have talked to Phil. They had been fraternity brothers. But why did Harry have to go behind David's back? His face warmed and he clenched his fist. Harry had it wrong. David was not about to go to his brother, hat in hand.

On the other hand, was he guilty of the sin of pride? He said cautiously, "It would be better to look locally."

Harry snorted. "There aren't any local banks. They're all branches of the big ones, and they go by the numbers. You know what our balance sheet looks like."

Dry-throated, David wished he had a glass of water, a cup of coffee. "I'm hesitant to involve my family."

"Come on, David. What's family for? If you won't call him, I will."

David cleared his throat. "I wouldn't want you to do that, Harry. It's a personal thing."

"I know about you and your father not getting along. That's why I'm the one to break the ice. You've got to admit, I have the power of persuasion."

He did, and that was the problem. Harry didn't know the depths of the hard feelings, how long they had festered. And David wasn't going to enlighten him. "I know that, Harry. But I ask you not to do it."

"Give me one good reason."

David forced himself to take the flint out of his voice. "Harry, I beg of you not to make things worse between my father and me."

"Bullshit, David. Won't happen. But I'll lay off for now. Just promise me you'll think about it."

He had no intention of thinking about it. "Thank you, Harry."

"There'll be a time you'll wish you'd said yes."

"I'm sorry, Harry, there's a call I need to take. I'll see you soon," said David as gently as he could. He hung up the phone and closed his eyes, a headache coming on.

He wasn't guilty about the non-existent call. He looked for a long time out at Quanasee Mountain and thought about his brother. They had grown up together as best friends, pals and buddies, always there for each other. He had stood up for David after the tragedy, but Phil would not blame his father.

David was angry at his father for disapproving of almost everything he wanted, and for cutting him out of his will. He was also angry at his mother for not fighting harder for him. It wasn't the money. It was the love the money represented. So the only thing to do was to live without them, to form his own family.

He did hear from his mother from time to time, but he only ever saw Phil these days at funerals. He hoped the next one wouldn't be soon.

Chapter 30

February 1991

The second Monday after Epiphany dawned sunny and chill. A whisper of snow had speckled the ground and the sky shone pale blue behind the gray-green hills. Exhausted from the vestry meeting from the evening before and anticipating the rest of the week without cheer, David spent the morning at home reading and writing and lunching on a solitary ham and cheese sandwich. It was around one o'clock when he pulled into the parking lot of St. Ninian's.

The meeting had been a circus. Tempers had flared. Members against buying back the property had different reasons. Nell thought Transmontane would preserve the house. There was the no-growth advocate who didn't want to buy property to expand "for those summer people who come and go." Folding chairs in the aisles were good enough.

Then there was the good soul who cautioned against spending money on "ourselves" by buying property and building new facilities when that money could go to the poor, and God knew the poor were always around just go down the road a bit and look at the old mobile home park.

David had fought hard to keep his impatience and defensiveness at bay and listen to everyone with a conciliatory ear. Harry had again insisted that Kip Hogarth's people were ready to move in and buy the property, and they had to act soon. In August the six months would be up. The owners had closed the B&B in December as usual, but they would not reopen in April.

The Johnsons would rather sell to the church than to Transmontane, but they were ready to look for a house closer to their grandkids. Harry even claimed that if Transmontane got the property they'd soon have their eye on the church itself, and who knew what might happen then?

David thought of Hogarth coming over to the cemetery, and he'd heard of "convenient" fires—one had occurred in Glencreggan, he remembered, in an old inn slated for renovation—but he couldn't believe such a thing would happen in Bow Creek. Not to this beautiful old church. Maybe he could raise some of the money himself by selling his Bear Lick property and lending, or even giving, the proceeds to the acquisition fund.

Kip Hogarth had barely disguised his lust for David's acres. But selling Bear Lick would be like selling all that remained of Lu, all that he had shared with her. The cozy wood-paneled house, the old cow and the chickens and the cats, the garden and the apple trees, raspberry canes growing in the sunny places, summer walks looking for wildflowers, evenings by the fire, her country cooking, and the house filled with the fragrance of pies for the church suppers. And especially the hugs when he came home from a hard day. Bear Lick cabin was his piece of the mountains—his foot on the earth, his storehouse of memories.

Alternative sources of money? The affluent members of his church could be counted on his pinky finger. The summer people visited but didn't join. Maybe he could track down some philanthropist, some "anonymous" donor. Who was he kidding? All those philanthropists knew his father and would ask him if Philemon T. Wilder was chipping in.

Or he could swallow his pride and call his brother.

He opened the door and smelled coffee. Lonnie was back on the job, and happy. Nell, now on Lonnie's side, had hired Chris to move furniture and do odd jobs at the antique shop.

David managed to quiet the devils sitting on his shoulder and spent a fairly peaceful hour working on correspondence. And then Harry called, wanting to come over right away. David put away the drafts of the letters and resigned himself. He said a small prayer that he would speak to Harry like a good Christian ought to.

Harry glanced around David's office as if searching for microphones before he hunkered down in the chair across the desk. "I won't beat around the bush. I've contacted Phil."

David's neck warmed and he dropped his voice to ice. "You went to my brother after all?"

Harry's mouth lifted at one corner. "Simmer down, David. I felt it would be better coming from me than you. I was doing you a favor."

David's hands fisted and he would have hit the desk, but Jane would have heard and come running. "Some favor, Harry. If we weren't such old friends, I'd throttle you."

Harry leaned back in his chair and steepled his fingers. "It wouldn't be the first time somebody's wanted to throttle me. It comes with the job. Believe me, we've been looking into other avenues."

"Behind my back? That's what I don't appreciate."

"We were going to tell you, but we knew you had a lot on your plate."

Yes, he had a lot on his plate. Human beings tended to heap it on, and, as Harry had said, it came with the job. "I've lost my wife, Harry, not my mind. What did Phil say?"

"He said he'd have to talk to you. And your father."

David shook his head. Now he felt like grabbing Harry's lapels and slamming him back against the wall. How could he have betrayed David that way? It took all his self-control to keep his voice level. He was supposed to be a man of peace, as Riley Clyde Summers had reminded him.

Oblivious of David's seething, Harry looked at him hopefully. "No hard feelings, David? We're in a hell of a sticky place here."

David had hard feelings, and he was entitled to them. "If that's all, Harry, I'll get back with you later."

When Harry left, David let out a long breath and paced the room. How could it get any worse?

At that moment, Evangeline Wilder, in white slacks and navy linen jacket, brooded under the warm Florida sun as she walked on the beach, wind-whipped waves foaming toward her ankles. The gusts tugged at her hat, and she reached up to catch the scarf ends lashing her face.

She passed a middle-aged couple searching for shells and a child and dog playing in the shallows. Glad for the walk in the sun and the breeze, glad to be out of the quiet rooms where Lem convalesced, her concern now was finding more questions than answers.

David was stubborn, as usual, and Lem more stubborn than usual. How could she broker peace between them? She'd tried so often.

She came upon a young family on the sand; the freckled woman's hair shone red, and the child beside her in a ruffled pink bathing suit sported her mother's copper curls. Copper curls that reminded her of Molly Westbrook. What to do about the strange encounter at the university coffee, of the girl's request about David? She gazed longingly at the child digging holes, tossing sand with her little blue shovel.

Keeping Molly out of his life was another example of David's stubbornness. What could be the harm in her writing to Molly, calling her, inviting her over for tea? If everything turned out as she hoped, it would be thrilling to hold a great-grandchild in her arms. Yes. She'd call Molly, and damn the torpedoes. Maybe Lem would get a kick out of it, after all. A tiny red-haired baby for Great-Grandpa.

She sobered, recalling what Lem had said to her earlier in the day. "Sometimes I wonder why I'm fighting to get well, Evie. I think I might just give up."

"But why, Lem?"

"Look what's happened with our sons."

"I think they've done just fine, my love." She smoothed his hair. "You expect too much of them. Nobody's perfect."

Lem harrumphed. "Phil is okay, but he's got the gumption of warm piss. David — bah. Turning his back on us. Some family I founded. I should leave all my money to the University."

Evangeline looked over at him, at his twisted and miserable face. She laid her hand on his shoulder and spoke with all the calmness she could muster. "Have you ever reached out to them, Lem? Have you ever tried to understand what they might be going through? Have you never considered you might be happier if you forgave them for not being what you expected?"

"What?"

Was his scowl from anger or pain? "Forgiveness, Lem. That's what I'm talking about."

He sat sullen-faced, gazing out the window, hands resting on his lap like dead fish. "I'm too old to change."

"No one's too old for love."

He said nothing.

When she'd gathered up her things for a beach walk and left the room, she'd left him staring out at the sea oats clattering on the dunes, at the roll and break of the sea. But his face had changed. The scowl was gone, replaced by a thoughtful expression.

Now, walking back, she glanced at their stucco condominium ahead. She'd convince him to go back to the city, tomorrow, even, and meet with Phil. Phil had called and told her of Harry's request, of David's reluctance to approach his father for a loan. *No favors*, David had said. Being hard-headed.

She knew without asking that Lem would not give or lend money unless David were to come to him personally, and maybe not even then. And David would not come. Or would he? The good of his church, certainly, would mean more to him than this family squabble. This old family squabble. The family squabble that had brought about the situation with Molly Westbrook.

"Miss Eva! Miss Eva!"

Startled, she looked up to see the daily caregiver running toward her, her uniform blue against the pale white sand.

Chapter 31

Heart pounding, David pulled his truck to a stop in front of the massive front door of Wildwood, leaped out, and took the four shallow semicircular brick steps in a single bound. He pressed the cold brass of the door latch, and it gave way. He pushed open the heavy door and strode into the hall. "Mother? Mother?"

His hoarse voice echoed in the tiled rotunda and then he caught the fragrance of lilies in the sun-dappled space. The hushed stillness of the house felt at odds with his agitation. He took a step forward, and the door to his father's study swung open. He stepped back, startled.

"David!"

"Jake?" David, overwhelmed with relief and gratitude, embraced his old friend in a bear hug. "What are you doing here? Aren't you supposed to be at Kanuga talking about touchy subjects?" He wished he could've gone to the church conference center in Hendersonville to hear him. It wasn't a long drive.

Jake gave him a sad smile. "I gave my presentation last night. I told the conference people I had an emergency and couldn't stay for the panel and that anyone who wanted to argue with me could write or call. I had to come, for Evie and you. Sometimes a stroke can follow a heart attack, despite everything."

"Jake, I really appreciate this. It'll mean a lot to Mother having you here." He glanced around as if she might be near. "How is she?"

Jake laid a comforting hand on his shoulder. "She's resting now. Let's go to the library." Before they'd reached the comfortable leather chairs, the phone rang.

"I'll let Junius get it," said David. "I'd rather not handle a call right now. Is Phil around?"

"I haven't seen him." The phone kept ringing, and Jake finally picked it up. "Wildwood," he said. "Thank you for calling," David heard. "No, she's resting." Jake glanced up at David—*do you want to take this*—and David shook his head. Jake kept talking to the caller, so David went to find Junius to ask if he needed help during this crisis. He was on the patio watering a huge arrangement of flowers.

"Hello, Junius. How are you getting along?"

Junius raised his eyebrows. "It's a sad time, man. Miss Eva's all worn out. I'm doing what I can."

"I can arrange extra help if you have school conflicts."

"Nah, I've got it covered," he said.

"Well, I'm going to see about an answering system, if Mother will let me. I know she's old-fashioned."

"Good luck," Junius said.

David went back to the front hall, waved at Jake still on the phone, and walked up the stairs to his mother's room.

She'd fallen asleep atop the covers, knees tucked to the side, still wearing her suit skirt and a light blue blouse. Her shoes rested neatly beside her bed. David gently pulled a delicate woven afghan over his mother—one he recognized from the Glencreggan house—and went back downstairs to see his father.

In the former guest suite on the main floor, the old man lay asleep in the bed. His big head commanded the pillow, but his mouth hung slightly open, his face sagging to one side. The doctors, his mother had told him, were guarded with their prognosis.

David found Jake still in the study, pacing in front of the fire, unlit pipe in his hand. He looked up. "That was one of your mother's friends on the phone. Wanted to rush right over. Sorry she hadn't been in contact lately. I couldn't stem the tide of regret." Jake took a box of matches from his pocket and lit his pipe, drawing in. "I counsel people not to let those relationships slide. You never know when the bridegroom cometh."

David shook his head. "I'm glad I have a friend like you, Jake. I wish I could have come down to Florida to the hospital. But it just wasn't possible for me to leave then, and they said he wasn't critical . . ."

"Don't beat up on yourself, sonny boy."

Junius had laid a blazing fire in the study, but the flames gave no comfort. Beyond the tall windows, the clear blue winter sky should have been cheering, but the contrast between this bright day and the greyness in his heart was cruel. The light should not have played so beautifully on the lawn nor wavily gleamed across the lily pond. There should have been a storm brewing with lowering clouds and deep rolling thunder, everything a shade past ashes.

Now David paced by the fire. "There isn't any time, is there, Jake?"

Jake leaned back in his chair and pulled on his pipe. "You tried to make peace when you saw him, didn't you?"

"He made me angry. I didn't try hard enough."

"Try again."

David raised his eyebrow. "Do you think he'll recover?"

"God only knows."

"I don't know what to say to him."

Jake leaned over and laid a hand on David's shoulder. "Ask for the words."

David went to the window and glazed at the bright sky. And then he was talking to God. *God, one more time. Let me have one more chance. One more time. It wouldn't be so much. At the end I want to know he loved me. Please give me the words.*

For the first two days afterward, David found that his father did not want, or was not able, to speak. David stayed by his bedside and read aloud to him, sometimes the Bible, sometimes one of David's own boyhood books such as *The Prisoner of Zenda,* or the book on airplanes of the world his father had bought for him. The old man did not respond.

On the third afternoon David sat beside the bed, watching the beams of the afternoon sun slant in through the Venetian blinds, a light breeze in the oaks outside stirring patterns of light and shade. He thought of the whole of their years together, all the episodes happy and sad, all the ways he thought his father had failed him, all the ways he had failed his father.

He closed his eyes and went back, back . . . to the big hand over his small one holding the fishing pole, the rainbow flash of a fish in the water, the old dock, the mist rising from the mountain, the glow of the fire, the glow of the cigar in the dark. The question was what it meant to be a man, what it meant to pass the torch, to be the propagator of his own dreams and the dreams of mankind.

Looking down at his father, David realized it was all up to him. This man could build no more bridges. He saw in a flash of insight—why had he been so blind before?—that *doing* was how his father expressed his feelings. David had to open himself, cast aside his pride, and risk rejection.

David leaned forward and said quietly, "Dad. I need your help." He could have sworn that the old man's good eyelid opened just a little, questioning.

"Wha . . ."

Was it a word, or just throat clearing? David took a deep breath. "I need to buy a building."

The eyelid opened again. Just a hair.

David began to talk about the old rectory. How he'd sold it so that the parish hall could have a new roof and repair the church. How the church now needed to buy it back. He told of the loan they required, and how Harry had contacted Phil without David's knowledge. How Phil had said that Dad would have to approve it. David told about the farm on Bear Lick he'd bought with the inheritance from his grandmother, the farm that held all those memories, the farm he was willing to sell if he had to. It would be a sacrifice, he knew, the loss of the place he loved, and he would grieve over it. Yet his life was changing, the town was changing. It was unsettling.

Was the old man even listening? But his eyes had now opened, and he gazed toward the windows, where sunlight glinted through tall trees. David talked of how much the old rectory place meant to Nell, and why, and his voice grew warm when he spoke of her. He said that he'd had differences with Nell over the rectory. He told how much he could have used his father's advice over the years.

And then he was quiet.

Lem's eyes met David's for a long moment and then one heavy eyebrow raised a fraction. The older man closed his eyes again. But his hand, the good hand, came up from the bed and reached out, trembling a little. David took it and clasped it.

Did the old man nod? He opened his eyes again and tried to say something. Then he pressed David's hand, let it go, and sank back.

His father had exhausted himself with the effort to communicate. David hoped he would understand what his father was trying to tell him.

He pulled out his handkerchief and dabbed at his eyes. Straightening, he walked through the French doors of the parlor and wandered the paths of the rose garden, his breath coming in shreds of vapor.

It had been a very long time since a gardener had attended it. Dead weeds choked the paths, and here and there bindweed was growing into the beds. The pine bark mulch had washed into the pebbled paths. The cut canes of the rosebushes, their thorns, seemed to glare at him. The garden was bleak and uncared-for and unutterably sad. And then on one of the stems, a tiny red leaf appeared, a leaf that would turn green in another month. All up and down the thorny canes he saw the swelling of the leaf buds, a sign of life renewed out of the dark, dead earth.

His father died the next morning.

Four days later David was headed back to Bow Creek. The concrete and grey haze of the city faded behind David's old pickup, melding into warehouses and signboards and automobile dealerships. Dressed in comfortable jeans after endless days in the clerical garb he always took with him, he was pushing the truck to its limit. Still, the motels and factories were slow to give way to farms and rolling fields.

After a couple of hours the last low blue foothills appeared on the horizon but soon disappeared when a downgrade took him through a few miles of forest and swamp. Climbing again, a faded billboard jarred him: PEACHES PECANS PRALINES 1 MILE. A few things hadn't changed in nearly thirty years.

Just down the highway a truck stop stood on a hillside, flags flying from its porch. STOP HERE, the sign read. He didn't want to stop but his mouth was dry, so he drove up the hill and parked under a shade tree.

After visiting the facilities, David pulled a couple of dripping bottles of spring water out of the tub and set them on the counter between a jar of pickled eggs in red brine and a box of packaged beef jerky. The woman at the register, a sooty-lashed blonde who looked as though she'd seen happier times, gave him a smile he didn't deserve. He paid for the bottles with a dollar, and she gave him a few cents change. "Traveling far?" Her cheerful voice didn't match her worn-out expression.

"Not so far."

She winked at him. "Cheer up, it ain't that bad."

He shrugged. "Does it show?"

She gave him a conspiratorial smile. "Honey, you just need to give your life to Jesus."

David walked out and drove away, speechless.

When he reached Bow Creek mist rolled down the streets, fogging the street lamps, shrouding the steeple of St. Ninian's. He felt disoriented, as though he had been on a very long journey, although it had been less than a week. He was heartened when he pulled into the church driveway, the light from the windows breaking through the miasma.

Inside, Lonnie was cleaning the kitchen and Jane was at her desk, squinting at a new computer screen.

"Where did that come from?"

"Tom got it for me," she said. "It sure makes things easier."

"When the cat's away . . ." said David, thinking of the tiny budget.

He had finally talked to his brother. Yes, Phil had said he would expedite the loan, but that was just the first step. The loan would have to be repaid, and David still had to convince those who didn't want to expand, and Nell, who thought the company would save the house. Was she naïve, or did she just want it to be true so badly?

He picked up a quartz crystal paperweight. He turned it over in his hands, rubbing his thumb over the smoothness.

"This came for you," Jane interrupted. David took a 9-by-12 envelope from her, glancing at the diocese's return address in the corner. He opened it and withdrew a booklet containing profiles of all the candidates for bishop. He read through it, regretting that Jake had left the conference and all those influential people because of his father's funeral.

David looked out on Quanasee, at the new green beginning to show. Phil had called and told him that his father had managed to tell his mother he wanted to change the will; that he wanted David to inherit his proper share. But nothing was on paper. A young lawyer in "Buffalo" Bill Kirkpatrick's firm had advised that the oral, or nuncupative, will might be valid, as long as the proper procedures had been followed. His mother had sworn that there were two witnesses: Junius Johnson and Jake Halsey.

David shrugged. He had no idea what the court would do. He would not dwell on all the problems that he could solve with such a sum of money, all the people he could help. As the written will stood, David had been left five thousand dollars, the same amount left to Nat, the long-time gardener, who'd had to retire the year before because of bad health. He wondered why his mother hadn't hired a new person. He hoped she wasn't losing interest in life.

Chapter 32

The morning in late February dawned with swirling mists, and David stood on the porch above the blanketed valley, mulling over what to do about the voice he'd heard on his answering machine when he came home from his father's funeral—the hesitant, nervous voice of Molly Westbrook. How had she found him?

Inside, the phone shrilled, shattering his thoughts. Early phone calls meant bad news. He made it back to his desk by the fifth ring.

Hattie's voice managed to convey both triumph and sadness. "It's Clover's time."

Not bad news, but good—maybe. "So soon?"

"By my reckoning, a mite soon. But you never can tell about the first one."

"Wouldn't you like me to drive her to the hospital?"

"Shoot, no. She looks just fine."

"Hattie. Just in case."

"Look, son. Don't you trust God?"

Hattie had played her ace, and David knew it would be useless to argue. Hattie had wanted to deliver Lu's child; a home birth had been planned, and then Lu had begun to hemorrhage and had to be rushed to the hospital. The loss of their child had been a crisis of faith that he'd barely survived, and he did only because of Jake.

He fought a rising anger at Hattie's stubbornness, even though he had forgiven her long ago. She had delivered plenty of healthy babies in her day, and he couldn't fault her for wanting to deliver her own grandchild—or great-grandchild. David had faith, but he did not believe in miracles. And now his belly clenched.

Hattie would never understand. "I'll drop by later. Tell Clover to hang in there."

"She keeps wishing after Riley Clyde. That sorry devil." Hattie sounded as if she'd like to take after him with the musket, or maybe even Vernon's .30-06.

David sighed. "I'll tell Clyde."

"He'll give you the runaround," Hattie snorted. "But you can bet he knows more than he lets on."

Distracted, rushed through his morning appointments, and as soon as he could get away, walked down to the barber shop. He found Clyde plying the scissors on the side hair of a man that didn't have much anyway. While the scissors clacked, David loitered, listening to the radio playing a Hampton Taggart song.

"When are you getting a TV, Clyde?"

"When they get something decent to watch." He nodded at the radio. "I kind of miss old Hamp, don't you?"

David felt his neck warming until he realized Clyde had been talking to his customer. Clyde finished with the old man, brushed and shook off his cape, and walked with him to the front of the shop. The old man paid and Clyde stuffed the money in a drawer.

Once the door closed, Clyde lit a cigarette. "Preacher, you look like something's on your mind."

"You're about to be a grandpappy," said David.

"Holy cow." Clyde slid his eyes over at Don, who was coming in the door. "Hey, Bubba, the preacher told me —"

"I heard," interrupted Don. He worked his jaw as if he was trying to make up his mind about something.

David knew a guilty face when he saw one. "I'm on my way out to Hattie's. She's delivering. I thought I'd drop in for a little while to give her encouragement. Do you know where your brother is?"

Don swallowed. "Don't know where the bugger is. Give us a call, okay?"

"All right."

"What a day for a birthin'," said Clyde. "Radio says a storm's on the way."

"Seems all right now." David glanced outside.

Clyde twisted his mouth into worry. "You might better ask Hattie to think again about deliverin' that young-un at home. She's a mighty peart old girl, but . . . You remember how quick them storms can blow up here? If there was any problem . . ."

"You know Hattie. Stubborn. I'm sure she'll be okay." He wanted to believe it, and Clyde was always preaching doom and gloom.

Brushing off the chair, Clyde didn't argue further.

When David reached the sidewalk, gray clouds were mounding, shading black to the southwest, and a faint moisture hung in the air. The sun in the east threw a thin shadow from the barber pole that Clyde had installed the previous week.

David walked toward St. Ninian's, hands in his pockets, glancing up at the gathering thunderheads. When he passed Nell's shop, he was tempted to ask if she was free for coffee, but Chris Larson was hanging around, and there was that matter of the rectory. He looked straight ahead as he passed by.

Approaching the church, he glanced up at the steeple, at the big oak, one a symbol of heaven, one of sturdiness. He wanted to trust Hattie. And he wanted to trust God. And who knew whose hands God would choose to work with?

The old Seth Thomas clock in Hattie's kitchen read a little after four in the afternoon when David walked through the back door. Hattie, peeling apples at the kitchen table, spared him a thin smile. Whenever Hattie had a spell of waiting to do, she hauled out the big crockery bowls and the flour to make pies.

"It looks bad out there," he told her. "It's getting colder."

"It's nice and warm in here." The big bubbling kettle of homemade soup smelled good. Hattie's tawny cat twined around David's ankles. He reached down to scratch the animal's ears.

Just then a rumble of thunder, very faint, echoed over the ridge. The cat slipped away to crouch under the pie safe.

"Pass me a few more of them apples, son. There's precious little else to make a pie out of this time of year."

"It'll be good, whatever you make," said David, digging into a bucket and filling the bowl on the table with green-yellow mountain apples. "How's Clover?"

"I hope it ain't a false alarm," said Hattie. "Go on in. She's sitting on the divan."

David found Clover in her usual spot, a crocheted blue and yellow afghan over her knees, watching game shows. "How are you feeling?"

"Not too bad," she said, "except every few minutes." From the TV, bells rang and shouts erupted. She turned to David. "Orabelle came over and told me all kinds of stories about pain and agony. I'm scared."

David remembered Orabelle Jenkins well. A widow and Lu's first mother-in-law, she lived in a small brick house just down the road. Unfortunately, Orabelle loved to tell horrible stories. He was sorry Clover had had to hear them.

He walked over and squeezed the girl's shoulder. "It's not too late to go to a hospital."

Clover's eyes widened. "That's not it. I'm scared of hospitals too." She paused. "I hope God's not mad at me."

"I've taught you better than that." David hoped nobody had been filling her mind with guilt.

Hattie bustled into the room so fast, David thought she must have been listening at the door. "Coffee's in the kitchen."

"Thanks, Hattie," said David. "Wish you had some of that pie ready."

"Just stick around, honey."

David, savoring the luscious oven smells, had nearly finished his coffee when a few raindrops, heavy as hail, clattered on the tin roof. He hurried outside to roll up the truck windows. He gazed up at the roiling, blackening sky over the mountains. And then the clouds burst.

They pummeled him with rain, spattering the ground, kicking dust like machine gun fire. Shirt soaked, he sprinted to the porch and leaped up the steps two at a time. Hattie thrust a towel through the door and he caught it. The rain sheeted down, hammering the roof.

Sitting with Hattie in the cozy kitchen, he listened uncomfortably to Clover's heavy panting in the next room. She must be having a stronger contraction now. Before the night was over he'd hold another baby in his arms, and he'd always looked on a new life with a sense of wonder. Over the years he'd held many babies as he baptized them, and each one held the secret of all that they would become. And each one had reminded him of Margaret Rose. Of David Ethan. He swallowed.

The rain howled and clattered against the panes, and the thunder rumbled again. Hattie went to check on Clover.

"Walk, girl," Hattie commanded, her voice echoing.

In a few minutes Clover was waddling up and down the hall, again and again, protesting, "They don't make people do this anymore, Granny!"

"Hush and mind me."

Through the noise of the rain David almost didn't hear the thumps on the back porch. He half-rose from his chair, alarmed, and the cat trotted away, tail fuzzed. The door squealed open and a figure in a cowboy hat appeared, silhouetted against the grayness. "Can I come in?"

Before David could leave the table, Clover had scuttled to the door and threw her arms around the wet gray ghost as best she could.

"Hello, Riley Clyde," said David.

Hattie stood, hands on hips. "What? You sorry devil. I ain't got no fatted calf." But neither Riley Clyde nor Clover was listening. They clung together, Clover crying, Riley Clyde awkwardly stroking her hair. "Hush, honey. I'm here now."

The boy's glance shifted to Hattie, and he nodded, "I'm sorry, ma'am." And then he noticed David for the first time. Clover had buried her face against her sweetheart's neck, and he put a finger under her chin to tilt her face toward him. David watched them, watched the tenderness spill like water over stones.

Maybe his visit had borne fruit after all. For a moment the room was quiet, peaceful, and then a flash, and he counted one, two, and the crashing of thunder.

"Take off your hat, boy," Hattie said, "but I don't know if I'm going to let you stay long enough to let it dry."

"Please, Granny," said Clover softly. "He's come back. That's what matters."

Riley Clyde removed the black cowboy hat and hung it on a peg by the door.

"You're lucky Hattie didn't bring out her .30-06," said David.

"Listen," said Riley Clyde, smoothing his hair nervously. "I had to work some things out."

"No word from you," said Hattie. "Doodley-squat."

"I ain't good with words," said Riley Clyde. "Preach here talked to me. I did some thinking."

Suddenly Clover gasped. "I think I need to lay down."

"Hold on, baby." Riley Clyde reached out and scooped her off her feet.

"I can walk," said Clover.

"Hush," said Riley Clyde, settling her in his arms. "You ain't no heavier than a sack o' cement."

He carried her down the hall to Clover's bedroom and disappeared through the door.

"He's such a fool," said Hattie.

"I believe he loves her," said David.

"What do that matter?" said Hattie. "He's still a fool."

Just then Riley Clyde hurried into the kitchen and, without a word, darted out the back door into the rain.

"See? Don't have the sense God gave a toadfrog." Hattie peeked in at the pies in the oven.

David went to the screen door and looked out. Riley Clyde stood half in and half out of the pickup door getting pelted by the rain. What the heck was he up to? And then he turned and dashed back to the house. He burst through the back door, clutching a brown teddy bear, and hurried back to Clover's room.

Hattie said, "Well, I'm going to find out a few things." She tugged at her apron strings.

David touched her hand. "Let them be, Hattie. There's plenty of time to sort all this out. Anyhow, aren't those pies ready?"

"Lord, yes." Hattie took folded dish towels and pulled the pies out of the oven. She set them on the pie safe, took off her apron, and hung it on a nail. "As near as I can remember he's got the law looking for him."

"Look, the boy told me he made a mistake. People can make mistakes."

"If he'd a-been behaving himself he'd be too busy to make mistakes. You're a funny man, David Wilder. I would've thought you'd be breathing fire and brimstone over this situation."

"The funny thing is, I thought I would too."

He hadn't intended to stay so long. He knew that Hattie considered menfolk to be just in the way with a birthing. Now, he didn't want to leave. He'd been far away when his own two children were born, the one who had lived and the one who had not. He would stay here now.

He and Hattie became quiet, David thinking of Tallulah, and maybe Hattie too. Riley Clyde bumbled back into the kitchen. "Clover wants some water," he said. "Me too."

"Help yourself," said Hattie, pointing to the shelf where a profusion of glasses in all shapes and colors crowded together. Riley Clyde took the biggest one, striped with red and yellow, filled it from the tap, and drank it down. He swiped his hand across his mouth and dusted it on his jeans. He filled it again and looked at David and Hattie, and his look made David think of a squirrel he'd caught once in a corn-baited homemade trap to impress Phil. He'd let the squirrel go without waiting for Phil to come home from football practice.

"Don't let my girl drink that much," said Hattie.

The rain strummed and pounded, trickled down the eaves, gushed across the back steps. A limb cracked overhead, and the tin roof rang when it landed. Clover suddenly shrieked, and Riley Clyde lurched out of the kitchen, dropping the water glass onto the floor, where it shattered into multicolored fragments. Hattie hurried after him.

David found a broom and dustpan behind the door, swept up the glass, and shook it into the paper bag that served for trash. Then he found a tattered rag to mop up the remainder and swished it across the floor. He had done a lot of mopping up in his calling. People did what people did; they got themselves in trouble; they lost the ones they loved. There was spilled milk all over the place, spilled blood, spilled seed. David mopped it all up, which was the best that he could do.

He rinsed the glass fragments out of the towel, wrung it out, and took it out to the back porch, where he hung it next to Hattie's washing machine. He met Riley Clyde in the kitchen, dazed. "The water broke," the baby's father said.

"All right," said David. "In the movies they'd have you putting on a kettle to boil."

"I'll do it, anyhow. I gotta do something."

Riley Clyde reached for the kettle on a hook above the stove, and David went to look in on Clover. He found her in a green hardback chair by the bed, Hattie taking care of the bedclothes. She whipped the bottom sheet out expertly and changed it, tucking the corners in, and then she spread an old quilt and towels over it. "Lay on this," she commanded.

Clover moaned. "Granny, I'm scared."

"You hush," said Hattie. "You got a spell of work ahead of you."

"Can we shut the window? The rain's coming in."

"Lord have mercy. So it is."

David lowered the window, brushing back the damp dotted swiss. Outside, it was already as dark as dusk, and fat raindrops pelted against the panes.

"It's starting to hurt bad," said Clover.

"Huff and puff," said Hattie.

Riley Clyde appeared in the doorway. "Water's on to boil." He stepped in and took Clover's hand in his.

The back door slammed just then, its crack syncopating with a flash of lightning that illuminated Clover's upturned face: a Madonna in a white sweatshirt against blue sheets, long hair braided back from her oval face.

"Jesus help me," cried Clover. Sweat beaded on her forehead. Through the drumming of the rain came a woman's voice. "Hello? Anybody home?"

David knew that voice. He hastened to the kitchen and found Nell McGarry in a hooded yellow slicker on the back porch. He opened the door wide. "Come in, come in. You came all the way out here in this rain?"

Nell left the dripping raincoat on a porch bench and stepped in, rubbing her hands. "Actually, Jane got worried. She asked me to come up here and see if I could pound some sense into you good people. She heard on the radio there's a bad storm coming. We think you need to take Clover to the hospital at once. There'll be power there and help if anything goes wrong."

"Come with me," he said. "Tell Miss Hattie that." Nell followed David to Clover's bedside, where Clover's eyes squinted shut against the pain.

Hattie and Riley Clyde regarded Nell uneasily. "Folks," David said, "Nell says we need to get to the hospital. There's a storm coming."

Hattie shook her head decisively. "Shoot, no. The road's no place to be in this kind of storm. It's too late, anyhow."

At that moment the back door squealed open, footsteps clattered through the kitchen, and then Edison loomed in the doorway, swiping a wet cap across his jeans. "Everything all right?"

"Your mama's being her usual stubborn self," David said. "Clover's in labor, and Hattie won't let us take her to the hospital."

"Who's going to pay for that hospital?" Hattie snapped. "I delivered my share of young-uns. Never lost a one."

Edison pulled his cap back on his head. "Can't go anyhow. We've got flooding. Bridge just gave way. Clean washed out. I got to the store by taking the truck through the cornfield yonder, but it's floodin' too. I had to leave the truck and walk back. Wayne's down at the store keeping it open. Batteries and canned goods are going fast. Bread and milk and jugs of water are already gone. You got enough stuff here?"

David glanced at Nell, then back at Edison. "Your mama's put up enough stuff to see all of us through a hardscrabble winter."

"I'll be getting on then," he said. He waved at Clover. "Hey, baby, how you doin'?"

Clover waved back at him weakly.

"I'll check back later." He ducked back out and then the back door slammed.

David looked at Nell. "Where's Sophie?"

"She's with Jane, who was tickled to play grandma. Chris Larson has gone to volunteer with the fire department if they need him."

David shook his head. "And you came out here knowing it was this bad?"

She looked at him with concern. "Somebody had to warn you, and the phone here seems to be out."

David picked up the phone. Dead silence.

Chapter 33

Outside the little house the wind screamed, and darkness settled around the two fitful candles like a thick cloud of soot. Limbs crashed against the cabin's roof, and twigs clattered on the gutters and drainpipes. David opened the door to Orabelle Jenkins, wrapped in sweater and raincoat, wet leaves tangled in her hairnet. She clutched a small battery-powered radio to her ample bosom.

"I'm too scared to stay t'home by myself. Radio says a tornado touched down near Greendale."

"Tornado? What happened?"

"Oh, honey, there's three people dead in one of them mobile homes."

Hattie came hurrying into the room. "Tornado, you said? Oh, Lordy."

"What if we all get killed?" said Orabelle.

Hattie turned to David. "Why don't you marry them two?"

"Now?"

Hattie wrung her hands. "They won't die in a state of sin."

Was she serious? "Hattie, it wouldn't be legal. They don't have a license."

Hattie picked the prayer book off the table and waved it at him. "It'd be legal in the sight of God."

David used his most soothing voice. "Hattie, Hattie. We're not in mortal danger. It's just a storm. It'll soon be over."

"So you say," chimed in Orabelle. "You don't remember the storm of '64."

Oh, he did, and it was a mighty storm, but his own storm had nothing to do with the rain. Something twisted inside, and from a great distance he heard Hattie. "Clover's scared, honey, mighty scared. It'd make her feel better."

He closed his eyes and then opened them. *I am not in the past. I am in this house with people who need me.* "Have you asked Riley Clyde what he wants to do?"

"The boy says it's okay with him."

What was the right thing to do? If they all died, nobody would know the difference. And if they lived, those two might regret it later. "Let me go make a fire while I think."

Nell sat with Clover while David walked into the front room. Away from the warmth of the wood stove in the kitchen, the chill in the rest of the house was bone-numbing. Hattie had taken care to lay the fireplace the day before, the kindling and the logs stacked just so, and when he struck a match to the resinous fat light'ard, the flames caught at once, crackling and snapping.

Hattie edged into the room and over to the fire and stood rubbing her hands. When she finally spoke, the words came hollowly, as though from a far distance. "She's not makin' much progress."

David gazed into the flickering flames. "How long has it been?"

"She started havin' the pains off and on this mornin'," Hattie said. "Pains got more reg'lar early afternoon. That'd be fine with me 'cept she's such a slip of a girl. I'm afeared we're in for a long wait." Hattie stood ramrod straight, boots planted, her jaw set.

David stepped out to Clover's room, where she lay pale and sweaty, knees tenting the damp sheets. Orabelle dozed, mouth slack, in a chair across the room. Nell perched in the only other chair, and Riley Clyde leaned against the wall next to the bed. David took the girl's hand. "How are you feeling?"

"It hurts. It's getting worse."

"That's what's supposed to happen. Now think of a happy time. Tell me about it."

Clover gripped David's hand harder than he thought was possible for a girl her age. "Uhh. There's one." She rode out the contraction, panting as Hattie had told her to do. She looked up then, eyes wide and moist. "I can't remember. Everything is one big hurt. Won't you do a wedding for us?"

Helpless, David wished he could stop her pain. What if she didn't survive? He stared at Riley Clyde. "Are you sure?"

The young man nodded but dropped his eyes.

"Do you have a ring?"

Riley Clyde shook his head.

He looked down at his own plain gold band. He had not removed it since Tallulah's death, forgetting that it was there. It had so much become a part of the way he saw his hands, his hands that soothed the brows of the sick, that closed their eyes in death, his hands that baptized a baby, that grew rough and calloused digging in the earth, his hands that had moved softly over Lu's body in love, and long before that, his hands that had held the hands of another and could not let them go, in the time when snow had traced patterns of lace in soft, dark tangled hair.

With a short glance at Nell, David tugged the ring off, put it in Riley Clyde's hand. "Take mine."

Riley Clyde stepped up and studied the ring. David thought for a moment he was going to hand it back. But then he smiled, tentatively at first, and held it so Clover could see it. He picked up one of her hands tenderly. "It's too big for them little skinny fingers."

"We'll give it back later," said Clover.

David shook his head. "It's a gift. I want you to have it. I'll have it sized to fit when all this is over." Still, he was uneasy. The boy didn't have a good track record. Was he telling the truth about setting his life straight? The rain was coming down harder now, pelting the windowpanes, roaring over the tin roof, gushing past the eaves in torrents.

"I want to do this wedding right," said Hattie. "Riley Clyde, go to the kitchen and fetch that bottle of blackberry wine. It's in the pie safe."

"Hattie, I don't have a prayer book with the service."

"Looks like you could remember," she said, "many as you done." She lifted a small green volume from the bedside table and handed it to him.

David gazed at it. "A 1928 prayer book?"

"I got that at the thrift shop for Tallulah, if she was goin' to join up with you folks. She told me you got her a new one, so I just kept this one. I like to look at it." Hattie paged through the book until she found the marriage liturgy and handed it to David.

"Now let's marry this girl right. I think these old words take better. All the problems these young-uns is having nowadays is from being married with those watery words that don't mean nothin'. That was what happened to her mama, God rest her soul. You know how it is, son. Them new words ain't got the power."

The power. Hattie believed what she said. When David first came to Bow Creek, it took him a long time to realize that, to Hattie and her kin, these Elizabethan words did have the power. The new translations weren't in Hattie's language. She knew perfectly well what swaddling clothes were, and to her there was no point in saying *distress* when you meant *tribulation.*

Riley Clyde came back with the wine and gave it to Hattie. "Come on, Preacher," he said. He stood by Clover's bed, holding her hand, scuffing his boots on the wooden floor. The makeshift altar stood ready. Hattie's best pewter candlesticks held two homemade candles that sputtered and wavered in the draft. The sky outside was storm-dark, mountain-dark, dark as the bottom of a river.

David opened the prayer book. "Dearly beloved, we are gathered together here in the sight of God . . ."

The wind howled, the rain rolled in torrents. " . . . if either of you know any impediment . . ." He glanced at Riley Clyde, but the young man's face was solemn, almost guileless. In the distance lightning was flashing, flickering, pinkening the roiling sky.

"Bless, O Lord, this ring . . ."

When Riley Clyde took Clover's hand the lightning crashed again, closer, freezing them in its brightness. And then the lights blinked off, and all was dark and silent, except the guttering of the candles, the drumming of the rain.

"The power," whispered Hattie.

He pronounced them man and wife. The candlelight quivered, casting Clover's radiant, tear-streaked face in half-shadow. The rain beat steadily, sheeting against the panes. David closed his eyes to blot out the pain of memory: the flash, the exploding gun. His heart hurt. His limbs grew weak. And then he pulled himself together. He had to be strong. For them.

"You may kiss the bride," he said, and turned away.

In the kitchen David watched Nell light a kerosene lantern, noted the deftness of her hands, marveled how the light seemed to caress her hair. Hattie served up a wedding feast of hambone vegetable soup and soda crackers and the four of them ate to the sound of the groaning and creaking of the pines, to the sound of Clover's moans. "I'll tell that boy to come and have a bite now," she said. And then Hattie left them to go back to the girl.

"Nell? What do you think about the baby?" David asked.

Nell sighed. "I'm no expert. I've only had the one, and she was easy. Look at these broad hips." She patted her hipbones with a sigh. "I'm afraid Clover ought to have a C-section. All this labor weakens mother and child both. Isn't there some way to get her out of here?"

"You heard Edison."

Hattie stormed into the room. "Nobody needs to cut on my girl. We got by in the old days." She squared her shoulders, took the lantern to the shelf, and began to look over her stock of herbs.

They died in the old days, David thought.

"Where's that boy?" Hattie grumbled. "I told him to come in here and eat something."

"He probably went to the front porch to have a smoke."

The kerosene lantern flickered, and David adjusted the wick, conscious of himself inside a circle of light against darkness and rain.

Ye are the light of the world. Light, like water, was a Biblical metaphor blunted and stripped of power by civilization. He had not understood it until he had gone to Israel, to the desert during the dark of the moon, where he had lain nearly naked under the pale stars, under the black, black night, blacker than any abyss. It was then he had understood the dark, and had understood the light, and had understood the light of the world.

He had forgotten. He would not forget again.

His reverie was interrupted by the sudden pattering of a fierce shower, then it subsided, trailed off, and was gone.

For a moment there was a silence empty of rain and then Clover screamed, and screamed again. David gritted his teeth, remembering the baby he'd helped deliver one day while he was in seminary. On the way to Chattanooga, he and a classmate happened to stop for a man waving frantically beside his car, who said he was on the way to the hospital with his wife and wasn't going to make it. He'd stayed to help while the friend went ahead to summon an ambulance. He remembered the blood, the rushing blood, the fluids, the screams, the woman's pale thighs and matted hair. The baby had been a boy. They'd cut the cord with a Swiss Army knife. The father had been grateful and nervous and poor.

Hattie's tawny cat stuck his nose into the kitchen from under the pie safe and wriggled out, stretching. David walked to the door and peered out. The sky was beginning to lighten into a dull gray dusk. He walked to the front porch. No Riley Clyde. He went around to the back and saw the stub of a cigarette smoldering in the mud at the foot of the steps.

Riley Clyde's truck was gone.

Disgusted, David stormed back inside to tell Nell and Hattie. "I don't know what's on his mind," he told the two women. "But I'll find him."

Flashlight in hand, David slogged along through the muddy cornfield in a pair of borrowed rubber boots. The boy was probably stuck somewhere in the field. He reached the top of the rise and saw beyond the downslope a spreading new lake, the pickup in deep mud at its edge. When he got to the vehicle, Riley Clyde was nowhere.

By flashlight, David made his way back to the dirt road, dodging muddy rivulets and deep puddles. He scanned the light back and forth across the road until he saw footprints in the mud. The heels were dug in deep. Why was Riley Clyde running?

Guided by the swollen creek's rushing, he followed the footprints through the mist toward the bridge. Past splintered timbers at the water's edge stood Riley Clyde, staring into the roiling mass of mud and foam. The creek bank supporting the bridge had caved away, leaving a jagged, raw concavity in the earth, a giant's bite.

The creek's ferocity drowned out David's first shout. The crushed bridge's timbers groaned, and splinters shook loose, bobbing through the current.

David cupped his hands to his mouth. "Riley Clyde! Riley!"

Riley Clyde turned back toward David. His eyes were wild. He stripped off his shirt. "I'm going for help," he yelled. "Helicopter, something." He hesitated just long enough for David to reach him and lunge for his arm.

David had him in a vise grip. "We need you here!"

"Can't help here." Riley Clyde wheeled and threw a punch.

David dodged it, but he lost some of his grip. "You'll drown! Don't do it!"

Riley Clyde swung again. This time he connected with a crack to David's jaw.

David staggered backward in pain, fury building. He leaped on Riley Clyde, shoving him into the mud, and they wrestled there on the bank, hardly a foot from the churning waters.

Riley Clyde struggled to his feet and came at David again.

David had been holding back, but he swung fully this time. Pain shot through his hand as knuckles connected with bone. Riley Clyde gave a yell and kicked out. David drew back, and Riley Clyde landed a chop to David's back, sending him sprawling.

Just as David pushed himself up, Riley Clyde dove into the rushing waters and was swept downstream. David saw only a leg, a back . . . under the water, a hand . . . heading downstream. He ripped off his jacket. He'd go after him.

"David!" He turned and saw Nell running toward him. She reached him, grasping his wet arm. "What are you doing? We need you at the house!"

He'd told Riley Clyde the same thing. He ran his hand across his dripping hair. "I tried to keep that crazy kid from diving into the creek. He said he was going for help."

"Oh my God," said Nell. She touched David's bruised face gently and rubbed his neck. "Are you all right?"

Her touch was soothing, and he wanted to relax into it, rest against her. He did not dare. For one thing, his clothes were caked with mud. He looked at Nell, her mouth open in dismay, with droplets of water on her damp hair, tendrils of hair curling on her pale neck. He reached up and touched her cheek. "I'm glad you came."

Nell shook her head. "David, what were you trying to accomplish?"

"I was trying to save his life."

"I'm going to pray he makes it for help," said Nell. "It's not getting any better with Clover." She raised her eyes to the scudding clouds overhead. "What do we do now?"

"Pray," said David.

He put on his muddy jacket and they walked back to the house. Hattie stood at the door to meet them, a knife in her hand. "We will deliver her," she said, "with the help of the Lord."

David stepped forward. "Hattie! No!"

She held up her palm, fixing David with a scornful look. "Just what did you think I was gone t'do? This knife goes under the bed to cut the pain."

They walked together into the kitchen, where a fragrant herbal mixture was steeping in a covered bowl. "Go wash yourself up at the sink," Hattie commanded.

Edison's wife, who'd trudged from home in muddy boots, brought cold fried chicken and fruit and cake and asked if she could help. Hattie murmured that the best thing she could do was to go back home and take Orabelle with her and see if she could find some clothes for David to borrow. David busied himself keeping the fire going in the front room and keeping water steaming on the stove. Nell volunteered as nurse.

Hattie and Nell were doing all they could, and after saying a prayer with Clover, David, muddy clothes in a washtub out back and wrapped in a blanket, slumped in a chair in front of the fire. He meant to stay awake and watch through the night, but his eyelids grew heavier and heavier and Clover's screams and moans grew fainter and fainter, fading away. He dreamed that he was trying to save her from the roaring current of the creek but couldn't quite reach her. She stretched out her hand to him. He grasped it, but her fingers slipped loose and a terrible wail came forth. He saw her face go under the waters, and it was no longer her face but Lu's face and it was Trilby's face. He awoke with a start, shaky.

How long had he slept? Glowing coals from the fireplace cast the only heat in the still-dark room. In the doorway to the hall faint candlelight shimmered, and women's voices were murmuring low.

And then . . . a baby's cry.

He jerked from the chair to his feet, his heart racing, and had to check himself, realizing he was wearing only his shorts and T-shirt. Shivering, he straightened slowly, his muscles stiff and sore. He found that someone had taken his muddy garments away and set out some clean clothes. He flung himself into overalls and a much-washed flannel shirt and went to see what was happening.

Clover, propped up in bed, held a tiny wrinkled baby in her arms. "A little girl," said Hattie and gave David a satisfied smile.

"Six pounds, by my estimate," said Nell.

Hattie shooed them both out so that she could supervise the first feeding.

When they were out of earshot in the front room, Nell said, "I'm afraid they ought to both be at a hospital. Why didn't you insist?"

David shook his head. "Ah, Nell. Perhaps I should have when Hattie first told me it would be a home birth. If Lu had been here, she'd have convinced them to go." He walked over to the fire and stoked the coals, coaxing out a flame, and then slid a few small branches in. "Hattie's feelings were on the line. She's still carrying a load of guilt from David Ethan. And nobody was at fault. What can the hospital do for Clover?"

Nell placed her hand on his. "She's lost a lot of blood. The baby is weak. I wish I could do more to help."

David blinked. This was serious. "We'll do what we can. First, let's move a cot in here by the fire for them. They're both alive, thank God." He knelt and fed two logs into the fire. "Let's get this room really warm."

Nell passed him a third log, not looking at him. "Still, you'd better pray hard, Preacher."

David stood and shifted the logs. "The rain has stopped. This mica soil drains fairly quickly. By morning we'll be able to get across the cornfield in my truck."

The fire was blazing now, and he walked over to the front door and opened it. A faint trace of ozone lingered in the air; a hazy curtain of clouds hung in the sky. Nell came to stand beside him, arms folded, so near he could smell the smoke in her hair. He reached to her tentatively, wondered what made him hesitate. He put his arm around her shoulder. "Thanks for being here."

She looked at him, smiling, but her eyes were troubled.

"What's the matter?"

"I'm afraid they won't make it. Hattie's doing all she can, and we're stuck here..." She took a deep breath and swallowed a sob. "I've got to stop that."

Once again he wanted to hold her, tell her everything was going to be all right. Instead, he cleared his throat. "Let's get that cot set up."

They found the rusty old folding bed filling a hall closet and rolled it out. Hattie met them with arms full of linens.

"Why don't you rest, Hattie? We'll do that."

"Pshaw," she said. "They're sleeping, finally. I don't want to move them now. I'll make this up and take myself a little nap."

David agreed. "We'll sit with Clover."

Hattie was having none of David's solicitousness. "No, get outside. You've been cooped up long enough. Just don't stay gone too long."

"I don't think we ought to go anywhere."

"Well, I'm going," said Nell. "I've got to move or I'll scream."

"We're fine as frog hair." Hattie looked at them. "You go with her, David. Look for that boy's body washed up."

"Hattie, Hattie. Don't say things like that. I'll go. We won't be long."

Along the road leading to the washed-out bridge puddles glistened in the faint light of dawn. Pearl gray suffused the horizon, softening the deep black shadows under the trees. David borrowed an old jacket of Nathan's from Hattie and walked beside Nell, her hands jammed in the pocket of her raincoat.

They walked without talking, words seeming superfluous in the enormity of it all. The sound of the rushing creek met them, and in a moment they stood on the bank, looking down on the melting mud shapes left by the scuffle. The water flowed past, swollen and turgid with mud. Old tires lay on the bank beside car parts, along with fast-food wrappers, plastic bags, and soda cans. A faint light shone from the store, across the creek and down the road.

"Edison or his son's probably sleeping there," said David.

"Or staying awake," said Nell.

They fell silent by the splintered bridge, David thinking of the damage it could do to a young man who might slam into it. "I hope he's all right."

Nell bit her lip and shook her head. "I hope so too."

They walked back facing east, and the glimmerings of dawn rose smooth and pale behind the hills, stretching across grass littered with torn branches and leaves and green pine needles. A faint breeze stirred, letting loose a cacophony of wind chimes.

David grew conscious of her nearness and reached for her hand, but they were approaching Hattie's front porch. Hattie, betraying her anxiety, was watching from the window. Nell touched his fingers briefly, then ran up the front steps.

David stood a minute longer watching the sun lift over the hills. His limbs trembled with exhaustion. He yearned for Nell's hand in his. He wanted someone to hold. He was the one who told people everything would be all right, and now he wanted someone to whisper those words to him.

Chapter 34

In the early light of dawn David and Edison and the boys laid planking and gravel across the worst spots in the mud-soaked cornfield. Nell was frantic to get home to Sophie, but waited to help David get Hattie and Clover and the baby, as yet unnamed, into the truck for the trip to the hospital in Greendale fifteen miles away. Then she followed the truck to the highway.

Though the emergency room was jam-packed with injured, the harried young woman at the desk admitted them without too much delay, especially after Hattie had had a word with her. Nurses came to take Clover and the baby through the double doors, and David left Hattie in a chair while he found a pay phone in the hall. He waited until the weeping woman ahead of him finished talking. She dabbed at her nose as she left, and the phone was still warm when he took it. He punched in Tom Wilkins's number, concerned about how the church had weathered the storm. After too many rings, Tom's mother picked up the phone.

"I hope I didn't interrupt anything," David said with concern.

"No, no, Father Wilder," she quavered. "You mean you don't know? Tom went over to the church to see about that big tree that fell."

"Big tree? No, I didn't know. I've been stranded. A bridge was out, and I couldn't get to a phone."

"Lordy. Smashed slap through the roof. I expect you'll want to get over there right now."

David thanked her and hung up. Hattie and Clover were now in good hands; he hated to leave, but he'd better see about the church.

Hoping for a miracle, he phoned the store. Thank God the line was working again and Edison was there to answer. He promised that as soon as they could go, he'd send his wife or one of the girls over to the hospital.

David's drive back to Bow Creek seemed endless, past broken trees and mud slicks and collapsed houses, wrecked cars and scattered real estate signs. The traffic slowed, snaking by the trailer park, where yellow police tape blocked the driveway. The place had been flooded and half buried by a mudslide. David craned his neck and saw Lacey's pink trailer upended. He wasn't paying attention when his lane of cars started forward, and a highway patrolman yelled at him to keep moving.

"Anything I can do, officer?" he asked when his car pulled alongside the tall man. "I'm a minister."

"Not right now," the trooper replied. "We're looking for survivors. But keep in touch."

He would keep in touch. But what would be left of his church?

A mile farther, falling rock had blocked the roadway, and he had to take a long detour. His stomach hard, he gritted his teeth and kept driving. Faith. He had to have faith.

By the time he arrived at St. Ninian's at mid-morning, he had calmed, but what he saw took his breath away.

The huge oak hung across the drive, new-leafed limbs splayed across the roof. Terrible yellow scars shot down the trunk, split and jagged with sharp splinters, and roots matted with clods of earth climbed into the pungent, oaky air. Pale leaves and acorn buds littered the ground.

He backed out of the driveway and drove around to the street behind the church, where a dirt driveway led to the crowded parking lot. He jockeyed into a remaining spot on the grass, and walking by the cemetery, he hailed Tom Wilkins and Wilfred Scoggins talking with two bearded workmen near a panel truck.

Tom wrung his hand and patted him on the back. "Thank God you're here. I was hoping you made it through the storm okay. We couldn't reach you. We've got a tarp, and we're going to take chain saws to the tree right away. We'd better cancel Sunday school tomorrow. The big 'un went through the roof of the Parish Hall."

David searched Tom's face. Was there anything Tom wasn't telling him? "You're sure the damage is confined to that one roof area? What about the nave?"

"The nave's all right. Be thankful for that sturdy church roof." The church roof that they'd replaced with the funds from selling the old rectory.

David knew that if the nave itself had been damaged it would have been impossible to replace the old native chestnut beams and paneling. "Thank goodness it wasn't worse. What else?"

"The Parish Hall inside is a mess," said Tom. "We may need paint and drywall work, but the roof is our number one priority. The insurance guy said to go ahead and do what we can to stop the damage. I've already been in touch with my cousin, and he'll put us at the top of his list. It might be a few days before he can get an adjuster out. The county inspector will have to look at it. There's been flooding all over the mountain, mudslides. You heard about the tornado in Sylva? Terrible thing."

David nodded. Surrounded by anxious, milling people, he recalled Nell's feeling of helplessness. People who hadn't lost anything to the storm wanted to help, wanted to give of themselves. "Let's ask for volunteers to come tomorrow and help clean up."

"My wife can call a few people about the workday," Tom said. "They'll spread the word." He looked closely at David. "You get caught somewhere last night? Wilfred went up to your place looking for you."

David slid his hand over his face. "My place? I hate to ask how it came through, Tom. I've been too preoccupied to worry about it. Tell me the worst."

"It's okay," said the taciturn man, waiting, clearly curious about David's whereabouts.

David sighed. "I got stranded at Hattie Holley's. Edison's bridge washed out." It wasn't the time to tell anyone about Clover.

Tom nodded, apparently satisfied. "Well, you go on up to Bear Lick and check on your chickens and such. We've got it under control here."

David felt a black cloud settling around his shoulders like that heavy wool cape his mother had given him. This was all he needed, right before the vestry took up the question of expansion. "How about the old rectory?" A damaged building would complicate the negotiations in progress.

"It's fine. Just lost a porch railing to one of them pines."

Relieved about his place, David took one more look around the church grounds before he left. If only he could be everywhere he was needed now.

He urged the old truck through the muddy rivulets up the road to Bear Lick. The washouts at the edge of the pavement had grown deeper, and he dodged a toppled boulder. Three fallen pines lay at an angle partially blocking the road, and their scarred limbs scraped the truck as he passed, the pine scent overpowering.

He bumped up his driveway in a cold sweat, crunching through the gravel, splashing through puddles, following the tracks Wilfred's SUV had left.

He parked and walked around the house. At first glance, he was heartened to see that the house was unscathed and his shade trees still stood. But in Lu's flowerbed, blobs of mud covered the young shoots. Still, that was nothing elbow grease and a garden hose couldn't set right.

Turning the corner, he came upon the forlorn apple trees. The tree that had sheltered Tallulah on the day he had sketched her leaned crazily, split down the middle. He should have pruned away the unstable Y-formation long ago, but he had let it grow out of negligence or sentiment. The second apple tree, just down the grassy slope, sagged with broken limbs.

Another link with the past broken.

With a feeling of emptiness, of heaviness, he trudged back to the barn. The barn cats peered out at him from the loft, then jumped down and twined around his ankles, mewling. He scooped dry food out of a bin for them and was glad the cow had a new home. Tom Eliot, his new buddy, dived for the food, but David knew he'd come to the house later.

The chicken pen was a mess of mud and leaves. A falling limb had torn the wire, and chickens were wandering around the yard. It was a miracle the cats hadn't chased them off. He filled the feed trays, then went to the barn shed and got a staple gun. He repaired the sagging wire and rounded up what he could of the chickens. By the time he finished his hands were raw and covered with scratches. He felt a bit better repairing the damage.

Finally, he walked over to the house. The back door swung open before he touched it. He hadn't double-locked it when he'd left, and the old warped door frame must have let the latch slip in the wind. Water and leaves and mud had puddled in the entryway. He flicked the light switch out of habit and was mildly surprised when nothing happened. In the shadowy natural light he saw the rug lying in the same place, the same dried galax rose by the stone fireplace. A trickle of water crept across the floor. He heard a loud meow and found Tom Eliot at the back door.

Heartened, he scratched Tom's ears and gave him more food. Then, with the cat watching, he worked steadily through his sadness and fatigue, sweeping the water and dirt from the back, cleaning and repairing until he was satisfied. He wanted coffee, and his camping equipment provided a Sterno stove and an aluminum coffeepot. Before long he had a steaming mugful that he drank with a cold ham and cheese sandwich and some potato chips. Luckily, there was one remaining slice of apple pie.

Hunger appeased, he walked out to the rick behind the barn and loaded his arms with firewood. He brought it into the house and stacked it beside the fireplace, then fetched another load to stack on the porch. When he had a fire going to his satisfaction, he poured another mug of coffee and sank into his easy chair. Tom clambered up into his lap. David took one sip of coffee, put down his cup, closed his eyes, and fell asleep to the loud purring.

He awoke three hours later to a setting sun and the sound of a car in the driveway. Tom Eliot had gone, and David pushed himself out of the chair. Before he could shake off his torpor, Wilfred Scoggins stood at his door.

"Sorry to bother you," said Wilfred, "but Hattie Holley wanted you to know they took the girl and the little baby to the hospital in Asheville in an ambulance. She rode with them."

Now he jerked fully awake. "Did she say why?"

"Greendale's full to overflowing, and the baby was running a fever. Clover too. By the way, she told me about you marrying those two." His taciturn face told David nothing about what he thought, and David was glad.

"Thanks for coming up to tell me, Wilfred. I'll get over to see them as soon as I can. Are the phones working at the church?" David took a deep breath, willing himself to stay calm.

"Yep, but the offices got some water." He shuffled his feet and looked away.

"And?" Resigned, David waited to hear the worst.

"Everything on your desk . . . sorry, David. It's a soggy mess. Some of your books too. Not sure how many."

"And that sermon I was working on." He gave a short laugh. "I can't use it now anyhow. The books and papers can be replaced. I'm just glad the old part of the church was spared."

Wilfred shifted his weight, as though he had something more to say.

"What else?"

Wilfred coughed, cleared his throat. "A couple of our people haven't been found. Lucy and Milford Bronson went to see about her old father, that cantankerous old cuss who lives down by the creek, and that whole area is flooded."

David's heart sank. "I'm coming to help as soon as I straighten up here."

Wilfred nodded. "Well, I'll get on back down there. My wife's trying to feed the troops."

Wilfred wound his way back down the driveway. Watching him go, David slumped against the porch beam. The church had a hole in the roof, the big oak was lying in splinters, some dear friends were missing, and somewhere out there was a woman named Nell, fallen as close to him as rain. Two women he'd loved had died. Did he dare risk loving again? His body and soul told him yes. A devil on his shoulder made him afraid.

But now he wanted to reassure Hattie and Clover. He called two hospitals in Asheville, but no one seemed to know about them. A woman told him it was mass confusion, with all the flood and tornado casualties.

He was going right back to the church, he told himself. To help. He just had to sit down for a minute. In the pitch dark, in the coldness, in the complete silence, he slept until dawn, awakened by a loud meow.

After an eight o'clock camp-stove breakfast of eggs, toast, and coffee, and a swipe at washing up, David put on a sweatshirt and jeans, tended the animals, and headed down Bear Lick to St. Ninian's to take a look at the damage. It was Sunday, the day he'd usually be standing up before his people.

The streams gushed muddy runnels, puddles laced the fields, tall pines cast jagged splinters to the sky. Slender saplings hunched almost double, arcs lining the road. Ironically, the sun glimmered in a pale blue sky, wisps of clouds drifting through the moist, cool air.

On the truck radio he found a news station. Seven people in the county were dead, and dozens had lost their homes. The trailer park was devastated and people were missing.

He gritted his jaw. Those people who died would be people loved by his flock—cousins, aunts, neighbors. Ties of kinship here were deep and lasting. What would he tell them this morning? They'd be looking for some word of comfort from him, and he'd have to find that somewhere deep inside himself. How could he say that God loved them, with all this destruction? He had to find the strength, the inspiration somewhere.

When he arrived at the church, he was surprised to see that trucks and cars were already filling the lot. Women trundled foil-covered dishes to a folding table in the courtyard. Members of the Men's Bible Class had rescued folding chairs from the damaged building, and teenagers piled branches against the cemetery fence. David got out of the truck and pushed up his sleeves. He walked over to his senior warden, standing beside the splintered remains of the big oak.

"It looks worse in the morning light," Wilfred said. "We were lucky. Look at the size of that damn thing."

David gazed at the oak and then up at the roof, at a ladder leaning against the side of the building. "What if it rains again?"

"They got another tarp up after you left."

"Good." David paused. "Heard anything about our missing people?"

"Lucy and Milford are okay. But the old man's dead. Heart failure."

David pitched in and began to drag limbs to a pile at the edge of the parking lot. One person manned a chainsaw, roaring and whining. Men, women, and children fanned out to the cemetery, sweeping debris off stone and raking between markers.

The mess inside was waiting for David, but the ladder leaning on the building caught his eye. An impulse seized him. He wanted to see the damage for himself, a God's-eye view. He grabbed the ladder and shook it, testing. "I'm going up there."

Tom Wilkins, standing nearby with a clipboard and pen, looked up. "What? You don't need to do that."

"I want to."

"David, you goddamn fool." There was a silence, and Tom Wilkins blushed. "Sorry. Take care. If anything happens to you, I'm no damn good at giving sermons."

David gripped the ladder again, and satisfied it was secure, climbed easily until he reached the top. He pushed himself from ladder to roof and stood.

Down below, more cars turned into the driveway: Harry Claymore's black Acura, an old Buick wagon, and then, Nell's van. He watched as Nell parked, got out, and pulled a faded red Thermos jug out of the back. She set it on a table among trays stacked with doughnuts and pastries.

Harry Claymore walked around the courtyard and stared at the roof, chin in hand, as though wondering if there might be anyone to sue. Then he spotted David looking down at him, and stood hands on hips, shaking his head as though to say, "About what I'd expect from you." He waved an arm in exaggerated arcs for David to come down.

David shook his head.

The pitch of this section was not steep, and he stepped forward. When he was halfway to the biggest oak limb, upraised like a swimmer's elbow, his foot slipped on a loose shingle and he skidded backwards. He leaned over, caught a vent pipe, regained his footing and eased himself over to the edge of the tarp. He steadied himself and lifted a corner. Below the gaping hole and the splintered beams, leaves and shingles littered the sun-splashed, waterlogged floor.

He clenched his fists and felt the sweat breaking out on his forehead. He was guilty, guilty of despair, the tragic undercurrent of his life. And why not? There had been things done and things left undone, and all the lost years. Gone were Trilby, David Ethan, Tallulah, his father. Perhaps even Riley Clyde. And Molly? Was she gone from his life?

He looked out over the hills, up at Quanasee, where cumulus clouds banked above the broken trees, the clods of earth, the muddy streams and the buried homes. He had been determined to keep his promise to Trilby, but Trilby had been trying to protect Owen, and Molly, and . . . him. That was then. What would she want now?

A cool spring wind ruffled the hemlocks' feathery branches. From here the mountains rose in their graceful blue-smoke majesty, their scars unseen. The floodwaters glinted almost beautifully. Here was God's handiwork in all its terrifying splendor. Here was the world they all had been given. It was a moment of luminous clarity.

The world had given him a father, a mother, a brother, good friends, a loving wife....and a daughter. Had he any right to keep her at a distance? She'd said in her letter that she thought her father, Owen, would understand, and she would ask for his blessing if David agreed to meet her. He wanted badly to meet her. But should he? How could he tell her about her mother?

A warm breeze rippled through the chill. David felt unreasonable joy at the beauty around him, a deeper warmth pervading him. He knew at once that he was part of it all: part of the sun and the shade, part of the trees and their brokenness, part of the roiling river and part of the debris it bore. Part of all that was life.

Life that was imperfect. Life that held loss. Life that held gain. And he could no more escape one than expect the other. What he had was grace.

How could he have missed it, how could he have been so blind? *He was forgiven.* And if God forgave him, he could forgive himself. He knew, all at once, that he understood—he *felt*—the soft wings of peace lifting him. He wanted to share this feeling, to tell the crowd below about what he had experienced.

If only they could feel it, if only they could share in his joy, a kind of resurrection, to become a new person in the warmth of the healing sun.

He took a few steps in the direction of the ladder, in the direction of the high distant clouds. He might have stepped right off the roof had not someone given a loud whistle.

Harry Claymore was underneath, standing by the ladder, and David came back to himself to find a sea of wondering faces watching him. The chainsaw had quieted, and work had come almost to a standstill. He nodded at Harry and descended the ladder, taking his time.

He knew what he was going to say to his people.

The hour before the Sunday service passed quickly. David walked up and down the halls and around the courtyard greeting people, finding how they'd weathered the storm. He would have helped with the cleaning, but Tom had organized everyone so well David wasn't needed. Even Harry was manning a rake.

Musing, he was almost knocked down by the small Miller twins, who ran along trying to fly plastic bags like kites. "Oops, it's Father

David!" They scurried away and began to pick up twigs. Children would be children, no matter how dire the circumstances.

When it was quarter to eleven, David went into his office, looked over the mess lying on his desk, and swooped it into a black plastic trash bag someone had left for him.

He hadn't expected the church to be full, and his heart swelled to see rows of hopeful faces turned up toward him. If only he could give them the words they needed. Young Melissa Wilkins sang the psalm, and as her clear voice lifted the sun broke through the shifting clouds outside, painting the stained glass luminous, eclipsing the candle glow.

When the time came for the sermon David looked out over his people, scanning the rows, meeting as many eyes as he could. He breathed deeply and walked up to the pulpit. He remembered Hattie's admonition. The old words had the power.

"The King James Bible," he said. "That Bible had a word for what we're going through, and that word is *tribulation.* We have been visited with tribulation, and that's always a wake-up call. It shows us where the fault lines in our lives and ourselves are located. It challenges us to be our best selves. It challenges us to have courage. And it challenges us to be diligent in prayer.

"And now, let us pray silently for those who are in distress: for those who have lost homes and loved ones to the flood." A hush descended over the church, while the sun streamed in through the clouded glass and a faint trickle of water dripped from the gutters.

David raised his head. "I want to say to you now that sometimes, when disaster strikes, we lose faith. We think God is hiding. We ask, how can it be? We can't see God in the disaster. But God is there. We don't know the nature of God, but he is bigger than our disasters.

"God will help us to take our disasters and become stronger from them, and that's one of our tasks in life. We live in an imperfect world. We're at the mercy of nature. Whenever man, in his arrogance, thinks he has conquered nature, nature finds some way of humbling him.

"That doesn't mean we can give up striving, give up helping. God is there in every one of you that brought food this morning, everyone who helped his neighbor. That's God working in our hearts, God using our hands.

"One thing I have learned is that we, as humans, are imperfect even as the world is imperfect. We all make mistakes. Will those errors define us, or, with God's grace, can we move on to live a new life, glorifying him?"

Out of the corner of his eye he saw Nell's face, rapt, glowing. His heart felt light, felt that the divine wind, Holy Spirit, had entered his soul.

"In a few weeks we will celebrate the glorious resurrection. We will have a resurrection here in our own hearts. We will have a resurrection in our community. Our church will never be exactly as it was, but we can have the same spirit as before, the same love, the same concern for neighbors and families. And maybe even more."

David spoke about Jesus, about his appearance before the disciples after the resurrection. "He was Jesus, not the same, perhaps, but still on his mission of love. Things change, and they change forever. We have to have the courage to grow with our changes, become a better person. I dare to say a holy person. Not a saint, but one in touch with on high.

"Whatever we have done—whatever nature has done—cannot be undone. But resurrection means forgiveness, means building, means comfort, means joy. It means the light of the world."

He talked, the sweat rolling down his face, and then he found he was trembling. And then he had run out of words, and he looked down at the people and they were looking at him as though they'd never seen him before.

Shaken, he said, "Amen."

The afternoon was brilliant with sunlight, the air cool. A breeze scattered redbud petals across the walkway while daffodils raised their heads from the sodden ground. High thin clouds quickened across the pale sky.

David stood in the Gothic doorway shaking hands, noticing that Nell and Chris were in line, talking quietly to each other.

"Good sermon, chief," said Harry.

"Yes, it was wonderful," said Nell, coming up behind David. He turned, and her eyes held his. "How are Clover and the baby?"

"They've been taken to Asheville," said David. "For some reason I haven't been able to reach them. I'm planning to drive over this afternoon."

"Please tell me as soon as you know," said Nell, the touch of her hand warm, comforting. But Chris was behind her, and she slid away.

David shook Chris's hand. "Heard you were volunteering for rescue. Thank you."

Chris shrugged. "The least I could do. This place grows on you. I'll be sorry to be moving on soon, but my grant's ending. Thanks for everything."

Before David could digest this information, the parish's grumpiest old man came up and slapped David on the arm. "That's the way to tell 'em, son. Give us more sermons like that."

"Like what?" said David, surprised.

"Short," said the old man, and grinned.

David had been invited to Sunday dinner at Edison's: hamburgers from the backyard grill, potatoes and carrots cooked in foil packets, and lemon icebox pie from the store's freezer. Today it felt like a feast, but he didn't have time to savor it.

After they'd finished dessert, the men were shooed out. He and Edison mounted the horses Edison kept for his two girls and rode down to the store, slogging through the mud of the field and across the shallow part of the creek.

All the phone lines, to his relief, had been restored, and he finally was able to get in touch with Hattie at the hospital.

"Oh, son, she's getting better in the body, but in the spirit? We're having a hard time here. That fool boy's disappeared, and she keeps turning and turning that big old ring you give her."

"Look, Hattie," he said. "I'm driving up there right now."

"No, I won't hear of it. Ain't it a mess down there? I heard about the church."

"Mess today, mess tomorrow. I'll see you soon." He hung up the phone.

Edison looked up from a box he was unpacking. "How are they?"

David shook his head. "Doing well in body, Hattie says. I'm praying for Clover's peace of mind."

"You call my daughter in Asheville if you need her. She'll come sit with them and let you get on back."

"She's a good girl," David said.

Edison let a smile cross his face. "She's made me proud, that work she does." He consulted a list taped beside his phone, scribbled a number on a piece of paper, and handed it to David. He folded his arms. "She lives with a guy."

David could tell this was the fly in the ointment, no matter how good a museum curator his girl was. "Do you want me to say anything to her?"

"Nah," said Edison. "One day I'll knock the son of a bitch flat."

"Guess I'll be off, then."

Edison cleared his throat. "If you don't clean up, Momma will have something to say to you."

David looked down, for the first time that day, at his dusty, mud-smeared jeans and sweatshirt. He'd looked like that from the rooftop. God and the congregation forgave his mud, but he wasn't so sure Hattie would. He rode the horse back to the house, and Edison's wife ran out to meet him. He told her what Hattie had said, and she took the horse's reins and told him to get on to Asheville. He thanked her for the hospitality and headed for Bear Lick Mountain and some fresh clothes. Maybe he'd have a few moments of quiet before he left.

The phone began to ring the moment he stepped inside the door. One parishioner wanted to organize a clothes drive and raffle for those who got wiped out; Harry's brother knew of a family that needed food and furniture; Tallulah's old mother-in-law was trying to find out anything from anybody.

He called Clyde Summers and the sheriff, looking for word of Riley Clyde, and came up empty. Between calls, he managed to change into a fresh shirt and a pair of khakis and took a clean windbreaker from the closet.

The experience on the rooftop still haunted him, and he wondered what Tallulah would have said about it. He wanted to tell someone about it, someone who would understand. But sweet Lu would have just given him a puzzled smile.

He took a long look at the picture above the fireplace. He walked over and took it down, then carried it into the bedroom and propped it against the wall across from the dresser.

He'd hang it later, in the spare room, maybe, when he got back.

As he was locking his back door, the phone rang again. He decided to let it go. For most of today's calls, there was nothing he could do, and he had no more information than anyone else. He wanted to get to Asheville.

Fever was a bad sign. Hattie wasn't fooling him.

Chapter 35

David drove out of the thin Bow Creek sunlight back into rising clouds, clouds that cast shifting shadows on the rolling hills that hugged the Interstate. He hurtled through chutes of green and came up fast on a big yellow eighteen-wheeler grinding up the mountain. He slowed, letting the traffic on the left pass.

When he'd called Clyde Summers, Clyde said he hadn't seen his son in weeks. David hadn't told Clyde about the tussle at the creek, just that Riley Clyde had shown up, gone for help, and hadn't returned. Randy Garvin, the sheriff, told David they were still searching for victims of the flood. Thus far Bow Creek had lost only one person, an elderly man, one life too many for David.

He knew how the rushing currents could carry a man all the way to a river, how a torrent could suck a body under and hang it on a ledge. He shivered. Underneath all of Riley Clyde's bravado and rebelliousness, a frightened young man lurked. Frightened enough to risk his life to help Clover.

David floored the accelerator, pulling out from behind the big yellow truck and passing it easily. The old pickup had life in her yet, and he was glad. Five thousand dollars his father had left in the original will. Wouldn't buy him a new vehicle for sure. He'd run this old trooper as long as it would roll.

And as for the new will, it wasn't something he'd expected, but he dared let himself hope it would stand. He could do so much good with that money. It wasn't the money that was important. The new will signified that his father had, at last, accepted the man David had become.

Signs began to appear: a big blue hospital **H**; ASHEVILLE 35; VISIT BILTMORE WINERY; JESUS IS LORD. The tall green hills rolled by and the clouds lifted and drifted away, and when he saw the tall buildings of Asheville he was traveling in sunshine.

David took the exit ramp down into the city. Not too much farther now. His faithful old truck gave a shudder, and David's foot pressed down on air. A tremendous belch of smoke burst from the exhaust. David feathered the pedal, but nothing happened. The truck rolled to stop, a brutish smell about it.

Grind though he may, he could not start it again. He should have had Herman check the whole thing when he'd fixed the muffler. He'd been in too much of a hurry to get it back. And he'd never thought about the battery in Lu's old van. Herman had wanted to take a look at it, too.

It was four-thirty by the time he'd found an open service station with a tow truck, had his old truck towed, and accepted a lift from the driver to the hospital.

Clover was sleeping. Hattie, calm and collected, said that her granddaughter, Rebecca, had already come over and stayed with them a good long while. Clover, on the mend and happy to see her cousin, had asked her lots of questions about the big museum house. Hattie was glad her mind was off "that fool boy."

Relieved, David asked about the baby.

"Poor little thing," said Hattie. "Come on, let's go to the nursery." David, saying a quiet prayer, followed Hattie through the hallways.

Plump and robust babies were displayed at the front of the window, like doughnuts in a bake shop. Behind them lay the tiny wrinkled baby labeled *Summers*, surrounded by tubing and monitors. Even so, David noted the faint fuzz of Riley Clyde's dark hair. "I hope she's going to have Clover's eyes," said Hattie.

David laid his hand on her arm. "Will she be all right?"

Hattie turned to look at him, her gaze candid. "That's what they say. Praying's your job, but right now it's my main occupation. That and listening to Clover talk about that fool boy."

"I want to talk about Riley Clyde," David said. "Let's have a cup of coffee."

They rode the elevator down to the ground floor café and sat across from each other at a table, hands wrapped around paper cups of hot brew from a large urn. "Nasty stuff," said Hattie, wrinkling her nose after a sip.

"Coffee's probably been sitting for a while," said David. He took a long swallow, caring only for the jolt it gave him. He told her what the sheriff had said about Riley Clyde. "He's still out there somewhere. At least they haven't found a body."

Hattie smacked her lips and grimaced at the coffee. "I never liked the fella, but Clover don't need any more grieving on top of this."

"Look," said David. "If we find him, won't you cut him some slack? We don't know the whole story. It's easy to condemn, not so easy to forgive."

"I ain't promising," said Hattie.

People around him talked in hushed voices, some with red, stricken faces, some unable to sit still, some downcast, all restless.

The coffee machine threw up steam and trays clattered. Maybe Clover was awake now. He rose to go and helped Hattie up. "When can they come home?"

"They want to keep her a couple more days," said Hattie. "They might keep the baby a while longer if she don't improve." She paused a minute. "You said somebody got killed back home?"

David nodded. "Unfortunately, Lucy's father. Heart attack. I think a tree came down on his place, but it didn't hit him."

"Scared him to death." Hattie shook her head. "You talked to Clyde and Ruby Lee?"

"They made it through all right. Clyde says he's not worried. Says his boy will turn up."

"Clyde's not the type to show worryin'. What about that woman the boy used to romance?"

David said, "Lacey? The trailer park got hit. That's all I know." He didn't tell Hattie about seeing the pink trailer overturned.

The elevator arrived, already full. They squeezed in and rode to the third floor.

In the hall Hattie said, "What're you going to tell Clover?"

When David hesitated, the old woman gripped his arm. "You better do some good, honey," she said. "Or she might just will herself to die."

Clover brightened when she saw David and Hattie. A bouquet of balloons bounced on the end of her bed, and her blue nightshirt looked brand new. She grabbed an open box of chocolates and held it out. "Want some? Rebecca sure was good to me."

David shook his head and gave her a big bear hug. "I'm glad to see you, honey. I can't wait till you and that baby come home." He settled in a bedside chair.

Clover grinned. "They told me maybe tomorrow they'd bring her in for me to see. She may be too weak for me to feed." She held up a small breast pump. "See?"

David nodded. She quieted, then, and David knew she was thinking about Riley Clyde.

"Have you heard anything?" Clover's voice became small, spoken almost to the blankets. She tugged on her plait, twisting it between her fingers.

"I'm afraid I haven't," David said gently. "But that's good news."

She wound the plait around her hand and looked up at the ceiling with vacant eyes. "I'm scared, Uncle David. What'll I do if . . ."

David leaned over and took her hand, patting it. "Remember the time you ran away?" he asked. "Remember how frantic we all were, searching for you? You weren't thinking of us, were you now? You were just concentrating on your goal, finding Riley Clyde. And this time, he was concentrating on finding help for you. That's what he was going for."

"He went in the creek," said Clover flatly. "Did he drown, and you're not telling me?"

"What?" How did she know about the creek? He looked at Hattie, and Hattie shook her head. Hattie hadn't told her.

"He went in the creek and didn't come up," said Clover. "That's what Rebecca told me. She let it slip. She didn't mean to. Nobody told her not to tell."

The floor dropped out beneath David. He swallowed. He was brisk with his answer, maybe a little too cheerful. "The sheriff hasn't found a body. I'm sure Riley Clyde's all right somewhere. Maybe he's on his way to you right now. He loves you, Clover. What did you name the baby?"

"I'm going to name her Jordan," she said, "after that song by Hampton Taggart, and Clyde, after Riley Clyde."

"Boys' names," grumbled Hattie. "I wanted Mehitabel."

But Clover didn't laugh. She leaned over and buried her face in the pillow, and David laid his hand on her cheek. "Have faith. That's all we can do for now. Have faith, Clover. He'll be found, and he's alive. That's how you can help your baby and yourself."

She rolled over and stared up at him, her cheeks wet. "It's so hard."

"Nothing's easy," he admitted, thinking of the rooftop where he'd stood Sunday morning, awakened to strength and purpose, to being at one with God's creation. He said softly, "Somehow I believe he's out there, and if you keep the faith your love will find its way to him."

She looked up with tearful eyes. "You think so?"

"I know so," he said.

She closed her eyes.

David kissed Clover's cheek. "I'd better be going now." To Hattie he said, "I'm not sure how long it'll take to repair my truck, and I need to get back to Bow Creek. I'll rent a car."

"You could call Rebecca. Maybe she can think of something."

"No, I need to get back." David made his good-byes and set out to find a car to rent.

He was asking for information in the hospital lobby when a woman walked by, her graceful stride familiar. "Excuse me," he said to the startled receptionist and ran after the woman. "Nell! Nell!" Visitors stared and smiled, but he didn't care.

He caught up with her at the elevators. She turned and gave him an astonished smile. "David!" She put a hand to her hair, windblown and tousled. "I tried to call you. We could have come here together."

David smiled ruefully, angry at himself for not answering the call that had come while he was leaving. And it wasn't just the broken-down truck. "I'm sorry I missed it, considering—"

Nell broke in. "How is she?"

"Much better, thank God. The baby . . . well, we don't know."

"I'm sorry. I interrupted. You said considering . . . what?"

"I was just going to find a car to rent. My truck broke down."

Nell placed a hand on his shoulder. "Why, David, I can take you back to Bow Creek."

"But you just got here."

"You can wait for me, can't you? It'd save you a lot of trouble."

David shrugged. "Of course. But surely you didn't come all this way just for a twenty-minute visit, did you? Don't you have other things to do in Asheville?"

"Well, you came all this way, didn't you? I'd planned to stay over and drop in on a couple of artisans who make things for the shop, but I'll call them and make plans to visit another day."

"No, no. Don't ruin your trip for my sake."

She touched his shoulder. "These are unusual times, sir. And they call for unusual deeds. This is no time for commerce, anyhow. You're going back with me, and I insist!"

David scratched his head. "Nell, I'd be grateful, if you're sure. Why don't I go around the corner and buy us a couple of sandwiches while you visit? I'm famished."

"It's my pleasure. And I'd like a sandwich. Veggie." She gave him an enigmatic smile and walked away.

David walked down the street and found a café and coffee bar that sold natural foods. He ordered two grilled veggie and cheese sandwiches, two packets of chips, some tasty-looking peanut butter cookies, and two large coffees, remembering that Nell liked hers with one sugar and one dollop of cream. He carried the bag back to the hospital. In the sky the sun was sinking, and they'd benefit from the last of the daylight on the drive back.

He'd timed it just right. She was stepping out of the elevator when he entered through the automatic door, paper bag in hand. Eyes shining, she walked up to him. "Clover looks so much better." She glanced at the bag. "Something smells good."

"Large coffees," he said.

"Oh, you're such a dear to think of this," she replied. They walked out into the parking lot. "You know, I've hardly slept a wink in the last twenty-four hours."

"Let me drive," said David. "I've had a night's sleep."

She nodded. "Gladly."

David got behind the wheel, and soon they swung onto I-40, and before long the swollen, churning French Broad River was receding in the rear-view mirror.

"So Clover's cousin let the cat out of the bag about Riley Clyde," Nell said, unwrapping her sandwich.

"I'm sure she meant well," said David. "She didn't want Clover to think he'd deserted her."

"He's a deserter, I'd say," said Nell.

"He's confused, immature, and unstable. Like another boy I knew once," said David.

"Anybody I know?"

David hesitated. Now was not the time to tell Nell about the young man he'd been, about Trilby, about Molly. "No. I don't think you'd like him very much."

"Somehow, I think I might," said Nell.

"Someday I may tell you about him," said David and wondered why he'd said those words. When was someday going to be?

He found himself treading safer ground: St. Ninian's. While Nell ate her sandwich, he told her about his father, about the inheritance, the strange will. "Phil will expedite a loan to buy the old rectory back, but how can we ever raise the money to repay that loan? I know you're not on my side here; you still think Transmontane will preserve the house. But we'll need that property in the future."

"Oh, David. I've come to realize that I don't really trust Kip Hogarth's word. Harry explained a few things to me."

He felt a surprising spike of resentment. "You had a talk with Harry?"

"We had coffee. But it was also your sermon, David. It made me realize that I can't go back to my childhood. Things change. And until we know more, I'll keep an open mind about how we can both win. Yes, I've seen new people in my shop. I can't pretend Bow Creek will stay the same forever, . Maybe we can try for historical status. Maybe we can get a grant. Where is the David who gave that sermon on Sunday? He would say *yes, we can raise that money.*"

"The sermon on the rooftop," he murmured.

"Tell me about it," said Nell. "What happened to you up there on the roof? I could tell something did. You had this *look* when you came down . . ."

He hesitated for so long that she said, "David?"

Why not tell her? He said in a voice full of wonder, "For the first time in my life, I had a mystical experience."

Nell turned and faced him. "A mystical experience?"

His voice edged into determination. "An honest moment when I felt I knew why we were put on this earth. A moment when I felt connected to everything there was. A moment when I knew that whatever I had done, I was forgiven."

Nell was watching him, open-mouthed.

David's voice fell. "I'm sorry. I can't explain it. Books have been written trying, and I never saw what they were getting at, until that moment on the rooftop with the broken earth around me."

"Try," said Nell. "I want to know."

They rode and talked, and the sun slipped down behind the mountains and the air grew cooler as the miles slipped away. The talk lapsed into a silence, and the clicking of a rock in the tire tread grew louder and louder. She unwrapped his sandwich and gave it to him, and he ate it hungrily.

Finally, Nell said, with a trace of apology in her voice, "David, we should have stopped at a restroom. I drank gallons of water on the way down, and now that coffee."

Outside the window were only black hills shadowed against the smoky sky of twilight. "Let's see what we can do. I'm afraid there won't be any service stations for a while. Can you hold it?"

Nell said ruefully, "I've been holding it. I didn't want to interrupt you. I was so fascinated, but now I'm afraid we have to stop. Please pull off at the next exit. Surely there's something."

David glanced at her profile out of the corner of his eye and felt her embarrassment. We can fly among the clouds but be brought to earth by our very human necessities.

He exited the next off-ramp onto a country road, traveling beside a wire-fenced field. They passed a farmhouse, then a sign pointing down the road to a Baptist campground and another sign advertising 12 ACRES. Behind the hills the moon was rising through shadowy clouds.

"What next, milady? Shall we turn around and drive to the next exit? Try the Baptist campground?"

"No," she said. "Just find a spot with thick bushes."

A football moon was climbing the sky, and clouds were floating in its wake. David found a wide shoulder next to overhanging laurel and pulled over. Nell popped open the glove compartment and retrieved a flashlight and some tissues. She got out.

"Be careful," he said.

"It's deserted," she whispered. Not even one car broke the quiet and stillness. He waited, tuning in the radio, listening to a Bach minuet from the Asheville PBS station. The music crackled and faded and he jabbed at the tuner. The bar ricocheted across the waveband, finally landing on "Wayfaring Stranger" by "our very own Hampton Taggart."

He switched the music off just in time to hear Nell's high-pitched yelps of pain.

Chapter 36

David threw open the car door and leaped from the car, landing in sandy soil, scrambling for footing. He raced for the underbrush, following the frantic light beams. Mountain laurel slapped his face and scratched his hands. "Nell! Nell!"

"Over here," she said, groaning. "Oh, I'm such a fool."

He jumped over a ditch and kept going, wincing as his arm took a gouge from a broken limb. He reached Nell and took the flashlight. She was trying to push herself up from the ground. "On the way back I tripped over a log, landed on some rocks."

"Hold on. Tell me where it hurts."

"My elbow. My knee. My hand."

She'd pitched forward and tried to catch herself, but her boots made it clumsy. David helped her to sit up. "Show me where it hurts." She pulled up her skirt, and his flashlight revealed a scraped knee. Her hand was scraped, and her elbow had taken the brunt.

He helped her back to the van and she told him where to find the first-aid kit. He smoothed a disinfectant wipe over the elbow, blotted blood with a gauze pad, and then wrapped the wound with gauze and adhesive tape. He smoothed disinfectant over her hand, and she winced. "Ow."

"You need it. Never know what's been on the ground. Animal scat, you name it."

Now he wanted to get her comfortable as soon as possible. He sped down the highway; fifteen miles later he saw the blue and white **H** sign of a hospital they'd passed on the way in. "I can take you to this hospital, see if they have an emergency room."

"No, that's not necessary. I'll be fine with a good night's sleep and a couple of pills."

He didn't want to argue with her, because she sounded firm, and he found a bottle of ibuprofen in the first-aid kit.

She'd said the pain had faded by the time they pulled into the driveway of the big white Victorian shop. All the lights were out save Nell's side-door light and a pale glow from an upstairs bedroom. She told him to park by the side door. "Sure you don't want me to drive you home?" she said.

"I don't want you driving yet. Let me borrow your wheels to get home. I'll bring the van back first thing in the morning and walk over to the church. Jane can give me a ride home later and I'll finally get that battery into Lu's old van."

"Come on in and have a drink," she said. "I think we both could use one."

He didn't see how he could say no. She needed somebody with her right now, because she was bone tired and still shaky. She'd hardly slept the night before, and driving all the way to Asheville? She always pushed herself too hard. "You won't get an argument out of me. But just one."

"Of course."

He turned off the lights and got out. The night closed in, cool and dark and heavy, and chill raindrops fell from the trees and slid down his collar. He walked around to open the door for Nell and help her down. He held her good elbow as they walked up the steps leading into the kitchen. She unlocked the door with a heavy click.

Inside, he inhaled the fragrant smells of potpourri and waxed wood, cedar and rose. Nell switched on a Tiffany-style lamp, drenching the kitchen in a soft pinkish glow.

David shrugged out of his jacket. Nell's comfortable house enveloped him, relaxing him. "It's so quiet. Where's Sophie?"

Nell hung both their jackets on antique hooks. "She's staying with Edison's girls for the night. Sophie was all excited, knowing they had horses."

David nodded. "Yes. Those horses came in handy when trucks couldn't get through the mud."

Nell nodded. "That was a long night. This was a long day. I'm so tired."

David took her firmly by the shoulders and turned her to the sofa. "Lie down. I'll mix the drinks. I think I know where you keep things." He walked over to the ornate cupboard that served as her bar.

"Good memory, you."

David found glasses and the Jack Daniel's. The faint noises of the quiet old house were memories crowding out emptiness.

He walked back to the sofa with two glasses of the amber liquid. He raised his. "To peace. And love."

"To peace." Nell sipped. There was an awkward silence. She asked him to switch on the CD player. "Just play what's there already."

The hypnotic strains of Eric Satie's Gymnopedie #1 crept into the room. She said, "Satie's what I play in the evening. During the day, the customers get fiddle and dulcimer. That's what they expect."

Cradling his drink, David wedged himself beside her on the sofa. "Classical? I thought you were a country music fan."

"I can see how you might have that idea." Nell shifted to give him room. "Hampton Taggart made me laugh. Just like my brother did. Maybe I was hoping to get my brother back. But Hamp didn't have my brother's good sense."

"I didn't know you had a brother."

"I guess I never told you. Tallulah met him. Before . . . before he died."

"Oh, Nell." He pulled her to him and held her close. "I'm so sorry. Has it been long?"

She gazed at him, eyes tired. "He was Lyle's roommate in college, both studying architecture. And then he started feeling bad, missing classes. When he finally saw a doctor, it turned out to be leukemia." She reached over, pulled a tissue out of a box on the table, and put her head on David's chest until her tears had stopped flowing. She rose and dried her eyes. "I guess I'm feeling a little fragile right now."

"You ought to stay home tomorrow."

She sniffed. "Easy. I work here."

"I mean, why not close the shop? No one will expect you to stay open. Half the shops are closed anyhow."

She smiled at him and touched his cheek. "You do have good ideas. Now if you'll just tell my daughter I need the day off."

"The schools'll be closed another day. I'll pick her up and then go with my plan to bring her here and then walk to the church."

"You sweet man." Nell kissed his cheek, and the music twined around them, its melody like a slow kiss, its sensuous notes spilling ever deeper, ever softer.

Aware of her scent and the heat from her skin, David fought the impulse to caress her arm. "It's nice being here with you," he said. "I wish things were different."

Nell's eyes met his. "Yes. You're still in mourning."

"Actually, I did most of my mourning before she died. I had to struggle to keep my faith during those dark days."

"I know what you mean," she said softly. "It was so hard watching her . . ." She looked away then, a flush rising on her cheek. Slow warmth stole over him.

He reached out and took her hand. "I need to tell you something," he said. "I think you might understand."

She gazed at him, waiting, calm, and that gave him the courage to continue.

And then he found himself telling her about Trilby, about Molly. She was quiet while he talked, and the rain trickled on the roof, and the music dropped its liquid notes.

"When I looked out over the land, standing on that church roof . . . I felt as though I had been forgiven for Trilby's death and . . . for not loving Tallulah as I could have. I did love her, very much, but not enough to let her into my soul. She must have known it. There's still a piece of me missing, and her name is Molly. All those women suffered because of me."

Nell patted his hand. "Love hurts. You helped me. I could have hit my head. I'm glad you were there."

"I didn't save them, Nell. *I didn't save them.*" His eyes stung and he grabbed a handkerchief.

"Look at me, David. Don't lose what you found."

He turned to face her. Her light brown hair fell across one eye, and he couldn't read her expression.

She brushed the lock of hair back and said slowly, "What happened to Trilby was an accident. She didn't realize how drunk her father was, how angry he could turn. She made a fatal misjudgment. And you were there because you were trying to right a wrong you had done, and you misjudged. So young, both of you. And from that came all the rest." She was gazing at him earnestly now. "It's just as you said. What's past is past. You're forgiven. If you meet your daughter, I'm sure she'll forgive you, too. I think you're afraid to meet her. You're afraid she'll judge you harshly. Resent you."

Nell was telling him the truth. "Yes," he said and looked away.

"She's your daughter, David. She just wants to know you. She's got a piece missing, too. And David . . . I want to know you better."

Her words had dazed him: perhaps it was the strain of keeping all those feelings for her at bay, telling himself he must not have them. His gaze met hers for a long suspended moment and then he reached for her and pulled her to him, breathing in her scent of violets and musk as he kissed away the rest of her words.

"David . . ."

"Don't talk." He kissed her again, to the faraway cannonade of the thunder. Then the rain began, a slow pattering on the roof, a smattering against the windowpanes. And she was warm against him, and he was holding her, and with her in his arms he was once again beside the lake of long ago as the waterfall thundered and the silver drops spun in the sunlight.

She nestled closer to him and he reached to touch her body, soothing it, smoothing it, gentle fingers stroking her leg.

She smiled softly and pulled away. "David, not yet."

Of course. She was exhausted. And for that matter, so was he. He closed his eyes.

Sometime in the small hours of the morning, he woke alone, a blanket over him, his joints stiff from the cramped position on the sofa. She must have gone up to her room.

Was she all right? He went up to see. When he stood beside her bed, her eyelids fluttered open and she reached out a hand to him "Hold me, please."

Shortly before dawn, David awoke to the smell of coffee. Groggy, he had a sense that something both wonderful and terrible had happened. But he didn't recall what until he saw the empty bed beside him. The room was all light and white and blue and looked exactly like her. She had left his clothes on a chair.

When he was dressed and had come down to the kitchen, Nell turned from the coffeepot and settled into his embrace. He kissed her with great tenderness and then she pulled back, smiling ruefully. "This was beautiful, and this was a mistake. We might get in trouble. I'll take you home right away, after you drink this." She handed him a mug of coffee.

"Nell, I was going to fetch Sophie for you—"

"Sssh. We can talk later. We've got to get you out of here before somebody sees you leaving. We're right here on the main street, or had you forgotten?"

David sipped the coffee. "Nell, I have something to say to you."

"It can wait," she said briskly. "Our reputations, David. Yours, mainly. I don't want to see you run out of town on a rail. And I'd prefer not to be considered the local Wallis Simpson."

He reasoned it would be futile to argue with her right now. He combed his hair and put on his jacket and shoes. He brought the coffee with him and finished it while she drove up Bear Lick Mountain.

No one spoke as the sky lightened in the east, lightening like his heart. He felt quite sure of what he was going to say. And then she pulled up beside his farmhouse.

"Turn off the motor," he said. "Please."

"But, David—"

He reached over and switched off the ignition. She stared at him, uncomprehending. And then he took her in his arms and kissed her. Long and hard.

Breathless, she said, "Was that hello or good-bye?"

He placed his finger on her lips. "Nell, I'm asking you to marry me."

She was quiet for a long moment. "David, I won't let you propose to me out of guilt. She looked down. "Anyhow, I'm not right for you."

"Are you saying no?"

She looked at him. "No, I'm not saying no. It's just that . . . this is a small community, David. I've made a mistake or two. You need a nice widow. Surely the casserole brigade has started now."

David smiled despite himself. "Nell, I'm not ready to marry again, but I don't want to lose you. You are a treasure. I was hoping we could be good friends, and then when the time comes, especially after your divorce becomes final, we can think about an engagement. And remember, the bishop will have to give us permission. Can you be patient?"

Nell looked at the house and said in a small voice, "I feel guilty about Tallulah."

"Don't, please. I think she would approve. I think I made her as happy as I could have, and it meant a lot to her to have you as a friend." He knew that was true, at last, and he felt the heaviness gone from his chest. The man he had been before could have done no more.

"What do you mean?"

David said slowly, "I'm just now beginning to see it. I never let her see my pain, and she hid hers from me. She never got over Leland's death. I found some letters." He felt his cheeks go warm. "I read one of them."

Nell nodded. "I can't fault you for that. It would take a saint to resist a letter from her late husband. I suppose you found out how much she adored her teenage sweetheart."

David swallowed hard. "Now she's gone to join him," he said.

Nell patted him gently on the cheek. "And now all we have to consider are Sophie, and the church, and the rectory, and Lonnie, and Jane, and . . .

"We can work it all out."

Nell shook her head. David, you're moving too fast for me.. And Sophie? I need to pick her up."

"Okay. For now. If you'll promise to rest today."

"I feel a lot better," she said.

"Tough girl."

He leaned over and cupped her cheek. "Nell. Please believe me. I love you more than I can say." He gave her one last, lingering kiss, and the rising sun burst over the fog-shrouded ridge.

She put her hands to her mouth, and he could see tears in her eyes. He held her close again, and it was hard, so hard, to let her go back down the mountain.

In his kitchen he drank a glass of water by the window, gazing for a long time out into the mist. Then he went into the bedroom and switched on the lamp beside the bed. He emptied his pockets onto the dresser, and as he laid down the crumpled, bloody gauze pad he looked into the mirror to see the picture of Tallulah staring up at him.

How could anyone know what she would have thought of his marrying Nell? More and more Tallulah was an enigma to him. He knew now he had married her because she had reminded him of Trilby. It was one more effort to make right what had happened those years ago, those years that had changed his life, changed him. But now he had forgiven himself and had to do only one more thing before his soul would be at peace.

Molly.

He heard a loud purr and felt a warm Tom Eliot winding between his ankles, heard his plaintive request for food. He scratched behind the ginger cat's ears, gave him a can of smelly fish cat food, and then went out to feed the rest of the cats and the chickens. Then he took a long, hot shower before he sat down to draft a letter to his daughter. He was toweling off when the phone rang. Nude, trailing steam, he walked into the bedroom and picked up the phone. "David Wilder."

It took him a minute to realize the voice on the line. "Sheriff? What's happened?" He felt as though a rock had lodged in his stomach.

"We found him, David."

"What? Who?"

"Riley Clyde Summers."

David steeled himself. "Dead?"

"Nope. He's in jail."

Jail could wait. Storm damage could wait. He had to write that letter to Molly.

When he'd installed the new battery and driven to town in Lu's van, David dropped off the letter at the post office. At St. Ninian's, he found that a crew was working on the big tree already. His good wardens must have cashed in quite a few favors.

Inside, Jane was cleaning and organizing her desk. "The computer is all right," she told him. He sighed with relief and asked her to please hold visitors because he had to make some calls. He hated to face the wreckage of his office, but at least he had a place to sit and talk. "Wait," called Jane as he was leaving. "I need to remind you—"

"Back in a minute, please," he said. He found he couldn't close his office door. The door frame was warped.

He called Clyde, who had also heard from the sheriff. Clyde told David that, as far as he was concerned, the boy could cool his heels in that jail, and he had customers waiting for a haircut. David tried to talk Clyde's anger down, and finally Clyde agreed David could go to Asheville and see if he could talk some sense into the young fool. "But I'm not paying any bail."

David understood. Well, he had to go to Asheville anyway and pick up his truck. Maybe he could offer to pay Chris Larson to come with him and drive it back.

He'd just picked up the phone to call his wardens and see how the repair estimates were coming along when Jane rapped smartly on his half-closed door. Startled, he rose and opened the door wide. She had the expression of a stern teacher with a negligent student.

"It's urgent. Dean Halsey called," she said. "He asked if you'd still be able to make it to the election. I told him about the storm and said you were all right. He's hoping you'll be there."

"Oh." The dean might have called him at home early this morning when he was . . . at Nell's. He took out a handkerchief and pressed it to his nose to distract Jane from his blush. He'd totally forgotten about the bishop's election. Today! He had to go. Maybe he could make it in time for the clergy vote. "What about the lay delegates?"

"They've already left. They're expecting you later."

Could he get to the Buncombe County Jail, bail out Riley Clyde, and still make it to the election? And what to do about the truck? Chris was nowhere around.

The answer was staring him in the face. If he could bring himself to do it.

Chapter 37

Evangeline stood at the front door of Wildwood, looking out at the stars, the glow of the city just over the horizon. The red lights of Phil's big prowler Mercedes slowly receded down the drive. She closed the door.

She and Phil had talked about the matter a long time, hammering out details, and they hoped the oral will would stand. "Buffalo" Bill Kirkpatrick assured them that it would.

She would move to a smaller place. She had no desire to remain at Wildwood, even though according to the will, she could live there until her death, when it would pass to Phil. Phil told her he didn't want to live there as it required too much upkeep, and he was over trying to impress people. He might sell it or donate it to the university.

Evangeline gazed around the rotunda. There were cobwebs on the high ceiling, and the chandelier was dusty. She'd have Junius call a service. In an earlier time, Albert would have noticed the dusty fixture and cobwebs and taken his very long duster to them, taking all morning. Junius, bless his soul, had had much to contend with lately. She was glad Lem had provided for Albert and Celesta in the will.

The clock read 9:05. She went into the small sitting room and switched on the television, then switched it off again. For perhaps the first time in her life, she had nothing whatsoever that interested her: not friends, not pleasures, not duties. She longed to see David. So many years had been wasted.

Once again she read the note from Molly Westbrook, the belated note of condolence. She picked up the phone.

Molly took a deep breath as Wildwood came into view: the tower, the turrets, the sculptured hedges, and beyond, the stables, the pastures. She navigated the winding drive slowly, drinking it all in. Could she possibly be related to these people?

She'd hurriedly dressed in a dark skirt, white blouse, and teal cardigan, set off by the gold necklace Paul had given her for her birthday. She hoped she didn't look too exhausted from taking care of the baby, an adorable boy they'd named Barnaby Paul. This morning he was with a babysitter, one of Paul's students.

Gathering her courage, she walked up the broad brick steps.

The door was answered by the tall butler she remembered, and he gave her a broad smile of recognition. "Mrs. Westbrook?"

"Yes, thank you." She smiled back.

"Mrs. Wilder is in the conservatory." He turned for her to follow him. Molly nodded. *The conservatory? Hope we don't run into Mr. Boddy.* She smiled as she remembered playing Clue with her friends. The only conservatory she'd ever seen was at the Biltmore House. No, that was a palm court, and there was a big greenhouse outside.

She was led to a large tiled sun porch with arched windows all around that gave a view of stables in the distance and the white fence of a riding ring. Molly felt a twinge of disappointment. So a conservatory was basically a Florida room.

Mrs. Wilder walked up to greet her, smiling. She wore a tailored gray pantsuit, white blouse, and black flats. She'd let her red hair go white, clipped short. Molly could see the tiredness beneath her flawless makeup.

"Hello, Molly," she said.

"I'm so sorry about your husband, Mrs. Wilder."

"Thank you, dear." She held out a hand in welcome, and Molly took it for a brief moment. "Thank you for coming. It's going to be very lonely without him."

How perfectly composed she was. If Paul were gone, Molly would be falling apart. She'd weep and wail and gnash her teeth and probably shred all the curtains, but here was Mrs. Wilder, seemingly serene.

The lady's hand indicated a faded wicker settee. "Please. Junius will bring coffee."

They sat together on the flowered cushions, and Mrs. Wilder made small talk, asking what kind of biology Molly liked best, when she would return to teaching, and what she'd named the baby. She raised her eyebrows when Molly told her the name but didn't remark on it. Junius brought the coffee and some pastries, and Molly eyed the jam tarts and cinnamon twists hungrily. She'd been unable to eat a thing for breakfast because she'd been so nervous.

Three pastries and two cups of coffee later the small talk skittered to a halt. Mrs. Wilder's voice dropped an octave. "You're from Glencreggan."

Molly fiddled with the hem of her skirt. "Yes, ma'am. I was born there. I left with my father when I was two. My grandmother looked after me before that. That's what they tell me, but I don't remember her. She's kind of a shadow."

"And who is your father?"

"Owen Ferguson."

"Ah, yes, the Fergusons," said Mrs. Wilder, not seeming surprised in the least. "You are the oldest?"

"Yes, ma'am."

"Tell me something about your mother."

"She was born in Germany, and her name is Hedy. She's big-boned like Daddy. She likes to cook, and she's . . . very loving."

Mrs. Wilder said gently, "She's your stepmother?"

Molly caught her breath, and her heart raced. "How did you know?"

Mrs. Wilder looked into her coffee cup as though an answer might be waiting there. "I know the strapping Fergusons. Two big people would have big children. My dear, you have delicate bones. Like me." Then she leaned over and looked at Molly intently. "Tell me about your . . . natural mother."

Molly shifted uncomfortably. "I don't know anything about her. That's what I'm trying to find out. That's why I asked you about . . . about your son. David Wilder. I've been searching and searching for him, because I heard something my aunts said, a long time ago."

Mrs. Wilder sat back, hands in her lap. "And what was that?"

Molly told her what she had heard on that porch so many years ago—the whispers, the forbidden topic of David Wilder. The admonition never to speak that name around Owen. The red hair. She supposed she had always known what they meant. But she'd never wanted it to be true. Until now, when it would help her to fill that void in her life.

Evangeline raised her hand to her throat. "Did you tell your father, Owen, that is, what you heard? And have you told him you were searching for David now?"

Molly shook her head. "No. I was afraid to say anything. He won't talk about my birth mother, and he hasn't been well lately." Her throat caught, thinking about her father, and she swiped at a tear on her cheek. She reached in her bag for a tissue. "He found out he has Huntington's disease, and I didn't want to give him anything more to worry about. And the disease is genetic. If he's my biological father, I might have it. So you see, I was kind of a wreck, and now I'm more confused than ever. "

She took a deep breath. "Mrs. Wilder, I was so happy that you called, because I just got a letter from your son. He wants to talk to me. He wants to see me. I'm not sure what to do next. I thought I'd be happy, but now I'm scared."

Evangeline's face glowed. She reached out and closed her hand over Molly's. "My dear. You have nothing to fear. I'll help you. I know you have to be David's daughter. You look like your mother, and like him." She smiled. "And you have my impossible hair."

Hope welled in Molly, and she could hardly contain her excitement. "Will you tell me what happened to my mother?"

Evangeline put her finger to her lips. "That's for David to tell you. At the right time. And he'll answer all your questions."

Molly's shoulders squared. "Yes, ma'am." She felt like laughing and crying at the same time. Laughing, for she had come to the end of her quest; crying, because she was afraid of what David Wilder would tell her about her mother. And what Daddy would think.

But she could do this because she had to.

"Come on, granddaughter," Evangeline said. "We have some planning to do."

Chapter 38

November 1991, One week later

David carried his duffel bag up a pine bark path through rhododendrons and hemlocks, the tinny murmur of a radio drifting through the twilight outside Jake Halsey's borrowed cottage.

The rough, dark-stained structure was tucked into woods about two miles from Glencreggan, just downhill from The Skylark Lodge, a rustic inn near Whitecliff Mountain. He stepped up to the planking porch, where a yellow light cast shadow into shadow, and knocked.

The door swung open to light and warmth and music and the heady smell of something Italian and delicious, of garlic, oregano, and wine. Jake stepped forward and grabbed David's hand. "Finally got here, you rascal!"

"Sorry. It's been a rough few days. Thanks for inviting me."

Jake stood aside. "Come on in. You can tell me about it. Give me your coat." Jake hung David's jacket next to two others on a wooden peg in the knotty pine hallway.

"David!" Emily's voice rang out, and there she was, wearing jeans and a red gingham shirt.

Foolishly happy, he laughed and hugged her. "I missed you at the election. I barely made it in time to vote."

"I'm so glad you were there. I was too nervous to watch. I went home to wait."

"Let me look at you," David said, resting his hands on her shoulders. Her hair, once dark brown, was scattered with gray at the temples, and she looked a little tired, a little heavier. But her eyes were as beautiful and merry as the eyes that had greeted him thirty years before, when he'd gone to stay with them after he'd fallen out with his father about theology school.

She searched his face. "How are things with you, David? Really?"

He gave her a bashful smile. "It's taking time, but I'm getting there."

"It's wonderful to hear you sounding happy. I'll have dinner in a jiff."

"I'll help. I know my way around a kitchen."

Emily fluttered her hands at him. "No, no, I won't hear of it. Shoo. Jake, for heaven's sake, give him a drink."

"Don't argue with her, she'll get mad," said Jake, winking. David followed him into a sitting room fragrant with the scent of balsam and oak logs, where a fire was blazing in a massive stone fireplace. Big, comfortable chairs awaited them. Over the mantel, mallards paddled on a glassy pond against a pale sky.

"What'll you have?" Jake motioned toward the bookshelves. A tray on the broad lower shelf held a bottle of Glenlivet, a bottle of Jack Daniels', one of Beefeater gin, an ice bucket, and four glasses.

"That single malt looks great."

Jake motioned to a chair. "Have a seat."

David settled into the old leather chair next to the fire and picked up a book from the side table. He leafed through it. "Thomas Merton? I haven't read that in years. Refreshing your spirituality?"

"What do you think I'd be reading?"

"The life of Teddy Roosevelt?"

Jake laughed. "David, David. That's done now. Yes. My spiritual side is definitely suffering from neglect. I've got a reading program lined up. Maybe I'll brush up my Greek."

"That'll be the day, Jake. You'll be a bishop yet."

Jake paused and spoke carefully. "I know I can do good, David. I have a vision of how I'd lead the church. But perhaps I'm not the one called."

"We all have our gifts, Jake. I wish I had your gift of leadership." With that gift, David wouldn't be mired in this rectory controversy now.

"I am humbled before your confidence." Jake handed him a glass. "The real stuff."

"Thanks." David took the single malt whisky and sipped, letting the warmth trickle down. He stared into the crackling flames, shadows dancing on the walls, He settled into his chair. How he needed Jake's advice now. Where to begin?

Jake gave him a knowing smile. "You want to talk about something, don't you? He pointed the stem of his pipe at David's chest. "First of all, where is she?"

"Where's who?" Jake's abruptness took David aback. *Molly*? Surely Jake didn't know... Jake, seeing David's expression, smiled wickedly. "Don't play dumb. You told me you were bringing someone to dinner. A woman. A dear friend, I think you said."

Oh, yes. David took a long sip of his drink. "Nell McGarry. She was Tallulah's friend, and I've known her for a long time. Or I thought I'd known her for a long time. I'm discovering more about her every day."

"Discoveries you like, I gather," said Jake.

David felt a flush rising in his cheeks. "She'll be here soon. She came separately with her daughter and they're staying at the Lodge overnight. I've hardly seen her this week. She's been busy at her store, and I had to help get a young man out of jail. That's why I almost didn't make it to the election."

Jake laughed. "I thought you had a pretty tame congregation."

David grinned. "Yes, most of the time they behave themselves. This boy's not one of mine. He's related to me in an odd sort of way."

"How so?"

"Did I tell you about that night of the flood? We were stuck at Hattie's house and Clover—my niece—was having a baby. That young man, the baby's father, couldn't take it. He dived into the creek, dived into that raging current, mind you, to swim across for help, and then he disappeared. Of course, we thought he was dead.

"That's what I've been doing the past few days. Trying to sort it all out. He almost drowned in the flood. Lost his wallet, all his identification. Got pulled out and woke up in a hospital. Told them who he was. Somebody mentioned the sheriff had been looking for him. He panicked. He thought he had killed me."

"Killed you, David?"

"Well, let's just say I wrestled him and he fought like a champ."

David pointed to the nearly healed bruise on his cheek, and Jake laughed. "Okay, David, then what happened?

"He ran out of the hospital, stole a car, and raced back to Hattie's place. When he found out that Clover was in Asheville, he hightailed it to Asheville with the highway patrol and the sheriff chasing him and that's where the law finally picked him up. He got wild and slugged a deputy. So with assaulting an officer and car theft, his daddy was fit to be tied. Said he could just stay there. I had to find a bondsman and bail him out of jail." David sighed. "He's turned eighteen and was charged as an adult. It's not over yet."

"David, if the rest of your life is like this, you're in for it."

"Frankly, I was hoping for quieter times, but—" David turned abruptly when the front doorbell rang. "There's Nell with her daughter."

When Jake opened the door, Nell, in a soft blue sweater and tweedy jacket, was standing with an arm around Sophie, wearing a plaid flannel shirt, puffy vest, and jeans.

Emily hurried from the kitchen and held out both hands to Nell. "Welcome, welcome. Hope you ladies like Italian food."

"Jake, Emily, Nell McGarry," David said.

Jake took her hand. "Delighted." Jake grinned and looked at David. "Lucky man. I think we've met, my dear." Nell, blushing, nodded and smiled.

David recalled the three of them standing in the wind after Tallulah's funeral, Nell's hair whipping about her face. It seemed an age ago. Emily warmly touched Nell's arm. "So happy to meet you."

The dinner was a grand success. Nell managed to charm both Jake and Emily, and David hoped she liked them as well. Sophie was quiet as usual, but she seemed pleased and dug into the lasagna and fresh breadsticks Emily had made.

Gazing around the table filled with those he loved, David felt warm and comfortable. So this was how it could be, surrounded by a family where you felt you belonged. Yet Nell had blushed when Jake called him a lucky man.

Did she not want to wait for him? What did he have to offer, after all? The farmhouse. Maybe she didn't want to live there, in Tallulah's house. Somehow he couldn't picture Nell and Sophie in the farmhouse. Of course, it wasn't big enough, but he could add on. And there was Molly, the daughter he had yet to meet.

He hadn't heard back from his letter to her, though he'd given her his phone number and asked her to call. Could she have changed her mind? Decided she didn't want to meet him?

When Nell felt it was time for her and Sophie to go, he walked out to the porch with them, and sent Sophie ahead to the car with a bribe of the Hershey bar he'd had ready in his pocket. Nell laughed. "You didn't have to," she said. "She couldn't wait to get back to her Pac-Man game." Her smile faded when she saw David's frown

The yellow porch light above cast them in half-shadow. "Were you embarrassed when Jake called me a lucky man?" David asked.

"I wondered what you'd been telling him about me."

"Nothing you wouldn't approve of, but I think he read between the lines."

She turned aside, looked down at her hands, fiddled with the zipper on her jacket. She bit her lip. "I'd like for us to have more time, David. I want to be sure that you're not rushing to replace Lu. And we still have things to talk about, you know that."

"Yes, I know," he said softly. "Do you love me?" He put a finger under her chin and tilted her head so their eyes met.

"David, I love you with all my heart . . ."

"There's an unspoken *but* there."

Nell glanced toward the car and looked back with surprise. "Sophie's watching us."

David took both her hands. "All right. I'll behave. "Nell, you're irreplaceable. If you hadn't been there for me, I would have been content to live alone in that farmhouse. Are you worried about living there?"

She pulled back and gazed into his eyes. He liked the way hers were crinkling at the corners. "Silly man. No. I'm worried about the church accepting me as your wife," she said. "And what about your daughter?"

"I've written to Molly," said David. "I want her to come to Bow Creek. We can welcome her together."

They heard a car door open. "Mom, come on! Why are you taking so long?"

"Pac-Man can't compete with this show. I'd better get her home," said Nell. "We'll talk later."

She opened her mouth to say something, but never got the chance. He brushed her lips quickly with his own. "There are two words I don't want you ever to say to me."

Her voice was husky. "They are?"

"Goodbye, David."

She wiped wetness from the corner of her eye. "No. You won't hear those words from me. I'll just say *au revoir* for now." There was a silly little smile on her face when she left and was still there, David imagined, as she was driving off.

Later, after the fire was burning low and Emily had gone to bed, the bottle of Glenlivet on Jake's sideboard was nearly empty. The night wind stirred outside, raking branches across the windowpanes. David shifted in the leather chair while Jake poked up the dying embers of the fire, cozying the room against the slap-slap sound, the menacing branches of the windy night. They'd been talking of the controversies that had roiled the last General Convention. Jake had been a delegate.

"Next time you'll go as bishop," said David.

"No, no," said Jake, shaking his head. "All that's behind me. There's something else Evie mentioned to me." He paused, as if trying to find the right words. "What have you done about your daughter? We haven't talked of that since . . ."

Since Tallulah's funeral.

David leaned forward. "I wrote to her, Jake. I told her that I'd rather explain in person what happened and why I never tried to find her. I said that I didn't want to hurt her father, who thinks she's his own child. And . . . I didn't say this to her, but I didn't feel I could ask Owen to forgive me."

"I have a feeling he already knows," said Jake. "I remember the look on his face at Trilby's funeral. He would have killed you if he could. He knew there could be only one reason you'd risk visiting Trilby after the baby came."

David sat for a minute, stunned, then shook his head. "And you knew before I confessed to you, didn't you? I believed I fooled all of you. Stupid of me."

"Not stupid, David, just young, like this Riley Clyde you've been helping. Maybe if you went to see Owen, it would help."

He had never in his life thought of talking to Owen. That promise he made? When he was on the rooftop, he'd realized that he'd used that promise as evasion. He needed to break that promise so he could help his daughter.

"I'd like to talk to Molly first. She said that he was sick, and she's afraid she's inherited what he has, what it might mean for her. For her baby."

Jake took the time to pack and light his pipe. He leaned back. "All the more reason to see him. It might ease his mind that someone would be watching over Molly when he's unable. You couldn't see it back then for jealousy, but he has a big heart underneath that gruff exterior."

"Nope. I thought he was a tough."

Jake shook his head. "David, you've been through a lot. But you and Molly will have years to get to know one another. Imagine it! You thought you were alone, and now, if all goes well, you'll have two daughters and a lovely wife. Pretty lucky, if you ask me." He raised one eyebrow. "Where's it going, this friendship?"

"It's too soon for both of us to make a commitment," David said. "But I have hopes. He let out a sigh. "We have issues."

"I'd be concerned if there weren't any issues," said Jake. "Are they serious?"

"Maybe. I told you about the situation we're in with the old rectory. You see, she wants to save the house. She thinks Transmontane should buy it, as they've promised to restore it. I don't believe they'll keep any promises that get in the way of their plans. And we need the property for expansion. We might save the house, but we might have to sacrifice it. The majority want to go forward, but the place was in Nell's family and she's attached to it."

"The answer is simple," said Jake. "Buy the property and move the structure elsewhere in Bow Creek. You can still find a reasonably priced piece of property there. That's what the developers will probably do, keeping to the letter of their agreement while building a shopping center right next to St. Ninian's."

"But that would cost a fortune for us," said David. "It'll be hard enough raising the money for expansion."

"Buy the house yourself," said Jake.

"Me?" David felt as if Jake had slugged him. "How can I? I'm poor, or haven't you noticed my rattletrap of a truck?" he laughed. "I had to ask Riley Clyde to drive it back to Bow Creek for me, and I'm glad it arrived in one piece."

"Poor no longer. Your father left you money," said Jake. "I was there. I'll testify, if it comes to that."

"I don't have any money yet," David said.

"You will," said Jake. "I know Lem's lawyer, and I'm not worried. What else?"

Jake had a way of knowing when people were cagey. Okay, he'd better get it out there. "Nell's afraid of what people in the church will say. It's a small town, and she's been divorced once with another one in the works. "Hmm," said Jake, examining his pipe. "If she means so much to you, you'll have to find a way. You could tough it out, or you could move."

"Move?"

"Yes," he said. "Remember those challenges I told you about? Are you ready to meet them now? Maybe you've done all you can do where you are. Maybe it's time to strike out for new territory. No one will know Nell's history at St. Augustine's, and I won't ask you to tell them. The church is changing."

"You want me at your church? Your big city church? Are you going somewhere?" David rattled the lone ice cube and downed the rest of his drink.

Jake's eyes narrowed and his expression became keen. "I've been thinking we need another associate. That would be a good step for you. My people need your gifts, David. Your insight, your courage, your concern for the less fortunate. Your mother will welcome you nearby, and your Molly will be there too."

David tried to digest Jake's offer. "Leave Bow Creek?" he said slowly.

"Sell the farmhouse," Jake went on. "Maybe you could be the one to buy the old rectory from the church and move it. Fix it up, stay there when you visit Bow Creek. For you will visit there often, I know. Nell can hire someone to run her shop, if she doesn't want to sell it."

Then he took his spent pipe out of his mouth, looked at it, and tapped the ashes into the brass ashtray, ringing hard. "See? That wasn't so hard, was it? I solved all your problems. And I'll be glad to officiate at your wedding." He leaned back, a satisfied look on his face. "I've planned a hike tomorrow, late morning. I've invited a retired bishop, Jack Willingham, and I'm hoping you'll join us."

"Fine," David said. "I don't have to be back in Bow Creek until tomorrow evening." This would be an interesting hike. Jake had lost no time making contacts. How was he going to reconcile his ambition with this new spiritual, soulful self? Somehow, he would do it, David felt, and when he did become a bishop, he would be a great one.

David rose from his chair and stretched. "You've given me a lot of food for thought, Jake. I think it's time to say goodnight."

"Goodnight, old buddy," said Jake. "We'll see you in the morning."

"I'm going up to the Lodge to have breakfast with Nell before she goes back to Bow Creek. I'll come back afterwards."

"And what are you going to say to her?"

David smiled. "Do I have to tell you everything, Jake?"

He turned back the speckled homemade quilt and stood at the window in his pajamas, gazing at the thin crescent moon high over the ridges, at the stars as thick as clabber. Such stars had been out the night that he had gone back in search of Trilby, on a journey from which he had just begun to return.

In bed, he drowsed and drifted into half-waking, a long tunnel on the edge of consciousness. At the end of the tunnel a broken apple tree stood in mist. The tree disappeared and Nell shimmered in his mother's rose garden, hair like sunlight through a violet haze, eyes tender and glowing.

He awoke at dawn to a faint pink glimmer above the ridge line. He had a lot to tell Nell. Somehow he knew she was awake too. But he wouldn't phone. He might wake up Sophie. He showered and dressed quickly, left a note for Jake and Emily thanking them for their outstanding hospitality, threw his things in a valise, and slipped out the door.

When he drove through a low cloud up to the lodge, she was rocking alone on the front porch, a heavy white mug in her hands. She did not seem surprised to see him.

He bounded up the steps and kissed her.

"You have something to tell me," she said.

He nodded. "I hate to leave right now, but I need to go into Glencreggan. It's not far from here."

"Yes, I know. May I ask why?"

"I want to talk to my daughter's father."

"Oh, David," Nell said, and her eyes were shining. She put down her coffee and leaped up to embrace him. "Oh, yes."

"Was that yes, yes?"

She gave him that Mona Lisa smile.---

Chapter 39

David went into the Spinning Wheel and ordered breakfast. Afterwards, he meant to get information from the sandy-haired girl he'd met before, Owen's niece, and go from there. He was even prepared to take the old truck back to Asheville, if Owen was there.

After he'd finished some just-right eggs and bacon and toast with local blackberry jam, he waited until the girl came to refill his coffee mug. "Yes, more of that good brew, please. Do you remember me?" He gave her a smile.

"Sure," she said. "You were in here a while back asking me about Uncle Owen. I'm Jenny."

"Good to see you, Jenny. I'm David Wilder. Know where he is now?"

She raised her eyebrows. "Sure. You want to go see him?"

"I'd like that," said David. "If he hasn't gone back overseas."

Jenny's smile grew wistful. "Afraid not. He . . . well, he retired."

"I heard he wasn't well. He's not at the VA?"

She sighed. "He was there. They ran some tests." She glanced around at a customer who'd just come in. "Be right with you," she called. To David, she said, "You'd better let him tell you about it."

So it was pretty bad. "Jenny. Just a minute. Where can I find him?"

She flipped her pad to David's check and scribbled on it. "Right here in Glencreggan. Granddaddy left him his house and couple of acres, and Uncle Owen's going to expand the house. He's living there until the building starts this summer. My aunt's gone back to Germany for a wedding, so it's just him right now."

She laid the check on the table. She had scribbled the address and phone number beneath the total. He paid with cash, leaving a generous tip.

After he left the café, David found that his cell phone wouldn't work on the mountain, and he didn't want to go back inside and ask to use their phone. He'd just show up and hope for the best.

The house was a mile or so down the cove road, and David missed the weathered mailbox twice before he found it. The two-track rutted dirt road snaked between two bigger houses that were going up. He bumped along until he arrived at a modest barnboard house near the creek. David admired the stone chimney, its wood smoke blending with the fragrance of firs.

He got out and slammed the door of his pickup, on purpose. You weren't supposed to sneak up on people up here in the mountains.

Before David took a step, Owen himself, still big, still muscular, appeared on the porch. He hadn't gone to flab like some men who'd been high school athletes, and David guessed the army had kept him fit. The big man crossed his arms and regarded David with suspicion.

David took a deep breath and stepped forward. Owen didn't move. David took another step, and another. And another. He felt the rush of blood in his ears. "Owen? I'm . . ."

Owen stepped forward.

He broke into a grin. "I knew you were coming, you sorry cuss. Jenny called me. What took you so long to come see me 'bout my girl?"

They sat by the fire in the front room and drank coffee and talked, or rather Owen talked and David listened. Jake had been right. As soon as Molly had grown out of babyhood, Owen's suspicions were confirmed, as she didn't look like anyone in his family. It didn't change the way he felt about her. She was still his daughter. His wife Hedy, a loving, uncomplicated woman, had treated the child as her own, and she never asked details about Molly's mother. Owen was sure Hedy had learned something or other from his sisters, but she never mentioned it.

David and Owen exchanged a few details about their lives. He told David that he'd seen duty in Vietnam; been lucky, he said. He'd retired recently as a First Sergeant. "Can't be out there and look weak," he said. "I don't know how long I can keep going, but I'm not going to fall down on the job."

He was glad David had come, was proud of his Molly for being so smart and brave about searching David out. He was thankful that when he got to a bad place with his illness, David would be there for Molly. Neither one wanted to talk about what would happen when his illness overcame him. And he was excited about being a grandfather. Molly was going to bring the baby to see him.

David took a deep breath and explained about the promise he had made to Trilby, and why he felt it was time to break it. After he had gotten the words out, Owen, only then, turned his head and dragged out his handkerchief. "Smoke got in my eyes," he said.

David knew it was time to go, back to his farmhouse on the mountain to wait for Molly's reply to his letter. He shook hands with Owen, surprised at the giddiness he felt, the lightheadedness, the lifting away of that burden of stone he had carried all his life. On the way home it began to rain, a light mountain shower that would pass on through and leave the sun behind.

When he walked across the porch to slide his key in the farmhouse door, the wet boards muffled his footsteps. Inside, the dark room smelled of old wood and burnt logs and dampness, overlaid with the scent of the sandalwood candles Nell had brought him.

He dropped his car keys on his desk and picked up the phone to call his mother and tell her what he'd done. Strange, she didn't answer, and neither did Junius. Had something happened to her? Was Junius rushing her to the hospital? Wait, she had one of those car phones, didn't she?

He found the number in the jacket of the suit he'd worn at Tallulah's funeral.

Chapter 40

The Lexus SUV with its three occupants sped along the highway under an overcast sky. The sun kept trying to peek through the rolling clouds, teasing them. "Faster, Junius, faster," said Evangeline.

"I'm going as fast as the law allows, Miss Eva," said Junius.

"Those trucks are going much faster." Evangeline sat back and sighed.

"Why didn't you let me answer his letter, Mrs. Wilder?" Molly asked.

"Call me Grandmother, dear."

"But I haven't met him yet. Are you sure?" Molly shifted in her seat and checked on little Barnaby asleep in the baby carrier. She hoped he wouldn't wake up hungry. It would be awkward nursing him here, but she had brought an extra blanket to drape herself with.

"Of course I'm sure! Anyhow, I want to surprise him. If I know him, he'll be stewing over what to say to you and whether you're ever going to forgive him."

Molly smiled. "There's nothing to forgive. I've had two wonderful parents, but I always felt like an outsider, never sure exactly who I was. Finding my missing father, and finding out about my mother, is more than I ever dreamed of. There's no more big empty space in my heart."

"David's going to be even more surprised to find out he's going to be a grandfather."

Molly blushed. "Yes. He doesn't know about the baby. But he may have seen me. When I went to . . . to Mr. Wilder's funeral, I saw a man with the family who looked at me for a long time. He had reddish-brown hair, and I felt it had to be him."

"You were there?"

"Yes, ma'am. I hope you don't mind. I slipped away quickly afterwards."

Evangeline shook her head. She didn't doubt that David would have stared at Molly. "You look so much like your mother."

Molly felt a shiver run up her spine. "I wish Paul had been able to come with us," she said, diverting talk from her mother. "I hope he does all right with the committee."

"I so enjoyed meeting him. He's a wonder, Molly, very sharp. He'll do just fine, I assure you. Coffee?"

"Yes. Please."

Evangeline drew a thermos out of a hamper. "I just have one more question. Why did you name my grandson Barnaby?"

Molly blushed. "In my research, I found that it was your son David's middle name. I just liked it."

"Or you had intuition. That was my father's name. Barney, they called him."

Just then the car phone sputtered a ring tone. Junius answered it smoothly, but before he could reply to the voice on the line he gave a deep sigh. "Phone's cut out, ma'am," he said to Evangeline. "It's chancy in these mountains."

"Could you tell who it was?"

"Think it was the Reverend, ma'am," he said.

"David? Oh, my goodness. I did give him this number. Maybe he'll try again when we're down the road. But now, let's have some coffee."

Smiling a secret smile, Molly's grandmother poured three cups. She handed one to Junius and one to Molly, and they raised their cups just as the sun reached its zenith, toasting the blessed blue sky, brilliant as a diamond, shining as a waterfall.

Molly turned her eyes to the spring green of the hills just now appearing, a trace of blue smoke in the heavens.

The fog that clouded her past was drifting away, and soon it would be no mystery. But there were other mysteries, mysteries hidden in the mountains, there for her to reclaim. And in that moment she embraced them all.

His heart thudding, David walked out onto the porch, trying to calculate how long it would be before they arrived. The rain had ended, and mist shrouded the mountains.

His mother had never come to the farmhouse, but she knew he lived on Bear Lick, if not exactly where. He found paint and a leftover scrap of wood and made another sign to add to the four-by-four pole. WELCOME MOLLY, it said, with an arrow directing cars to the fork that led to his house.

Inside, he tidied the house, room by room, making it as neat as if his mother was planning to give it a military inspection. With nothing else to do, he found himself pacing the floor. He'd just sat down to read yesterday's *Citizen-Times* when he heard a car rumbling over the ruts in his road.

He tossed the newspaper aside and hurried out to greet them, full-hearted with wonder of the day finally arriving, a longed-for day of near unreality—a day of joy and a day strangely calming, as if he had finally come home.

The car stopped. Molly didn't wait for Junius Johnson to open her door. She sprang out first, while the driver helped David's mother out of the car.

Molly and David gazed at each other, and David's throat grew thick. She was very much like Trilby, a red-haired Trilby. She smiled and gave a tentative wave, then leaned back inside the car to take the fussy baby.

For a moment they remained like a tableau, no one moving. Then David walked slowly down the wooden steps to the yard, kissed his mother, shook hands with Junius, and then stood face to face with Molly, for a moment suspended in time.

At last he nodded toward the bundle in Molly's arms and smiled. "Can I hold the baby?"

"Barney," Molly said, in a breathy whisper.

His grandson. A thrill coursed through him as he took the infant, holding him as he had held so many others for baptism. The baby stopped fussing and reached out a tiny hand to touch David's beard.

Amid laughter, Evangeline took her great-grandson, and now he pulled Molly close. His spirit soared. The sun crept out from behind the clouds and the fog sifted away in shimmering droplets like the tears in both their eyes.

Epilogue

Bow Creek, 2002

Molly had dropped off Barnaby with David and gone over to Glencreggan to visit with Owen. And today, David was out in his waders on the rocky Quanasee River, teaching his ten-year-old grandson how to fish with a rod. Nell was watching over their gear and the picnic she'd packed. Sophie was away, spending some time with her father. Lyle had become a much more attentive father now that David had come into Sophie's life, and Sophie, now a college student, avidly soaked up knowledge from Lyle, wanting to study architecture like her dad and late uncle.

The afternoon sun glinted on the waters, and as David instructed the boy how to hold the rod, how to position it, he felt a surge of pure joy. "Smile!" he heard Nell call, and he glanced back at her.

"Now, hon," he said. "Barney needs to focus on the fish."

"All right," she said, "but I want to get some pictures to send to your mother."

"Sure, but no smiling at the camera until later, okay?"

"We will all be glum, sir."

Pictures for his mother of her great-grandson. He wished she could be here with them, but she'd taken to traveling with Phil and Betsy, "while I still can," she'd said. The three were now in Greece to observe the classical architecture. Phil had become involved with historic preservation, and he and Betsy had found a passion they could share. They had sold the overdone house that Betsy had insisted on, way back when, and bought a neo-classical one to restore, with lots and lots of bookshelves for Phil's reference books. Their marriage was strong for the first time in years.

Their son, the former slacker Thad, had shown a talent for banking after all, and Phil was glad to let him carry the load for a change.

"Grandad!" Barnaby yelled. "Help!"

David snapped back to attention. The boy had a bite! He helped him work the fish, helped his reel it in. It was a nice one, not one they'd have to throw back.

Nell snapped a few more pictures. "If you catch three more, we'll have them for supper!"

By the time the sun was sinking to the mountaintops, they had four fish on ice.

As they were packing up their gear, an SUV pulled to a stop beside their van in the tiny parking area.

At first David didn't recognize the couple who got out and called to them and then he recognized their voices. "Riley Clyde! Clover!

A girl of about the same age as Barnaby slid out of the vehicle. She was pretty, like Clover, with the dark hair of her father and hazel eyes of her mother.

"This is Jordan," Clover said.

"Mama! I want to be called Jorie," the girl insisted. She and Barnaby regarded each other warily at first and then she went right over and asked to see the fish he'd caught.

"She's a handful," Clover said.

"I wish Hattie could hear you say that," David said. Hattie had died two years back, and David was unable to go to the funeral, much to his dismay. Hattie's big heart had given out, and nobody thought to tell him until it was too late for him to rearrange his obligations. She was buried by her own Baptist pastor.

He hadn't seen any of them since he'd left Bow Creek to go to the city as Jake's associate. He and Nell had stayed on another year at St. Ninian's, spending time together as friends until David could work through his grief and Nell's divorce was final. And until the rectory question had been resolved and the property bought.

Then David knew it was time to leave.

He and Nell were married in the chapel of Jake's church, and afterwards he joined Jake as his associate. He and Nell and Sophie had spent happy years in the city, and they traveled to Bow Creek from time to time to check on Nell's shop and the old rectory, still being used for Sunday school and meeting rooms.

David had offered to buy and move the structure, and the vestry had agreed. The church was growing under the new leadership, a second-career clergyman who could relate well to the newcomers, including summer people, artists and craftspeople, new residents seeking a simpler way of life, and old residents seeking a new church.

David had sold the farmhouse and acres, found homes for the cats and the chickens, and kept Tom Eliot as a friend and rodent patrol. And then, after seven years, once again there was need of a bishop in North Carolina, and this time Jake was elected.

David stayed on at St. Augustine's until a new rector could be found, but knew he needed to think about a new calling. He missed the mountains, and so did Nell. And then one day, a call came from Jake.

"David, this must be strictly confidential. I can't say too much, but you might want to reach out to a friend in Bow Creek and ask what's happening there."

David called Harry Claymore. After some hemming and hawing, Harry told him that the new man had done a good job for a while, welcoming the new summer residents, working on fundraising, and making plans for the eventual new addition, but he seemed to have an arrogant personality. Then they found out he'd been hiding some "irregularities" in his background. Harry did not want to elaborate, and said they'd gone to the bishop for advice.

"Wish we had you back," Harry said. "Any chance . . ."

"Nell, too?"

"Especially Nell. I think everyone misses her, even the gossips."

David didn't have to consider it, even for a minute. "Harry, if you're serious, I'll talk to her. We'll stay until you're ready for a young twerp."

But where would they live? Above the antique shop would be an odd place for a rector, and the old rectory had just been moved to its new location. It was far from being habitable, and Sophie couldn't wait to get her hands on it to plan renovation. This weekend, they had come to Bow Creek as a getaway and to look at available houses to rent.

Watching Barnaby and Jorie kid around, David smiled when Riley Clyde told him that he and Clover had expanded the barber shop to include a beauty salon, and Clover had trained as a stylist.

Everyone was doing well, and they had another child, a boy, who was at his cousin's for the afternoon.

"Take our picture for David's mom?" Nell handed Riley Clyde her camera. "Quick, before it gets too dark."

Standing in the light. That was what it was all about, wasn't it?

David folded one arm around Nell and one arm around Barnaby, and in the mellow late-afternoon light, the river rushed alongside them, and the pine-scented air was sweet, and the evening wind was soft. David, smiling between his past and his future, knew that in embracing the present, he accepted grace, allowing him to break the bonds that tied him to the past, letting his soul fly free.

THE END

Acknowledgments

First of all, thanks to the clergy who helped me begin this journey, those I have learned from and worked with during my days on the Vestry and as a volunteer in several capacities. I'll call them by their Christian names —Fathers, Reverends, and even a Bishop. I am thankful for Bob, John, Eddie, Greg, Claiborne, and Louis, and I thank Charles and Ruth for their early advice on this book. I also thank Martha and Joe for more inspiration. I met Barbara Brown Taylor only once, but her books also inspired me.

Thanks to my husband, Joe, for his steadfast support, eagle-eye proofing, and keeping me straight on car mechanisms. Thanks to my first readers, including Annette Mayfield and the late Peter Mayfield, Sally Parsonson, and Anna Montford Shepard. Heartfelt thanks to my cheering squad at church for support.

Thanks especially to my Words of Passion editor, Nanette Littlestone, for helping to make this book the best it could be, and designer Peter Hildebrandt for the marvelous layout and cover. And of course, thanks to Shaun Loftus for sage advice and her team for helping to get the word out!

Author's Note

This book could not have been written without fond memories of time spent in Western North Carolina, especially when I was young. Memories of hiking on trails, ducking under waterfalls, exploring forests and streams, picking blackberries and wild blueberries, breathing air that seems to sparkle like Champagne, fishing in a lake where petals float, glorying in a sunset from a mountaintop, and talking with people from all walks of life, will stay with me always.

Beautiful mountain regions have always attracted visitors, especially those from hot and buggy places. These treasures of nature were usually settled early on by rugged farmers and woodsmen and women. The descendants of these old families love their patches of heaven fiercely, and have their own way to doing things. Sometimes an uneasy relationship arises between the visitors and the descendants, and that's part of my story.

I'd like to quote from Heart of the Blue Ridge: Highlands, North Carolina (Faraway Publishing, 2004), by Randolph P. Shaffner, regarding his use of mountain dialect in his book. He asks speakers of the dialect not to take offense: "Sometimes an idea cannot be better expressed in plain English… There is a certain simplicity, irreplaceable humor, and courageous, self-effacing understatement that only mountain English can convey with a poetic dignity that speaks to the heart…"

I also ask North Carolinians to forgive me for a bit of liberty with geography—though not as much as some writers have taken—in David's travels. All of my towns except Asheville, Raleigh, Durham, and Sylva are fictitious, but readers may have their own opinions about what places inspired them.

Thank You

Thank you so much for buying this book!

I hope you enjoyed it. If you did, please consider writing a review so that others can find it! Reviews mean the world to an independent author, and I enjoy sitting down with a cup of tea and reading your comments.

If you'd like to find out more about me and my books, please visit my website at www.annelovett.com. If you sign up for my newsletter, you'll be the first to know about new releases, new appearances, and writing and history trivia!

More by Anne Lovett

www.annelovett.com

Rubies From Burma

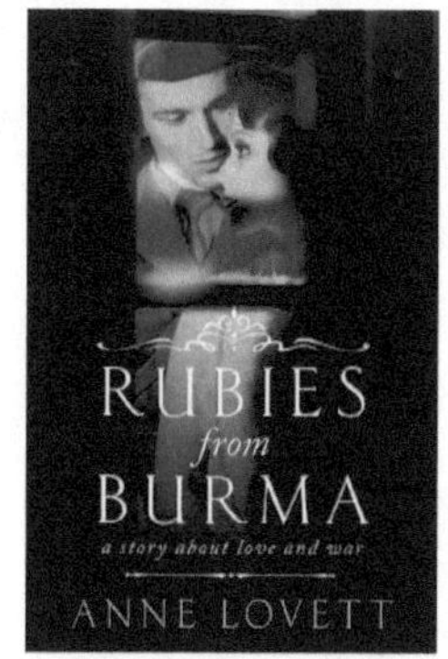

A world at war. Romantic tension. A forlorn girl determined to win over a man she cannot have.

"Exceptionally satisfying."

—Kirkus Reviews

The River Nymph

A fleeting glimpse of a girl bathing brings love at first sight. But will they ever meet again?

"Thoroughly entertaining."

—Kirkus Reviews

Saving Miss Lillian

She was just looking for work. What she found was an eccentric old lady, a murder plot, and an unforeseen romance…

"A closely woven tale of green and deceit…a winner for sure!"

—Fran Stewart, mystery author

Snakes and Lovers

She's done with commitment. Until a whole pile of complications coils its way around her life.

"A fun and fast paced book, sure to delight."

—Netgalley reviewer

www.ingramcontent.com/pod-product-compliance
Lightning Source LLC
LaVergne TN
LVHW091248150826
845673LV00006B/1354